Cold Streak

Lewis Aleman

Megalodon Entertainment, LLC.

Published by Megalodon Entertainment, LLC. (USA)
www.MegalodonEntertainment.com

First Printing: December 2007

Visit LEWIS ALEMAN and the world of COLD STREAK on the web at:
www.LewisAleman.com

Printed in the United States of America.

ISBN 978-0-9800605-0-8

BULK INQUERIES:
Quantity discounts are available on bulk orders of this novel for educational, fund-raising, promotional, and special sales purposes. For details, please contact www.MegalodonEntertainment.com

Chapter I

Can't see the shadows under the dust
Could patience exist if there were no lust?
Always asking why is this and why is that?
Too often we miss the point, and it's gone in a flash…

Reality seems to come in swirls. A word. An echo. A smear of sound. The words fall on her ears like needles. She can't comprehend their meaning, but each little piece slices into her, keeping her pinned to the floor where she has fallen. Phone at her side she stares at it as if she could make it take the words back. Somehow it can't be right. As soon as she can understand she'll know it's all over.

Her brain fires, and a light goes on that she'll never be able to turn off. Her soul responds as her torso crumbles forward onto her knees. Her eyes send out wet streaming messages constantly telling a story she's only just heard. When the call first came, it was just one lone damp scout scaling down her thin cheekbone waiting to see if the story was real before it wailed its sad tale to the world. Now that scout is drowned in an ocean of droplets that all scream *no* as reality wrings her out.

Murdered? It was something for the headlines. Something to shake her head about, but nothing that she is supposed to know. To taste. To grieve. Her thoughts repeat in circles: *How can they be dead? Who would want to kill them? How could someone kill my babies?*

All on the inside, her consciousness focuses on her questions. Her eyes are aimed at the overturned phone, but she can't see it or hear the voice that continues to call her name over and over again. Nor does she feel the cool of the hardwood floor below her. So fixed on her questions she can almost see the words in her mind.

I should never have left them. I shouldn't have left. God, I pray all the time; why weren't they protected?

In a brief moment of clarity, she notices an opened drawer. Not the checks that she had just wrapped up in a rubber band, nor the bank envelope, or the electricity bill that is still unpaid. But, she sees past them to the gun underneath. Her mind opens its black curtains for a flash of a memory. How they had pleaded with her not to buy the gun. *The city was safe enough—the gun would just be dangerous.* The gun would be dangerous…

Had she not just lost everything that made her happy in life, maybe she would've smiled at the irony. Now, she feels that, if her lips ever move in that upward direction again, it would be most profane.

So many miles away. Not that she could do anything even if she was there. But…she still aches to be. *There's nothing to go home to. Nothing. Nothing...I don't want to live...*

For the first time since both she and the phone crashed to the wooden planks below, she moves quickly lunging for the drawer. Customers' signatures and various papers scatter to the floor as her hands reach down to pull something into the light. Her hands fully stretched, fingers extending downward and out like a doctor in delivery or the opposite of prayer. She still doesn't feel the floor on her knees, but she does feel the coolness of the steel.

Dropping back from her knees onto her haunches, she shoves the barrel in her mouth. The sight cuts the tender roof, but she's not aware of the blood it strikes. Trembling, quaking, her body is motion. Every part of her moves in quick jerking sobs. All except her left hand. It holds steady. It holds the gun.

Her thoughts still swirl around and downward as she tries to keep her mind from disappearing with them down their spiral. She struggles to get a moment of clarity. One pause from the vortex to focus before she acts. There's a word, some code, something to scream. Something more than help, but she can't grasp it, and she's beginning to feel that she may never grasp anything again.

Something fires from within her chest to aid her failing mind. Is it word, or is it just sound? Her lips throw open and cry out, "God."

Repeating it over again seems to be conveying all that she wants to say. She feels as if there is something with her now, although she still keeps the gun tightly in her mouth.

With her teeth pinging on the barrel, she whimpers, "What if I take it out? Then, what? What is there for me?…Nothing…Nothing…Why? Why did this happen? Why should I stop? They're gone…"

The swirling thoughts subside slightly as if they were pushed into the distance. They move from being a hurricane in her face to storm clouds floating ominously over all her thoughts but farther away on the horizon. She thinks of her daughters and of the horrendous words uttered through the phone receiver, and for a moment, just a moment, she envisions those words being acted out on her children.

She screams, and the barrel cracks a tooth in the rear upper right side of her mouth, but the gun stays inside, never slipping away. Speaking, there is no gap between her broken feelings and her words. She doesn't know what word is coming next until it slips from her lips and around the barrel.

"I can't. I can't live. I have to kill myself…no…no…nothing…no… … or…God, please, make me into something to avenge this. Turn me into something so unnatural that I can destroy the monsters responsible for this. I am woman. I am mother. I can't live past this. If I take the gun out—if I don't do this, it is only for vengeance. For the strength to kill. Please, do not trick me or stifle me. Give me this, make me more relentless than those that I seek, or do not stop my hand."

The gun flies across the hardwood floor, bounces three times, swirls around, and stops.

Chapter II

The sting starts to fade away from the freezing feeling that rocked her body for a seemed eternity. Although only forty-five minutes have passed, it felt like it moved as slowly over her as the shade in the evening, but the stinging chill squeezed and stabbed like no shadow. At least like none that she has seen yet. Something in her skull felt the most odd. She felt a line being etched into her scalp. All she could do was shake her head to try and get past the icy pain, but she had no idea what was being meshed into her skull.

After the cold was done with her head, it moved on to her chest and rampaged outward through her, like expanding ripples from a rock thrown into an icy, nearly frozen, but not quite solid lake. The waves of it had rocked her back to the floor, pinning her shoulders, legs, and arms down flat against the wood below. Despite how intense the freezing became, she could not move at all. It gripped her completely.

She was not able to budge for some time after it had started to fade. When the icing-over seemed to reach its climax, she lost all consciousness except for the fact that she couldn't stand to be anymore and that it would be the end for her. Just as her soul was about to slip away, the cold started to wane. Still in intense indescribable pain, but the sting was ever so slowly creeping back to wherever it came.

Now, as the stinging finally begins to fade, the first thought that springs to her is that she still exists in some state. Is she dead? Is she alive? Is she still in the office with the phone lying on the floor? She doesn't know. She just knows that *she is*. Second, she tries to open her eyes. Her face is still too numb to feel or move.

Her eyelids feel as if they are open, but darkness is around her and inside her sockets. She can sense her eyes are still there, but she can't see. There are some passageways that we can't view but that we can be pulled through in the dark.

Even through this unnatural internal blizzard that courses over her body, she can hear voices calling to her. Not even on this bizarre journey has her soul found comfort. Her children seem to call to her from within. Despite her deviant condition, she won't turn off their voices inside of her. And, often, another voice calls. This one is not pleading or wailing like the children. It is comforting. It is stronger. And, she can't allow herself to acknowledge it yet, or she'll truly come undone.

Desperately wishing she could see something—anything, her mind drifts to a poem that she wrote for a college class eleven years ago. The lines come to her in order. It is the first clear recollection that she has had since she first fell down.

"In a world full of darkness,
I look for my light
Wandering aimlessly
Through the never-ending night.
Never getting closer
But no further away
I keep searching
To find light, for that I pray.
Stumbling clumsily
Through the darkness I fall
Like a blind man in a maze
I walk into another wall.
Though I have sight
This eternal black cloak makes me blind
Yet, I keep searching
For the light I'll never find."

Pulling her from the poem, pins and needles like never experienced before begin to swarm over her. It feels as if she is an ant pile erupting. As more and more ants pour out, more and more sting covers her body. The stinging is far more than she can stand, but she can't move her mouth to scream. The stinging spreads downward through her neck and chest. As it creeps through her, she slowly regains feeling of her body—even though the pricking is causing constant pain, the returning feeling to her skin seems different, somewhat numb.

Finally, vision returns to her eyes. Color seems to be in some tainted form. Everything is covered in a bluish-gray coating. Colors exist—but not as before. Surprised by the sudden sight, but even more surprised by the fact that she is still in her office on the floor and not in some celestial place. Even though she feels constant stinging—a cold burning—something about her body feels too still. Something is definitely askew, but she can't figure out what it is. Too much pain is already upon her to go looking for more problems.

Eventually she is able to turn her head. She looks around the room as if there would be some kind of a map or clue as to what she is supposed to do now. As she turns her vision around the room, she notices she can see the tiny writing on the calendar fifteen feet away on the wall. It reads,

"Daniella's B-Day." While reading the name Daniella antagonizes her sorrow, she is aware that she should not be able to read the miniscule writing on the small calendar from such a distance.

Soon, she begins wiggling her fingers, and eventually twitching her entire arm. By the time she can reach a hand to her face, the stinging reaches her thighs. Her face feels numb to her hands as if she were wearing mittens. Her torso regains enough feeling for her to roll off her back and onto her side. Her fingers begin to move more freely, and she returns them to her face. To her disheartening surprise, her face feels very light pressure as her fingers press firmly on it, and her fingertips seem to have no sensation of touch at all—she just feels resistance and pressure on the tips when they hit her face.

She drags herself a few feet over, pulling her still unmovable legs along with her. She rests her back against the desk and begins to remember her words before the freezing came. The request before the change. She slaps her legs in hopes of speeding up their return to mobility; the sting is tremendous. Suddenly, she can't wait much longer. She has a long drive ahead of her.

Chapter III

Her neighborhood looks hazy to her, mistier than she has ever remembered, even for the hour before dawn. Yellow tape is wrapped around the front of the house; smoke rises from around the side of a van—she can smell the coffee as she is halfway down the street. She rode the entire trip home with the windows down, and she never felt the slightest bit cold from the unseasonably wintery outside air. She has always been one to turn on the heat at night to remove the chill—even during summer months. She would notice it to be odd, if her focus were not on yellow tape ahead of her.

Glancing around for black, lumpy bags, she doesn't see any. She's not sure whether she is happy or sad not to see them. She walks around the van to the side on which the two officers are leaning and drinking their coffee that steams into the cool night air.

As she draws near, she can hear a strong feminine voice saying, "How can someone deal with something like this? I'd like to think that I'm tough, but I think I would…," the voice stops as both of the officers are startled since they did not hear her approaching.

No matter how long a cop has been on the job, it never gets any easier for one to talk to a parent who has lost her children. A short extremely thin woman with an astonished countenance stops in mid-sentence as she looks at the worn figure that has just walked up to her. The cop's face looks young but hard, and it doesn't seem accustomed to being taken aback. She says, "Mrs. Bonney, I'm so sorry."

Her counterpart, who is roughly twice her size and looks completely unsure of himself, offers, "Yeah, M-Mrs. Bonney, we're terr-terribly sorry." His response is as sloppy as his appearance. He looks far too harmless and soft to be an effective cop, like the antithesis of his partner who is harsh and sure enough but without the size to back it up. Perhaps if they were mixed into one person, they would make for an impressive authoritative force. Apart, they just look vulnerable.

It seems odd to hear her name aloud, almost like it doesn't belong to her anymore. *Mrs. Bonney*—it seems so strange to hear. All she can do is nod her head at the two officers.

She looks back to her house and then at the police, who could not be any more uncomfortable, and asks, "Are they, are they in there?"

The sloppy cop looks at her and then at her feet. The female cop looks at her face and is stunningly shocked by something that she thinks she sees. She says, "No, ma'm, they've been brought to the morgue already."

Silence. The female cop continues, "The incident took place around 11:45 for the best that we can decipher."

Mrs. Laura Bonney looks again to the house and then back to the tiny, uniformed woman standing in front of her. "I have to go in there."

Laura turns around as "there" leaves her mouth and steps directly toward the house. Her voice sounded scratchier than usual. Her feet hit the ground three times toward the house when she hears a step and a voice behind her.

"Mrs. Bonney, you can't go in there. It's a crime scene. You can't…," the female cop stops mid-sentence, which is something she is very unaccustomed to doing.

Her partner, the clumsy one, had tapped the side of her arm in as fast of a motion as he could make. He so rarely makes such a forward move that it took his partner completely off-guard. As she glances at him, he shakes his head side to side. She begins to understand what he is trying to do, and she glances back in the direction of the house and the woman that is halfway up its walk.

Laura stares at the female cop, which makes her step back awkwardly. Something in Laura's eyes looks colorless and gray to the officer. Laura sees terror in the policewoman's eyes and assumes there won't be any more words coming from her in the next few minutes. So, she turns back to the house, nears the door, and touches the handle. As she turns it, she remembers all the times that she would open the door and scratch her hands on the flaking gold paint on the handle. As she turns it now, she feels nothing.

I guess the cops don't lock doors…What else could happen here that would be worse than what's already been done?

Her thoughts are quickly interrupted as she steps inside. The house looks normal enough in the foyer. Pictures of the family are on the wall, although some look to be crooked. She instantly looks away. As she walks into their living room, she feels as if her chest has been crushed. Blood is everywhere. Splatter covers their couch so completely as if it were a pattern in a new style of decorating. Her husband was obviously sitting on the right end of the sofa, because there is an amoeba shape where he must have been with puddles of blood in it but no splatters. And, the splatter is thickest closest to the amoeba outline of his body, and it is thinnest on the left side of the sofa away from the body shape.

What did they do to him? How could this much blood come from his body? His poor precious body...Oh, God, did they beat him after he was dead? Ohhh, God. Oh, God...

Walking toward the tainted sofa, she sees slashes in the black fabric. They certainly weren't there before. Gabe was far too orderly to have tolerated a couch with slices in it. Even after she had been gone far longer than expected, he still would not have kept a sofa in such condition—it wasn't his way.

Oh, Jesus, they stabbed him. They stabbed him...My God, look at all the times they stabbed him...

This revelation seems to rock her body, and she feels dizzy.

Got to move on...gotta get through the rest of the house.

She walks past the sofa and into the kitchen. Nothing seems out of place. Gabe always kept the house painstakingly neat, much neater than she would have on her own. Her personality would not mind leaving dishes to be washed until the next morning, but Gabe would not be able to sleep if he knew the mess was lingering there. So, she always made the effort to keep things in order to keep him happy. Always. And, he rarely forgot to remind her how much he appreciated it, and he was never too tired to help. Shaking her head, she feels like she'll fall down and die right there on the kitchen floor. But, she turns herself back the way she came, making a direct line through the living room without looking at the couch again, and goes down the hallway leading to the bedrooms.

The only lights turned on in the house were in the kitchen and in the living room. As she walks into the darkness of the hallway, she knows she is entering another level. Something heavier that she may never walk back out of.

Only a few steps into the hallway, she can see the faint haze of the night-light still burning in her daughters' room. She opens the door and sees the twin beds that have their blankets flung off onto the floor. As she steps in she can see that stuffing from the pillows has been scattered in various places. She can see glistening pools on both beds: one at the head of the bed and another about 2 feet down. It's the second pools that widen her eyes and consume her focus.

She stumbles rapidly and awkwardly between the two beds. There are pieces of light brown hair on the floor next to a teddy bear with its face to the carpet. She winces and puts her face toward the bed. Then stops, pulls her long black hair behind her head and ties it in a knot that will serve as a hair clip. Something is very different about her hair, yet she certainly has not noticed, nor would she care about it at the moment. Returning her face just inches from the lower stain on the bed, her jaw begins to tremble, and her eyes want to roll back. Shaking her head, she pulls together her courage and forces herself to focus on the tiny bed below her. The sight of wild, curly hairs in this area causes her head to fly back uncontrollably, and she wants to scream; but, her throat quivers too much to control, and what word could she possibly find to capture what she feels? She swings her arms around wishing there is something to punch or something to hold. A driving from within causes her to close her eyes for one tight defining time and then turn to glance at the other bed. This bed has two similar stains but also a plush toy from a children's television show that seems to be staring at her. She focuses once again on the lower of the two stains and sees the same horror, but, this time, it comes in a slightly different color and consistency. At this, her entire body falls backward cracking her head on the carpeted floor beneath her, stirring up three pillow feathers from the floor. Laura feels tremendous pressure at smacking her head so soundly, yet it doesn't feel like pain. She can't feel anything in her scalp or on the surface, just pressure deeper within her head. On her back, she stares at the ceiling, which has fluorescent stars that they cut out as a family last year and placed them above the girls' beds. The girls were having terrible nightmares after watching horror movies at a classmates', Buffy Tyler's, sleepover party—the type of movies they are never allowed to watch at home, and it was the last time they were allowed to go to Buffy's house. They put up the stars to remind the girls that there were not evil things hiding in the darkness to get them—that all things were under the stars in God's universe and under His reign. They always shined brightly with the night-light on. She winces her head to the side once again when she realizes her girls must have still been looking up at them while they were being violated.

Never wanting to get up, she could die right there, just as she felt in the kitchen. It's just too much to comprehend what happened to her angels. They were only seven and nine.

Something drives her to move. There is much for her to do although she is not sure what. She gets up on her knees between the beds again and places a hand on both of them.

Out loud, she pleads, "My babies…Oh, God, my babies…I'm so sorry. Mama should never have left you…Dammit, why? Why my children?…Mama's sorry. I should've been here…where I belonged…It's all over for you now, my girls, they can't hurt you anymore…" straining her fists tightly closed, she continues, "I'll get them…I promise…Mama will make it right…I'm so sorry…so sorry…I'll be with you again…I'll be with you again…"

Without thinking about it, she is back on her feet and moving toward the doorway. Down the hallway, moving into the light. She sees the couch again and is completely compelled to go to it. To touch it. To do something.

Kneeling before it, and running her fingers along one of the long incisions, she begins to speak in a tone that is not a whisper and not regular speech, but one that is reserved for the most sacred of moments, "Oh, Gabe, sweet Gabriel, I'm so sorry. I should never have left. I should never have left you here alone…I don't know what this was about. Why didn't they take anything?…How did they do this without the children hearing you struggle, or you hearing them scream?…Jesus, Gabe, why?…I'll get them, Gabe. I promise. I will send them to hell. In fucking pieces."

After uttering her first curse word since she had children, she rises, and she looks down at where her knees were pressed against the carpet in front of the sofa. She had put them down right in a blood splatter on the floor. She wonders how she didn't feel the sticky moisture below as she kneeled there for so long. The blood is caked to her black jeans, and she has left two oval shapes in its puddle where her shins had been resting. They almost look like wings that hook to nothing. Blood angels.

She stands up and walks toward the foyer. As she passes the wall with the pictures, she looks this time. All of the pictures are hanging. Some are crooked, and one has a bloody handprint on it in a smear. Holding her hand up to it, she realizes it is one much longer than her own. And, the fingers are far too slender to have been Gabe's. Seemingly too long for woman, but too thin to be of man.

Someone must've left this mark leaving in a hurry…Unless if they've left this earth, they didn't leave soon enough…

She walks out the door into the further awakening dawn. Suddenly, she becomes aware that, as wracked as her soul feels, she is not physically crying and has not been since she left her office hours ago. It baffles her. She sees both cops leaning on the front of the police van. Surprised that they stuck around for what must have been an hour, she walks up to them. They nod their heads in acknowledgement at her, but they look away from her face. The female cop still seems afraid to lock eyes with her again.

Laura starts to speak and stops. Then, feeling something push her forward, she asks, "Do you guys have any idea what the hell happened here?"

Clumsy looks at her with the face of pure compassion, discomfort, and hopelessness. He opens his mouth in a choppy motion, but it is his partner's strong voice that speaks up first.

"Ma'am, we were just here locking down the scene when you arrived. Actually if we had worked faster, we would've been gone before you got here…I hate to say this, and I'm sorry, I'm so, so sorry, but something in there shook me and I needed some time to get myself together before I could go back in there…"

There is a long silence, and Laura stares at her waiting for her to finish.

"Mrs. Bonney, your daughters…I'm really not supposed to say anything…I heard the detectives say…rape…I'm terribly sorry…"

The officer raises her hand to reach out to Laura's arm, but she stops halfway—not comfortable with shows of affection and still a little afraid of what she saw in Laura's eyes earlier.

Laura, who has been staring unflinchingly, turns her head to the side and mumbles, "I know."

The female officer starts to look up; and the question of “How?” pops into her mind, but she dares not ask it. Not asking a question is something she is very unused to, and it is only one of many reasons why she wishes she were home now.

The clumsy one opens his mouth again, and, with a sorrowful tone, he says, “Mrs. Bonney, we don’t know any of the details. We don’t know who or why. We overheard some things, but we’re not even supposed to know them. The person that you need to speak to is Detective Andarus. He’ll have all of the information for you.”

As soon as the words leave his mouth, he immediately feels stupid as he realizes the only “information” that Mrs. Bonney would want to hear is that her family is really alive and that all of this is some torturous fantasy. For the first time in her recent memory, the female cop simply nods her head instead of voicing her own approval or opinion. The clumsy cop stares back at the ground. At this point, Laura looks in their direction again, staring at the tops of their bowed heads.

“So, where’s this morgue?”

Chapter IV

The morgue pathologist lies in a sideways crumpled mess on the floor, and Laura feels nothing for him. He may as well be a blouse thrown off her tired shoulders and onto the carpet after a draining day of work. Her fingers grab at the zipper and let go only to grab it again and again. It doesn't feel right in her numb hands, but that is not why she lets it go. She knows the water can't be any colder than what she already feels, but she is still too afraid to jump in.

It seems to roar, or moan, as she finally yanks it along its toothed course. Surprisingly, she's still conscious after taking the initial plunge. Looking down at the sight far beyond horror on the table below her, consciousness is not something that she wants. Not any consciousness in this reality.

In all of her years, she has never seen a more empty-looking vessel than her husband's torn and motionless upper body. What used to exude so much energy and passion has been reduced to an already decaying and obsolete shell. For a moment she feels hopeless. She has to look away to remind herself that he still *does* exist with energy and emotion, but on another plane.

Her hands instinctively reach for his face, but she thinks of the possibility of accidentally erasing traces of evidence that through police findings may lead to her reaching her destination. As much as it aches her spirit, she holds her hands mere centimeters from his face, but never actually touching him. As she feels she can't possibly bear this burden any longer, just as she is about to call out and plead for providence, she looks down to the blood still caked on her knees, then up to the fluorescent lights above, and finally back down to her spouse. With a firm continuous motion, she opens the zipper all the way down to its stopping point. Without pause or whimper, she flips the top portion of the bag off her husband's body, exposing its haunting carvings to her eyes.

Sometimes our minds pick and choose what they want us to remember; occasionally we remember ourselves as being a little braver than reality can verify, or that our enemies were a little more malicious or evil than they were in deeds, and sometimes we forget things that were all too real to spare ourselves the recollection. Laura doesn't have any of those tools to filter what is violating her retinas. As the vision singes past her eyes and fires toward her brain, she can almost smell the burning as it etches itself into her being. She asked for retribution and, through its course, to find the truth. As her innermost feelings are thoroughly being fried, she realizes reality is an emotionless master; expensive, torturous, and hard to hold; but the only pillar that can uphold justice.

When her eyes allow her to move them again, she follows his bare neck to his right shoulder, its violent gash, down his biceps and slowly over its gnarled, uneven, fleshy wound, down to his elbow which begins a long scratch running its way down the top side of his forearm, and then to his hand. Knuckles are busted and raw—he must have tried to fight back. Glancing across his body to his left hand, she notices it is perfectly smooth. It wasn't a long fight. Studying his body as if it were a ravaged battlefield, she looks for signs to conclude what happened to him and, more importantly, who did this to him.

If Gabe could only use one hand, someone must have been trying to hold him from behind, but they couldn't keep him completely wrapped up...he knew the girls were in the bedroom...God, what were his thoughts like as he was dying knowing the girls would be next...

Looking up from his unharmed left hand to his shoulder, she notices there are no knife wounds on this arm, although it is splattered with blood. The arm is unharmed until his upper biceps. Raw-looking nail marks scream from out of the flesh of his upper arm. *Someone must have been holding his arm back from behind...could it have been a woman?* She had first been thinking that she was hunting a man, and then several men, but until this very moment, she never considered that she might be searching for a woman too. But, there is little joy in discovery, since, in every new piece of information that brings her millimeters closer to his killers, she learns more details on how he suffered. She has to piece the entire picture together to achieve her vengeance, but there is nothing that she would rather never see and nothing else that would wrack her body so turbulently than the image that her pained efforts slowly bring to her mind.

Truth is said to be a straight and narrow path, but how often does it follow such a treacherously steep fault line? With every action, she sees her next step ahead of her, but she feels as if she could fall over the edge with each onslaught of tainted imagery and never return to truth or reality again. The path is certainly clear at least one step ahead at all times, but her own threshold of endurance, and the limits of her soul for that matter, are shrouded in shadow.

The other haunting shadows ahead of her lie in smaller zippered black bags on tables across the room. She is well aware that they are there and awaiting her, but she tries out of necessity to keep the thought of her next task behind a floodgate in a separate, enclosed channel of her mind. She's barely treading water now. To immediately breathe the blood of the two looming atrocities of justice ahead of her would certainly cause her to drown.

Chapter V

As the second evening falls on the longest twenty-four hours of her life, her mind has closed certain recent memories just so she can be. Her eyes have seen it all and stored it in places in her cerebrum, but her brain will not let her begin to decipher any more of the horrendous images. Numb is all she has become. If she lets herself feel, she knows it will rip her apart. Even though she would like to let it destroy herself and crucify this demented nightmare, she knows she needs to finish this task, as impossible as it appears.

As her soul seems to hibernate, the droplets skate down her face, which rests on top of her arms that lie atop her bent knees. Crouching in an alleyway, back against the wall, she is completely unaware of their motion or moisture. Her eyes are open and staring at a brick wall seven feet in front of the one on which she leans, but all she sees are the ugly visions that her brain cannot yet translate into something that she can understand. They should be tears but are merely raindrops crashing indirectly from the darkened sky overhead. The roof's ledge sends the rain shooting off the rooftop and into the alleyway. Within the droplets are flakes of rust. Somewhere between corrosive and beautiful, they shimmer in the falling water, but her opened eyes only see the images from earlier that day. Hours she stared at them, and she sees them as clearly as if they were still in front of her—screaming out the ultimate injustice inflicted upon them. Be it insanity or clairvoyance, she can hear it too.

During better days, she would have known where she was, and she especially would have the cognizance to recognize the danger of the neighborhood. But for all mental concerns, she is not here right now. Rustling a little further down the alleyway, closer to the street, paper and trash are crumpling. Within the dilapidated dumpster with rusted holes in all four of its bottommost corners, a tail slithers back and forth as its owner tunnels through the refuse. The sounds of paper creasing, Styrofoam cracking, and bottles clanging are barely audible over the rain above. If it only realized what crouched just yards away from its metal enclosure, it certainly would not make a sound.

A door swings open loudly slamming against the brick building. For a brief moment smoke and the sounds of a partly busy bar pour out into the rain. Then, the shouting begins.

"I told you, Chris, to stay the hell away from people when you're in here drinking! Now I've got a guy with a broken nose bleeding all over my bar! Get the" rain noises break up the conversation, "here! If I ever see you on this," more dripping noises, "street again, I'm gonna smash your drunk head in and bury you where no one'll find you."

The drunk doesn't respond, partly because he is intoxicated, but mostly because the guy doing all the talking has him from behind in a tight headlock with massive biceps closing his windpipe. Letting go of the drunk's throat and delivering a furious kick to his lower back all within the same motion, the bartender sends the drunk flying into the wall before him. His face hits first.

Door slams, drunk lies on the ground groaning, the rain still rains. Both creatures stop rustling, and Laura still crouches unaware that anything else exists or moves besides her thoughts.

Eventually, hunger takes over, and the sounds of paper and trash resume slowly in spurts, as if they were testing the environment. When no thing answers the initial movements, the tail moves again without fear. After all, its motion sounds much more natural and in tune with the rain than anything that came out of that angry door mere moments before.

Difficult to tell where the drunk's face starts and his nose ends as he begins to move his head that erupts with crimson, still lying where he crashed from the wall. The blood pours out his busted nose and into his open mouth until reflex causes him to begin coughing. The coughs spatter blood on himself and onto the ground next to him. The tail and its body keep wiggling around in the bin just a few feet down the alleyway from him. In an inebriated logic, he decides that the sounds of the creature in the container are mocking him.

He sits up, shoves his body closer to it and kicks his leg at the dumpster. Missing horribly, his foot goes underneath the bottom of the receptacle, scraping his ankle and calf area along its edge. The jagged, corroded edges dig into his skin through his jeans. After dropping his back against the ground again, he mutters a few curse words at the box of refuse and its unknown inhabitant. The tail still moves along, unflinchingly looking for sustenance. Rocking in feeble jerking movements, the drunk tries to roll over onto his side in a hope that he can get back to his feet. The dumpster is his new focus. Even in his hindered state of consciousness, he is aware that it will provide an easier target than the angry, muscle-bound barkeep beyond the door through which he was forbidden to cross again.

By a process of spastic body crashes, he gets onto his side. A few crashes more, and he fumbles himself onto all fours. Rising up awkwardly and flailing his arms trying to grab a little balance, his slanted, crooked shadow falls on the dumpster like a swaying banzai tree. Thrusting both hands onto the top of the trash container, he grabs hold and sends a loud thud echoing through the bin. The tail and its owner freeze from instinct and fear.

Blood runs through the cracks in his teeth as he smiles a seemingly demonly smile. Is it humanity or is it just stupidity that causes us to taunt things senselessly even when we are in dire circumstances? Possibly the same weakness that prevents us from making a decisive conclusion to this question is the same flaw that compels us to act that way. However, the running blood and the falling rain are the only things that parallel the primal brain activity of the lush. As his fly sputters down, he falters and stumbles with his underclothes for far longer than what should be necessary. Before he is actually free of his clothing, he releases himself in his pants and eventually all over the front side of the dumpster. The noise that was inside its walls is still silenced, much to the banal pleasure of the drunkard. Gluttony and perversity consummate in a vile marriage, making the misplaced caveman feel some degree of achievement and victory despite his bloodied face and urine soaked pants, standing in the rain in the alleyway next to the bar from which he was so forcefully ejected. As a blood soaked smile, which seems to dream of haughtier circumstances, indicates in this dark place, perception is the most powerful of drugs. A hoarse-sounding laugh-grunt-cough-taunt rattles some mucus in his chest.

Finally, within the container of leftovers and unwanted and forgotten items that were tossed aside, the little body decides that it needs to dart as far away as possible from the alcohol-fueled disturbance that is currently defiling its maze of garbage and metal. With a jerk, both body and tail wriggle their way to the back of the receptacle. The sudden sound of rustling and panic sends a jolt to the nervous system of the drunk. So startled, he jumps backward, loses his balance, totters in vain attempting to remain upright, and falls on his back. With brain impulses weighted down by the menace of barley and hops, it takes him a moment to comprehend what has just happened. Another spell in the alleyway passes, and he becomes cognizant of the excessive amount of warm moisture around his lap and thighs. Rising to his feet as quickly as his condition will allow, he begins kicking the bin repeatedly. As shoe-sized dings are being violently pressed into the front of the metal bin, fur and eyes and then tail exit through a rusted hole in the left rear of the container. The scampering of little pink feet cannot reach through the rain and over the clanging, drunken attack to the ears of the assailant. The patter moves faster than the rain, but it seems to be in a perfect double time rhythm, as if it were a natural aural camouflage. Swaying in a rodent motion, moving down the alleyway, and getting slightly farther away from the calamity with each tiny step, it approaches an object crouching against the wall. Unslowed, undaunted, and unharmed, it alters its course from running along the bricks to moving around her. Just as it is passing in front of her, its tail touches her right foot. Instantaneously, the rat doubles its pace past her to the end of the alleyway.

All the while, the kicking and swearing have persisted at the other end of the alley. Dings cover the façade of the trash bin as if it were bombarded by a hailstorm. His breathing has grown heavier until it has become the short uneven breaths that he gasps now. Feeling that he is going to vomit, he pulls his last kick down from the air and drops to his knees. As his head spins, the alley seems to be more like a cylinder than a squared, brick-walled enclosure. As it turns and spins, the rain makes it appear lubricious, alive, and organic. He stares into the alleyway cylinder, his drunken vortex, until he thinks he sees something. It is an obstruction in the rain; something that is preventing the falling droplets from hitting the wall. He feels compelled to investigate. Choppily rising to his feet once again, a bastard phoenix, he staggers toward whatever it may be, but not before he gives the bin one last kick as he walks past, taunting a creature that has long escaped him.

Past the dumpster, his shoulder hits the wall, and he pauses momentarily before continuing toward what now looks like someone crouching. The possibility of an easy fight brings a strange crooked smile to his still-bloodied mouth. As he steps closer, his feet spatter the water below, and, as he inches closer almost touching her, they unintentionally fling water onto her shins and knees. No movement from her. Thinking this will be easier than he thought and looking at her drenched hair matted to her face, neck, and shoulders, his cocked smile grows slightly more out of whack, and, placing one hand on the slippery bricks, he leans closer to peer into her face. Spraying her countenance with searingly toxic breath, he glances between the strands of hair that block her face, trying to obtain a glimpse of her eyes. If she is unconscious, it will be all the easier. Glancing at her hair, there is a different consistency in the color that even shows up through the wetness. He looks at it closer, his nose almost touching it. There is a streak stemming from the root—beginning way deep in the scalp. He closely follows the hair as it clings down her forehead and to the brim of her nose. Then, he searches again for the eyes. Through the darkness and the rain, it is hard for him to focus on them. He leans down even closer, straining to see. Suddenly, a flash of light crashes from within her eyes although she does not move. Completely shocked and falling backward rapidly, his shoulders and head smack the ground with tremendous force. Some blood comes from the back of his skull, but he breathes. He and the rat.

While the rodent looks on from the shadows, his tormentor lies with his zipper down, reeking of a mix of beer, vodka, and cigarettes, and soaked in blood from within, urine from below, and rain from above. When he wakes in the morning, she'll be gone, he'll meander home, and the rat will remain.

Chapter VI

Laura sits on the park bench from which she has witnessed many games and adventures of her children. Princesses triumphing over evil adversaries twirling and dancing in just victory, grand weddings, concerts so powerful that the girls' voices seemed to mark the world, and even the occasional freeze-tag. But, all of that had been over two years ago. The paint flaking off the worn wood below her has deteriorated from minor cracks upon her last visit to large gaping holes.

There is much for her to do, but her mind only recently returned to her. Her consciousness came with the morning, slowly restoring her basic bodily control. She does not remember much of the alley and none of the rank, wheezing, and snoring body that she stepped over as she walked out of it. She seemed to have been lead to the park as she does not remember thinking to go there. Nor does she recall the walk. Nor the route. But, she has been on the bench for most of the day, and what an unusual morning and afternoon it has been. A dank, misty haze has hung over the park keeping most of its regular inhabitants away. The sun has shined above, but it has been muchly weakened after filtering its way through the opaque sky to hit her face. Nevertheless, even with the depleted sunlight, her mind did thaw slightly and slowly from its icy hibernation of the evening before. She began processing the retinal paintings from the prior day at the morgue, images of her most horrific fears even beyond her worst envisioning of Hades. She had taken these unwanted portraits, which were wrapped in black zippered bags, like they were small doses of poison. Each insight, each observation pulled her somewhat closer to the end, but every bit of understanding only made her more aware of the hell her family went through. Every flashing, graphic scene sickened her from the inside, rotting at her resolve, rusting her determination; eating *her*. For hours every profanely poisonous image scorched her mercilessly, and then the next recollection would drop a few more burning, drowning droplets of toxins onto her consciousness. Once the trickling doses added up to a pool of more malignancy than her mental tolerance could tread, as if she were drowning in it, the sights nearly stopped her system altogether, but something inside her shut down her mind until she could digest all the bane she had taken in. This afternoon her eyes slowly turned from looking inward, and she can now see the park, which makes her think of things from the past.

Often, Gabe would be sitting next to her watching their miracles perform for them. It was as if they were watching a theater of that day in their children's lives every time they came here. Even when her gym started taking off downtown, she would still love to watch their performances, even the sleep-deprived ones that she yawned herself through. Of course, she would turn her head to the side when her body would force herself to yawn, always trying to hide her fatigue from her children and fearing at the thought of hurting their feelings through some sign of disinterest or passive discouragement. Sometimes Gabe would see some of his students there playing football or soccer. They would always come over and say hello. His pupils loved him so much that they would occasionally briefly join in with the girls in their adventures. Watching high school and preschool merge was something rare and odd that was only brought together by Gabe's fantastic relationship with his students. Maybe they lowered their teenage wall of aloof coolness in an attempt to somehow repay Gabe's kindness upon them by giving their goodwill to his children. A trade of being given a warning instead of a detention in exchange for pretending to be the prince of a five year old for five minutes. It was beautiful and unusual. A flower on a bare branch in the winter. Now it's all dead.

As the setting sun throws a pinkish hue onto the dense damp air from over the tops of the trees that line the park's perimeter, a figure is walking in her general direction. This is the first occurrence of another presence this entire day. The dreary weather has kept all others away, including the usual landlords of the park, the squirrels. But, this one closes in, and it is no squirrel. With every encroaching step that he takes, her visions of a better past existence seem to fade away. The pages of her daughters' stories evaporate into the dampness of the air as he approaches.

Even with her vision that seems to be inexplicably and unnaturally sharp, she cannot make out the exact details of the intruder's appearance. From the broad outline, she assumes it is a man, but she can't be sure. It is not fear that she feels. It is the pesterance of distraction. She had just begun to ponder why she was not crying while remembering vivid memories of her daughters who will never breathe again. How could she dare not shed a tear while the purest movies that she has ever watched were replayed in her brain, shaking her emotions to pieces on the inside; how could she not bawl or wail aloud? She certainly loved her girls—what could make her act so coldly? And now, she has to put down this twisting emotional puzzle to deal with whatever is creeping upon her through the haze.

The timing of his steps seems slow, but it is in pace with the movement of the breeze and just slightly slower than the flight of the pigeons overhead. It is as if at this moment she has two minutes internally to the outside world's every one. Even as his lower limbs rise and fall and push toward her bench—her family's bench, her mind wanders back to the puzzle. She feels no urgency as the snail's pace of his steps wipes away any possible threat or interference.

Why am I not crying—have I cried at all?...Did I cry at the morgue?...At the house? Why not as I remember them playing now? How can I sit at this bench and be so dry? Am I?

Raising her hands to her face, she places her fingertips directly below her eyes. She tries and fails to feel some moisture—any hope that her emotion is still natural, still human, and still woman seems to have dried up. Although her fingertips continue to feel as numb as if her prints were just burned off them, she is nevertheless quite sure that there is no moisture on her face. Closing her eyes momentarily, she tosses her head in confusion. Opening them again, she sees that the approaching figure has come slightly closer, and, still shaking her head, his shape seems to bounce sideways with her vision, as if her thoughts and disdain for his presence could physically move him and make him flutter.

As the figure walks toward her, he thinks that he recognizes her, but he cannot place from where. As he stares at her, he wonders if she was a childhood friend since he knows he has seen her before but something has changed so much that he can't firmly recognize anything except the familiarity. He has trouble focusing on her face. It is as if she is sitting still and moving at the same time. Her cheekbones, eyes, thin chin, and girlish nose look like they are the work of an artisan who can produce things so beautiful that they don't even appear to be human; some unnatural masonry, a moveable unmoveable, a bioanachronism; she looks like a statue yet she moves, and she moves yet she looks as rigid as marble. He notices that there is something grayish about her appearance that he cannot place yet. Something stone-like. He wonders if she is homeless. Then, he passes the thought off as her clothing appears to be too nice, her jacket appears to be too new, and she doesn't look to be frail. She is lost in thought as he moves closer, and she does not act worried about him in the least. But, when he reaches about five feet from her bench, her eyes shoot up at him like spotlights, as if he has tripped a sensor on an invisible alarm. He notices that something is definitely odd in her eyes, but he sees the horrifically odd every day in his work. He steps; she stares. His need for some human interaction after walking through this deserted and overcast park for the past two hours has pinned down his social insecurities. He had stayed around the rim of the park along the two-mile walking track looking for anyone else to nod, wave, or smile to. After there was no one for so long, he decided to cut through the center of the park and break his circuit. He had passed the gym and was sorry to see that there were no basketball games going on. The empty tennis courts reminded him of the picked-over and meatless corpse of a cleaned bird on Thanksgiving. He had continued further and ended up near the playground, and that was when he saw her sitting there on the bench. Her hair pulled back in a single, mane-like ponytail, leaning forward with her elbows on her knees, and looking out over a field seeing things that he could not see; she looked as lonely as he felt. There are many images and memories from his work that he would love to remove from his mind and some things in his personal life that he regrets during every moment of consciousness. These iniquities so dominate his mind that he feels detached and separate from all that goes on around him. Kindred forces broke fears of crossing lines of etiquette, and he knew that he must talk to her. So, he had started walking directly toward her.

His hand touches the armrest on the opposing side of the bench as Laura, all the while her eyes keep a direct line on him. As he turns his back to her slightly to sit himself down, a shiver of fear snakes its way up his spine and into his neck. It is a feeling that he has grown accustomed to. Every day in his work, he sees underlying warning signs of things horrific and menacing, yet he has found a way to disconnect himself and disregard their strong warnings. Very few people could do what he does.

For a brief span, he gazes straight ahead over the field. He sees through his sunglasses that it is gloomy and lacking sunlight; the light that still breaks over the trees is faint and fading. He doesn't see what she was so focused on before his arrival. Uncomfortable, he feels as if she is staring at the side of his face, which adds to his social anxiety of being too afraid to turn and look at her. He thinks that maybe if he just sits for a moment that she will say something.

Laura continues to stare at the side of this interloper's face. She deeply wants him to leave, having much more desperate things to attend to than some ill-guided, lonesome man in a park. But, there is something more: more than she wants him to be gone, she does not want to say a word. This strong dreadful desire to avoid any interaction dominates her will for him to go anywhere else but here. She doesn't know exactly what she needs to do next in her mission, but she is deeply distressed that this stranger is sitting next to her hindering it. She knows she was guided to the morgue, to the alley, and to the park without any thought or navigation on her part. She has definitely been lead to every subsequent step, so she wonders why she is now stuck here in the park without any innate navigation telling her where to travel next. Then it hits her…

Still looking directly forward, he says, "What a strange day." He pauses waiting for an answer. When none comes, he turns to look at her. As his head turns toward her, her head turns away at the same pace, moving her vision from his profile and back to the field. This obvious sign of a lack of interest only makes him smile, as there is no reason to hide his awkwardness anymore. He continues, slightly less than undaunted, "Lousy, rainy, overcast weather. No wonder we're the only two here."

...maybe he is the next puzzle, she thinks. Why else would he wander up on her in the middle of a lifeless park on such a dank day? But, what could he have to do with anything? A harshness in his voice reminds her of how her own voice sounded back at the house. The difference that she

noticed in her timbre—as if her words were pushing past the tragedy in her soul—making them wheeze out as a whispery sorrow-laded rasp. She could hear it even in the few choppy words that he has uttered, and it is no comfort. She knows she no longer has compassion to offer anyone. So, what could the sound mean in his voice? Is he the one she is looking for?

Continuing in his uneven rhythm, "Hey, I—I know this sounds like a line, but I think I know you: I know it. I—I was trying to figure it out as I was walking over, but I can't seem to place you."

Without moving her head, taking a breath, or even blinking, she says, "Maybe you can't place me because I don't belong anywhere."

Briefly happy at hearing her say something, the corners of his mouth turn up to form a smile, but they drop back down as soon as he realizes what has been said. He exhales softly, and replies, "Yeah, I haven't felt like I've belonged anywhere for a long time. The only time I feel any sense of inclusion is when I'm working. I have *total* control at work," pausing uncomfortably, then continuing, "So what do you do?" He asks leaning forward so he can catch a glimpse of her face that refuses to look at him; she still focuses on the empty field.

She pauses for a moment, shakes her head to acknowledge that she is going to respond to the question despite her longing for no conversation, and says, "Nothing seems real anymore. I don't even feel like I'm here right now…like I'm just kind of drifting in-between." The density of the color in her eyes changes as she speaks, like clouds circling together making the sky a little darker.

Fascinated by the change in her eyes, he finds himself opening up to her, at which he has never been good and absolutely has not done in recent memory. He hasn't initiated a social conversation with an unknown woman since he met his ex-wife, much less to say, "I know exactly what you mean," which causes Laura to look at him. He can see she is highly offended with his comment by the intensity of her iris storm. He is startled, as is evident in the quiver in his breathing, but he continues, "I don't feel like a person. I'm just a robot following directions. My feelings seem to be gone like I can't even make my own choices anymore…besides, work's been murder lately."

She stares into his face hard as the last line cuts into her ears. He doesn't mind her probing stare. His face looks tired and drained, yet almost relieved. Like a long-denying patient who admits for the first time that he has a terminal disease. Those words bother her.

Is it him? Is he the one responsible for this? Is that why he is here now?…Why else would he be here talking to me if he was not involved? Why would we be thrust together on this rotting old bench with no one else around, wasting my time, unless he has something to do with this? Unless if I'm here to talk to one of the squirrels, he has to be one of them…Why else?…Maybe the chase has come to me…

He says, "What an odd park conversation," then looking to the sky, "But what an odd day."

A red flickering flashes in cinders and highlights her pupils. He is not sure what he sees in her eyes; he doesn't really know if it is the setting sun being reflected obscurely through the overcast sky or if it is something that terrifies him. Her thoughts remain most sinister and unnatural, and she is comfortable with it.

After watching intently for a moment, he definitely is afraid of the churning red sparks in the pupils that stare at him. Not even in his line of work has he seen something like this. It can't be explained scientifically or forensically—those things he understands. Supernatural is something in which he has never held much belief. All he can rationalize is that he has gone insane—too much work, negative and morbid work, too much loneliness and torment. But, he doesn't believe his alibi; he knows he is stronger than that; he knows he is not broken yet. And, the alternative terrifies him. He doesn't want the responsibility of knowing something else; but he has already seen it, and, even if he could look away, he could not forget it. More importantly, he can no longer close his eyes to the world that they prove exists. So, he sits and stares at her silently.

Continuing to look at his awestruck face, something does not feel right. The welling up of her hatred and thirst for vengeance feels out of place. She wants it to be him. She searches her feelings for it to be him. She calls out to the maker for some affirmation. No confirmation comes. She is not happy.

Why waste my time bringing me to this park to talk with this idiot??? We made a deal—we have an agreement. You promised me that I could have my mission, that justice would be done—that I could avenge my family. Why in the name of all that's holy am I here talking to this man if he's not the one...

Suddenly, she feels a pull to get up and walk away from the bench immediately. Some urgency is moving her again. Still unhappy with no confirmation that he is one of the people that she is looking for, she forces herself to let go of her targeted rage and follow the direction she is being given.

When she stands up, he looks at the back of her head, still unable to bring himself to speak again after he saw the subtle glowing in her irises. He discovers a white streak that runs down her scalp from the brim of her hairline to the tip of her ponytail. He wonders how he could not have noticed it earlier as he makes it a point to study every detail of people with whom he comes into contact. This observation only makes him feel more uneasy and unsure of himself in this strange interaction, as his normal strengths have deserted him while talking to her. He wants to call after her and ask for some explanation to all of it: the eyes, the hair, why he is acting so out of character around her; he wants an answer so that he might have some hope of putting this behind him and going back to his lonely, yet predictable and understandable, life. But, he has no idea what to ask.

As she leaves him sitting on the bench, the clouds semble to follow her, and the sun peeks out from behind the overcast horizon. He sees red stains on the back sleeves of her jacket, which remind him of his particularly gruesome work waiting for him the next morning. It is yet another detail that has escaped his normally keen awareness. Something triggers as he watches her exit through the flaking, black, iron gate of the park. Just as she moves out of his vision turning from the gate and onto the sidewalk, he calls in as loud of a voice as he can currently project, but it is as if his body was under strain and can only muster a whisper, "Laura."

Chapter VII

She can't let it go. It keeps coming back to her like a child begging for attention, yet she does not stop walking. As she slogged out of the black iron gate of the park, she heard her name called after her. It was at so low of a volume that it was little more than a muttering whisper, but she is certain that she heard it. Whether it came from the man on the bench or from within the troubled walls of her head, her name registered on her eardrums.

Her feet follow an unseen path down city streets as her mind wanders and focuses on those five familiar little letters. She is not aware of where she is headed, but she can feel that she is on the trail that she is supposed to be walking. She can sense that she is going with the pulling and not fighting against it. It still is a dank and dying dusk, but the thickness of the haze is now slightly broken by the setting sun. Not enough to illuminate the landscape, but, it is just enough light to remind the people below that it is still there behind the clouds. As the streetlights begin to flicker and flash above her, she wonders if he could have possibly said her name. It sounded like a whisper; how could it reach her ears so far away at such a quiet volume? How could he possibly know her name anyway, as she has never seen him before, and she has been out of town for the best of the last two years? Unless, he is one of the ones she is looking for. Maybe he knows this, so he was looking for her. He did seem somewhat disturbed. Her thoughts circle around the same questions as she steps off a curb and crosses the street in front of her. Her feet navigate the sidewalk, curbs, and all interfering items with more grace and balance than she should have for the lack of attention that she is giving to her travel, especially as she instinctively steps over the curb when she reaches the other side of the street without even a glance in its direction.

The street is familiar, and she is not sure why. It is a long strip of town houses that have all aged together for generations. Her mind will not let her focus to remember when she has been here before. It races as if it were hunting an idea.

...Why didn't he try to kill me then if he was involved? If he knows I am the wife, why did he let me go? He didn't try to talk me into going somewhere private; he had no weapons—at least none that he tried to use...What would be the point of him just trying to talk to me? What could he gain from a dead-end conversation with me if he already knew enough to do what he did to my family? ...wretched...maggot...There is no reason for him to make contact...maybe, he's not involved. Maybe, he's just some sad and desperate park pick-up guy...then, why was I made to waste precious time talking to him? Why were we the only people in the park? Too bizarre...It had to be set up; he has to be involved—I was lead to the park just like the other places before...has to be a reason. This makes no sense...

As she walks down the street, she can see the last rays of the sun falling behind a tall pointy building a little over a block away. As the beams of light are submerged under the harsh points of the imposing, shadowy edifice, they have no effect on her emotion. Frustrated from the inability to decipher the meaning of the park events, she is tempted to kick an overturned trashcan that has been left vacant and hanging off the curb. The temptation hits her as if it is also calling her name, taunting her to focus on herself and her own anger for an instant in order to pull her momentarily away from her purpose. As she glances at the targeted can, which is sideways and jutting out slightly into the street, she can envision kicking it and feeling the release. She hasn't been able to cry; she hasn't screamed; she feels like it is taking all of her strength of being just to keep from erupting. Although she feels enough anger to do so, more than she has felt in twelve years since she was a teenager, more than she could have ever imagined, and more than one should be able to feel and yet still live, but, she does not want to vent. She wants to hold it all dangerously pressurized inside of her, so she can release it like a floodgate when the time comes. No matter what the events in the park pan out to be, she will have her vengeance—her family will have their justice; she will not lose sight of that. Without that, she does not want to do anything, much less kick a trash can.

The quiet of the neighborhood that is retreating for the night is broken by footsteps. Harsh footsteps. Man footsteps. Laura turns in an animalistic manner somewhere between hasty and agile to see what is coming up the street behind her. While she is in rapid motion, the crimson sparks return to her eyes like lava. She sees a man in a light blue shirt with his collar opened and his gray tie thrown over his shoulder lackadaisically. The five o'clock shadow has returned to his face from his shave some eleven hours before when he left for work. It has been a long day, especially for a working Sunday. But, the smile that he left at home when he started walking for the bus suddenly returns to him much like the last beams of the sun breaking through the hazy sky at the end of the day just moments ago. Her chest aches tremendously. It is not the man in the park—it's much worse. He looks so much like Gabe when he would come home from a long day of school, followed by meeting with his writing club, and topped off with parent/teacher conferences. If she could only run up to this man and tell him the many things that she wanted Gabe to know, maybe she could release some of her pain. Maybe she could seek some respite if there were any benefit to the dead through a vicarious conversation with the living. Just as her insides begin to sear from the memory and the hurt of things not said, she hears a voice, one that cuts.

A girl of about seven bounces on the small, concrete porch of the aging townhouse. She looks like she may explode from joy. The sound was a squeal that escaped her without any deliberate effort upon seeing her father. She tries to hold herself to the porch, as she is not allowed to go off the stoop after the streetlights come on. The smile that she resurrected on her father's tired face is pointed directly at her as he calls her name. At this, she jumps off the steps and runs to the sidewalk to meet her daddy. He crouches down, hugs her tightly, and then grabs her hand and leads her back to the steps.

As she takes her first step up to the tiny porch, she asks, "Daddy, I miss you when I get home from Sunday school. Why do you have to work so long?"

The man drops his undone tie around her neck and responds, "Princess, if I didn't have to, I would be here every second."

The girl's question ignites all that was left of her insides that were not being burned before. The bonfire is so much that it causes her to drop her head and stagger briefly. No one is outside to see her, as the screen door of the man's house swings shut. She hears the tiny voices, which have been calling to her since she first received the dreaded phone call, repeating the little girl's question to her. Every time it repeats, it lacerates her a little deeper like the fabled falling pendulum.

Still looking at the ground, she feels no awkwardness in speaking out loud to answer the slicing query. "I'm sorry. I thought I was—I thought I was helping. It was supposed to be for you. I'm—I'm so sorry. Daniella, Susanna, Gabe, I am so sorry…should've been with you...should've been with you…"

She didn't hear the elderly woman as she opened her door and walked down the sidewalk with the heaving, black plastic bag. So enthralled, she didn't even hear her pick up the overturned trashcan, open the lid, drop the bag inside, and place the lid back on top of it.

But, the woman heard it all. She first decided to look in the opposite direction and get back into her house as quickly as possible. *She must be crazy; this city is falling apart—neighborhood's not what it used to be,* thought the woman as she heard Laura's twisted whispers. But, as she turns to walk back up her sidewalk and return to her own little sanctuary behind the screen door, she knows she can't walk away. Not without saying something. So, she turns around.

The woman asks Laura in her colloquial yet soothing dialect, "Honey, are ya awright?"

Laura's head stays facing the ground, chin on her chest.

The woman steps closer and tries again, this time correcting her natural speech, "Honey, are you all right?"

She reaches a hand up to Laura's shoulder, but, before she can touch her, Laura raises her head halfway to its upright position, still sheltering her eyes from the woman. And, she tells the venerable lady, "I'm nothing, ma'am."

The old woman's facial expression dances from surprised to awkward to sympathetic, as she cannot think of anything else to say.

As she still sways in front of the woman from the emotional singeing, Laura feels the pulling again, like fingers on her shoulder urging her to turn away and keep walking. Keep moving, keep searching, keep preying. The old woman's mouth opens, but, before any sentiment is allowed to sound out of it, Laura responds to the pulling and steps around her to head up the block, towards the pointed building blocking out the expiring sun. The old woman holds still for a moment, considering going after Laura, but she feels some fear of the way Laura spoke and the eeriness of her demeanor. The woman scampers back to her house and hurriedly flings the screen door open. She scurries inside, barely getting the end of her robe clear of the shutting door. She stands against the wall in her living room, breathing heavily, trying to decide what she thinks of the whole interaction. Back against the wall, she focuses on the sound of her excited breathing. As she stands, she can hear a little voice next door laughing and squealing, "Ready or not, here I come, daddy," and her heart and mind slow down and are reassured by it.

The woman sighs, pats at her heart, and says, "Jesus, please, help her." Then she returns to the kitchen where she finishes cleaning the place setting for one.

Laura continues to walk up the street. The sharp points of the large building stick out into the deepening darkness of the growing night, looming over the feeble streetlights below. It is familiar. It seems monumental, as something from years ago, yet she doesn't recognize it specifically. Too distracted. The pulling is slightly more powerful and persistent as she steps closer to it. She can almost feel its presence as she reaches the corner. She is at the point where the street that she has been walking along is crossed by another. Across the side street is the pointy building, and her street dead ends a short block after the intersection. She can now see that it is made of brick.

The pull is amazingly strong. She can feel it and even hear it beckoning her. Halfway across the street, she glances over its structure, and it begins to come back to her. A wedding years ago—that is when she was here last. A fancy wedding of Gabe's sister. It bothers her. She shakes her head at the recollection. She feels deeply disturbed by the force of the pull and equally uncomfortable with the destination. It doesn't seem appropriate even though she is being drawn to it through means that come from beyond her. She continues to shake her head as she focuses on a cross high up on its rooftop. Clenching her teeth, she turns herself around with much effort, like she is fighting a current. She feels the pull still on her, summoning her to turn back around to the building.

She looks over her shoulder without moving her body around, still facing the opposite direction, and she says in the harshest tone that she has ever heard from her throat, “This wasn’t part of the deal. I have a job to do.” She can hear an inner screaming—the pull actually calling her. But, she walks away from it and up the dark street, not knowing where she is headed. And, still clenching her jaw, she wonders why she is feeling no pain from the tooth that she chipped back at her office. The thought makes the darkness seem a little darker.

Chapter VIII

A slender hand with meticulously manicured maroon nails drops a small stack of papers onto a desk. The hand belongs to an arm that is bare up to the short sleeve of the simple, yet stylish, gray business suit. The suit leads up to shoulder-length blonde hair that frames a beamingly smiling face.

"G-o-o-d morning, boss man," she says without sacrificing her smile in the process.

It's almost too much for him to bear on a Monday morning. He knows she is looking at him in appraisal. She'll see his bloodshot eyes, and he'll have to listen to her talk about it again.

"Detective," she says as she makes her away around to the back of his desk and slides her arm gently around his shoulders, "I know you're sick of me telling you this, but you have got to take better care of yourself. Your eyes look like something out of a horror movie. You need more sleep. You have to let it go; it's not health-"

"Irene, that's enough," he interrupts gruffly and then sighs. Her arm drops off his shoulder, and it makes him feel terrible. He looks up at her, but she has already turned her head away from him facing the wall of his past accomplishments, a gray file cabinet, and a framed photograph that is turned facedown on top of it. He starts, "I mean, I appreciate what you're saying; I really do. I just can't deal with any of this now. Not after all that's gone down this weekend."

Still not looking in his direction, she breathes in deeply and replies, "I know. I know you're right. I just worry about you; you know that. It has been a terrible weekend. Horrible for all of us. I just don't want anything to happen to you." She sniffs, quickly wipes at an eye, turns toward him, forces a smile, and says, "So, where do we get started on this one?"

"I've been thinking about that all weekend. Ever since what happened to Debbie; it's like it's been haunting me…I think we need to go to his school, ask some questions, try to find out what he was like—did he have any enemies? And, we need to try to get a hold of his wife again," he pauses uneasily. Glancing away from her, he asks, "Has anyone heard anything from the Houston Police Department? What did they find out?"

She answers, "Yeah, a Sergeant Burgis called this morning and said they found the front door to her gym unlocked, the office open. There was a gun on the ground, and the phone was still off the hook. He said Mrs. Bonney's gym specialized in helping women get into shape after pregnancy," she pauses for a moment trying to remember if she left out any of the details, "Oh, yeah, and there were no cars in the parking lot."

"Hmmm...she must have freaked out and left...wonder what's up with the gun...that's strange...we need to know where the hell she went...," he says hopping up from the chair to his feet with surprising speed for his apparent lack of rest.

He walks around the desk, passing extremely close to Irene—near enough to smell her shampoo as he crosses by, but not observant enough to notice how closely her eyes follow him. As he sticks his head out of his office door, he inspects the area and appears to be mildly frustrated.

Looking back into the room, he asks, "Where are Jackson and DiNardi?"

"They both are taking a sick day. They called not too long before you got here," answers Irene.

He grunts; she fidgets awkwardly with her fingers. She traces figure eight patterns repetitively on her thumb with her index finger. She is usually not aware when she starts doing it, and she has been doing it in certain situations for most of her life. She does it around Detective Andarus frequently.

When she sees that he is not going to comment, she continues, "I guess they're both trying to deal with the Debbie thing—I know I am."

"Yeah, I guess," he says in a low voice. Then looking up to her, he continues, "but you're here today. And so am I."

With that he walks out of the room. She stares at the empty doorway momentarily; then she glances around the small room in which she has spent many hours of the last two years of her life. Mostly happy hours; some bittersweet. She glances around at his worn chair that he vehemently refuses to replace, the file cabinet that has drawers that are quite stubborn to open, and she stops on the overturned picture on top of the file cabinet. She usually does stop and focus there.

She thinks, *Why doesn't he just take it home, or throw it away? It's been upside-down since I came here. Why can't he let it go?...He needs to let it go...I need...*

Her thoughts are interrupted as he walks back into the room. He says nothing, but he did notice at what she was staring. Steam rises from the coffee cup in each hand. No matter how busy or stressed they have felt or what hour of the morning or night they were working, he has never asked her to fix him a cup of coffee. She has picked up food for the both of them on many occasions, some at his request, but most of the time because she wants to make sure that he eats. But, he has never asked her to make the coffee. It is a detail of which she often reminds herself.

He hands it to her, and she blows on it knowing it will be too hot for her for at least a minute or so. Detective Andarus always drinks it immediately; he likes the bite of the heat. He will wince every time; but he never complains, and he never waits for it to cool down. Maybe it is because the pain causes him to focus and clears his head of other thoughts hovering around his consciousness. Possibly practical. Possibly savage. Savagely practical? He has quit trying to figure out those things well over three years ago. Now, he just tries to get through the week through any means necessary. He has stopped worrying about the how.

"So, you wanna go on a field trip?" he smiles for the first time that morning as he asks. She can see that he has not shaved since she saw him last on Saturday night at the hospital. She had told him then that he should come back to her place to keep each other company, and she would fix him something to eat while he was there. His eyes had gleamed for a moment and then faded away. With a pat on her shoulder and a shake of his head, he had turned away from her and walked off without a word. She left feeling foolish again. She is almost getting accustomed to it. Almost.

"Back to high school again, ugh. Not looking forward to that," she says slyly trying to make him smile again.

He does and says, "Yeah, right, weren't you Miss Irene Bauchan, the Homecoming Queen, your senior year?"

Shaking her head and motioning with her hands, "No, no, no. That was my friend, Tracy. She won. Seems she was a little friendlier with the football team, and that helps in high school elections. I was too shy. I only made it to the court."

Touching her shoulder with his free hand, coffee still vehemently clutched in the other, "Well, it was their loss. I'm sure you were the prettiest girl they had ever seen. People often go for second best because they're not afraid of it. Going for the best is too scary for the majority. Besides, you're too smart for that stuff—it might've made you think about becoming a model or a wanna-be actress. I need you here as my partner," pausing momentarily, "eh emmm, *my brilliant partner*; so, it all worked out."

She blushes and glances at him, then away from him, and back again, as she never does in the most shocking and nightmarish instances on the job, but as she consistently does in his rare moments of sentiment. Still smiling, "All right, sweet talker, let's go back to school."

With that comment, she extends her elbow jestingly for him to escort her out the room, to which he timidly slides his fingers around the outside of her arm's hinge. He walks her out of the office, never sliding his arm through hers as she would like, but he doesn't let go of his tenuous hold on her elbow. She contents herself with the thought that it is enough for now. Enough for a sad Monday morning.

Twenty minutes later. Clear across town, on the outskirts of the city, close to the suburbs and not far from her family's former home, Laura waits leaning on a tree as she has since just before the sun came up this morning. She has watched for anything unusual, something to explain the travesty that drove her into this madness, much like a rabid animal hanging around the outskirts of a town watching for an opening. The breeze has blown all morning, quite unusual for Riverview, but she has not felt it. Her skin remains numb, but, even if it did feel as it used to, she would still be unaware of the wind blowing, unable to enjoy its touch. Her eyes have focused through the chain link fence in front of her and across the small grassy field to the buildings beyond it. The school structures are uninspired and plain in design like large versions of miniature model buildings, perfectly rectangular in shape, created for efficiency, as bland as a factory. But, this factory is missing something, and that is why she has been here for the last few hours. She watched as the disciplinarian arrived first to open the building and turn off the alarm system. His name is Ken Ohler. She knew him as he had been over to her house several times for parties and dinners thrown by Gabe. The next appearance was two members of the janitorial staff, arriving in the same car. Then, some teachers began filing in, the principal, and eventually teenagers. Some were crying, most of the girls, several of the guys. No one was smiling. Conversation was uncommonly expensive as it came in few words and at low volumes. Bells rang, the classic tin-like audio sound of the announcements rolled on for at least ten minutes—which is about seven and a half minutes longer than what is typical. Laura paid no attention to the words, but she focused her eyes on the grounds. The announcements were only a bee buzzing in her ear; she did not let them distract her. The pull was holding her sight to the property. Then the students moved class by class into the gymnasium, which is the giant rectangle across the field closest to her vantage point. They marched in small groups up the steps and through the gym doors as they had many times before for pep rallies and assemblies. Their heads are reverently looking toward the ground, and the only words spoken come not in cheers but in soft comforting whispers. After the last student and teacher had entered the building, the doors shut and echoed slightly across the field. This echo is still ringing in her ears as she continues to lean her shoulder onto the trunk of the lone cypress tree just outside of the fence of the school's enclosed property.

She knows what they must be talking about in the gym, yet she does not know how to feel about it. Surely, she does not want them to forget about Gabe easily. He gave so much of himself to them. Every day. But, she feels burning and twisting inside of her as the assembly is another reminder of his gruesome murder. And the children. The pull is keeping her here, and she will not let herself retreat from it. She believes she must be here for a reason. So, she stands and rots. And, then, there's the other thing. She feels that she is breaking an obligation by standing under the tree instead of being inside the assembly honoring her husband. She thinks herself to be an abandoner of her spouse in the most sacred of times to pursue this quest. Not being in that gymnasium and not adding her words to the unified voice speaking out on the goodness that was her husband aches her so heavily that she must place most of her weight upon the tree to remain standing. But, the quest is for justice, retribution, and the truth. And, it is for him too. For all of that, she hangs onto her burdensome choice as she trades publicly honoring her husband's legacy, or even being in attendance as others do so, for unnatural knowledge. So, she stands under the tree like a modern day Eve and focuses on the grounds while she singes on the inside.

Her eyes burn. It is a combination of the daylight, although it is still too dim for this time of year, and emotion. She can feel the irritation in her sockets, but her hands do not leave her sides, still propping herself against the tree. She wishes the sky were black. The contrast between the colorless void that she feels and the sun above only reminds her of how damaged and twisted she has become. How far she has been removed from what she used to know, how she used to feel, and the entire world around her. The cypress tree on which her shoulder rests looks like it is perennially weeping. Bare forsaken branches, brown drooping stems. It looks like death grows from within it. A creeping death sprouting from another world into this one, pulled through its gnarled protruding knee-like roots, up its skinny trunk, and out its bony, arthritic, and balding branches. If not for the weeping leaves upon its tips, it would appear to be already dead.

Now, there are two walking across the blacktop yard that is on the other side of the grassy field, between the packed gymnasium and the temporarily vacated school building. Laura's eyes capture the rumples on his shirt, the loosened collar with the disarmed tie wrapped through it, and the coat draped over his extended forearm. Casual, yet keeping within an arm's reach of formality. Halfway to giving up on decency but lightly clinging onto it out of uncertainty, not wanting to completely abandon it, or hope.

The woman's appearance at his close side is less remarkable. It is adequately professional and neatly worn. As they continue to walk, only the woman's noticeably close proximity to her associate garners Laura's attention. A man slightly irreverent, whom she can now see is also unshaven, and a woman willing to closely stand beside him are both walking into a school building adjacent to a memorial service for her deceased husband. She wonders if the killers have come to her. Then it stings through her. It's him.

Moments before in a meticulously clean car, Irene parks the vehicle in the horseshoe at the back of the blacktop yard. The detective pops open his seat belt and reflects on how his car has not looked as clean as hers in quite some time. There was a time when every Sunday afternoon would be spent washing and waxing two cars. Sometimes his wife would help him too. He always found her at her sexiest when she was in the driveway with him in a pair of cheap shorts and an old shirt. Whether she pulled her hair back in a ponytail or wrapped it under one of his baseball hats, he never cared as long as she was working there with him. But, those memories lie buried under the layers of dust on his dashboard, dust that he hopes would never be seen in Irene's car.

It has been a quiet ride in the car for her. The radio was turned on softly, and even softer was her voice occasionally singing along. Not perfect in pitch was her accompaniment, but it remained perfect in warm sentiment, which is the only reason that the detective did not request for her silence. He has never been a morning person, and he is slowly becoming a nocturnal creature with a day job. His mind races restlessly throughout the night, constantly reviewing things that he should not have done and debating whether he should now do other things that spin around in his head. All of this unwanted nighttime activity equals even harder mornings for him now. She is well aware of his condition, which is part of the motivation for her care and tolerance of his rough demeanor. Most other people would not peer into him straining to see the bright spots; they would simply declare him lightless and rotted from the inside out. Despite it all, none would criticize his professional strengths, as he is an amazing detective. His hunches consistently beat the odds, mostly due to his uncanny ability to think like a criminal. His dedication to his work and the many tedious hours that he has poured into each case are not questioned by any. However, his personal life warrants a different diagnosis. One that has kept most people away from him, sneering at him, or in the least raising a puzzled eyebrow. But, Irene looks past it for something more, some kind of a spark. Sometimes she swears she sees burning glimpses of it, and at others she is terrified that she has been staring at a blank canvas for years of her life only to find that there is no obscured picture and that its emptiness has infected her too.

The sky has remained overcast, but not as dramatic as the day before. The sun can be seen breaking through, and that is the part on which she chooses to focus. As she steps out of the car, the light is mildly refreshing. After the weekend that she has been through, it is most welcome. The detective has had his sunglasses on his face since before his first step out of their office. The light is hardly enough to necessitate their presence, but his worn eyes seem to call for them with an almost vampiric dependency. She knows he will only remove them while talking with people. He still has respect for a level of professionalism despite what goes on during his long nights.

She waits for him at the rear of the car as he slowly makes his way. Cracking a joke about his pace being that of a constipated beast of burden crosses her mind, but she passes on the idea and smiles instead. He throws his coat over his forearm, and she watches to see if he will extend his other hand toward her as he closes in. It happens the same way it always does, and she walks close to him without his arm in hers. On the rare occasion when she could convince him to go out into the populace and watch a movie or come with her to buy him a new shirt or tie, her gait exuded so much compassion and familiarity that they were always mistaken as a couple. To which, he would look the other way, while making a comment like, "Don't wish such horrible things upon her," and grinning a quick and fading grin. She would always smile as if she had just won the Nobel Peace Price or graduated valedictorian. Inevitably, his rapidly retreating smile would slowly pull hers down along with it, and they would go about their business as before.

As they walk up the steps to the school building, the detective reaches out for the door handle first. He opens it and holds it for her to walk through. She has never thought it odd or considered that he may be doing it to watch her from behind as she goes through ahead of him because he just as readily holds the door open for DiNardi on a routine basis.

When Laura leaves the tree, a subtle breeze pulses like a natural form of life support through its emaciated, rheumatic branches down to their decrepit stems. A little more light breaks through the clouds and illuminates some buried green from the dangling cones. As she steps further and further away from the tree, the brownish-reddish-purplish trunk gently sways with the wind like an exhale of the earth, rustling its bark-covered arms and shaking off a dark sleep that had been leaning on it.

She moves like the light or the total opposite of it, dancing and intertwining with it as its mirror image. She doesn't remember getting herself over the fence. The grass seems to bow down before her shoes press upon its blades, and they spring her feet back off them and into her stride. Maybe, it's comfortable and accommodating, maybe nature is helping her in her quest, or maybe the grass wants no part of her touching it or pushing into its soil and roots. But, she is unaware of the assisting or rejecting nature of the earth below her. Nor could she care any less about anything that remains on this planet except for grasping vengeance. She focuses on their bodies walking into the building, slinking into it, and, before they know anything, she is upon them.

The dark blue door opens with a creak and a whoosh of air condition. The industrial tile floor that can only be found in factories, warehouse offices, and school buildings is worn in a faded and scuffed arch that turns in front of the stairs, which are directly ahead, and toward the doorway on the left at a ninety degree angle where it meets the carpet of the hallway. The sound of two dress shoes slapping and a pair of modest heels clacking on the hard off-white tile floor bounces around the vacant stairwell. They step toward the doorway to the hall in which they can now see the glass doors of the office, dark gray carpet, and long rows of dark blue lockers. Just as Irene takes her first complete stride in the bright, carpeted corridor and Detective

Andarus places his first foot onto the carpet, the dark blue door pulls shut behind them. He turns his head to glance over his shoulder at the motion of the door. Despite an odd feeling, he does not see anything, but something slipped inside. As Irene approaches the glass door with the lettering of Attendance Office, she steps to the side waiting for the detective to open it for her. This is an odd occurrence since she has never expected or waited for him to open a door for her before. He'll hold a door open for her if he reaches it first as he did earlier, but she doesn't usually step to the side waiting for him to take care of it. On the past occasions when she has reached the door first, she typically has swung it open and waited for him to grab it and follow behind her. But, Andarus almost smiles at her unusual request and reaches to open it.

From the darker stairway, Laura watches as he grabs the door handle. Sparks. He quickly jerks his hand back to his side and grunts loudly. Irene snickers and then laughs uncontrollably while choppily grabbing at his shoulder. Suddenly, his facial expression changes as he begins to realize what has just happened to him.

"I'm, I'm sorry, Paul," Irene says between laughing convulsions, "I couldn't resist it."

He barely grins and says, "No, it's okay," still fighting a smile, and he continues, "It's about time you got one over on me."

"Really, Paul, it was too much for me to resist. Every day in grade school, I would shock myself on a metal door handle getting into a classroom. I hated that hallway—had the same kind of rough carpet as this one. I couldn't take this shock; I had to pass it on to you," squeezing his shoulder and stopping the laughing, "I'm sorry; I know it's lousy timing with Deb and all."

"It's all right, Irene. I promise," he responds while opening the door for her. He smiles briefly as she walks into the office ahead of him, but he makes sure to lose it before his head enters the room.

Laura continues to look on from her vantage point in the darker stairwell, not really concerned if they see her or not, but she is trying to gain as much information as possible before they know she is around. Besides, the pull is on her to remain in the stairwell, which is also more comfortable for her than the bright corridor through the walkway ahead of her.

As she waits in the stillness, she realizes how odd it is. In years past, she had been down that hallway numerous times to visit Gabe, to bring him lunch or a stack of papers that were left at home. On every trip, the hallway was stirring with life. Students opening and slamming lockers, heading off to their next class, or conversing about and within the social microcosm of high school. Even while classes were going on, there was still an electric murmuring of questions, answers, and youthful activity shooting through the hallway. Now, it is like a deserted stable. She was always a little jealous that she never got to attend Gabe's high school. It was a brighter, safer place than the world in which she grew up. In fact, she never thought that she would ever feel anything as empty and tormenting as she had in her youth. She never could have imagined, even in her darkest moments, that she would feel as she does now. As she stares upon the hallway stripped of its hope and magic, it is all too obvious to her; Gabe is gone, and nothing will ever be the same. And, it does occur to her that she is gone too, at least in some way. Part of her was gone forever a split second before the phone hit the floor three nights ago. On that same night, another part flew from her some dark moments later.

A sob and a whimper interrupt her thoughts as the glass office door opens again. A flash of light bounces off the moving door toward the stairwell in which Laura lurks. At this, she slinks her way onto the stairs. The walls of the dark blue stairwell lift up memories of a long weekend four years before when Gabe organized a fix-up-the-school crew. Of course, he bought the paint and did the majority of the work, but six parents showed up too, which was a welcomed surprise for Laura as she had envisioned Gabe and herself alone slaving over painting lockers and walls in great detail that would certainly be doomed to endure scratches and scrapes before the end of the next semester. It was a particularly taxing chore for Laura since she had been painting and setting up her first gym that entire week. They painted classrooms, hallways, and bathrooms, but she remembers this stairwell especially well because the trim was painted dark gray and proved to be quite difficult to cover without dripping onto the dark blue walls. By the time they were finished, she was beaming with happiness for Gabe and his students who would be in a building far more welcoming than the intimidating, graffiti-covered compound that she had attended.

She climbs higher on the stairs. The steps go halfway to the second floor to a little platform where traffic would make a one-hundred-and-eighty degree turn to the second partition of stairs. She crouches on the first step of the second partition.

In a private whisper, Irene says, "My God, she was so broken up that she could barely speak. Poor woman. Makes you wonder why she even came to work today."

Detective Andarus thinks that she is not doing the school much good by being at her job today anyway—*how can she answer any phones or assist anyone if she can't bring herself to speak*? He does not utter a word but merely nods his head, which was already focusing on the tiles ahead of him as he steps off the carpet of the hallway. He reaches into his coat pocket with his pinky and next bottom finger curled inward, and he pulls out a plain-looking, black pair of sunglasses between his extended index and middle fingers and his thumb. The movement is executed with the smoothness of an old-west gunslinger effortlessly flinging his weapon from its holster. Laura skillfully slides her position lower on the stairs to place them within her sight as they move toward the door. The sunglasses reflect the tiniest amount of light as he slides them over his ears, but it catches Laura's attention. The placement of the sunglasses was timed so that he did not need to pause or slow his pace before opening the door into the beaming daylight beyond. She wonders how often he has needed to hide from the sun for it to have become a familiar ritual for him.

As Laura glances at the worn path where it passes through the doorway continuing from the tile floor onto the carpeted hallway, maybe she should pause and consider what doorways her path may be crossing into and which ones she may not be allowed inside, but instead she turns her head away and focuses on following the pull which is now after the two that just walked out the dark blue door. She waits for the door to nearly touch the frame before she stops its retreating motion. Her movement to the exit was not a conscious thought but a mere action, just as is her waiting momentarily before she pushes it back open. The reflected light from the glass office door in the hallway begins to fall again into the stairwell. Laura quickly pushes the blue door in front of her open and exits as the woman from the office steps into the hallway. The woman, with sad pink skin around her eyes and a crumpled tissue clutched in her left hand and held tightly against her chest, stands still in the corridor and stares into the stairwell watching the closing dark blue door. She thought she saw something, but in her drained state of mind she is not sure what she saw.

She whispers, "Laura," and not being able to remember for what she was going to the copy room in the first place, she turns her troubled head back to the office.

The tissue has more work to do.

Outside, Irene walks briskly beside Andarus, making a direct diagonal line from the building they just exited to the gymnasium. While Irene is still thinking about the sobbing secretary that they spoke to just moments before, Paul pulls the door open for her and smiles in a miniscule fashion as he remembers her uncharacteristic ruse earlier with the glass office door. She feels like she is entering a church as she steps onto the wooden gym floor. A solemn hush hangs like humidity over the room, and she feels something sacred. Andarus is just glad that his eyes no longer have to contend with the sun as the door is shutting behind him.

Laura watched as he stepped through the door after his comrade. While the door is still closing, she stares at what she can see of his face past the scruffy hairs and behind the sunglasses. She is sure it is he. And, she will wait.

As Laura leans on the only lamppost that is burned out on the block, she watches the door of the 3rd Precinct. While she waits, she recalls the events she watched outside of the school. Earlier, she had watched as the detective and his cohort shook hands with the principal, expediently walked around the corner of the gym, and talked with her as the remaining students flowed out from the assembly, returning to their classrooms. The detective, facing the principal whose back was close to the wall of the gym, took out a small notepad and a pen from his back pants pocket, which Laura noted was farther away from his heart, eyes, and mind than the coat pocket which is reserved for his sunglasses. It also occurred to her that the more she closely obeys the pull, the easier these observations drift to her. He wrote something quickly upon meeting Mrs. Andrews, and then, about two minutes later in the conversation, he wrote seven more words according to the number of times that Laura counted his pen being lifted from the tablet. Moments after, the principal escorted them back into the building, through the dim stairwell and the bright corridor, and into her office.

Laura had an easy time viewing their outside conversation. With all of the sadness choking the exuberance out of the school, the teachers were busy looking after their students. She had been away for the best part of two years, so many of the faculty that knew her had retired or moved on. Four years ago the students would have all recognized her from her frequent visits to see Gabe. Now, only a handful of observant seniors might have been able to remember her from her visits when they were mere freshmen or sophomores. Even if someone did recognize her, she should have been expected to be there. It was a tribute to her recently deceased husband, and no one had more of a right to be there than she. But, she still did not feel it time to reveal herself to Andarus. Either way, no one was rushing off to look a new widow in the eyes and offer a brief word to fill an unholy rift. Laura stayed about seventy feet away as she observed them. She watched from the other side of the stream of passing students as where the detective, his assistant, and Principal Andrews were standing. The pull gave her no alarm as she peered at them, so she felt no concern about her visibility. She turned from them and started walking away as soon as they began making their way toward the school building, not knowing where she was headed—just that she had somewhere to go.

Part of her desperately wanted to burst into the office and demand to know everything from all three parties, but especially the head detective. By then, she knew well enough who he was. But, the part of her, that was crying out to force her way into the office and grab onto the truth, to fight for it, to demand, to beg for it, had grown quiet, and she had learned to follow the guidance of the pull. Bleeding and burning all the way.

All of these events from the past afternoon tumble in her brain as she leans on the burned out light pole and stares so hard at the door of the station across the street that it appears she is trying to rip it off its hinges with her gaze. There is a parking garage behind the building, but she is quite sure that his car is one of the four parked in the reserved spots by the curb in front of the building. His assistant parked her compact import in the front of the building between a police car and a gray, unmarked vehicle in the same style as the police car, which all are followed by another police cruiser on the end. Laura is certain that the third car parked along the curb, the gray one, which is immediately behind the assistant's car, is the detective's vehicle.

Thunder pulses like a heartbeat. It reminds her that she is creeping closer to her prey whose heart is still beating. She doesn't remember when the rain started falling, and she is barely aware of it as the drops roll down her forehead, through her thin eyebrows, down and back up the slope of her lids, and splashing into her eyes, causing her vision to blur slightly. There is a wretched, silent delay between the rolls of thunder screaming across the sky. Boom. Nothing. Boom. Nothing. Boom. It reminds her of three hearts that beat no longer. Three black bags. Three bloody bags. Three ripping scars behind her eyes under a darkened streetlight that hold their stare at a closed door across the street.

Beyond the door and beyond her plagued sight, in an office that smells of stale coffee and half-eaten fast food, a confession is spoken.

"All right, let's admit it."

Andarus waits for the heart of her statement to come out. He notices an expression that he has not often seen on her face. He doesn't like seeing her like this.

"This case is scaring the hell out of me," Irene says looking determined as always but worriedly cautious, afraid. Having been amazed numerous times at how tough she could be and still maintain her feminine demeanor while staring at a nightmarish crime scene, interviewing suspects, and tracking down a murderer, Andarus is startled by the expression on her face. He thinks it looks like a great white shark feeling the shadow of a larger, forgotten, and mythical creature approaching stealthily. Her persevering attitude reminds him that he is not alone on this one, but the uneasiness in her countenance gives validity to his own thoughts that they have stumbled on something odd. Even for him.

She raises a single eyebrow at Andarus awaiting his response. Anxious to hear what harsh reality he will smack down on the comment and wanting to add some levity to the creepy tingling that runs in her brain and up her forearms, Irene raises the eyebrow to a ludicrously higher level.

Whiskery lips twist in a pensive sideways motion, seemingly ignoring her cocked brow, and he utters, "Mm—yeah."

Her eyes drop from his face to the floor, uncomfortable with her guide tossing her request back to her. She has always been respected and considered an equal, but he has never before been without any insight to add to her questions. Equality is something desirable in every situation except an emergency. Her lip quivers for the first time in two years in the office about something work-related. It doesn't go unnoticed.

His voice breaks the chilling void, "So, the question is, 'What are we going to do about it?'"

This is the call back to the battlefront, and she pulls the arrow straight, readying herself, "Okay, what do you think? We have to find the mother right?"

He looks away from her, as he did earlier on every occasion that she mentioned Mrs. Bonney, "Well, let's review what we know again. At approximately 11:15 on Friday night, Craig Augury, a neighbor, reported the murders in such a horrified manner that the operator could barely get the address from him. After coaxing the story from him later, he says he heard doors slam, a car take off—claimed it sounded like a cheap import muffler, he knocked on the next door to check on Mr. Bonney and the kids: no answer and the door handle is locked. He goes to the back door and finds it locked too, but through the kitchen window he can see the father is a bloody mess on the couch…"

"Paul, we're missing something with the neighbor's story: they slammed a door and sped off. Why? They got away with the murders: they had their way with the girls. They did it all without leaving any signs of breaking in or attracting any of the neighbors' attention. Why would they draw attention to themselves at the end? It's a stupid move."

"Or, it's a scared teenager. But, let's not rush ahead. Crime scene led us to believe that at least two males were involved in the murders due to the rape. Unless one male managed to detain one of the girls while he raped and killed the other girl. We'll know that for sure soon. Flesh under the girls' fingernails indicates that they were not dead at the time of the raping. But, the wounds on the father also imply that there were at least two people in the house: one holding him back, and the other stabbing him. After initial investigation of the scene, Debbie called the missing mother who was in Houston. Debbie was found when we returned to the station in some sort of a seizure repeating the name, 'Mrs. Bonney' over and over again. She was taken to the hospital, and the only diagnosis given by the doctors was that she was in shock from some serious stimulus. Three days later and she is still in the hospital whispering the words, thanks to her medication, instead of shouting them at full volume as she was before. Which brings us to the same dead end that we've been rushing to all evening: what in the hell happened on that phone?"

Irene shudders just as she did when he mentioned the raping. She has become desensitized to some parts of the job, but there are other aspects of the work, like juvenile, rape with which she hopes she will never become comfortable.

"Paul, what if it is much simpler than we are giving it credit? Mrs. Bonney had to be in an amazing amount of pain at hearing the news: all of which Debbie had to hear over the phone. Every outburst, every wail, every sob. And, this is one of many calls like this that Debbie has had to make over the last fifteen years that she's been here—I mean she was doing this when I was graduating from grade school. Is that not enough to make someone have a breakdown?"

He stares at her for a moment before speaking, "Sure, of course it could be enough to make someone have a mental breakdown," pausing again, "But, you don't believe that, do you?"

"No," she responds as the brief hope deflates from her, "It wouldn't explain why Mrs. Bonney has not shown up anywhere, why a pathologist also went to the hospital with a broken jaw and collarbone, bruises and a concussion, yet nothing was stolen or disrupted, or why…" she stops suddenly.

"Why what?"

"Why I have this pressing feeling of dread all around me."

"You're not the only one, Irene. DiNardi and Jackson didn't show up today, and I promise they don't have the flu, and our secretary is incessantly whispering a name like an owl in a hospital," his level of emotion reaches a pinnacle when he mentions the secretary. Irene has learned that Debbie Lambert cared for Paul greatly in the year that his wife left him and his mother died. She made sure that he ate and heard a kind word every day at work. Debbie assumed those duties right up until Irene was hired. At that point, she encouraged Irene to make sure Paul took care of himself.

Reaching out as she always does, she touches his hand with a soft firmness, "I know, Paul, I know," pausing for a moment, "That's why we're gonna nail this one. This thing needs to end here; we can't let it affect anyone else."

With his left hand, he pats her hand that remains on top his right, and he suggests, "We'll start tomorrow morning with talking to the suspects. Early. Let's wake them up and see how they respond without any time to prepare themselves. We've been over all that we know so far all night long: we're not gonna do any more good tonight except spin our wheels and wear ourselves out. Let's get some sleep and meet up here at six in the morning."

"Yeah, detective, let's get some sleep," she says slipping him a maternal glance as she turns to the desk and tosses all of the remaining fast food into the bags.

He takes the bags from her and tosses them into the trash.

"Irene, I've got a few things I want to do before I leave, so why don't you get going and I'll be right behind you?"

Raising her eyebrows as she did earlier, "All right, boss man, as long as you promise me you're leaving here within the next half hour."

"Uhhh," he responds turning away.

Crossing her arms and shifting her weight to her left knee, "P-a-u-l?"

"I'll be gone before too long. Don't worry about it."

"Don't make me come down on you, *Monsieur Dupin*. I can be more relentless than anyone that you've ever brought to justice; now promise me."

Smiling briefly, but turning his head away from her so she cannot get a clear view of it, "You know I love it when you get literary, but get out of here; I'll be gone in twenty minutes."

Not hearing any movement, he glances at her, "I promise."

"All right, if there are lights on in this office in a half hour, there will be hell to pay."

"Yeah, yeah, yeah."

She walks out of the office, but her thoughts remain on the scruffy man alone in the room.

Twenty-one minutes and fifty three seconds later, Paul turns on the ignition, instantly bringing a darkness-cutting illumination to the gauges in front of him and the sounds of rock radio into the cockpit of his car. He looks at his eyes in the rearview mirror trying to see the wear that Irene has been harping on. Without a thought, his lips move along with the familiar words of the radio, "*One who doesn't care is one who shouldn't be,*" words that he sang new in his youth that have now become classic, *"I've tried to hide myself from what is wrong for me."* His door flings open and the darkness grabs his arm.

It is she, she from the park. He sees the face, the streak in her hair, something gathering in her pupils.

"Laura," slips from his lips involuntarily just as it had at the park.

Quickly rushing her face uncomfortably close to his, she demands, "How do you know who I am, detective?"

"I could ask you the same thing," retorts the investigator.

She does not speak, does not move, does not blink. Stares. The mix of the persistent rain and the statue-like resolve of her eyes causes the detective's self-imposed silence.

Breaking the wordlessness, "It's from the pictures in your house," he rapidly explains, noticing the eye of the storm in her irises gaining speed and growing in intensity, forcing the truth out his mind and through his tongue, "I'm investigating your family's murders."

Silence. Swirling, penetrating eyes. He notices the droplets streaming down her face, blotting and running and blurring. Covering her with a thin, lucid layer: a watery skin. Like rain on a glacier. She is so consumed with her stare that she doesn't pay the droplets any mind, as if she had control over them like they were a part of her body. Andarus is filled with pure awe: sheer amazement and hellacious terror. It dawns on him that it must be the same feeling that he saw earlier in his office: the great white shark, the perfect natural hunting machine facing the unknown giant that was thought to be forgotten but only lurking in deep freezing waters. Irene. He must handle Laura himself, or she might go after Irene. His plan offers no comfort as he has no idea how he will do it.

"I'm sorry," he offers.

She stares. His breathing is loud; he cannot hear hers at all. Andarus sits motionless behind the wheel of his car, facing the interloper who had flung his door open just a few long moments before. In eight years on the job, he has never once sat motionless waiting helplessly on someone involved in an investigation and allowing anyone to stand threateningly over him.

Her voice shrills through his nervous system like a knife on its sharpening stone, "Who are your suspects?"

Without thought or mental consent to do so, his mouth opens and utters, "Murdstone and Legree."

"Who are they? How did they know my family?"

Mouth opens, words fire, “Students of your husband.”

“No, Gabe’s students loved him. *They loved him*. Why?” The harshness of her voice trails off at the end.

“He gave them their last detentions that caused them to be expelled,” as the words slide out of his mouth, he wishes he could grab them out of the air and yank them back to safety. Discretion has become too frozen for him to drink in Laura’s shadow.

Shaking her head, she poses, “Do you think they did it?”

He sits still, unstirred, trying to fight her from pulling the answer out of him. He tries to look toward the light of the gauges, but the spinning whirlpool pupils suck him into them like the eye of a hurricane.

She repeats with intensity, “Did they do it? Did they kill my little girls and my husband?”

With trembling lower lip, “I…I don’t know.”

“What do you think, Andarus? Tell me.”

Hearing Laura say his name that he never told her adds another level of despair to the situation, another layer of frost on the ice.

“Now.”

“I—they—”

The stare stares.

“Yes, I think they might have.”

Silence.

“Nothing was stolen. Your husband had no criminal record, and, according to Principal Andrews, he had no other enemies in the world. And, a neighbor’s statement indicates that the malefactors were likely juveniles. I don’t know, but it points to the two kids.”

She closes her eyes for a moment. Andarus feels like an outdoorsman stepping into a cabin escaping a frosty winter wind. But, it is fleeting as they soon pop open again and swirl upon him.

Trying to regain a shadow of his professional behavior, he asks, “Mrs. Bonney, where have you been? Why haven’t you—”

Whirlpools intensify; in a blaze a slender hand reaches to the back of his head, and his forehead smashes the rim of the steering wheel at an extreme velocity. His eyes shut, and he shivers as if in a draft.

Chapter IX

The dank streetlights strain to cut the darkness that is night. The street itself was the dream of three generations past; Planeline Highway was to be the crowning architectural and commercial thoroughfare of the suburbs of Riverview. Somewhere along the line it became antiquated, signs faded, hotels turned to motels, stores closed, houses became dilapidated, and commerce of questionable means became as easy to find as its roaches; time has pressed its thumbprint on the old dreams.

She walks along the broken sidewalk of this street that brings back horrible memories from her younger years. The moonlight is thin, not much more than a hazy, faded yellow aura in the night sky. Clouds still linger. Out by the curb, a brush-painted white sign with uneven black writing says "$100 a Weak, $35 a Nite." The smell of dust, garbage, cigarettes, and spilled alcohol rise up to her nostrils, and it assures her she is in the right place as she walks up the driveway that is hedged off by a latticework fence on the left side and the motel office on the other. Atop the latticework fence and running to the office is a wooden canopy that is about ten feet high. The driveway is barely wide enough for one vehicle to pass. A sign on the fence to the left with some type of unkempt vines running over it reads "Honk before entering." The tinted glass windows that make up the walls of the office are caked with dirt from the highway and the winds of recent storms. The hue of the words "Cash Only", written in drippy, bright, crooked, red letters on the window next to the office door, stirs up some movement within her pupils. Through the dirty veil of tint and dross on the windows, she can see someone abruptly rise to their feet from a chair. A hand reaches out to grab something on a solid block of furniture that could be a desk. Laura slows her pace and stares in the person's direction. The hand goes back to rest on the hip, and the body lowers itself back to its chair. Laura's regular pace returns, and she does not look back to the office again.

Crossing through the threshold into the inner rectangle that is the No-Tell Motel, all of the pink doors are shut and locked. Rodents fear storms, even those that claim to be human. She passes a pool in the dead center of the rectangle that is full of opaque water. Brown and black leaves sway in the bottom of the pool resulting from the untimely breeze blowing on its surface.

The top of the water has a thin film that bubbles along the edge of the pool where the gust causes the tiny current to crash. Faster than fast the pool is lit up from an angry sky. For a still moment Laura sees the entire contents of the murky swimming bowl; a boy's lost tennis ball, suspended and twirling particles, a forgotten pair of goggles, small branches wrecked upon the bottom hopelessly wishing they could plant root. The thunder following the flash strikes with such force that the pool bounces as if trembling before it. Laura devises that all of the items in the pool are trapped, as if frozen, in an artificial plane, stuck between the concrete floor and a sludgy, inhuman membrane upon the surface of the water. Before the thunder is done its scream, she lets the thought pass. She seeks something foul lurking around the corner.

The night is silence, except for the approaching storm. No crickets, no frogs, no voices except the persistent pull inside her soul. She turns a corner. It is a small walkway that leads from the center of the rectangle to the edge of the side street. The motel rectangle is made up of four buildings. The building on the right runs the entire length of the rectangle consisting of the hazy glass office followed by six rented rooms. The far end of the rectangle is one narrow building with only three rooms in it. Then the left side is made of two buildings with a small alley between them, which is where she is now. Just inside the alley at its corner is a cigarette machine. Next to the tobacco dispenser is a soft drink machine with an "OUT OF ORDER" sign taped over the bottled water button.

A dangling light bulb rocks with the breeze revealing exposed wire crimped into quick disconnects. Her hand reaches up and malignly taps it with her extended pointer finger. The bulb flickers out, and a piece of a filament floats toward the bottom of its glass casing. There is a window on the right, and past it is a door. A half-inch past the doorframe, the wall ends. Connecting the two buildings at the end of the walkway are long vertical iron bars with a horizontal crosspiece every two feet until it meets the ceiling. The last crosspiece has a large nest, which looks to be a home for absent birds. The pull sends her to the dirty window with a broken set of blinds that the management had purchased twenty-seven years before. The inner windowsill is littered with dead mosquitoes, flies, and cigarette butts. The blinds are bent and missing pieces, resembling the sly-looking long plates in the mouth of a baleen whale, but these battered blinds more accurately resemble the baleen plates of a whale beaten, toyed with, and killed by a great storm or perhaps a mysterious predator no longer seen or believed in by man.

The light inside the room is minimal. Through the holes in the blinds, Laura can see that one faint bulb hangs from the center of the ceiling, and one lamp with a crooked, stained shade is placed on the floor next to three dirty pillows. The floor itself is a brown color with many amoeba-shaped stains. A stack of speakers stands about seven feet high next to the lamp. She can hear loud talking, but cannot see anyone yet. The voices are coming from inside the bathroom, whose light is on and its door set against the frame but not shut. Maneuvering her body to look through the different breaks in the blinds, she can see television sets on the floor all over the room. Numerous smaller sets sit atop larger ones. Car stereos, home audio components, and various computer equipment bespeckle and crowd the small room. Smoke pours out of the crack between the doorframe and the bathroom door. There is no mattress or even blankets in the room, but there is an area of about six square feet in front of the three cruddy pillows that is cleared of any items. Two Styrofoam boxes of Chinese takeout lie on the floor mostly uneaten. A line of ants has made its way to the box closest to the door.

"So, where is your little slut, Simon? We talked about this—today is the day," demands Ed, flinging the bathroom door open and sending the smoke to disperse and pollute the room.

In a meeker, but annoyed voice, Simon responds, "She's not at her old man's house—the drunk told me he hadn't seen her in two days. I don't know where the hell she is."

"Have you talked to her since the house?"

"No, I haven't seen her since she ran out of the car when we pulled up here after we were done."

Anger growing, screaming starting, Simon spouts, "Dude, you have got to get that bitch under control. She's still pissed about the girls—you should've handled her when she started acting up at that worthless teacher's house."

Laura's fist squeezes the wooden windowsill tightly as the last three words were grunted, barely able to hold herself still. Were she not so fixated on their faces and the sounds they utter, she would have noticed how little she can feel in her fingers. She stares so intently through the window that she thinks they will surely feel it on them before long.

"We needed to get out of there—she was going nuts. What did you want me to do, Ed, kill her right there? They'd trace her to us right away. You're the one who peeled outta there like an idiot—no one knew we were there at all—now, 'cause of you, they might. What do you want me to do about it now?"

"Don't you start yelling at me 'cause you can't handle your woman. She's gone nuts over this thing, and I told you two days ago I'm not gonna go to jail because she can't keep her woman mouth shut. And, you, how can you even still think about her? This whole thing wasn't about getting him back for what he did to us—it wasn't about us getting expelled. She was still burning for *him* because he shot her down last year. That's what this was about for her—that's why she did it."

"Go to hell, Ed."

"It's true."

"Go to hell."

Simon looks away, and Laura can see a twitch on his left eye raging out of control as his hand goes to his forehead to try to rub some relief into it.

Laura wonders if he had this mental struggle when Ed decided to violate her defenseless daughters. Did Simon twitch, fight, and then cave under Ed's push as they ripped stuffed animals from their hands and replaced them with filth? Or, had he twisted himself into the demonic idea before he entered the house, thinking it, planning it, and lusting in its brazen unholiness?

Her anger shuts her eyes and blocks her hearing momentarily, and all she fears is that it will shut her down again like after the morgue. She strains for control, and her ears open to Simon growling, with his head trembling, "…her, forget her, I h-a-t-e her. Said she loved me. Said she loved me! It was all to get him—it wasn't for me! It was never for me!"

Ed smiles broadly at hearing Simon sound exactly like himself, enjoying that the button he pushed produced the desired effect so quickly, so completely. So obediently. Falling so far only seems reasonable when one has dragged another along with them to break the inevitable collision with the ground, and it only seems enjoyable when ripping someone far above them to pieces in perverse mockery. Ed smiles at the thought of Simon accepting such a perfectly forbidden target; he gloats internally at the manifestation of his growing power over Simon.

Acting on his gloat, "You're right, Simon; she played you. You were her toy to get over the man that broke her heart. She's not here now, and she's never coming back. She's never coming back to you, Simon! She's going to try and end this, and turn you in now—and me with you. If we take the fall, she'll get even with you for what we did to the girls. And, was it so bad? Should they have died without ever knowing how it felt, without ever experiencing the thrill?"

Words fall from Laura's mouth without guidance or thought, "They spew out swords from their lips, and they say, 'Who can hear us?'" She feels as if she could vomit out her soul, but she squeezes the windowsill tighter. Her pupils spin like a tempest, completely out of control. The dizziness begins to overtake her. But, she grabs onto the pull, which is still on the sill. She cannot allow herself to go out now; or, they will surely have her, and what they will do to her will be another inhuman horror thrown on top of the scorched carcasses of her family in the consuming and desecrating fire. But, for now, the whirlpool is stronger than her, despite her resolve.

"And, think about this, *my friend*," Ed continues smiling so broadly and pointedly that his self-sharpened canine teeth gleam in the dirty light of the room—the right one with saliva streaming from it, "without your money—our money to pay for her next hit, what do you think she is doing right now to get her next fix?"

An animalistic, defeated scream and the sound of a television smashing into the ground echo through the tiny room.

Talking from behind closed teeth, sitting on the floor in the center of the room next to the shattered television and his fractured and lost emotion,

Simon offers, "We have to; we can't go down for this because of her. She can't do this to me…she can't…bitch!"

Grinning wickedly, Ed explains, "Patience is for the timid and the unsure; act now. Do it. We'll find her; she doesn't have any friends or many places that she could be; we need to get on the hunt while her rotten stink is still fresh and she hasn't run to the shelter of the police. Do it. Do it, Simon," reaching at his forearm to help him off the ground.

As Ed pulls him to his feet, Simon looks to the ground and says, "We have to; she's given us no choice. I looked for her; she knows where we are. She has to know this is coming—unless she is planning on turning us in. Let's do it."

Ed slides his arm around Simon's shoulders as he helps him to the door. They stumble to exit the room arm in arm; Ed smiling, Simon struggling. As Ed's hand reaches out and unlocks the deadbolt, Simon stops walking and says, "Ed, I have to do it. All by myself. Don't you touch her, Ed. Don't even think about it. She was mine; I want to do it alone—I *need* to do it alone."

Still with the mouth of a frenzied wolf, Ed says, "Sure, sure, Simon. No problem. I wouldn't *dream* of it," then with a much sterner voice that is devoid of compassion, "As long as you get the job done, Simon. Make no mistake; we're taking care of this tonight."

"Just stay out of the way, Ed. I have some things to say to her first. She's gonna hear me scream before she goes, so she'll understand."

"Whatever, pushover, as long as it ends with a bang tonight," with a forceful pull of the door, that scrapes its way through the uneven frame, and a tug at Simon's shoulder, "Let's get this rolling now before the rain drowns us."

Laura is aware the door has opened, and she scrambles to gain control, but the pull of the whirlpool rocks her. She drops her chin to her chest with her hair covering her face and eyes.

Ed lumbers through the doorway slamming Simon's left shoulder on the edge of the doorframe. He sees a woman standing two feet in front of him still facing his window.

"If you were looking for what we've got, baby, all you had to do was knock; we'd've treated ya right, wouldn't we, Simon?"

Simon glances up and only nods his head meekly in response. Laura stands perfectly motionless.

"You have to excuse lovebird here, my fine female customer," Ed says shaking Simon at the shoulders with his arm that still lies there. Noticing that she has not responded in anyway whatsoever, Ed wonders if she is already out on her feet, "What can we do for you, bitch-face?"

Ed chuckles to himself, Simon sighs as if crying, and Laura does not make a sound. Utterly frustrated at the lack of a doting audience, Ed swings his hand to smack Laura in the forehead. Her body stumbles backward keeping his approaching hand millimeters from touching her retreating body and face.

Ed staggers mildly, but his arm around Simon's shoulder prevents him from falling to the ground. Laura stops in the exact position in which she needed to move to avoid the blow. The uneven motion causes Simon to stir and look up to see what is transpiring above his dropped head.

Staring in amazement at Laura's well-kept body, Ed focuses on her head, whose chin still rests against her breastplate.

"Damn, Simon, this one's already out of her box. *This is gonna be a well-deserved night, my boy.* We're gonna have some fun with her."

Ed waits one last time for a reaction, trying to gauge her level of consciousness. Satisfied, he says, "Simon, look at her hair; she's got this long white streak running down—that is the hottest thing I've ever seen. Look at that body on her; momma, does aerobics."

He reaches out to touch her streak, but his other arm is still around Simon's bony shoulders, which tether him, barely preventing his hand from touching her. Ed irritatedly lifts his arm from Simon's shoulder, and, pulling the arm around as fast as he can, he shoves Simon into the room with both hands.

"Get the hell out the lady's way, moron. Can't you see that she needs to make some business wit us?" following Simon into the room and leaning very close to his ear, he whispers, "Other business can wait, hombre. This one's ready to party. Got it?"

Ed turns around to see Laura standing about six inches in front of them, head still resting on her chest. Stumbling back again, he says, "Oh, there you are."

She flips her head up, flinging her hair out of her face, unveiling her eyes that are full of violently twirling maelstroms. The sight sends Ed reeling backward into the seven-foot stack of speakers, which tumble on top of him. Her left foot flies backward slamming the door tightly in its warped frame. Simon looks up in disbelief to watch Laura's left leg land, pivot, and send her right foot crashing into the unprotected, bony side of his knee, sending a bone-crunching snap bouncing off the walls of the filthy room. He drops to the ground screaming, and she walks to Ed, who lies pinned to the floor by a large stereo speaker that has broken his left forearm and has held it trapped there against the carpet. He cries silently, breathing heavily as the mystical-eyed creature in the shape of woman stalks closer to him.

Gulping loudly, and with a higher voice than he has ever spoken in the presence of Simon, Ed pleads, "You can have all the junk you want—it's in the bathroom under the sink—it's in hollowed out cleaning bottles. Ju-just don't hurt us anymore."

She steps closer. Slowly. Intentionally.

"Just take the smack and go," steps closer, "Take it and go," one step closer, "*For the love of God, just take it and go!*" squealing at the end.

In a voice like he has never heard before, she states, "How dare you? *You*? You inhuman, rotting bag of flesh. How dare you call on *Him*? We haven't even begun."

Ed squeals in an incomprehensible tone.

"Two little girls, seven and nine, and a man like no other will have their vengeance."

As his pupils expand to an absurd level, she sends her fist flying with her entire body behind it. Her toes arch, her legs lock at the knees, and her torso flings around in a blaze crashing her fist into his filthy mouth. Teeth buckle, two fly out, blood bursts forth like an explosion, and his jaw snaps out of its joint on the left side, hanging crooked and looking lobo-like. The punch shook his body with such force that it knocked the heavy speaker off his shattered forearm.

Wheezing sounds gurgle out of his jaw. Reaching down, she grabs the lower mandible with her left hand and digs her fingers into the broken mess tightly. His eyes stare and strain, but his body is frozen in response to the shocking pain. She pulls the jaw back to its original position and shoves what is left of the shattered bone into the socket. At this, his body convulses and screams from within his throat.

Leaning in closely with her eyes directly in front of his, still clenching his destroyed jawbone, she says in a crazed whisper, "Get used to it…Feel it…Feel what you did to them…Going to be a long night for you…Long night for you…"

Shrieks pound, echo, and splatter the room for the next three hours and thirty-three minutes.

She walks out of the hallway of terror into the open rectangle into which the enraged sky breaks, flashes, and unloads its vicious ferocity. The disgusting film that covered the pool's surface slimes its way over the walkway as the grimy water overflows. Within seconds her hair is matted to her head and clings to her face, chin, and neck. The long white streak in her hair shimmers in the lightning revealing running red streaks sliding down her face, chest, arms, and into her mouth. The spaces between her teeth are tiny rivers of blood, and they run more vehemently as she smiles. The pull has abandoned her as it tries to pull her inward, to suck her inside of herself, to vortex the beast it created into a nothingness. But, she is far too full at the moment to be crushed. Her smile jerks erratically between the maniacal smirk and the empty dropped lips of a fresh widow, and her soul feels like it is falling at a faster rate than the bombarding rain. She does not feel much of anything besides an explosion of everything except love and peace. Hate, vengeance, the thrill of violent restitution, pain, sadness, and shock fill her veins as they struggle not to explode. The shrieks, the spewing, the organ-twisting, face-ripping horror that she brought to life in that room have never been seen outside of hell in the long, muddied history of man. It scars her deeper than the phone call that she felt on the floor of her office some days ago. She can almost smell herself burning, and her eyes scream out for her humanity's scalding; but her smile feeds on the rage of having beaten the memory of all that she ever loved into two mounds that should never have been on the same planet as her raped daughters and lacerated husband.

Chapter X

Andarus looks at Irene for a response. The door to the office is shut behind her as she rubs her temples, trying to make sense of what Paul has just unloaded on her. The detective knows what he saw, and he is not afraid of the judgment to be cast down from the slender fingers massaging her forehead. By describing the event to Irene, he has handed her a puzzle that he cannot solve; a procedure that he cannot complete on himself. On the surface level, it merely has to do with bizarre circumstances in a case, but there is a much deeper-reaching verdict that will be linked to her analysis. As crucial as it will be, he still does not fear it. He feels as if he could welcome the worst. If he truly is insane, if she deems him to be mad, he can quit pretending. He can quit trying. He can let go and drift away, open-mouthed swallowing the waters of apathy, hoping that there is some solace in the notion that he does not have to fight anymore, that he doesn't have to believe any longer that his sorrowful condition could change, that he will no longer strain his eyes at the sun looking for a miracle to change his poisoned reality.

As soon as her eyes open, he knows his hope is thwarted. Even past the dangling pinkies in front of her eyes as her hands are still at her pulsing temples, he can see what her response will be. It is going to be crushing, but not the ultimate crush that he was looking for. Not the release. She has not given up on him; she hasn't said a word, but he can see it. Her eyes are warmth. Tired warmth: half of him and half of her. For a moment, he does hope. He hopes that her eyes never become completely like his, and he fleetingly wishes that he had never breathed, as he knows he is responsible for the worn half of her. But, he can see it in her eyes. She has warmth still. And, he waits for her words to prove his instincts. After all, communicating with women has never been his strong suit.

"Paul, I've been telling you for the longest time that you need to take better care of yourself. You never get enough sleep, you pump your body full of caffeine, and you don't eat properly," taking a deep breath, "You work nonstop, Paul. This can be a very morbid job at times. Even though we help keep the city safe and catch the bad guys, we look at death every day."

He goes to softly protest, but stops and waits for her to continue.

"I just can't believe it, Paul. I can't bring myself to think that there is some boogeyman, I'm sorry—boogey*woman*, out there hospitalizing a secretary over the phone and forcing you to tell her details of a case just by staring at you. Then, she slams your head into your steering wheel and knocks you out until I find you at 5:50 this morning. Paul, I'm sorry—it just can't be."

Andarus shakes his head in agreement. He doesn't accept her explanation, but he cannot imagine a way to make her believe what he saw. He rubs his fingers over the stubble on his chin creating a rough grating sound.

"It wasn't the first time, Irene."

"What? What first time?"

"I saw her in the park Sunday afternoon. I sat next to her on a bench. Tried to talk with her. It was strange…There was no one else in the park that day. I talked to her about my personal life—how I felt inside," leaning forward and lowering his voice, "You know me, Irene, I don't do that. Ever. It was like it was pulled out of me. I didn't even realize that it was her until she was walking away. The pictures from the house—it was definitely her. I couldn't get up to go after her. It was like I was held there—the wind knocked out of me."

"Paul, you watched a woman, who we were trying to track down to obtain information about her family, walk away from you without asking a single question?"

"Yes."

"I don't know what to think about this. I definitely think you need a rest," she waits to see if he will respond—he does not. "Paul, you need some time off. This work, this lifestyle that you're living is starting to affect you," pausing again, "Maybe we all need a break."

The noise of cabinets opening and closing in the next room can be heard through the wall.

Andarus asks, "Are Jackson and DiNardi here, yet?"

"They haven't called in, detective; I think that would be them making their morning coffee," she answers pointing her finger to the wall to her left that is shared with the other room.

"And DiNardi is eating his morning donuts. Wonder if he has any extra for me?"

Irene smiles and says, "No sugar for you, crackpot. We've got to figure out exactly what happened to you last night. We can't have our head homicide detective knocked out with his forehead resting on the steering wheel of his car in front of the police station."

"It's amazing that no one stopped to check on me."

Chuckling, she says, "Yeah, I guess our force is getting pretty laxed not to notice a man with his head on his steering wheel about twenty feet from the front door of the station."

He notices that the word should have been "lax," but he has no desire to correct her, "Most of them come in the side door from the parking garage anyway."

"Paul?"

"Yes, sunshine?"

"I'm not interested in talking about sugar, DiNardi eating donuts, or how observant our local police force may be," placing both hands on his desk and leaning over to be face-to-face with him, "Paul, are you seeing things, darlin'?"

"Well, if I am, what happened to Debbie? And, if Debbie broke down too, what happened to the pathologist, Irene? If it's so, then we've got a mental health and unexplained physical illness epidemic."

"Yeah, but there has to be…Paul, there's got to be some…This can't be something supernatural going on. There is always a logical explanation—even if it means that someone involved has gone insane, there is always a reason. Paul, you know this; we do it everyday, and you've been doing this five years longer than me. Don't you think that you could have had some type of episode? After all that you've been through, after all the non-stop work, after the lack of sleep and food, after all that has happened with Karen?"

Andarus looks solemn for a moment, "No, she hasn't done that to me yet," pausing momentarily, "Irene, I would love to tell you that all of this was an episode—some breakdown or fever dream. If that were true, then we wouldn't have to deal with this problem. It's out there, and it knows me. *She* knows me. I wish I could tell you that it's not real, then she would never know you."

Irene shakes her head softly, "I know, Paul, but…"

"Debbie knows her. The pathologist knows her. *I* know her; doesn't that mean something to you, Irene?"

With a quiet sob, "Of course it does, Paul. That's why I can't accept it so easily. I know that you're right—I believe you. I just don't want to; I wanna believe that we can fight this like any case we've ever had. And, I want to believe that you're gonna be safe. What are we gonna do?"

"Well, I know what I have to do. I have to finish this—I've been pulled into this whether I like it or not. I don't think I'd walk away anyway; I need to be here for Debbie. I can't let that stand. I have to find out what happened to her—it may be the only way that we can help her."

She nods, and he continues, "But, you, Irene, you don't need to be in on this one. You're right; something is creepy about this case. It touched me—I can't deny it. I felt it. It laid me out."

Slowly, she says, "You'll have to shoot me to keep me off this one. I won't leave you. I don't understand any of this, but I believe you anyway."

"I might not be the best person to put your faith in," slower still.

"Well, that part is up to me, detective. And, unless if you're willing to shoot me, we are pursuing this one together. Now, are we going to wake up those teens, or are we going after the mystery woman?"

"I think we better go after the kids and hope that the mystery woman hasn't found them first. At least we have an idea where they might be."

He pats his pants pocket to retrieve his notebook.

"I can't believe this."

"What? What happened?"

"She stole my notebook. Last night, she must've taken it from me after I passed out."

"Passed out, tough guy?"

Smirking irritatedly, "All right, miss sensitivity, after I got knocked out. Happy?"

Closing one eye, looking upward with the other, and crinkling her nose, she says, "Mmmm, not quite. Throw in breakfast and a foot massage, and you might have a deal."

Andarus opens the long, narrow wooden drawer in front of him, which makes a squeak as it chugs along on its old, crooked guide rail. Quickly grabbing a fresh, unused notebook and roughly shoving the drawer back to its closed position, he gets up from his desk, grabs his coat—the same coat from the day before, and starts walking toward the door.

Irene follows suit and says, "No, I don't think I'll be happy until we shine some light on this specter lady. We can't have you getting knocked out every night—it'll kill our credibility."

Quietly chuckling, he says, "You just can't leave that one alone, can you?" As they walk through the doorway, he breaks his own protocol and holds her elbow tenderly. But, it is dropped as soon as he sticks his head into the small lounge area next door.

"DiNardi, Jackson, can you guys shoot by Riverview High School and ask to speak with anyone on staff who knew the late Gabriel Bonney?"

From her small frame, Jackson speaks up quickly, "No problem, sir."

Andarus adds while throwing Irene a subtle glance, "Oh, yeah, while you're there, ask if anyone has seen or heard from Mrs. Laura Bonney."

Irene purses her lips in a manner that says 'I would stick my tongue out at you if no one was looking,' and Andarus turns away from DiNardi and Jackson to walk toward the front door.

"Detective, we, uh, saw her Friday night at the house. Is there a problem?" explains DiNardi in as concise a speech as he can execute.

Irene spins around on the heels of her pumps, and asks before she comes to a complete halt, "What house?"

DiNardi looks to Jackson who is looking directly at Irene. Somehow Jackson knows her partner is sweating for her to take over, "At the crime scene. She showed up and wanted to go inside the house. The bodies were already gone. We were just closing down the scene."

Losing the cheerfulness to her voice, Irene continues, "What did she say to you? How did you know it was her?"

Jackson stumbles on that one for a moment; Irene has never seen her falter before except when asked about her personal life. Her reaction is not comforting.

"I don't know—I guess we recognized her from the photos in the house."

"And?" prods Irene.

DiNardi steps up to help his partner, "She—she wanted to go inside the house. Jackson said no, but I told to her to go ahead. We had already collected evidence, forensics had gone, the bodies were gone, we were done, she was so up-upset, I, I'm the one who let her go inside."

Irene asks, "Guys, you know better than that. What if we missed something and needed to go back?" The scolding gives birth to silence, and then she continues, "Was that all? Did she leave with anything?"

Jackson jumps back in, "No, she didn't leave with anything. But, she did want to know where the bodies were."

Andarus is stunned at the comment, but Irene continues, "Do you guys know that the morgue pathologist is in the hospital—he was attacked?"

"Oh, oh, m-my God," says DiNardi, while Jackson stares blankly. He takes a full breath and adds, "And she said that she knew…she said that she knew the girls were raped…I thought that was strange."

Jackson, "Yeah, me too."

Andarus coughs and says, "Guys, don't worry about it. Don't tell anyone else about this. She can be awfully persuasive, can't she?"

"So, you've seen her, too, detective?" asks Jackson.

Andarus looks at the two of them and says, "Just ask at the school anyway for me. See what you can turn up," as he turns around with Irene right behind walking toward the elevator.

When they are about forty feet away from the lounge and in front of the elevator, Andarus pushes the down button and asks Irene, "The suspects' names are Simon Murdstone and Ed Legree, right?"

"Yeah, I wrote down their addresses and printed up a street map on the computer while you were on your third or fourth venture to make coffee yesterday."

"Oh, great, thanks. That saves us a phone call back to the principal, and it keeps me from looking like an idiot."

"That's my job, boss man," she says as they step into the elevator, "By the way, it is duly noted that you're not the only one seeing the mysterious Mrs. Bonney and acting strangely around her."

"Yeah, I guess we're all going nuts."

"But, Paul, what is she doing? She wasn't at the ceremony for her husband. She's apparently been back in town since late Friday night—early Saturday morning, and hasn't contacted us…If she is the one who bent up the pathologist, what was she doing there? I think we should go talk to him in the hospital."

Andarus glances at her and asks, "That should be quite interesting since he hasn't spoken a word since the accident."

"You leave that one up to me, Dick Tracy. There are other ways of getting information from people than tough-nosed questioning."

Paul looks away from her and closes his eyes in pain. They step out of the elevator and walk toward the front door silently. When they are out of earshot of numerous people walking around the first floor, he says, "You really don't have to get involved on this one. You've been on every disgusting case that we've had over the last two years; you don't have anything to prove to me. I know you're competent, capable, and reliable. And, brave. I can't explain what is going on in this case, and it's already been brought to my doorstep...well, my car door."

"Paul," she says softy, "If you shut up now, I can pretend you were never talking, and I won't have to put rat poison in your coffee."

Paul slides his sunglasses on his face and winces when the frames hit the mildly swollen but plenty tender areas where his forehead met the steering wheel some six and a half hours ago. He pats her on the shoulder as he holds open the door to the station for her to pass through ahead of him.

A misty twenty-two minute car ride brings them to a house that sits on cinder blocks. They get out of the police cruiser and walk toward the house in the persistent drizzle that has hung around since the early morning's powerful downpour. The old chain link fence in the front is rusted and tarnished with strong weeds growing through its diamond-shaped holes. The grass is high and uncut. Overrun, dominated, and littered with cigarette butts that were never stomped out when they were discarded, is the walkway to the front door. The house itself is of good construction, relatively level, but ill kept; the dim, yellow-painted wooden siding is flaked and cracked, and the gutter is disconnected and hangs off the roof mere feet from the front door. The concrete steps guiding one's walk to the front entrance are solid and in good condition, yet the metal rails that enclose the steps are both ripped away from where they used to bolt to the house. They rock with the slightest touch, rendering them completely unreliable and serving much more as a trap for unsuspecting visitors than assistance to anyone's step. One weekend of painting, fifteen minutes of re-drilling and bolting the rail, an hour of gutter repair would transform the house into a distinctively more welcoming home. But, the dust-covered yet brand new Cadillac in the shell driveway clearly demonstrates where the owner's priorities lie. No lights are on except for the flashing bluish tint of a television glaring on the window shade closest to the front door. Irene steps up to the door and knocks three times. Coughing and incomprehensible wheezing are the only response. The coughing and wheezing come closer, sounding as if they are originating right behind the door. There is a break in the hoarse rumbling, which is replaced with a faint turning and flickering sound. Then, the coughing resumes, a dead bolt flips, and the door opens.

A haggard-looking middle-aged woman drags intently on a newly lit cigarette, holding a drink in her other hand and standing in the one-foot crease that she has left the door ajar. Exhaling she asks, "Who the hell are you?"

Pulling his badge out of his coat pocket, Andarus explains, "Mrs. Legree, I'm Detective Paul Andarus, and this is Detective Irene Bauchan. We would like to ask you some questions about Ed."

"Oh, Lord, what has he done now?" she coughs deeply and continues, "Look, before you go'an get me inta this, you need ta know that *that boy* has been outta *this house* since he turned eighteen tree munts ago dis fifteenth."

Irene asks, "Well, ma'am, we need to talk with him immediately about a case we are investigating. Do you have any idea where we might find him?"

She takes a long drag on her cigarette without the slightest sense of urgency as they wait in the thin rain for her answer. She smokes with the presumed eloquence of a wine connoisseur, with her top two fingers holding the cigarette and outstretched somewhere between the style of a salute and the attitude of a lone extended middle finger. Turning the side of her face to them in a pseudo-regal gesture, she blows the smoke into the air as if each polluting particle was a word rolling out a poet's mouth.

"As I said be-four, Mrs. Officer, Edward is outta my house, an' I have an aim to stay outta his affairs altogether." Her voice is a combination of two sounds—two tiny men working away in her throat: a carpenter sanding away furiously and an aged crooner trying to hit dusty, raspy, and distanced notes in a smoke-filled lounge.

Backing up his partner, "Mrs. Legree, we asked you a very simple question; could you please answer it? It is essential to our investigation."

"Well, young man, what kinda detectives are you anywayz?"

"Homicide, Mrs. Legree."

"Mmm-hmm. Uh, no, I don't think I want to answer your question atawl. My legal RE-sponsibility is done wit dat boy, so I think I'm-a fixin' ta have ta bid you two offa my property."

While Mrs. Legree speaks, Irene's teeth grind at the battery of deliberate and accidental verbal violations. It is not a problem of accent or colloquialism, nor is it a dislike of a particular dialect. It is not to be confused with the French or Cajun accents found within a two hour's drive from Riverview, nor is it a product of geography, heritage, lineage, or anything else about which to be gratified. It is a verbal profession of the proudly uneducated, a vocal symbol of a simple, self-minded lifestyle, a badge of idiocy in which one surrenders to life at the first hint of the opportunity to become an adult; and instead one accepts alcoholism, ignorance, low wages, and social and emotional dysfunction as if it were some claim to a simple man's purity. The jarring speech traits include deeply accented vowels which are so cartoonishly exaggerated that each word sounds like it comes from another language, deliberately choppy speech, which often turns a simple word into two separate words complete with pause and all, placing the accent on the wrong part of the word, which mutates words like insurance into "IN surance," a street named Helios pronounced as Helloice, and a simple name like John into Jawuhn. The butchered speech is only a symptom that may or may not indicate the social disease. By themselves, the mispronunciations have minor significance and might even fool a visitor into believing it to be some type of quaint charm. The danger is in the disease itself, which can be verified by the harsh treatment of one's children followed by a wink or a nod to another adult in the room, some adverse pleasure in failure and bragging on how bad one's life has become, and through the continual baffling behavior of putting forth significantly more effort to avoid any type of work than it would take to accomplish the task or to learn something new. It is a difficult diagnosis to decide upon, but Irene has known both sides very closely in her life to be able to smell out the difference. The biggest resentment that Irene has for the abusive, gluttonous, simple-man syndrome is that she saw simple purity first hand during every fair-weathered summer weekend of her youth. A fishing camp that she would go to with her father was neighbor to many outdoorsmen who worked during every moment of sunlight: fisherman, hunters, shrimpers, tour guides, bait shop owners, and marina operators. She may not have been able to discuss Faulkner or the thin line between abstract art and inanely thrown color on a canvas, but these people were intricately familiar with dignity and the human condition that both mediums are intended to portray. Despite living near poverty and having a limited formal education, they knew the importance of family, generosity, and the struggle of every day honest living. Many of the men, who would come home wind-beaten, sunburned, and with battered and worn hands, would often return singing to their wives, rubbing their shoulders as they cooked, or playing with their children as if they had done none of their tiresome labor all day long. In spite of the squalid conditions, no one locked doors, and it was not from a faith in all of humankind; there was no witless naivety. All of the people in the gaming community had guns, lived a half-hour from the nearest police station, and had no qualms in handling their own problems. Furthermore, news spread quickly in the town, and no one would have to face a violator alone, at least not for long. They recognized that there were things worse than dying, and Irene never saw it expressed so plainly than in their unfailing bravery to protect what was theirs. She gleaned most of her optimism and respect for maintaining justice from these people, as she certainly gained none of it from her own father. It is the love of that genuine spirit that causes her to so dislike imposters like the one in front of her now. The poor imitations are the ones that cause most of the world to misunderstand and have prejudice against the honest, hard-working laborers that she knew. But, despite it all, she manages to place her thoughts out of the way in order to unbiasedly perform her job. They will surely come back to her that night, but for now she needs to focus.

Scanning the woman's clothes that can be seen through the door opening, Irene formulates the best way to field the woman's comment, "Mrs. Legree, we can talk about this now, or we can make you get into the police car in front of your house, come down to the station, and answer our questions there."

Mrs. Legree holds her cigarette burning idly between her fingers and looks away from it and toward Irene for the first time. She slowly opens the door widely, steps down to the first step, watching to make certain that her cigarette does not hit the doorframe, but dragging the long pant legs of her oversized pajama bottoms along the step and spilling an unnoticed drop from her drink. She stares at Irene in a bit of a huff, pushing her bottom lip up and down by playing with her lower jaw.

"Well," Mrs. Legree starts with a glint in her eyes and a crack in her voice, "I guess you two are gonna do as ya please whether it's fittin' or not. Let's get dis overwit. I doan wanna be out here in my night clothes any longer than I hafta."

Despite her shirt being easily three sizes too large, Andarus has acute visceral discomfort with her lack of a bra. In her right hand, there is a small glass with the distinct smell of whiskey and Coke, devoid of ice, but there is another element in the mix that is not standard. After a moment's inspection, Andarus is relatively sure that it is an unmixed egg settled at the bottom, converting a drink into breakfast. Her eye-makeup, no doubt from the night before, is excessive and dramatic, but it is merely an observation, not a judgment. After all, Andarus wears the same clothes from the day before, even though it is due to circumstances out of his control. Surprising considering the time she must devote to her eyes and hair, but fitting the style of the social disease, a thin mustache is growing in of long slender black hairs.

"When was the last time you had any contact with your son?" Andarus pursues.

A cough and a laugh start, "Last I seen him was when I chipped this glass."

"Ma'am?" asks Irene.

"Bout a week ago he got hisself expulled from the school. Too many DE-tentions—he'uz still on da PRO-bation from da last year. I ta-old him long be-four that that he'd be no longa welcum here if he did dat. He'd done moved out be-FOUR den, but he'd come 'round for dinner or to pick up sumtin' from outta his room. That Mrs. Andrews called me dat day to pick him up. So, I's told her if he could get hisself kicked out that he could get hisself home too. That Simon that he bums round wit brought'im on home 'bout eight'clock. When he stuck 'is head through the door, I was sittin' on da couch watching da box, and I let my drink fly at da wall right next ta 'is head. Ha! Splashed what was left o' the drink on his stupid face. Boy had that a one a'comin' to him."

Irene presses, "Mrs. Legree, what happened after you threw the drink?"

"That lil' wuss ran back out da door so fast dat he fell down dese tree steps we on righta now."

Trying to get to something useful, Andarus directs, "And, that was the last time that you saw him?"

"Well, sorter," she starts, relishing not answering the question in a useful manner, dragging on her cigarette, exhaling casually, then continuing, "He came back da next day when he knew I was going ta be at da casino; I play da slots once a week wit my sista. He took his stuff, fifty dollars that I had a'hidden in da pantry, and he stole muh TV. My new big screen TV he took. Now, I'm watching dis lil kitchen TV in my den. You catch dat boy—you bring me muh TV back, ya'hear?"

Irene responds, "Well, ma'am, that is what we're trying to do. Do you have any idea where we might find him?"

"Nah, didn't I tell you he's got muh TV? If I's knew where he a-goan off ta, I'da beat his dummy head from one end o' this city to anotha. Shoo, I'da got dat TV back, missy."

Irene continues, "You mentioned a boy named Simon, do you know where we can get a hold of him?"

"Well, I ran into his maw down at da grocery an she told me dat she tried to get him inta da re-hab and he took off with some skank he'd been keeping up wit. I'd figger where Simon is, Ed ain't far."

Andarus interjects, "Ma'am, do you know Simon's last name?"

"His kin's name is Murd Stone. His people always been a lil strange, but dey keep to deir own bizness, gotta 'preciate dat much. But they are a odd group. Been for at least three generations down da road."

Irene quickly unfolds and consults a computer printout from her business suit pocket, and questions, "Would that be at 1102 East Andover?"

"Shoo," Mrs. Legree responds with a mocking chuckle, "You axin me questions you already kna da answas to. I'm glad ta see da po-lice spend deir leezya gettin' so much important werk done and botherin' innocent tax payas in deir pj's on deir stoops in front o' da huh-ole neighbahood."

She chuckles at the delivery of her comment, giving them the side of her face again, and returning her lips to the small, burning cylinder in her hand. Irene pauses for a moment, mildly agitated, but knowing Paul will wrap it up; he is quite skilled in questioning challenging individuals.

"Well, Mrs. Legree, we can assist you on that one right away; we only have one last question for you. Do you know the name of this girl that was, Ed's buddy, Simon's girlfriend? If we can track her down, we might be able to find the other two."

"Ooo, now what did dey say her name was? I saw the little thing a couple 'o times. Well, she ain't exactly a lil thing eitha. She's a tall one, bout an inch o two taller than Simon—I figga she's bout five ee-leven, maybe up ta six foot. Skinny as a Eee-thee-OHP-an. Nah, what's er name?"

She scratches her head a moment, seeming much more willing to provide her name than any of the information about Ed or Simon.

"She was an EYE-talian girl. I think her last name was Sly-kov-sky, or sometin' like dat. Yeah, I believe it was-a Sly-kov-sky. Not an EYE-talian name; her momma musta been EYE-talian. As far as findin' err, she didn't get kicked out wit da two dummies. She might be at da school. Doan know where she's from. Ya might catch err strollin' down Pla-ayneline Highway late at night," she ends again with an odd snicker.

Irene nods to Paul.

Paul says, "Well, thank you for your time, Mrs. Legree. We may have to contact you again if more questions arise."

She raises her cigarette at them in a toast of smoke. Walking toward the police cruiser that they took with them this morning, they are about three feet from the car when the hoarse, polluted voice earnestly calls after them.

"Nah, you two doan forget to call me when ya fine mah teevee."

Andarus holds back a smile, turns to face her, and says, "No, ma'am, we won't forget to call you," as he raises his hand to say goodbye.

Unusual as it is, Andarus is smiling as he slides into the driver's seat. It is also out of the ordinary that he is driving in the a.m. hours of the job. Irene usually volunteers since she is aware of his erratic sleep and she enjoys driving anyway. But, something in the forcefulness of when he grabbed the keys this morning gave her a signal that he needed to drive.

Putting the car into gear, he asks Irene, "Should we go pay a visit to Riverview High now and see if this Slykovsky girl is there?"

"Yeah, I think that's our best bet. If Ed's not at home, it's likely Simon isn't either. But after checking out the school, we should go to Simon's hou…"

Interrupting, the radio blasts:

"Two 187s found at No-Tell Motel at 4116 Planeline Highway by motel owner. Scene described as…"

Andarus's mobile phone rings. After looking at his number, he turns the volume on the radio completely off and answers the call.

"Andarus here, go ahead."

"Detective," says the voice on the line, which makes Andarus relieved that it is not DiNardi, "We've got a hysterical motel owner on hold at the No-Tell Motel. Did you just get the radio message?"

"Yeah, Jackson, Irene and I just heard it. What do you know?"

"He says he just went into the room this morning because the door was left wide open and another tenant claimed he heard loud screams all night long."

"Jackson, is he still on hold?"

"Yes."

"Ask him for the name the room is under."

“On it,” she replies with a slight click as she puts him on hold.

Irene waits patiently, straining her ears to hear what the answer may be.

“Murdstone. Simon Murd—.”

Before she can finish the name, Andarus is pushing the accelerator and saying, “Forget the school for now. You and DiNardi get down to the No-Tell.” Andarus hangs up as the last syllable leaves his mouth, carelessly tossing his phone onto his lap.

As he speeds down the street, Irene asks, “Oh, my God, those are our boys, aren’t they?”

“Well, whatever is left of them,” Andarus replies.

Chapter XI

Blood-soaked, she leans her back on the same brick building on which she had shut her body down after visiting the morgue two days before. Unknown to her she leans on the same exact bricks, essentially on her shadow from the other night. Her pupils fluctuate from excited swirls to a gray-colored exhaustion. Her mouth is crooked as the left side is raised and pointed and the right side is dropped and rounded. The twitching rocks her body as images flood her mind. Her thoughts are a flashing phantasmagoria of twisted, screaming bodies and blood. Some of the images, the more recent in chronology, make the pointed left side of her mouth rise wickedly and her eyes sparkle; images of pulsing, spewing, severed veins; sounds of screaming, squirting, and choking on blood, and the feel and sound of fingers ripping roughly and animalistically into flesh; these excite her wildly. The other images that weigh her down, still fresher on her mind and soul although further away in time, crush the left side of her lips and extinguish the burning energy in her pupils. These images of blood on her couch, specific stains on the twin beds of her daughters, the desecrated mess that she saw in zippered black bags; these images choke the oxygen out of the blazing fire in her eyes, causing a sizzling that fries her tormented soul. Circular, the fire is soon relit with the sparks of the cycling images of two massacred males in a motel room. The images of unholy tragedy and gluttonous vengeance intertwine and overlap, wrestling for dominance and wearing her so thin that she barely is. The pull has abandoned her, trying to suck her within herself, to cause an implosion that will wipe all evidence of her from the earth that she has stained. The crazed energy that she created still swells and swirls inside her, trying to make her explode and throw one last spatter of blood into this world, ending the tale of Laura. Fighting the pull of the two powers constantly stretches her in opposite directions, leaving her so drained and thin that it aches to be. Giving in would be a release. At this point, she could care less as to which direction she falls and fades away, but her bloody work is not done yet: one more remains.

Her walk to her alleyway was covered in thick angry rain, much heavier than in any other part of the city. The streets were empty, dark, and blurred in the kaleidoscope of raindrops. Her vision of the journey was something similar to a swirling color but not exactly, like trying to see the green grass of the graveyard through the misty midnight maelstrom fluttering and flinging in her face maddening and mystifying her mind, giving mere glittery glimpses of what is gone and things that never should have been done. Now, squatting in the damp alleyway, she has no peace, no restful hibernation, no relief. The mercy that she was given the last time she was here has gone away with the guidance of the pull, which is proving to be far more treacherous than she could have imagined.

Chapter XII

A fast, silent ride gets them to the motel first. The Legree residence is only a mile away. Pulling into the motel, nothing seems out of the ordinary to them; its appearance is consistent with the deterioration and grime of its neighboring competitors. Its hand-painted signs of crooked letters indicate the level of quaintness and lack of decor that one could expect in the service and facilities. It is a street frequented by Irene and Andarus. After responding to countless fatalities there, he wishes the Earth would open up and swallow the entire street into its molten core.

The police car slows its frantic speed on Planeline Highway to a crawl as it rolls through the motel's narrow driveway into its inner rectangular parking lot. The tires splash several puddles on the uneven surface of the driveway. Before Paul removes the key from the ignition, the motel owner rapidly walks through the office door toward the car. His face is blank and pale as he closes in on them.

Paul, now standing, shuts the door, and the motel owner is approaching him quickly through the thin but remaining rain.

Looking at the man nearing him, Paul asks, "Sir, are you the owner/manager?"

The man raises his hand in a wave that ends with pointing in the direction of an alleyway on the left side of the rectangular parking lot, and he commands, "Come."

Paul waits for Irene to make her way around the rear of the vehicle, and they walk briskly after the motel owner, who is ahead of them and making a beeline for the alleyway with the cigarette machine on its corner. A tear in the shoulder seam of the owner's shirt winks at them, beckoning them to come forward as it opens and closes with the pull of the material. It resembles the long, skinny opening between a crookedly mounted motel door and its upper frame to their left. Several stains can be seen on the back of his shirt; some appear to be paint, others are not easily discernable. These shirt stains are also similar to some counterparts on the walls of the building; scars of the outline of a long-removed payphone, discolored paint and wood rot near the gutter, and various graffiti on the off-white wall that contrasts the pink doors and doorframes. The man disappears with an abrupt left turn around a corner. Andarus and Irene increase their pace to stay close behind him.

As the man fumbles with a jingling key ring, Andarus asks, “Sir, did you find the bodies?”

“Yes, I found them,” he says softly as the deadbolt flips open, but he holds tightly onto the handle to keep it from swinging open.

With his fresh, new notebook removed from pocket and in hand, Andarus asks, “What is your name, sir?”

“Al, Albert Lott,” the man says as he nods his head for Andarus to step to the side to let him pass between Irene and him.

Andarus steps back, his shoulder pressing on the dirty white wall to his left. The owner takes a step forward in between Paul and Irene, and, when his hand can no longer hang onto the door and continue to walk away, he releases the handle but keeps walking without looking back to them.

As he is about to reach the end of the short alleyway by the cigarette machine, he says, “Officers, I’ll be in the office when you are done.”

Irene and Paul stand looking at the open doorway to their immediate right. The manner and urgency in which the proprietor walked away and in which the door eased itself open in front of them causes a foreboding to creep over them both as they briefly hesitate to move, like it is the gates of hell opened for them by a retreating attendant who has an appreciated fear for what lies beyond. Andarus slowly slides his new notebook into his pants pocket, and they pretend that is for what they are waiting to enter the room. Paul steps forward and peers into the doorway. Leaning forward, he sees a familiar shade of red sprayed onto the wall just past the opened door. He hopes it is some type of graffiti but knows better. He takes off his glasses as he crosses through the doorframe. Merely a yard into the room, his feet stop short, as he gazes upon the blood-soaked walls and floor and the two horrific lumps within. His glasses slip from his fingers and drop to the floor. Despite years of desensitization, Andarus’s eyes swell and absorb the hellishly rich scene before him. His vision grabs hold of a lacerated body directly in front of him with a pile of overturned and smashed televisions around him. The corpse lies with his legs open and head down upon his chest, which is unevenly and hideously torn open. His entrails are stretched out before him with certain areas of them smashed and squeezed with such intensity that the imprint of the crushing fist can be seen like the handle of a knife. Blood has been splattered on all in the room as if it rained down from an apocalyptic cloud. His right hand is ripped off at the wrist. The top of his head, which is aimed directly at Andarus, has many wounds and abrasions on it. Some of his hair has been ripped out, and his ear has been wrenched off his head leaving an angry, fleshy hole. Quickly, his sight is directed across the room to the other lump, which hangs from a noose made of a torn, electric extension cord tied to a plant hook in the ceiling. A syringe is shoved through his bottom lip and out his top keeping them held tightly together, piercing his mouth like a jewelry stud, and his right eye socket is bloodied, beaten, and hollow. A slime runs from the misshapened eye hole down his face, and the remains of the eye lie on the floor below his dangling corpse. His body is marked with cuts and tears, and his right hand has also been ripped off at the wrist. The fingers on the remaining hand are bent in impossible directions, jutting outward like dead branches on a fire or like the beckoning hand of the ferryman, Charon. Bruises can be seen over any inch of the body that is not torn open or stained with the red from within. Shards of broken glass from the smashed televisions are stabbed randomly into their bodies. His intestines are the only part of his carcass to reach the ground below him.

As these images race through his mind, causing total sensory overload, his only thought is to reach around with his right arm and push Irene out of the doorway. His arm hits across the top of her chest, and it does indeed knock her back a step. But, it is all too late. He sees that her eyes are as horrifically wide as his, and he aches more at the thought that they will never return to their normal state than at the indescribable terrors he has just witnessed in the room. He pushes her with all his might, spinning her around to face the doorway and pushing her through it into the alley. In any other situation, she would not have stood for it, and he would not have even thought to do so. As they step into the dirty alleyway, a heft lifts from their chests, but they both shiver. Violation is all they feel. Recovery is not even a thought. Andarus holds Irene's head to his shoulder with a hand placed at her cheek and his other arm wrapped tightly around her back rubbing her between her shoulder blades. They have hugged before, but Andarus was always mindful to keep it brief. Now, since the scene in the room has sent them reeling for decency, upholding professional distances is not a thought to him. He clings to her as much for himself as it is for her. She squeezes his shoulders intently. Their breathing is consistent and regular, but they know it will not last for long. They brace themselves against each other waiting for the reality of the darkness in the room to fall upon them.

An hour later, DiNardi slushes the mop in its wheeled bucket. It has been used for five separate accidents so far this morning, and its repugnant water is in need of being removed. Jackson sits on the ground with her back against the wall, facing the drink machine in front of her. DiNardi has already tried to buy her a water from the machine, but he soon found out that none were available. She nods in his direction to let him know that she appreciates him cleaning up her mess. She fought the convulsions for quite some time, but when the chief forensics investigator lost his breakfast, she could no longer contain herself. Of the four homicide officers, only DiNardi has not vomited at the sight of the room, which has much more to do with his restraint over his curiosity to see its carnage than it has to do with his intestinal fortitude. Unlike DiNardi, Jackson could not keep herself out of the room despite Irene and Paul's warnings. Before this, she has never seen anything to cause her to lose control; the next closest incident was at the Bonney house days before. DiNardi's only exposure to the chamber was his brief excursion to retrieve Jackson when he heard her gasping erratically only moments after walking into the room lone and defiant. Irene and Paul stand further down the alley near the doorframe waiting to speak to the forensics investigator and being extremely careful not to look beyond the door. Despite all the horrors that they have digested professionally in the past years, all four of them feel as if they have lost something and are forever less clean from having seen it. Andarus is the only one to have taken a second and even a third trip into the room to check on forensics.

Al Lott, the motel owner, has remained inside his office the entire time. If an officer happened to walk near enough to the glass bureau where he could see them through the window, he would ask questions on how much longer they would be, how was the investigation going, and who would clean up the room. But, he dared not leave the glass office, just as he had the night before when a mysterious woman walked past it into the rectangular courtyard. He saw the room once this morning, and something inside of him screams to never gaze upon it again. He cannot logically rationalize to himself why he cannot see it again; it is his motel, he has always protected his investment in the past, and there is nothing alive in that room to possibly harm him. But, he is content to abide by his inner warning just the same and at any cost.

After a long wait, Mr. Lott sees a police car drive past his office with a small woman driving and a large man in the passenger seat. The car turns onto Planeline Highway. Andarus and Irene are walking to the office door through the lingering drizzle. Lott is excited to no longer be waiting, but he is fearful of hearing any more details about the room.

Andarus opens the glass office door with a spider-web crack about a foot and a half from the ground—the perfect height for close-range kicking. They both step into the office. Mr. Lott stands and nods, looking in their direction but no higher than their knees.

"Mr. Lott, do you have any surveillance cameras on the premises?" asks Andarus.

"Yes, detective, I have a 24-hour video that runs on a loop."

"Excellent. What part of the building does it record?"

"The entrance to the street."

Irene asks, "And that is also the only exit?"

"Yes, ma'am, that is the only way in or out. Let me get the recording for you," says Lott as he hurriedly walks through a doorway behind his desk into another room.

They look around the office while waiting. Andarus stares at a plastic-looking sofa against the glass wall that is easily twenty years older than he is. Irene glances from an archaic looking television set, that is well dusted but not turned on, to the rack of keys behind the desk. They hang on a neatly arranged pegboard, each with its room number printed on its plastic fob in such an orderly fashion that it resembles letters made from a stencil. The order and cleanliness are out of place for this part of town, and the contrast provides a point of interest for Irene. She glances at Paul to see if he has noticed it too, and she sees he is indeed looking at the pegboard of keys.

She looks very serious for a moment and leans in to whisper in his ear. Andarus waits for a well-observed fact. She places four fingers from her outstretched hand gently on his shoulder and says in a voice much more sultry and drawn-out than her normal speech, "Fancy seeing you in a place like this, sheriff. Looking for some company this evening?"

He laughs, but ropes it back to a smile, and finally to a mere smirk. He is not a fan of laughing or smiling while at a scene, but he is relieved to feel anything except the intense grief and disgust that has clung to them like a malodorous fog since they stepped foot into that room. She is quite happy with his reaction.

The room spins unexpectedly in Andarus's perspective. His eyes slam shut, and his head wobbles slightly with his body following suit. With a strong shake of his head, he throws off the dizziness, but the pounding in his brain remains. Irene, who is staring at him but no longer smiling, notices it immediately. It is not the first time that it has happened today, but it is the first time that she caught it with all of the chaos surrounding them.

"Paul, you have a concussion; you have to go to the hospital."

Andarus shakes his head trying to cast off her insistence as he did the dizziness, "No, I'm fine. We have work to do."

Pursing her lips tightly before speaking, "This is not a joke, Paul. You have to have someone look at it."

Having begun shaking his head in disapproval from the moment she said no, his mouth opens to give a rebuttal, but she cuts him off, "If this were me, Paul, if it was me who might have a concussion and black out on the job, possibly in a very dangerous situation to myself and in endangering the case, you would not let me refuse to go to the hospital."

Without hesitation he offers, "No, we'd already be at the hospital if it were reversed."

Her reaction is mixed. There is a tiny relief in that he admitted the truth, although Andarus has never made it a habit of lying to her. But, she is also irritated that he so readily admits that he will not risk her health in the same manner that he will risk his, and she is not sure if she should feel loved or disrespected. She bites her lip to stop a smile.

Leaning closer to her ear and whispering softly, "But, this is not a normal case; two of our people are in the hospital over this. If for no other reason than keeping it from becoming three of us laid up in the hospital, I'm not going to get checked out. I will not give this murderer one more to person to add to their list," he waits, looking at her face that grows solemn, and throws her this, "Look, I'll take an aspirin; will that make you happy?"

His feeble offer achieves two things: enough time has passed where Irene knows the motel owner will be coming back at any moment, and, if he is willing to take any type of pain reliever, she knows his pain must be really intense.

Within a few long seconds of the two staring at each other, Lott returns to the room and hands the video shakily to Irene, whose hand had quickly extended to grab it.

Lott starts to speak three times, but only succeeds on the last attempt, "Detective, I saw her come in last night. This woman…It had to be her…She walked right through the entrance. I always check who is coming in or out—have to be careful of people breaking in, causing trouble, or trying to hang around for free. But…" he pauses there and looks at the floor.

"But, what, sir?" coerces Andarus.

"I don't know how to explain it, officer, but she gave me a look…I'm embarrassed to say it, but it…it scared the hell out of me. I stayed right here by the desk, and she walked on through. Didn't see her leave—it was stormin' by then."

"Mmmhmm," says Irene, "Do you remember about what time this took place, Mr. Lott?"

"Well," he says thinking, "It had to be between twelve-thirty or so and one a.m., because it was just before the rain came down last night. You'll be able to see her on that video—she came right up that driveway on side of us. The time will show up on the bottom corner of the screen—the right side."

Andarus scribbles the times down in his notebook.

Still avoiding any eye contact, the motel owner adds, "I been here a long time on Planeline, always been a rough street; I ain't never seen nothing like this," pausing, "Wish I never had."

"Me too," says Paul uncharacteristically allowing any emotion to penetrate his firm demeanor in front of a witness on a case. Andarus gives Lott his business card and instructs him to call if he can remember any more information about the night before.

"Well, I know when those two started renting that room by the week that there was a bed in there. Didn't see one this morning."

Irene answers, "No, there was no bed in there. Looks like they tossed it out to make room for TVs and stereo equipment."

Moments later, leaning on the car in the parking lot, Paul makes the phone call from his own phone. It rings. He hopes the message recording picks up. This has always been Debbie's job; the occasions when Paul has had to make the call for her have been very remote, and he has never gained any poise, confidence, or immunity to the harshness involved. Leaving the actual message on the answering machine is never an option, but leaving a message to call the police department is acceptable. Paul would love to not speak with Mrs. Legree for a second time today, even if it would only be a brief interim before he would have to call her again to deliver the morbid news. It may only be a day of temporary relief, but it would at least allow him to spread out her poison over more time, a breather between shots of arsenic. But, a cough and a rasp on the other end of the phone bring all hopes of a delay to a dead stop.

As the coughing continues inordinately, Andarus asks, "Mrs. Legree?"

"Ugh, ugh, yes, 'tis Missez Luh-gree."

"This is Detective Andarus; I spoke with you just a little while ago."

"Yes, I knows who ya are, nuh whatchya got ta say ta me nah?"

"Mrs. Legree, your son has been found dead at the No-Tell Motel. I'm terribly sorry."

Silence. Even her incessant wheeze-cough gargle is silenced. Then the wheeze hisses out subtly like a popped balloon, "Did yah find muh tee-vee?"

Shocked to a pause, Andarus slowly replies, "No, no, ma'am, we did not find a working TV."

Click.

Chapter XIII

The explosive energy has drained out of her body and soul leaving her more tired than the dead and as colorless as the streak that runs through her hair. The brief euphoria of grabbing justice is no more than memory, merely a distant crack of light in the abyss into which she has fallen. Laura knows that it is not complete; the squealed name that she wrenched from a putrid soul some hours ago echoes and swirls in her mind, reminding her that there is still one more to bring to justice, one more to hold a mirror in front of her face and force her to see the hell inside to which she has nurtured and given birth.

The torture attacks Laura from two fronts. Violent actions, while expedient, come at a steep price, even when they are justified. Every ripping, tearing, squeezing, punching, and twisting that she delivered has put a weight on her body. Although she has felt numb since she rose from the wooden office floor some days ago, she now feels much more so with the cost of the vengeance added to it and crushing down upon her. Perhaps this is why criminals never appear content. Every movement from her feels as if it is being done in the deepest trench in the ocean under the constant crushing force of unfathomable gallons of water. To move her eyes to look in another direction is to move a mountain. And, tangled into this problem is the second torture, the disappearance of the pull, which is the only tool with which she could combat the resistance of the weight around her. The weight is terrible enough, but the lack of a tool to fight it leaves her nearly hopeless.

The female name bounces in her head. It taunts her like the sound of the waves breaking on the beach in the ears of a man who has swum the whole ocean only to drown in the surf, within yelling distance of the shore. It mocks her as she has seen much and done much more than what is natural and feasible only to be stuck, trapped in a brick alleyway as if chained to a dungeon wall.

So, she sits immobile in the rain. The moisture, although she is not paying any attention to its presence on her skin, only contributes to her feeling that the entire girth of the ocean remains on top of her. She feels so far down within its depths that the light of the surface is only a faint hint of a hue far above her. As the darkness of the dense chilling void closes in on her, she wonders what primordial terrors lurk there besides her.

Chapter XIV

As an acute shock runs through Andarus's fingers, he glances at Irene who has been standing several feet to his right waiting for him to touch the handle first. She is giggling through her hand, which is placed daintily over her mouth. As he opens the door to the office for the second time in two days, his laughter is strong but entirely internal since he is on location working on a rapidly escalating murder case. But, as she passes in front of him, he gives her a deliberate wink to ensure that she is aware of his appreciation of catching him with the same trap two days in a row. As he steps into the office, no one can tell by the seriousness of his face that he ever smiles.

The secretary behind the desk stands in a clumsy motion and looks at the detective and Irene with a troubled countenance. While walking toward them, she accidentally knocks a small stack of homeroom attendance folders onto the floor as her sweater drags over them. She smiles awkwardly and then looks at their chests instead of their faces; homicide detectives seem to have that effect on some people.

Andarus sees her trepidation, and initiates the conversation, "We're here to see Principal Andrews. We called on the way over—it is extremely urgent that we speak with her now."

"Yes, yes, sir. She's in her office now. Just let me tell her that you are coming in," she offers as she walks toward the wood-paneled bureau two doors down to the left of her desk. The vice principal's office is to her immediate left between her desk and the principal's office. Turning and glancing at them over her shoulder, she adds, "Just one moment, detectives."

She raps on the door softly three times. She opens the door with enough space to poke her head through. It disappears from their sight for a moment between the door and its frame, as if it were locked into a guillotine. She pulls her head back through, opens the door widely, and bids the detectives to enter. They step quickly into the room and see the principal is sitting at her desk with an open file folder in front of her.

Principal Andrews rises to her feet and quickly shakes their hands as she explains, "I pulled the file that you asked. We only have one student with the last name of Slykovsky, Daisy Slykovsky. Daisy's been absent yesterday and today, which is odd for her as she has had perfect attendance two of her previous three years here."

Irene asks, "Have the parents called in her absences?"

"No, they are unexcused. We've tried to contact her father both yesterday and today with no response. He has been unreliable and uninterested in her schooling—the only parent-teacher night that he showed up to he was drunk."

"Mrs. Andrews, can you tell us if she was ever in Gabe Bonney's class?" questions Andarus.

"Well, she would have had him last year as a junior in American Lit. Let me see if she had him or Mrs. Henrick's class," flipping papers and then holding up a class schedule, "Yes, she was in his class last year. Detectives, you don't think she had anything to do with this, do you?"

Irene answers, "We can't discuss that, Mrs. Andrews, but would you be surprised if she was involved?"

Mrs. Andrews removes her glasses from her face revealing some crow's feet from hours of staring at paperwork over her career. She blinks and exhales before answering, "Well, yes and no. Daisy has always been the child that we've rooted for. Little lamb's mother left when she was in the third grade, never to have contact with her again. Her father is an abusive alcoholic—never could get any evidence to help her and she would never admit it was going on. She would be picked on because she was always so tall—she was six feet in the seventh grade. We tried so hard to make sure the other kids left her alone, but it's impossible to hear every harsh word whispered at a lunch table. Despite all of that, she has been an honor roll student since she came here. Quiet. Kind. We always wanted her to succeed."

"Who are her friends?" asks Andarus.

"Well, for the most of her time here she kept to herself. She loved to read—kind of in her own world. But, this past year she was hanging around with Murdstone and Legree—those two that I was telling you about yesterday—the two that Gabe gave the detention that got them both expelled. That's when we really started worrying about her."

"We've been told by Mrs. Legree that she was Simon's girlfriend. Is this true?" asks Irene.

"Yes, ma'am, I think that is accurate; I did see them holding hands in the hallway quite often. It was one of the few times I remember seeing Daisy smiling."

"Has she ever been in any trouble? Have any teachers ever complained about her?" continues Andarus.

"No, not that I can ever remember," responds Principal Andrews.

"Well," says a timid and shaky voice from outside of the opened door to the office, "There was one complaint near the end of last school year."

Andarus and Irene turn around to face the doorway and the incoming voice. The secretary steps into the opening and says, "I'm quite sorry, Mrs. Andrews—I didn't mean to eavesdrop. I just heard what you were saying, and there was one incident."

"Please, continue," encourages Irene.

The secretary looks at Principal Andrews, and she nods in approval, "Go on, Mrs. Guess."

"Well, it was about a week before exams started, and Gabe came into the office."

Andarus interrupts, "Gabe, Gabriel Bonney?"

The secretary responds, "Why, yes, sir, he is the only Gabe that we have here," she pauses for a moment, and it seems that she will inevitably break into tears as she realizes the inaccuracy in what she has just said.

Noticing that she is near the edge of falling into an emotional river, which would render her useless to them, Andarus leads, "Gabe came in with a complaint?"

Snapping back into the conversation, Mrs. Guess elaborates, "Yes, sir, he did—the first time that he came in to complain in seven years here. Only it wasn't really a complaint—he was concerned—he needed help. He said that Daisy Slykovsky dropped a note on his desk expressing how much she loved him and wanted to be with him. What really upset him was the way she talked about it—she said she wanted to give herself to him—that no man has ever", lowering her voice to a whisper, "*excited* her like he did." Then, returning to her normal speech, "That they were meant to be together. He was so nervous—didn't know how to handle the situation. He looked like someone asked him to perform brain surgery. He was so sweet about it—he didn't want to hurt her feelings, but he knew he couldn't handle it by himself—that someone in the administration needed to know what was going on, and that a female staff member should talk with her about the note."

"And, what happened?" asks Principal Andrews as surprised as Irene and Andarus.

"Well, ma'am, he wanted to talk with you about it, but you had Mrs. Legree in your office about that PE incident with the eighth grade boy getting roughed up. And, Gabe was very concerned with this being kept very private to spare Daisy's feelings. So, he asked me if I could talk to her about it, and I did. I called her in and used the conference room to talk with her. She sobbed for a moment when I brought the subject up, but then she blew it off claiming the note was a joke and that she was embarrassed that I even had to hear about it. I explained it to her that it is very inappropriate to talk to a male teacher that way, and she apologized and said she understood. It's never come up again until now."

"So, that was the end of it?" asks Andarus.

"Yes, well, almost. There was never another incident or another word about it, but she did seem to look at him—stare at him in the hallway. You could tell she still had feelings for him, but there was an anger in her eyes. She looked like she had been betrayed. Maybe she was angry because he told me about it—she is a very shy girl," starting to tear up, "Maybe I didn't handle it properly, but Gabe didn't want her counselor to know because he is a man—Mr. Sheridan. He didn't want Daisy to be humiliated any further. Somehow, he thought I could do it gentler. Why did he trust me?—I am such a fool," sobbing takes over the end of her words.

Principal Andrews quickly moves around the corner of her desk and places both of her hands on her secretary's shoulders. Then, she says, "You're not a fool, Sandy; you did the best you could. Gabe trusted you for a reason—none of this is your fault."

"Poor Laura," sobs Sandy Guess in a choppy speech, "I can't imagine how she felt at the ceremony yesterday."

Irene and Paul look at each other astonishedly. Principal Andrews begins to explain, "But, she wasn't here yesterday, I was loo—"

Her words are cut off abruptly by Andarus's louder question, "You saw her here yesterday?"

The secretary is even more jittery and nervous at the sound of his voice, but his urgency prompts her to a quick response, "Yes, I thought I saw her in the stairwell just over there," she finishes by pointing at the wall of the office in the direction of the stairs.

Andarus looks directly at Principal Andrews and says, "We'll need to take this file with us now—there is no time for copies. We'll return it to you as soon as we are done."

As the principal watches Irene collecting papers and closing the file folder quickly, she nods her head while still holding her sobbing secretary at the shoulders. As they are about to exit her office, she asks, "Is Daisy in danger?"

Andarus quickly looks back at her while still walking out the doorway and nods in affirmation, but says, "Ma'am, I can't answer that."

The knocks reverberate through the second floor apartment, hollow and unanswered. The warped, rotting, thin door jolts in its frame with each rap of his knuckles. The apartment number H shakes with the movement.

Andarus and Irene have been standing on the slanted balcony that leads to the apartment door for slightly more than two minutes. The rain runs out a hole where the tin overhang, that attempts to cover the balcony, meets the brick wall of the building. It filters its way down the wall around the protruding and slightly uneven bricks until it hits the angled platform and slicks past a pair of brown dress shoes and a pair of pumps. Lastly, the feeble stream crashes into the round base of a medium-sized pot that holds a dead and withered plant, and it slides around the planter and over the rail to the bottom floor in a tiny waterfall that goes unnoticed in the rest of the downpour.

Andarus sighs as the knock fades without a response. He turns around, gazing through the drizzle and over the parking lot. The building houses sixteen small apartments, and the parking lot below only contains nine cars. One has a horribly cracked windshield, busted headlights, and small caverns where the side mirror housings used to be. Another car sits on its rims atop four flattened and sliced tires. The entire lot can only fit sixteen cars; it is as if the builders knew people renting an apartment of this caliber in this part of town are not likely to own more than one car per family.

After sizing up the vicinity from the balcony's view and seeing nothing to help him, he asks, "It's eleven forty-five on a rainy Tuesday night. Where else would she be? According to Principal Andrews, she didn't have any friends beside Legree and Murdstone."

She says, "With the weather being as lousy as it's been, she's got to be seeking shelter somewhere. Maybe we should check some of the girls' homes to see if someone matches her description. Her height might make her easy to find."

He grunts and says, "Yeah, that's what I'm worried about. If Mrs. Bonney has found out about her, she is going to be easy for her to find too. And, she's been beating us to the punch so far."

The tension with which he speaks is from chasing to find the nearly dead, which makes him nervous and uncertain, questioning every second that he may be wasting by making the wrong decision; choosing the wrong lead to follow. He is quite used to hunting down the dead's secrets and through it finding the living killer, but he has never been comfortable with tracking down someone whose immediate existence depends on his choices. He is far more comfortable working for the dead.

"Do you think she knows for sure?" asks Irene.

"Based on what that motel room looked like this morning, I'd bet she got everything that she needed to know…I mean, assuming that she is the one doing this."

Irene stares at him despite a slight breeze sprinkling raindrops onto her face, and says, "You can't be serious that you think this could be someone else. Paul, tell me you're not serious."

"Of course, I think that it's her; she did knock me out. But, we can't assume anything until we're sure. She may not be working alone either."

"Well, when we screen the video from the motel, we'll know for sure if it was her."

There are no sounds but the soft touch of the rain.

"She's out there, Irene, waiting for us to find her," utters Andarus staring into the rain, "Waiting for us to do something," he continues as he clenches his fists.

"Yeah," says Irene thinking about the Daisy. As she scans her mind of the area's girls' shelters that they have visited far too often through the course of their work, a thought occurs to her.

With an intensity in her tone that he has not heard in a while, she asks, “Hey, Paul, which one are you talking about?”

Chapter XV

She did not want to, but she had to. Laura had to force herself out of the alleyway. The terribly nightmarish events of the day still burn at her. The thrill of vengeance no longer consoles; in fact, it only burns at her further, as it is not done. The last two words that she needs to find and destroy grant her no reprieve, not even a moment to rest or plan. Its command is uncompromising, and torture will follow her until it is met.

It is evening, and a dark evening at that. She seems to slide through it as it is still slick from the unceasing rain. Large puddles line the street curbs as the city drains fail to swallow the wet anger from above. She is unaware of where she is heading, much like all of her traveling between her awakening days ago on her office floor in another city and this very night. But, different from all of her other recent wanderings, she is now unguided and lost. There is no pull directing her one step at a time to a destination. Her steps are controlled by her own mind, which at the moment is a blind guide. She pays no attention to her surroundings. Her focus is on internal thoughts; the only external stimulus of which she is aware is the perpetual wall of rain around her. The only aid that she has is that the weather is so nasty that few others decide to venture outside.

He did not want to, but he had to. Irene had to trick him into it. When the doctor walked down the hallway up to Irene and himself standing just outside of Debbie's hospital room, Andarus asked, "So, what can you do for Debbie?"

The doctor gave him a puzzled look and glanced to Irene for assistance. She looked both uncomfortable and fiendish, and the doctor started to piece it together.

Looking back at Andarus, the man in white said, "I'm Dr. Lowe; I was told that you may have suffered a concussion, detective?"

The awkward exchange of looks continued as Andarus moved his vision from Irene to the doctor several times.

Irene chimed up, "Paul, tell the doctor how you feel. We're already here, and he offered to examine you right away."

“So, this is where you were when you said you were going to call your father?” he asked neutrally.

“Eh-emm,” cleared the doctor’s throat, “How did this happen, detective?” he continued as he removed a narrow flashlight that resembled a pen from out of his coat pocket.

Andarus reluctantly returned his attention to the doctor, “Head trauma while pursuing a suspect.”

“How were you struck?”

Andarus looked to the floor as if he would not answer, and Irene poked him in his side with a fingernail, “The suspect caught me off guard and hit me in the forehead with something—I didn’t even get to see what it was.”

“When did this happen?”

“Late last night.”

“Have you experienced any bouts of dizziness? Headache?”

“No, nothing to complain about.”

“Let me look at your pupils,” explained the doctor as he raised the tiny, yet powerful light to Paul’s eyes.

Irene’s voice broke in, “That’s not true, Paul; tell him.”

Andarus’s mouth did not move, and the doctor focused on his adjusting pupils.

“Tell him, or I will.”

Exhaling, Paul explained, “I’ve had a little dizziness, but it’s been a long day. Nothing to worry about.”

“Uh-huh,” responded the doctor in a tone that did not convey belief, “detective, we are going to need to get you into an examination room. We need some x-rays to determine,” Andarus’ phone rang, “how severe your trauma may be.”

He flipped his phone out of his pocket with unnecessary speed, looked at the screen quickly, and said, “Doc, I have to take this call; I’ll be back in several minutes—I’ll come find you.”

And with that he walked away, straight to the elevator and down to the parking garage, never having been more glad to receive a wrong number. That was four and a half minutes ago. He leans on the car staring at the elevator doors, and finally sees Irene walking briskly in his direction. Her face looks more concerned than angry, which makes Paul feel like a jerk.

“You were just going to leave me up there, Paul? Waiting for you like an imbecile?”

Smiling, Andarus replies, “Well, you’re an amazing detective; I knew it wouldn’t take you long to figure me out.”

“Uh-huh,” she responds without the slightest hint of humor as she opens the passenger door, but she does not sit down, “Where are we going, Paul?”

"There is a surveillance video that needs to be reviewed back at the office."

"Paul, it is eight thirty; you've had a concussion, you've been up all night and day; go home. Get some sleep."

He looks down at the keys in his hand as if there is something suddenly fascinating about them.

Lightening her tone, "Paul, if you drop dead, I have to handle this one all by myself. Is that what you want?"

Seriousness falls upon him, "No, Irene. You know that."

"Do I?"

"What else am I going to do? You know how it is for me. Go home to an empty house. Toss and turn all night—aggravating myself because I can't fall asleep. I'll be thinking about the case anyway. What do you want me to do?"

"Damn it, Paul; I'm driving. Give me the keys," she demands as she walks around the front of the car. Then, defeated, she continues, "Since when have you ever done what I wanted you to do?"

"Irene, I'm sorry. I know that you worry about me—I know that you do a lot for me. I wish I could do the things you ask me to; I wish I could be normal, have a normal life. But, I don't think I can get out of this. This is how I am. This roving lack of peace is how I live; there may be no cure."

She begins to despair as she feels there may be no cure. What solace can she gain even if she can muster the strength to finish the task without the pull? How will she feel any better after killing the third when the first two have left her in her current condition? And, the rain, the incessant rain, only convinces her that she is drowning. Hopeless.

The word hopeless sticks with her. Hopeless like her husband dying knowing that his daughters lie helpless in the next room. Dying to the cries of two-thirds of all that he held dear being defiled. Hopeless like her daughters lying on their tiny backs clutching at stuffed animals that were unable to protect them as they had dreamed and pretended. The darkness ripped them out of their clutching hands and cleared the way for disgusting evil to penetrate their innocence. Hopeless. She screams like an animal returning to a devoured den, and its sound fills the street. Chilling the air. It is such a shriek that only two brave souls even dare to look out the window at what could have made that sound. Where the pull has fled and ceased to guide her and give her fire to go on, she lights her own flame. She ignites the fatigue, the horrible images, the hatred, and the hopelessness. The doubt burns the fastest inside her, and the rage tingles throughout her, quickly spreading out of control. Her mind drains of its distractions, and finally she is pulled where she must go.

Chapter XVI

The metal doors slide shut, entombing him. He sighs embracing their temporary relief. Slowly he extends a single finger toward the cold, shiny wall in front of him. He blinks his eyes lackadaisically sheltering them for a precious second. His finger pushes the worn button before him, and he sighs again, still quite surprised that he was able to convince Irene to leave him alone in the building.

As the metallic cube moves upward, Andarus's head throbs, and the dizziness returns. He was hoping the latter would not resurface and hinder his work. The light above the doorway ascends across its dial steadily until it stops with a ding. The doors sink into their opposing caverns, and he steps wearily down the isle toward the kitchen area beside his office. Shaking his head along the way, he tries to sift out the throbbing and ringing.

He grabs a thermos from the bottom of the sink and begins rinsing it off. His thoughts drift, and, as the water rises in temperature, he shudders at acutely scalding images of broken glass, lacerated eyes, and dismembered corpses. Persistent memories from earlier in the day seem much more menacingly vivid now that he is alone. He closes his eyes tightly in a futile attempt to banish the horrid recollections from his mind. He knows they will return and linger like the taste of poison; he only wishes to stretch out the interim between their attacks to give his frail faculties as much time as possible to recover before dealing with the next strike. The water running over his hands holding the mug in the sink is an uncomfortable burning, but he welcomes its heat as a sign of life.

As he shakily pours coffee into the mug, he reminds himself that the sound of whispering that he hears in the next room is just the hum of computers and the ever-running ceiling fan. The chain had broken off the fan base some three months before Irene came to work there, and it has been left to run ever since. He also tells himself that the hellish coughing that he hears is only the air conditioner's uneven rumbling as it shuts itself off. Furthermore, he persuades himself that the chilling cackling that startles his nerves is the sound of frozen cubes dropping and settling in the icemaker across the room. And, he tries to convince himself that the thick silence between the noises is only an empty office and not death wrapping itself around him.

Andarus is not sure if it is a result of too little sleep, horrific sensory overload, or an accumulated immunity from years of abuse, but his first long gulp of coffee does nothing to rejuvenate his awareness. The uncomfortable heat numbs his taste buds, warms his chest, and burns his tender stomach, but his thoughts remain frostbitten. Cold. Stalled and stuck on things humans were never meant to see.

He opens a cabinet, pops what he needs into his hand, and closes it. He tosses both pills into his mouth and sends them on their way with a sip of coffee. As his head's throbbing causes him to wince, he doubts that the tiny capsules will grant him any relief. He takes another deep drink from his mug. But, before his left hand places it back onto the counter, his right hand already grasps the handle of the coffee pot. He rapidly refills the mug and tops it off with creamer and a half packet of sugar. He folds the top of the packet over and places it on the counter, knowing he will soon return for it.

Andarus walks out of the break room and into his adjacent office. He turns on a small television set, inserts the surveillance video and presses play. As he sinks down into his chair, the driveway entrance of the No-Tell Motel pops onto the screen with the time of 12:01 am and the date in white letters in the bottom right corner. He can see the side of the glass office windows and one lane of Planeline Highway within the camera's frame. He kicks his feet on the desk. Grabbing the remote control, he sends the video racing, and the numbers turn faster as his eyes struggle to focus on them. Having scanned many videos in the past, Andarus sips his coffee without taking his sight off the screen. His eyes are dry. Even the air around them feels like an intrusion. An abrasion. A splinter. He holds them gratingly on the screen. Even though his mind is in an exhausted and stagnant condition, he is innately aware that his physical and emotional states are something less than what should be called life. Nevertheless, his mind focuses on Daisy, Debbie, a traumatized pathologist, and Irene. He cannot let himself think about what he would do if there were no more cases to solve and no more people to protect. Besides, he has to keep his mind on the screen.

A "bing" bounces unchallenged through the long room in front of his office, over small rows of desks and computers, through the opened private office door and to Andarus's ears. He feels nothing, aware only that something has happened. Then, *could it have been the elevator?* His mind sprints wildly. Lunging. Panicking. Spinning, he grasps at thoughts like branches as if he were suddenly pushed off a cliff. Fear itself. Then, Laura. The motel room. A sad woman walking away from him. Irene's face. A quick choppy breath.

"I-r-e-n-e," he sighs in an ah-hah manner. He thought he had convinced her too easily to leave him by himself tonight. A smile threatens to break through his stone lips, but a throbbing surge in his head and an abrupt bounce in his vision of the TV screen throttle any chance of it taking shape on his face. He rubs his eyes violently—cannot let Irene see him like this.

"All that caffeine'll kill you, detective," the words freeze the air as they pulse from the doorway across the small office to his stinging ears.

Frantically, his fingers pull out of his eyes and smack down upon his lap. His vision is an unfocused camera as he struggles to see what is in his doorway. No one could have gotten from the elevator and down the long isle of the computer room that quickly. His panic, whisper, and rub of his eyes lasted less than four seconds. Impossible. And without a sound. He reconsiders that maybe the silence in-between the other noises truly was death wrapping her fingers around his throat as he recognizes the voice from the doorway while his eyes refuse to see her. The pinnacle of years of excitement on the job, and all he can feel is fatigue. All he can think about is her.

The ripples of his vision smooth to reveal the doorway. But, she is not there. In fact, no one is. Just as he begins questioning his own sanity and the validity of his concussion, a firm hand presses down on his right shoulder rapidly spinning his chair around. The chair stops abruptly, but his head still spins.

He sees a pale white streak in a sea of black, like a waning moon in a starless sky. He knows her hair as one knows the setting of a recurring nightmare. He sees the eyes through the torn, black curtain of her mane. Mesmerized, he does not think he can move. He cannot uncloud his mind to scream, nor is he aware of how futile it would be if he could cry out. He stares. Anesthetized.

Her hand stops just before touching his face. It looks as if she will grab Andarus by the chin to command his full attention and to hold his head so she can stare into his face. But, she makes no move. Something inside commands her to touch him not. Not yet. The hand remains before him, as she reluctantly obeys the pull.

Cranial gears turn, and he ponders why she waits. If she wanted to kill him, she could do it at any moment. Why wait? He remembers that it is not what she wanted from him last time. Information. He braces for her to rip it out of him again. As he tries to gather his mental strength to resist her, his exhausted mind is silenced. His resolve is laughable as his brain strains to operate, grinding, producing only mental shrapnel.

Her voice slices into him, "Daisy," his eyes widen and his body stirs slightly, as she steadily presses, "Daisy Slykovsky. Where is she?"

Her voice is drenched with disdain as she utters the name she wrenched from a tortured mouth the night before. Andarus's eyes ache to turn away from her, yet he does not look elsewhere. He mumbles something that is not quite words but is soaked in desperation.

Her fingers rage to throttle his incoherent voice, as every mumble is another wasted moment. Another moment of her wrestling the pull, her aching fatigue, and long seconds added to the separation of her estranged family and herself. Seconds more that she has to be aware of what has been done to her daughters and husband and to also know that it is not finished. It is unnecessary time given for the noxious taste of unwanted knowledge to linger in her mouth. It is that much more time for her to *be*. She wants to rip his tongue out of his mouth and pull the unsaid words out with it. Stretching closer to his face, but still not touching, her fingers long for it—to lustily grab her retribution violently from a violent world. It would be a strike against so much more than Andarus; it would smack the face of the pull that commands her not to give into the growing malcontent inside of her. The pull knows she needs the information from Andarus, yet it stokes the fire of impatience and anger, reveling in her discontent and commanding her to tolerate its torture. One watching her menacing fingers and swirling crazed pupils would never be able to trace the line between her current condition and the patient, loving, and reformed mother and wife of just a year before.

"Where does she live?"

Andarus squirms, fighting a spasm. The words are ready to jump out of him. His body is all too willing to give her anything she wants. Maybe then she will leave. The "detective" in his mind has always been dominant, easily putting the pursuit of a perpetrator or the protection of the people above his own feelings and needs, but now his "detective" side struggles to suppress his strained humanity like a fool trying to hold back a stream with his hands.

"Where…is…Daisy,…detective?"

His flesh gains control, "She wasn't home," he blurts timidly.

The corners of her mouth move neither upward nor downward, but they slide straight out, widening her lips and pushing them into sharp points. An image of a Shakespearean queen-to-be flashes in his brain, but it is immediately discarded. Laura usurps his entire focus. He sees power, but beyond that he sees hellish pain inside of her.

She leans forward, moving her hand to the side of his head and placing her face directly in front of his. It is close enough where one should be able to feel the other breathing, but Andarus feels nothing. The proximity adds to her intensity, and she says, "I didn't ask you how you spent your day, Andarus. I've wasted too much time looking for this one. This has to end; Where…is…Daisy?"

At the sound of his name being spoken through her icy voice, his resistance is destroyed. The word "end" that she has spoken rings and echoes through him as it gives him a glimpse of an inclination that he may possibly be able to get out of this situation. "She lives with her father."

"Address."

"1604 West Palm St.," flies out of his mouth before he consciously tries to recall the address, "Apartment H."

His thoughts are like a shuffled deck of cards. She grabs them and sends them flying into the wall, and, with the mere command of her voice, the one card for which she is looking lands in her opened hand. He would realize he is part of the game had he played a willful part, but never is one truly played who realizes the game is on.

She turns from him. The "detective" in his pride jumps to attention, as she is about to slip smoothly through the opened doorway. Feeling as if it will shrivel up and disappear from his personality forever if it does not act now, it grasps the reigns of his mentality.

"How?" he starts.

Her body pivots instantly flashing him a façade that changes from being full of irritation to a sly, calculating smirk. The second look has none of the seriousness as she had earlier—no focus on business. It is wild and maniacal, and it is set on the man in the desk. There is no pull holding her back now.

Andarus has a unique adrenaline-fueled rush coursing through him like a speeding daredevil who has just realized he has gone too far to stop himself from going over the cliff. So, he stomps the accelerator to the floor. Her demeanor scares him as if it were a deep, looming canyon awaiting his fatal crash.

He stomps, "How did you find Legree and Murdstone so quickly?"

The sound of his voice speaking freely both annoys and intrigues her. But, the utterance of the two names sends her anger over the edge. Paul sits helplessly as she seems to slide around the desk toward him. His adrenaline has left, his hands sweat, and there is only miniscule relief in knowing that he took his shot.

Blur, sting, and darkness. As his eyes see not, and his brain dreams not, the words, "What you don't know might save you," swirl and spiral, fading away into nothing.

A "bing" bounces through the long computer room and through the office causing the unconscious detective to stir scarcely in his chair. His vista is a blurry, shapeless haze, and he is not sure of where he is. He is not aware of much. All that he knows is the "bing" means something is coming, and last time it was not good. He slides his hand to his gun holster, but he stops there as he fights to keep his eyes open. Even though his vision is skewed, it is better than darkness.

When she can see his face, his eyes are Debbie's eyes from the hospital, and his mouth repeats the same dreaded words. Her heart is shattered, and the tears fall before she can reach out to touch him.

"Laura…Bonney…Laura Bonney…Bonney…Laura…Laura...Laura Bonney…"

Her curled hand draws to her mouth as she squeals, "No," whimpering through her fingers.

"Laura Bonney…Laura…"

"No, God, no," she whines. Her thoughts grow dark. God is on her mind, and she is about to pray for something she never would have imagined before. She takes her hand from her mouth and touches his face with it and places its counterpart on his chest.

"Yes…" utters Andarus.

Her mind is awakened from its dark thoughts and thrown onto that one word.

"What??? Paul, talk to me!"

His lips struggle, "Irene, yes," deep breath, "Yes, Irene."

Those are words that she has longed to hear for so long, but never has she imagined them to come from this situation.

Jerking her body forward, she presses her lips firmly against his. Pulling back, she says, "Yes, Paul. Tell me. Please, tell me."

Sigh, "Yes, Irene, it was Laura. Laura Bonney. Daisy. Daisy needs us."

"My God, are you all right? What did she do to you?"

He lifts his head off the back of his chair. Swelling and throbbing quickly convince him to rest it back where it was. His eyes are still wild and unfocused; but, at least they now stay on her when he speaks, and they don't wander randomly.

"Paul, what happened?" she persists as she runs the front of her fingers across his cheek.

Grunting softly, "I'm fine, Irene. I'm—I'm so glad that you came looking for me." He grabs her hand and squeezes it for a fleeting spell.

"I'm not so sure about that, Paul. What did she do to you?"

"It was all a blur. It doesn't matter now; I'm all right. What is important is she got info out of me about Daisy. Laura's going after her, and we have to find her before she does. God, she could be home in bed right now…Irene, we have to go."

"Paul, I'll go after Daisy; you have to go to a hospital."

Sitting up forcefully, he says, "No."

"I'm not playing with you on this one. You're going to get help."

He shakes his head and struggles to maintain strong conviction as if he were making a dying request, "No, Irene. No."

"Yes, Paul."

"No. I'm going with you. We're going to find Daisy. Then, I swear I'll go to the hospital. You can drive me, and I won't fight. But, I am not going until we get to Daisy."

"Oh, Paul," she sighs full of worry, her eyes threatening to rain on him again.

He smiles at her, barely holding back wincing from his pulsing head, "Just fix me some coffee, and let's roll."

For the first time ever, she goes to make his coffee, and, despite the terror around them, there is something nice about it.

Chapter XVII

Nearly a replay of the day before, except it is now two a.m. and the weather is worse, Andarus's knocks go unanswered on the wobbly locked door in front of him. He, typically calm and professional, is currently at the end of his patience. With two blackouts, sporadic minimal eating, no sleep in two full days and far longer since a restful night's sleep, a friend and a pathologist in the hospital, a bizarre murder case, and a seventeen-year-old girl's life depending on his actions, not only does Irene anticipate a breakdown, but she will not blame him for it when it comes.

His last knock is inordinately loud, and he flings his hands to his sides in frustration and turns away from the door. Irene thinks for a moment that he may curse; something she has never heard him do. The expression on his face also indicates that profanity is on the way, but he fights the urge and suppresses it temporarily at least. However, his zealousness has not left him to get into Daisy's father's apartment.

"Where the hell is he?" says Andarus in a voice too loud for two a.m.

"Maybe, he's out looking for her?"

"Yeah, right, maybe he's given up drinking too."

"Well," asks Irene, starting to shiver from the damp weather, "what are we going to do?"

Andarus scans the area with his eyes, and, glancing back to the door, he says, "Back up," motioning with his hands for Irene to step out of the way.

Surprised by the commanding response, she does step back and watches him intently as he plants his left foot firmly down in front of him and cocks his right foot back, preparing to kick the door with it.

"Paul!" she jolts, "What are you doing?"

"I'm kicking this lousy door down."

"What? No!"

He turns out of his kicking stance to face her, "Irene, we don't have time for this. What are we supposed to do—wait for this drunk to come home and ask him if we could please search his daughter's room because she might be in trouble? Come on—we can't do that. The girl could be in the morgue by then."

"Paul, I know this, but, you can't just kick the door down. We could get shot by a neighbor, or what if he's in the house passed out and you wake him up by kicking the door down? We're in plain clothes—this is dangerous for us and the outcome of this case. We can't do this, Paul. Not this way. If anything does happen we are going to have a hard time explaining why we broke into their apartment in the middle of the night. What if the dad is involved in this somehow? We can't just break into his home and then have him convicted."

"I don't care. I just don't care what they'll do to me; I have to help her before it's too late—there is no other way. Laura ripped information out of me about this girl. Irene, I am responsible for this."

Her face brightens suddenly, "I'll go find the landlord."

He nods, "Two minutes. I'm kicking it down in two minutes."

Without looking back at him, she makes her way down the metal steps and says, "Make it three, tough guy."

"Hurry. I can't have this girl's life hanging on my head."

Irene nods, understanding his urgency, but what he did not tell her is that he is unsure of how much longer he can keep looking for Daisy before his body says it's had enough. He stares over the parking lot—the same two immoveable cars are there from the day before. As he leans, exhausted, on the door, he thinks that just as no progress has been made on repairing the dilapidated cars below, neither has any progress likely been made in any of the lives of the tenants who are stuck here. The door behind him likely has not opened since they left. Not by father, not by daughter. And, it only makes him want to kick it in more. The rail along the edge of the stairs sways with the rain-heavy wind, completely unhooked from the first step. Interrupting his thoughts, he watches Irene make it safely to the ground and turn left to the other side of the building.

After looking frantically at similarly warped doors, she finds one with a drop slot with the letters R-E-N-T unevenly carved in its tarnished, bronze-colored flap. Hating that she has to do it before she even does it, she knocks steadily five times on the flimsy door. Waits. Just as she cocks her hand back to knock again, a light flips on and is reflected on the shrouded window to the right of the door.

It opens, and a woman of about fifty stands in it, looking annoyed but not entirely surprised that someone is at her door after two in the morning. She makes no attempt to wrangle her hair that she has been sleeping on. Without a word, she gives Irene a what-do-you-want stare.

"Ma'am, I'm Detective Irene Bauchan, and my partner and I need to get into Apartment H immediately," she explains waving her badge.

The lady does not stir, but asks, "Why are you bothering me with getting into that apartment? That is not my responsibility to let people in or out of there. That is a rental unit, and you need permission from the renter."

“Ma’am, I understand that, but Mr. Slykovsky is not at home right now, and he was not at home earlier yesterday evening either.”

“Well, now, he wouldn’t be. He’s a night watchman over at the Sears. If you were an acquaintance of his or someone who had his permission, you would know that you couldn’t find him at home at this hour.”

“Ma’am, this is essential to our investiga…”

“Do you have a warrant?”

“No, ma’am, but under life-threatening circumst…”

“No, I didn’t think you did have one. I don’t know what kind of investigation you are trying to run, but this sounds phony to me. I ain’t never heard of the police coming to search a residence in the middle of the night.”

“It is highly unusual, but…”

“It ain’t happening neither,” says the woman as she starts to close the door.

Irene shoves her foot in front of the doorframe, and the door smacks her rain-dampened pump with force.

The woman opens the door back up with a serious look and says, “Now, what do you think you’re doing? Do you think I’m an ignorant slumlord who doesn’t know the law? You got no right sticking your foot into my apartment like that…”

“Ma’am, you’re absolutely right, but if you don’t help us a girl is going to die tonight.”

After a slight pause, the strong downward arch of her eyebrows loosens to reveal a face of compassion, and she asks, “Daisy? Sad Daisy?”

“Yes.”

Moving close to Irene, she whispers, “Is it her daddy? Did the son-of-a-bitch hurt her again?”

“No, ma’am, but she is in terrible danger.”

The landlady looks around to see if anyone is watching, “Okay,” then as if convincing herself with the repetition, “Okay, let’s go.”

The landlady grabs a large key ring off the wall and leads the way with her thin robe fluttering in the windy rain. As they are about seven feet from the stairs, a loud thud is heard.

“Damn it,” says Irene quietly, which is the second time today that she has slipped with that phrase and a sure sign to anyone who knows her that it has been a remarkably trying day.

The landlady certainly heard it, and she turns to look at Irene. Instead of explaining, Irene steps ahead of the woman, quickly covering the distance to the stairs, and she goes up the wet, metal steps first. When she reaches the top, she throws Andarus a dirty, accusing glance and then looks to the door, only to see no damage. Looking back at him, his right pants’ leg and shirtsleeve are drenched, and he is smacking at his clothing trying to knock some grime off.

Stepping onto the narrow terrace, the landlady poses, “May I ask as to what that loud noise was?”

Looking at his soaked, dirty pants and grabbing the leg with his hands, he says, “I was pacing back and forth, and I tripped over this pot with the dead flower in it.”

The pot indeed had been knocked over and stood back up as its soil has spilled over its edge and onto the terrace.

“Well, you be careful, officer; it’s dangerous weather out.”

The woman faces the door and fumbles with the keys. Irene faces Paul and grabs his forearm rubbing it softly. Although he could use a laugh, he is glad that she did not make a joke. The door opens, and they follow the woman inside to a living room with worn, discolored carpet and dim lighting. Irene turns on a nearby lamp, which casts a small amount of light but throws huge shadows on the far wall. Beer bottles cover most of the coffee table and the kitchen table, which is adjacent to the living room, and used ashtrays are scattered in various places. The room is weighted down by the smell of cigarettes, which only makes it seem darker and denser than it is.

They walk across the living room to an unlit hallway that has three doors; two lead to bedrooms and one to a bathroom. The first bedroom door has divots about the size of a man’s fist in it. Flipping on a light reveals a room with a bed, a small TV atop a dresser that has several of its handles broken off and some hanging from one side, and one small nightstand with an ashtray and a lighter on it. The light is flipped off.

They pass the bathroom without inspection. Moving to the next room, the light switch is flipped, which does no good. A breeze blows through the room. Andarus steps into the pitch of the chamber, noticing it is disheveled; there are things that he cannot decipher that he hits with his feet as he steps. He bumps into a dresser and follows its surface until he finds a lamp. Turning on the lamp reveals that the window has been shattered. The only things preventing the rain from blowing across the entire room are the deep purple curtains that block most of the broken window’s opening. The objects on the floor are cds that fell out of an overturned rack, which apparently was in the way of whoever came through the window.

Andarus looks at Irene in disbelief.

To the landlord, he asks, “Did you see anyone with a ladder tonight?”

“Of course not.”

Irene jumps in, “Anyone strange hanging around tonight? Out of the ordinary?”

The landlady laughs, and says, “In this neighborhood? Are you kidding me? There is always somebody strange hanging around. But, no, no one mentioned anything weird happening today, and I can promise you no one came to that window with a ladder.”

Thinking out loud, he asks, “How in the hell did she get in here on the second floor?”

Scanning the contents of the room, the only thing that seems to be out of order are the scattered cds. The posters on the wall are of fantasy artwork and gothic music groups, and they are all hung perfectly straight. The dresser has been recently cleaned, and the only items on it besides the lamp are a few small makeup containers, neatly arranged with their labels facing forward, and a bottle of perfume called Autumn Rose. The mirror at the back of the dresser is covered mostly with stickers of the same images that are on her posters. Very little space is left to view one's reflection. Between the dresser and the far wall is an incomplete bed. The bedspread and pillow are missing, but the mattress is still wrapped in black sheets. Schoolbooks are stacked on the floor in front of the bed like a pyramid with the largest book on the bottom and the smallest on the top. She has a small bookshelf of cheap make that is filled with worn books that have obviously been read more than once. The bookshelf is directly across the room from the dresser, and the window is to its left. Some of the books on the left side of the shelf are wet due to the incoming rain from the window. Glass and water are on the floor on the window side of the bookshelf.

Growing tired, the landlady asks, "Are you sure someone didn't just break the window? Nothing seems to be missing. And without a key, no one could've locked that deadbolt after they went out the front door."

Irene answers, "No, ma'am, there'd be a rock or a baseball or something in here if that were the case."

Adding, Andarus says, "Besides, this window is broken too cleanly. If it were an accident, the entire pane wouldn't be broken out. Someone kicked this in completely so they could get through easily."

With a tremble in her voice, "That's impossible, officers. No one could've gotten up this high to kick that back window in. A ladder would've woken up the people below us; that's their bedroom window that it would've been in front of. And, I live just two doors down—it probably would've woke me up too. We had roof work done a few months back, and it made a loud racket inside my apartment every time they moved those ladders. It just doesn't make any…"

Irene interrupts, "Ma'am, we have to look around and figure this out. Would you mind stepping out and giving us a few minutes?"

Seeming afraid to leave the room by herself, she offers, "Well, okay, I'll be in the living room trying to find a clean place to sit—if there is one."

As soon as she disappears from the doorway, Andarus slides up next to Irene and asks, "So, what do you think?"

"Well, I'm starting to understand how some woman knocked you out cold twice in about twenty-four hours. I was beginning to think you were losing it, Andarus," looking to the window, she watches the dark purple curtains rustling with the incoming rain and wind, "How in the hell did she get in through that window? Did she climb up the bricks in the rain?"

"I don't know. I don't understand how she has done any of the things that she's done so far…but, we don't need to figure it out now. Now, we need to find Daisy. Then, we can deal with Mrs. Bonney."

"All right, let's see what we can dig up."

They scan the room in different directions.

Within seconds, Irene says, "Hey, come look at this."

She points to the trashcan that contains a torn photograph. Upon closer inspection, Andarus asks, "Is that Simon Murdstone?"

"Yeah, I think it is, boss man. I guess they had a falling out. Maybe, that's why she wasn't at the motel room with the others."

"That might have been one of the smartest breakup decisions in teenage history."

"No kidding," replies Irene as they turn away from each other searching separately again.

Novels of various kinds—mostly fantasy, music and band magazines, sketch pads filled with drawings of gothic princesses and slain monsters, video game magazines but no gaming console, no pictures of friends, no signs of any other girls. Within ten minutes they leave.

In the car downstairs, Irene sits behind the steering wheel, and Andarus sits shotgun with his head pressed back and upward against the headrest, shoving out his Adam's apple.

"Well, that was a waste of time," she blurts.

"Not entirely. We know she had a split with Murdstone. So, she's probably trying to avoid him. She may not know that he's been murdered either, which might make her easier to find. If she knows he's dead, she's gonna try to disappear."

"Okay, but where do we look?"

He sighs and says, "I don't know…but…"

"But what, Paul?"

"I don't know if I should even mention it."

"Are you serious? We're in a case where we don't know what to do next, and you don't know if you should mention something?"

"It's not about the case…not really…I didn't fall. I blacked out—I'm a little dizzier from the shots to the head than I let you believe."

"You blacked out? You fainted?"

"And, when I got up, I was angry and frustrated, because I know this girl is counting on me to find her—whether she knows it or not. And, I'm in no condition to take care of myself much less save someone else…so, I kicked the pot over. When I heard you guys coming, I picked it back up."

"Paul, that's so not like you. I've never seen you lose your temper. My God, you blacked out just standing there? You've got to get to the hospital."

"Right after we find the elusive Miss Slykovsky."

"I'm here too, Paul; you can go to the hospital, and I can look for the girl. You're not alone."

Sighing softly, “No, that’s not what I meant, sunshine. You’re absolutely the one who will be carrying this investigation—you found the picture in the trash, which was the only useful thing out of coming here, and I’m certainly not on my best game right now. But, I’m the one who gave away her personal information to the murderer. This doesn’t rest on you, because I’m the one responsible for it.”

He clenches his fist as if he will punch the dashboard. But, he looks at his partner and slowly releases his hand.

“Well, if you won’t let me take you to a doctor, where are we going next?”

“Hmmm,” pausing, “well, if she was in tight with Legree and Murdstone, she’s probably hooked on the same junk that we found in their motel room. Maybe, we should cruise down Planeline, and see if we can find her or find someone who has seen her…Unless you have a better plan.”

“No. I don’t know what else to do. Jackson and DiNardi came up with no leads today at the school either…She obviously loves to read; we could check with the libraries tomorrow and see if she has checked anything out lately—maybe catch her there. But, that does us no good right now...this truly is a wild goose chase…but, I don’t know what else to try either.”

“Well, let’s go trolling on Planeline.”

Chapter XVIII

An October breeze passes through five weeks premature. If not for the drizzle and the foreboding clouds, it would be downright beautiful. She watches the people walking through the parking lot into the small arena. Some have branded themselves with pretense; some have a morbid fascination; some are so misused, misunderstood, and subsequently jaded that all they want to see is black; and others wear the noir clothes and eyeliner as a membership card, conforming into a nonconformist club. Some are there for the music that both peaks and provokes their melancholy spirits, and others that merely want to play out the role of the pseudo-hip and semi-intelligent outcast to garner some attention from others whose lives taste the same way. Many wear t-shirts of the bands playing that night; some are worn, tattered, and as loved as a child's security blanket, and others are crisp and new, seemingly bought yesterday to wear to the show tonight. Subtle differences that only an insider would decipher, but distinctions that divide the crowd the distance of an ocean. Strangely enough, the true fans of the genre are kind and tolerant toward the hangers-on despite their annoyingly silly behavior, much like they are younger siblings struggling to play an adult game. Or maybe, they've been so scarred by the unaccepting world that they cannot bring themselves to ostracize someone else.

With all of its festive celebration of blood and death, it is one of the few places in creation that Laura with her crimson-spattered clothing and angrily streaked hair would not raise suspicion or attract a crowd. If anyone has ever had need to listen to a lamented dirge, would it not be her? But, she remains scouring the crowd with her eyes, leaning on a sad-looking oak tree just outside the parking lot.

She cannot spot the one she is looking for, but she is content to wait as the pull holds her to the tree on which she leans. She has been very wary of trusting its guidance since its unexpected return. Her faith and comfort in it through the handling of Ed and Simon had left her vulnerable and defenseless when it turned from guiding her forward to trying to suck her inward and inside of herself, imploding her into nothing, trying to clear any evidence that it had helped her. She has not forgotten the long hours following the horror of the motel room, the struggle to hold onto herself, keeping herself from being swept up in the same force that used to guide her, nor has she overlooked the unguided, hellish hours that she forced herself through the streets looking for her last target and ending up at Andarus's office. She is fully aware that it did not return to give her supernatural aid until she had dragged herself onto the path of the third vengeance, seeking what should be the last murder. The promise of more destruction is all that keeps it to her, and she has no doubt that there will be more treachery to be dealt with in the instant that the last bloody justice is enacted. Knowing that she needs the pull's help to find and pluck the one flea off the decaying carcass that is the parking lot before her, full of humanity, music, and a celebration of the macabre, she keeps the pull as a deadly bedfellow. For the moment, she is focused on plucking Daisy, and she will embrace the pull until she has her, the wilted flower that she seeks, content to not worry about the devil until she has him by the tail. She stares at the parking lot as the stream of people walking into the building grows thinner and eventually dries up, leaving empty, lifeless cars behind like the tide leaving abandoned and outgrown shells of crustaceans searching for a larger and more comfortable home, all the while never realizing how vulnerable they are in the interim to any predators lurking about. For the moment, Laura lurks leaning on an oak tree. Looking. Luring. Looming in the latency of the tree's shadow.

The hum of electric keyboards sounds like a synthetic mass. The muffling of the music as it passes through the structure of the building and into the night air only makes it sound more forbidden and otherworldly. Despite its haunting aura, the music makes her feel nothing new aside from being just one more reminder to think of Gabe, Susanna, and Daniella, along with their suffering and her loss to which her mind is already devoted. The sun turns its gaze, sliding its rays to another story, and nudging the drowsy night sky to commence its vigil. Laura does not care nor notice the change in the celestial ceiling; her only focus is on the closed and unmoved doors to the building.

The fatigue has not left. It grows. It is a weariness, a lust for sleep. She is not sore or bruised from her activities in the motel room. Yet, her eyelids press downward with a force that has gained momentum with every passing hour since she has left that bloody chamber on Planeline Highway; every movement has been weighted down as if yoked to an invisible burden. It is a mild torture simply to keep herself upright and leaning on the tree. Were she not so focused on staring at the closed doors ahead of her, she would worry what strength will she have left when her target walks through them.

A piece of paper is clutched in her hand. It is a small flyer that she found on a dresser top in the early minutes of the morning; she has grasped it tightly since. The moon moves steadily across the sky, and she waits. The last note fades away from inside the arena, and the constant drizzle quickly turns into a formidable downpour. The doors open, and the crowd funnels out under the overhang. They edge to the end of the shelter and stare into the thick rain that drenches the parking lot before them. Some of the ones with brand new t-shirts venture into the parking lot. They dance around and pretend to be enjoying the pelting rain, at least as long as there is a crowd. Excessive black eye makeup runs down their faces resembling some type of war paint or Halloween decoration. Their baggy clothing becomes drenched and clings to their bodies in such a revealing way that would normally make them feel mortified in public, but in this case acting cool somehow overrides looking cool. And, they dance as if at a ceremony.

Most of the crowd, the ones with the worn shirts, stare at the lot and wait. An umbrella is not standard concert-going equipment, and most of them have long abandoned their desires to impress strangers by doing silly things. The two parties, of which the crowd is made up that were difficult to distinguish earlier, are plainly separated now into those that dance for attention and those that wait for the rain. It is all of little help to Laura, as she does not know to which group her prey belongs. She is not even sure of what she looks like, as there were no pictures of her to be found in her apartment. Not even a yearbook. However, she is content to wait, believing her target will reveal herself.

Many of the ones running aimlessly in the rain are picked up several at a time by parents or older siblings who are usually shaking their heads as the young, soaked bodies pile into their previously dry vehicle interiors. Some of the older ones make quick dashes to their cars. Many still wait under the shelter. The rain slacks ever so slightly, and a tall, skinny girl with long brown hair walks unescorted into the parking lot. Within seconds the rain turns her hair to black. Laura shoves off the tree with her shoulder into a standing position, and her eyes light up and follow the girl's movement. The girl keeps her head aimed down, looking only several yards ahead of her as she navigates the parking lot that is beginning to resemble one large puddle.

She shudders softly, but it does not slow her pace. She is not looking around to find anyone, but she seems intent on making a straight line out of the parking lot to the street. Laura moves.

"Hey, princess, do you need a ride?"

The girl looks to her left to see a car filled with three boys under the age of fifteen and a much older male driver who does not appear to have gone to the concert by his attire. The car is driving toward the street in the same direction as she is walking. She sees their giggling faces, and she can taste their sour laughter as it is familiar.

As she looks away from them and back toward the street, she can hear several voices interacting into one jumbled conversation, "Roll up the damn window, Trevor, it's raining outside…come on guys, she's kinda tall, but she's cute…I don't know if there's enough room for her back here—she's a beanpole…" there is the sound of an older brother smack, "Trevor, put the window up now!"

She can hear whimpering and the sound of the window meeting the weather-stripping. The first sound almost makes her smile as a small restitution, but the rain and the daunting prospect of her long walk, coupled with the strong possibility of more heckling, convinces her that the smile is not worth the effort.

As she reaches the corner of the parking lot and the street, she notices a woman standing on the other side of the car stable. The woman stands perfectly still as the wind tosses her clothing and the ends of her wet hair that extend well past her shoulders. The woman stares at her as if there is nothing else around them. She stands below a streetlight, and it reveals a pale, white streak running through her drenched mane. Even from the distance of thirty-some feet, the girl is sure that the woman's eyes are sparkling unnaturally as if the light from the post above is moving around in them. She feels a shortness of breath as she stares back at the woman wondering if it is some new type of contact lens. Many people at the concert were wearing bizarrely colored contacts; some even matched their outfits. But, none were like these. She and Daisy are the only two standing in defiance of the weather. The woman looks to be at least five to ten years older than her, and it reminds her of something that she is missing. But, with a fling of the woman's head, throwing water and hair, all of that washes away; the woman's face looks as serious as a statue and equally as cold, and it is definitely focused on her. The girl stumbles at the sight, feeling the smack of the sudden movement and the harshness that it implies.

"Watch out, sasquatch!" yells a voice through a small crack in the window of a car that whips around the curb to which she has stumbled dangerously close.

The tires tear into a large puddle and send a wave of discolored parking lot water crashing into her thighs, splashing her torso and running down her legs. She could just cry, and she knows she will once she gets to a place where no one else can see her. The rear tire barely clips the edge of the curb, riding up on it for a few inches, and bouncing back down onto the cross street as they speed away from her. Her friend, panic, hits her and brings her to attention as it has on so many times in the past when she could hear her father's keys jingling at the front door or the subtle floor squeaks of footsteps coming down the hallway toward her bedroom. This time her panic sends her looking across the parking lot under the streetlight. It is vacant. She scans the surrounding area and sees nothing. She spins around checking out the entire panorama of possibilities, but she cannot spot the woman. It is disheartening that she cannot see where the mysterious figure has gone off, but she would not feel any better if the woman was still standing there staring at her. Taking in a couple of quick breaths and a last look around the parking lot and the street, she turns quickly right and walks briskly.

Several hundred yards away in the opposite direction at a red light, Laura knocks firmly on a closed window. As the window rolls down, she leans forward slowly, and the skinny, pale driver's face broadens with a smile as his car only contains a single male passenger. He is clearly one of the worn shirts by his self-contained demeanor, the obscure bumper stickers on the back of his car, and by the music coming out of his speakers at a reasonable volume. All that he can see is her long hair covering her eyes, an outline of her nose, and her full lips—all of which are covered with a running layer of water. He is already interested.

"H-," is all that he can muster, as "hi" is a heavy word for him to deliver to people with whom he is not comfortable.

"I need your car," say the pouty, female lips in front of him.

His hesitation is there, but it's not a choice, as he has no skill in coed bantering. "Look, my name is Jeff, and this is Myles. We can br-bring you wherever you need to go. Just hop in the..."

"No, Jeff, I'm gonna need your car."

"What—do you want to drive?"

"No, get out," she says as she opens his door.

He stares at her fearfully, the thrill of talking to a girl fleeing from him. The light turns green, but the car in the lane on side of them is not even looking at the signal. All of the surrounding cars are watching her as intently as they can through the wall of rain. She quickly grabs him by his hair and throws him onto the grassy median on which she stands. Hopping into the car, she glances over at the passenger who sits in a daze.

"Myles, get out."

He jumps out of the car, and, without bothering to close the door, he runs behind it to the median where Jeff lies facedown, not having moved since he was thrown there. She speeds into the intersection and makes a u-turn back toward the arena and in the direction of a lone girl.

The force of the acceleration slams the passenger door shut. A phone sits in the drink holder in the center console. She grabs it, rolls down the driver's window, and throws it out onto the same median in which she has tossed the car's owner. Several wet, blurry moments later, Laura spots the girl walking alone down the sidewalk. She slows to the speed limit, rolls down the passenger window, and then she brings the car to a crawl, pacing the girl walking. The girl looks straight ahead pretending to not see the car.

"Daisy? Daisy, that's you, right?"

The tall girl turns in amazement at hearing her name. The car is not one that she recognizes, but a small sticker of a band that she likes on the rear passenger window puts her at ease. She bends down and looks into the vehicle at the driver. It is a woman smiling at her who looks familiar but she cannot place from where.

"Daisy, I'm Laura; I used to be friends with Simon and Ed."

A look of fear falls on her face, and she says, "Simon and I broke up—I don't talk to them anymore."

With that Daisy turns away expecting a harsh retort. Laura calls out, "Good for you. They're both douche bags; I *hate* them."

The intensity with which Laura said the word hate makes Daisy believe her, and it makes her smile. It is enough to make her look back to the car and the driver.

"Yeah," is all that she can think to say without saying too much.

Laura says, "Hey, girl, let me give you a ride; get you out of this rain."

Daisy steps up to the opened window and places her hand on the door handle. Bending down to stick her head in the space, she asks, "You're sure you can bring me home? I can't go anywhere else."

"Don't worry; I know what you're thinking. I wouldn't bring you anywhere where those losers would be—I don't want to be around them myself."

Daisy smiles.

Laura assures, "Yeah, I can bring you home."

The door opens, and Daisy plops her wet body down on the seat. The window goes up, and Laura asks, "So, where are we heading?"

"Go straight ahead until you hit Planeline."

"Andarus, get in the car; you have to hear this!" shouts Irene as she sticks her head inside the small building scattered with a few gamers.

Andarus quickly ends the conversation that he was having with a security guard in the front of the arcade and heads outside to the cruiser with Irene. She is already in the driver's seat as he slides into the passenger position.

She simply points to the radio as she gets onto Planeline, cuts across three lanes and turns left at the first light.

The radio repeats, "Car jacking outside Riverview Arena at the intersection of Arena Drive and Annunciation. Blue 4-Door make unknown. Witnesses spotted a female with long, black hair throwing the driver onto the median and taking off back toward the arena. Suspect is said to have a noticeable streak in her hair…"

"That's her! That's her!" shouts Andarus.

"I know—I knew it had to be her."

The radio continues, "…was alone when she took off…"

"We should be running into her. She should be coming from the other direction, if she hasn't turned off."

Irene nods and keeps her eyes focused on the road in front of her and the oncoming traffic to her left. Her head turns quickly in the other direction.

Andarus asks, "Did you see anything?"

"No, no, two girls were in that car."

"Hmmm…look! Lights ahead!"

Police lights flail two blocks ahead of them.

"Maybe they've got her," says Irene hopefully.

"Maybe," offers Andarus without as much enthusiasm. "Pull alongside them," he instructs as they approach the Riverview Arena Security Car on the shoulder and the apprehended car in front of it.

Andarus's window is rolled down, and he holds his badge in it. He takes one look at the driver and shouts to the security guard who holds her license in his hand, "It's not her. The one we're looking for is closer to thirty than twenty."

"How do you know?" questions the security cop back toward the car, but Andarus and Irene are already moving on.

They see lights ahead of them again.

"What kind of event did they have down here tonight?"

Irene answers, "I think they said it was a rock concert. Don't know who was playing."

As they near the next vehicle pulled over, Andarus says, "Slow down."

He points to several bumper stickers on the rear window of the car, and asks Irene, "Those look familiar?"

"Oh my God, she was going after Daisy—right here. We were only a few minutes away."

"At least she was alone in the car a few minutes ago. Maybe she hasn't found Daisy yet."

"Take a right here, Laura," says Daisy in a voice that sounds so relaxed it surprises herself.

"Okay, right on Planeline. Where to after this?"

"Keep going straight toward the airport, and take a left toward the river on Sanctuary."

"No problem."

They sit in silence for a few blocks.

"Say, Daisy, didn't you live on the other side of town not too long ago?"

Daisy stares out the window with tingles running up her neck at that question.

"I thought that we dropped you off at an apartment on the other side of town one night after hanging out with Simon and Ed."

"Yeah, yeah, I used to live with my dad," she says quietly.

"Who are you living with now?"

Hesitation, "My aunt."

"Oh."

Three more blocks of silence.

Laura asks, "So, great show, huh?"

Warming up again, "O-o-o-h, it was a-maz-i-n-g!"

Laura forces a laugh, and bites her bottom lip tightly when she remembers her daughters stretching out the word the same way when they would describe the stories their daddy would make up for them to put them to sleep at night. Her face winces grotesquely at the memory, but Daisy is too excited in talking about the show to notice anything else.

"It was s-o-o crowded. And, it was s-o-o loud. Especially after the two tabs I bought from this girl in the bathroom. It was a-maz-i-n-g."

Laura turns her head to look out the driver's window, so she can hide her reaction from Daisy.

"It was s-o-o emotional. It expressed all the things I've been feeling lately."

"You have no idea," grumbles Laura.

"What'd you say?"

"Nothing, nothing. It was a great show."

"I didn't see you inside. Where were you during the show?"

"I move around. There was a lot of people in there."

"Hmmm," says Daisy, "I was by the stage…I hang out next to the speakers all the way on the left side, because people get mad at me when I stand in front of them, but I still want to be close to the show."

"Hey, I really gotta pee. You think I can go inside your aunt's house?"

Hesitation returns.

"Oh, come on. I really gotta go, Daisy."

"My aunt's sick, and…she goes to bed early. She'll freak out if she sees anyone else in the house with me."

Silence.

Feeling like she has insulted a friend, "I'm sorry, Laura. It's not me—it's my aunt. Can't you stop somewhere on the way home—after you drop me off?"

Brief silence, then, "No problem. I'll stop somewhere…Whoops!"

The car wheels around, sliding a little as it makes a hard left turn.

"Almost missed Sanctuary. You should've told me it was coming up."

"Sorry, I haven't been here long…look, you can just drop me off here, and I'll walk the rest of the way."

"No way—it's still raining. I'll bring you to your house."

"Mmmm-kay, it's a half block down on the right. The one with the weeds growing in the garden…ugly weeds…my aunt used to plant flowers, but she doesn't have time for that anymore…not since she's been sick."

Pulling up to the curb in front of the house, "Well, here we are."

Daisy looks around to see if any neighbors are awake and possibly watching, and then toward Laura, "Hey, thanks for the ride."

"Look, Daisy. I seriously have to pee. You have got to let me inside—I'll tiptoe."

"U-h-h, it's not a good idea—my aunt…"

"Yeah, I know but I gotta go now."

Laura can see the urgency in Daisy's eyes as she scans the neighborhood.

"Look, Daisy, I'll pop a squat on the front lawn if I need to, but I'm going now."

"No, no!" exclaims Daisy, "I don't want the neighbors to see that…o-h-h, just come in, but wait for me; I have to go in through the back door, and I'll come open the front for you."

"Thanks, but hurry."

"Okay. Okay," says Daisy as she jogs gingerly to the rear of the house.

Laura closes the car door quietly and then waits several feet before the front door on the lawn, allowing the rain to once again have its way with her hair. As her hair covers most of her face again, she no longer suppresses the energy in her eyes, and the release awakens every inch of her that has lacked power since the last two slayings. All of the gaps between her and the pull, all of the struggle, all of the doubt have left her. Her rage feels stronger than when she was at the motel. The unkempt garden reminds her of her own house after she moved away: the garden in which she used to plant flowers with her little girls, the garden that was neglected and allowed to die when she left. She feels as if she will burst.

The door slowly opens and a long, slim hand beckons her to come inside. The fingers remind her of something. A smear. Long, slim, red streaks across the glass of a family picture in her foyer. It takes all of her strength not to scream out, to grab those fingers and wrench them in obscene directions that all somehow point to hell. But, the pull commands her to go inside the house. Maybe, it is to get out of the sight of innocents who may hear the noise, or maybe it's just one more moment of torturous waiting for the pull to force her to endure. Either way, she is content enough to wait to get inside of the house to have the girl within her grasp.

Laura steps into the dwelling, which has only one light on, none in the room that she has stepped into.

Daisy points to a light down the hallway, "The bathroom is down the hall; the room with the light on. Be quiet, and please go quickly."

Laura makes a point not to look in her direction but just raises her hand in acknowledgement and walks to the light. The bathroom doorknob is made of glass and is in the style of several generations prior. The old design is also reflected in the style of the pink sink, mirror housing, and toilet. Laura closes the door quietly and flips the lock. The bath/shower area has sliding glass doors, and through their blurred visibility metal assistance rails can be seen attached to the walls. The sheen of the sink inexplicably attracts her attention, and she turns to see it head on. When she gets in front of the sink, her vision is pulled up into looking directly in the mirror. Her eyes blaze and turn wildly, and her own soul races in fear. The streak in her hair appears electric and pulsing in its reflection. A sting races through her eyes into her head, and she falls backward, smacking the rear of her head against the wall and crashing to the ground.

Tiptoeing feet can be heard approaching the door. Then, a frantic whisper, "Laura, what the hell are you doing?"

Shaking her head and opening her eyes, "Na-nothing. I'm a little sick—I might be a little while."

"Oh, Jesus, hurry up. Hurry up."

Cracking her neck and climbing back to her knees, she grabs the shiny, pink sink and struggles to pull herself back onto her feet, knees quivering. She stares down at the sink and lifts her perspective high enough to see her head and her bangs hanging down blocking her face. Obstructed, her reflection is not as strong as before. In a quick jerking motion, she flips her hair out of her face, and the eyes rage again. They are all she can see. The whirlpools within them spin, pulling her in closer, and she feels as if she is just a spectator. Sting rockets through her eyes into her skull again, and she flies back into the wall and to the tile floor. A crazed laughter echoes in her head; but, it sounds not like her voice, and her mouth is closed.

The thud is much louder this time, and the tiptoeing feet are also a little less cautious and quiet in the their motion.

In an exasperated whisper, "Laura! Laura, what in the hell is going on in there? Get OUT of that bathroom now."

"U-u-h-hm-m-h-h-h-m-h-m-h," groans Laura softly, unable to open her eyes this time.

Feeling the intensity of the moan, Daisy whispers, "Laura, if you're that sick, take your time. Just be quiet. For the love of God, no more crashing noises." The feet step away and come back, "But, be neat in there, okay?"

"I'm com-ing, Daisy," sighs Laura forcing her eyes open, "I'm coming."

Her head is a cyclone as she gets herself to her knees. Pulling herself back to her feet takes two tries, and she stands again staring at the pink sink. The pull calls her like a siren to stare back into the mirror. This time she feels like one more shot might end her existence altogether, and that does not sound like a bad idea. No more burning, longing, missing, hating, regretting, feeling…

Her hands squeeze the sink tightly, and her forearms strain to hold her body standing. None of her veins stand out, but she can feel immense pressure in her limbs. The two straining hands clutching the sink remind her of her couch, and the violent nail marks dug deeply into Gabe's flesh. She can hear the screaming of two children from down the hallway floating to the sofa where a dying man lies in torment. Then she thinks of Daisy in the darkened house, probably not far from the door with the glass handle. She shakes her head at the mirror while still looking down at the sink. Raising one finger to the reflective surface, she turns from it and opens the door. The only light in the hallway comes from the bathroom behind her. There is no sign of the flower.

She grabs the doorframe as her body sways, still weakened from her bouts with the mirror. She has no plan, and Daisy has disappeared. Dread comes over Laura, but something pulls her to walk farther down the hallway, away from the front door. A kitchen is behind her at one end, illuminated in a faint green light from the clock on the microwave. Ahead of her, the door to the immediate left is closed, and the door directly at the end of the hallway is slightly ajar. Her fingers feel numb as she slides them on the door, but her eyes get a jolt of energy as she pushes it open. Peering into the room, she sees a bed with the covers pulled back awaiting someone to come to sleep. A Nathaniel Hawthorne book sits on the foot of the bed, and she is aware that she should not be able to read its title in the darkness. Scanning the room, it appears to be decorated in the taste of an elderly woman—the curtains, the furniture, the carpet, the headboard, and the antique television. The few items out of place are a pair of black boots on the floor by the bed, the black pillowcase on the pillow, and the black bedspread.

Turning in the other direction just past the TV is a closet that is also barely ajar. Laura steps toward it slowly, still shaky in her movements, and flings it open. A scream, a falling forward, a glittering in the near darkness.

Laura grasps the limb that ends in a shining blade. The scream grows worse as she intensifies her grip. Her arm is attacked from another direction—it is her assailant's free arm, and it smashes its nails at Laura's bare forearm. The sound of four cracks and another scream follow. The blade shimmers as it falls to the ground. It strikes a foot and rips through its socks, spewing a thin stream of blood. The pull's hunger wells inside of her as the wound opens, and Laura almost shouts aloud in lust. Still holding her attacker by the forearm, she swings the body onto the bed and into the dim, intruding light from the hallway.

Daisy immediately grabs at her forearm that looks twisted in the light. Her mouth is fully open-hinged while high-pitched whining echoes out of it. The pain in the slender arm must be great, as she has not noticed her foot.

Standing over her, between Daisy and the light, Laura asks, "What's with the knife, Daisy? Why would I want to hurt you?"

Daisy looks at Laura's face, but doesn't utter a word, the same indecipherable whining bounces out of her throat. Laura reaches down and squeezes the throat with force. Daisy's eyes roll back, and the sound stops.

"It's time for talking now, Daisy. Answer me."

She loosens her grip on the girl's throat, but keeps her hand close enough so she can throttle her again if necessary.

"I-I-I've been through a lot lately," says Daisy breathing in quick uneven gulps. As Laura's hand moves toward her throat, she starts again, "I-I thought you were—convinced myself you were someone else." The hand moves closer again, "Someone who would want to hurt me."

The hand stays stationary, "Who would want to hurt you?"

Staring at the hand before her, "People," pausing, but feeling the hand touch her throat, she continues, "We did a terrible thing."

"Who?"

"Simon, Ed, and me," she gasps once for every name that she mentions.

The hand crushes her throat again; she can feel each finger's mass on the inside. Then, it releases.

"We—we—we killed," gasps, "Killed someone."

"Who?"

"I used to love him. I used to love him."

The fingers attack again, Daisy's eyes feel as if they'll turn completely around. Release.

"Say his name."

"Mr. Bonney…Gabe Bonney," she cries like a child as she mentions it.

"Why?"

The fingers move forward, and she blurts out, "He hurt me. I loved him, and he didn't love me. I never loved anyone before him. He was kind to me, and I—and I loved him. But, he told other people and embarrassed me…"

The crushing and squeezing is immense. Fluid runs out of her nose.

"What does that have to do with the others?"

Gasping and gasping. Laura grows impatient and wants to pound her into a nothingness, but the pull urges her to wait.

"He got them expelled. The only boy I loved after him—he expelled. He crushed my first love, and hurt my second one…I couldn't take it…couldn't take it…"

Laura steps back for a moment. The light from the hallway hits her face.

"Look at me, Daisy. Don't you dare look away."

The girl looks up into the face. The eyes burn, turn, and twist, pulling her into them. She cannot move.

"Oh my God…Oh my God! You're the woman from the parking lot—I saw you standing in the rain. You looked so much different when you picked me up…I didn't know it was you…"

"You still don't know…" whispers Laura, "There is no aunt here, is there, girl?"

"No," squeals Daisy wishing she could look away.

"Whose house is this?"

"Simon's grandmother's house. She died five months ago, and the family's been fighting over what to do with the house ever since. I came here to get away from them. Simon and Ed are evil. My dad is evil. I had to get away."

"What about the girls?" bellows Laura.

"What?"

"The little girls down the hall from my dead husband? What about them? Why didn't you get them away from the evil? Why, Daisy?"

Her eyes grow grotesquely wide, "Oh my God, you're the woman in the pictures. You're *his wife!*"

"And the mother. Why, Daisy? Why my children?"

"It was never part of the deal. We were supposed to take care of Gabe, and that was it. We didn't even think about the kids being involved—that's why we went late, so they'd be sleeping."

"Why, Daisy?"

"Simon and I were with Gabe, and Ed slipped away to the girls' room while we were in the den. We didn't know what was going on. After we were done, Simon went to get Ed."

"And?"

"At least a few minutes had passed, and I went in after them…It was horrible…One head was dead and flopping around…and one's eyes were open and looking at me, blood and tears running all over her face…"

Laura's head spins at the images, and she feels as if she will fall out. Daisy sees it and springs off the bed and onto her feet, still grasping at her misshapen forearm.

"It's not how it was supposed to be. I screamed. I screamed at them. And, I ran out the house. They looked like my dad—both of them. I screamed, and I ran. Simon ran out after me and tackled me to the ground holding his hand over my mouth. I couldn't move; I couldn't fight—all I could do was cry."

Laura staggers where she stands, not even looking at Daisy anymore.

Now, screaming hysterically, "Ed came out and we left. We left. I screamed at them. And I screamed at them. They both punched me to shut me up, but I screamed. Ed peeled out down the street…"

Watching Laura intently as she sways, about to swoon, Daisy steps quickly toward the door. She enters the hallway; closer to the light. Pushing hard with her feet, she feels as if she is pulling the world behind her—her steps are so slow. She is finally beside the light, but she wants to run half way around the planet before she'll even look over her shoulder.

Her hair is grasped from behind, and she is thrown down to the carpeted floor next to the opened bathroom door. Her head smacks the wall before it hits the ground. She lands facing the bathroom and sees two divots in the wall that were not there before tonight. Laura stands over her and leans forward, bringing herself face to face with Daisy. Her eyes are hatred as they twirl like saw blades.

Grasping Daisy's throat with one hand and digging savagely into her stomach with the other, "You…you brought hell into my house…into my babies…into my husband…

…now it's here for you."

Chapter XIX

"Paul, it's time."

"It doesn't even hurt anymore."

His eyes have never looked so recessed. His entire body appears to be sinking into itself like an apple left too long in the sun.

"We've been working since six a.m. yesterday morning. Enough is enough. We're going to the hospital; then, we're getting some real food to eat. I'm going to take a luxurious shower, and, for the love of God, you are changing those clothes. Day 3, boss man, you're going to be attracting flies soon."

Smirking for a fleeting, undetected moment, "We had a deal; no hospital until we find Daisy," explains Andarus, not believing for a second that the girl is still alive. But, he keeps it silent as Irene could never understand how he could be so sure that Daisy is now dead without her having seen Laura in action as he has, even if for a few quick moments. After an entire night and morning, he does not doubt that Laura has plucked the flower from the weeds that she lives in, and he is convinced that they are now looking for a corpse. But, he will still look, as he is not willing to place his certainty over a girl's life.

"Every working officer is looking for Daisy, the license plate of the stolen car, and Mrs. Bonney. There is nothing left to do; there are no more excuses, and I'm too tired to be nice. So, let's go."

The "too tired" hits something deep inside Andarus, and he says in the best little kid's voice that his powerful tone will muster, "But only if we stop for ice cream on the way home."

"So, you're not going to fight me on this?"

"No."

"And you're going to let the doctor examine you?"

"Yes."

Forty-eight minutes later.

"What a quack!"

Laughter and concern wrestle within Irene as she jumps from her plastic hospital seat and walks alongside Andarus. Her body peels off the seat, leaving her dainty imprint behind.

"What?" she asks.

"Psychiatrist? What a brilliant solution."

Now, the laughter takes her, "Well, tough guy, I've been telling you that you're nuts for two years now."

Andarus stops walking and stares at her with a bland facial expression shared only by those who realize that they have become the victim of harsh irony, those who have expected disappointment from a loved one and received it on cue, and those experiencing an unbelievable series of mishaps who ask, "What else?" only to have the greatest indignity fall upon them next. The look cuts.

Nudging him in the arm, she prods, "Come on. Tell me what the doctor said."

"He's more worried about my insomnia and eating habits than the concussions. He said the crucial hours have passed but to try to not exert myself for the next day or two."

"Where does the psychiatrist come in?"

Groaning, "He thinks the shrink can help with my insomnia."

"Well…maybe it's not such a bad idea."

He stops walking again, turns to face her, and the look returns to his countenance.

She continues, "I just want you to be healthy."

"Yeah, yeah, I know."

"Paul, you know your lifestyle has to change; you can't go on living like this. Maybe, this is something that could help you. You need some kind of outside help."

"Well, it's not this."

"Well, living like a zombie is not an option either…What is that anyway? 'Living like a zombie'? It's a contradiction. Being alive yet always feeling dead. Up all night and hiding from the sun all day. Walking around but not experiencing things like everyone else. Are you getting the picture, boss man?"

He keeps looking straight ahead, sighs, and says, "Sometimes I sleep."

"Yeah, maybe two or three hours on a good night."

"No, there was a night not too long ago that I slept for five hours straight."

"That's still not enough. And, what's sick is that you've been in this sleepless cycle for so long that you think five hours is pretty good."

"Can't we talk about this case?"

"No, Paul, three days—three long days with no breaks, nonstop on this case—no talking about the case."

“Okay, well can we talk about anything except my impending insanity—how’s about calculus, soap operas, celebrity couples, menstrual cramps—anything else that might drive me a little less crazy than talking about my craziness?”

“Anything except something that might actually help you.”

“We should pop in and see Debbie while we’re here.”

“Paul?”

“Come on, ‘Rene. We’re here already. Let’s see her for a few minutes, and then we’ll get breakfast, hose off, paint Easter eggs, and do whatever other frou-frou activities you have planned.”

“Sleep, Paul. After eating and showering comes sleep.”

“Sleep. Sure. My old friend sleep. Right after we visit my old friend Debbie.”

“Okay, Paul; look, I care about Debbie, too, you know?”

“Of course.”

“Well, you don’t always have to make me the bad guy when I’m trying to make sure you take care of yourself.”

“Well, in life, some are bad guys and some are good. I can’t help it if you see yourself as one of the bad guys. Perhaps, you could change your actions to alter your perceptions, or maybe you should go see a psychiatrist about that.”

With a crooked, agitated smile and holding both of her hands out like a child reaching to grab a cup, “Sometimes I’d really like to choke you, boss man. Especially when you’re delirious from sleep deprivation like this, I’d really like to wrap my hands around your throat and squeeze.”

“Well, you know the shrink could help you with that too.”

“Paul,” thirty percent agitation, seventy percent amused.

“I know. I know: Debbie. Eat. Shower. Bed. I got it.”

“Well, if it’s done in that order; it doesn’t have to end in death for you.”

“I’ve been meaning to talk to you about this violence/death fixation; you know who can help you with that…”

“Paul!”

The woman lies on her bed, back down, seemingly staring at the ceiling, but a closer look reveals that she is not focused on anything in the room. Her lips move in blips of two at a time, but the spaces between them follow no rhythm. Some come close together as if links in a chain, and some have long spells in between. But, it is always the same two words being uttered.

Andarus sits in a chair pulled up to the metal rail of the hospital bed. His hand clasps the rail tightly, releases, and then clutches it again leaving his prints on its surface. Irene, sitting sidesaddle on the other side of the bed itself, rubs Debbie's forehead gently. Not many words have been spoken to her except, "We're here." "We love you." and, "Hang in there."

Dust particles
in the sunbeam
over Andarus's
shoulder
seem to defy
gravity as
they float
around.

Awkward silence is not a phrase that accurately portrays the situation. It is silence, and Andarus does not know what to say; but, it is not awkward. It is helpless. Debbie is one of three people around whom he has felt entirely comfortable in the last seven years. Cracking a joke or asking about her life has come easily. But, what has he to say to her now that her lips incessantly repeat the two words that have become the bane of his mental and physical condition? What can he say to her that could make any of this better? What words can he find that would not fall so short of amelioration that they would sound insultingly trite? And, even if he can find words tailored just for her, can she hear them?

Compassion pumps out of Irene: her eyes, her lips, her hands grasping Debbie's hand. Wordless. Andarus wishes he could exude the same warmth, but he thinks that if he were to grab Debbie's other hand it would only steal some of Irene's warmth instead of adding to it. As he watches Irene, she picks up his uncertainty and curves her lips at him.

"Debbie," he says leaning close to her, "you need to pull through this soon; we miss you. Irene here is cracking up without you. In fact, we have to leave now to get her to a psychiatrist appointment."

In the unique tone of whispered exasperation, "Paul!" voices Irene, smiling and fuming simultaneously.

The two words stop repeating, and Debbie smiles.

Chapter XX

The contentment of the vengeance, the icy retribution, and her relief in finishing it make her clench her eyes tightly together, not wanting to see anything in this world again. With the weight crushing down on her, she thinks. She can still see this world. No door has opened. She still is. Pressed against the brick wall in a filthy alleyway, she still is. And, that is a horror that she did not bargain for.

Rain persistently plinks around her. In itself, she cares not for it either way, but it is a reminder of something she dreads. Any details of her return to the alleyway elude her memory. She had paid no attention to her surroundings and is not even aware that she has come back to the same alley. The spattering rain is all of which she is cognizant outside of her thoughts. It falls around her in a thousand clicks, like a torturous, sped up clock.

Behind her eyes, shrieks and screams echo through her soul's chamber. Images pass of a crimson-soaked motel room and a desecrated flower. The sounds and the dismembered recollections bring a near peace to her. A tainted solace hovers around her giving a partial satisfaction. She has finished what she ached to accomplish. Her plans for revenge are done, but she knows something is not right. Something feels undone, but all for which she is concerned is accomplished. Maybe that is why she instinctively wandered back to the same alley to lean on the same bricks on which she has composed herself before, looking for some direction.

Nearly a day before, she crouched over Daisy. She soaked in every detail that she wanted to witness. Every squeal, every gasp, every tear, every drop of Daisy's trampling seeped into Laura's being, filling her. Sometime during this absorbing of Daisy, the pull fled from her again, and she could feel the weight coming back onto her. Now, the crushing heft of the things she has witnessed threatens to consume her. She feels that it is after her. Now that there is no more blood to spill; it has no use for her. More than that, Laura is a threat to it. The pull works in shadows, unsolved phenomena, and old wives' tales, and Laura is a glaring proof that it exists. So, it presses on her, relentlessly trying to pull her into a nothingness, wiping away its fingerprints once again, calling her down to hell.

Hell is not where her children are. Hell is not where her husband resides. But, neither do they live in the world in which she is trapped. As she sits spiraling down recycled screams and horrors, no doors open for her, only the pull pressing down…down…down…

Chapter XXI

He is surprised that he has agreed to come along, because he has always feared dying alone, despite his lifestyle. The hallways that Andarus walks down are occupied yet empty, holding a mirror up to his fear. Clustering the lonely elderly into one building fails its purpose as it does not create family or community. It only makes for hundreds of lonely dying people under one roof. Life itself is painfully tentative to each one as self or neighbor could slip away any moment. And for many, memory is a Dali painting and reality an unfinished puzzle. Acquaintances have become too heavy for arthritic hands, and true friendship has departed somewhere in a past decade. It is much like a waiting room where conversation is simple and interaction is minimal, because they know one by one they will all be gone when their name is called. Only in this building, all those around Andarus are waiting to see the physician of all.

"My dad's room is at the end of the hall," points Irene, sliding a delicate finger into the air that has a faintly aged smell.

He's been here with her a handful of times before, and on each visit she points out in which direction the room is. Andarus notices tire marks from wheelchairs and carts on the floor below, intersecting each other and forming nests of indecipherable paths. He wonders about his own path and if it is decipherable to the rest of the world. Do his decisions and life create a path toward an end, or has it all been crisscrossing and rambling pointlessly? He also wonders when his path will cross again with its most recent and violent interloper. He glances at the darkness of the night sky out the window at the end of the hall, half expecting to find her eyes watching him.

A female hand squeezes his shoulder, which should cause a faint shudder given the dark thoughts it interrupts. Fatigue stubbornly clings to him as if it were ash. Irene indeed made sure that he ate, showered, and laid down for six hours during the day, which was quite an undertaking to restrict Andarus's mind to a pillow. But, a mere six hours of rest and even less of sleep is far too little to combat seven days of unrest and acutely heightened awareness, and three days of work without a break.

She smiles, and he pats her hand on his shoulder. She is not sure if it is affection or if he is pushing away her touch. And, the uncertainty of it aches. She is already emotionally fragile as visiting her father is either a sweet-tasting poison or a foul-smelling flower. She has not decided which it resembles more: a mostly good thing with a sour lining or a terrible experience with a faint hint of goodness. Her heart squirms.

She looks from Andarus to the open door as his hand lightly drags hers off his shoulder and to her side. The gloom permeates through her as his gesture and the door both lead to sad results. But, a gentle squeeze stops the squirming. His fingers slide through hers as she steps into the doorway with him right behind. Holding hands is not an action that Andarus employs lightly, and two long years of close work have taught her that. She has always smiled when she walked into the room to visit her father, but for the first time it is real.

The man sits on the bed. His expression is bland with a slight glint of excitement in his eyes that he tries to hide. As Andarus steps into sight behind Irene, the old man smiles and extends a hand with deep, rough grooves.

"Now, what the hell is this walking in the door? Irene, don't you have better taste than that?" asks the old man smirking.

Andarus smiles back and says, "Hey, Martin, how are you doing?"

"Can't complain, but I do anyway. What have you been up to, Paul?"

"You know, same old, working myself to death."

Chuckling, the old man says, "Except for solving murder cases. Heh heh. Seems like you've got a serial killer on your hands: two high school kids, a teacher and his family. And, it doesn't sound like you guys have a clue."

"Daddy!" exclaims Irene as she quickly but gently smacks his knee. It is an action that Irene has not used before, and Martin stares at her with hard eyes even though his face is still smirking.

As Andarus thinks to himself that it is probably three kids, not two, Irene and her father still stare at each other. Feeling as if things could explode between them quickly, Andarus interjects, "Been following things on the news, Martin?"

Relieved to have an excuse to look away without backing down, the old man's eyes relax and return to his one-man audience, "You know it, detective. The TV news, and that rag of a paper that we got here; all they wanna do is bash the president. I've got one of the girls here that brings it down to me at five a.m. when the paper boy drops it off; I get it before anyone else mucks it up. I like to keep up with what's going on around here. Especially with the police," quietly glancing back to Irene, "seems like they let anyone on the force now."

Irene looks hurt and vulnerable. Andarus sees it, and feels helpless. Before long the old man is kicking the show back into gear as he begins talking again.

"Paul, do you want some coffee?"

Paul has never accepted Martin's offer for black, steaming liquid caffeine, half because of being polite and half not wanting to extend the conversation with java fuel. But, the old man asks every time before he gets the dialogue going very far.

"Paul, did I ever tell you about the time that I drove my pickup across Jake's Pond to take Tommy Pickering's fifty dollars?" Without waiting for an answer, "The police were clueless, then too, as to how my truck got there in the first place. Now Tommy was always daring people to do this or do that, and I was the type of guy to take him up on it…"

Paul has seen Irene's dad exactly eighteen times for various reasons over the last few years, and he has heard this story exactly eighteen times. It has always included the same euphemisms, expressions, and exaggerated pauses for effect. Paul nods politely, but he sneaks a glance at Irene every chance he gets. While Martin speaks, Paul notices a thin line of hairs just above his cheekbone that he missed when shaving. Paul had noticed it before on a previous visit, but considered it a fluke. Apparently, it was not. It is a thin, wiry trail of gray whiskers that extends from his highly shaved sideburns down the slope of his cheekbone toward his nose. Some wild ones run between his bushy eyebrows and the sideburns as if they create a thinly connected Bering Straight between the two bodies of hair.

Bits of the story flash in and out of his thoughts; some are cringe-inducing as he waits for the next line that he has unwillingly stored within the banks of his mind. "…and that Tommy said I'd never get past the middle of that pond without stalling out, so I said, 'Put your money where…that truck stalled on the incline on my way out of the pond, but, darn it, I was past the middle by then…." Paul glances around the room. It is slightly larger than what he would have expected for a nursing home. It looks much like his college dorm room in its size and shape, but it is filled with items from over two decades before. He spots a sink on one of the walls. It has a small round mirror in front of it that has some type of a haze or grit on it: cataracts and limited visibility in the mirror. At this, he thinks he has solved the mystery of the stray hairs escaping the old man's razor. "…it took two trucks on dry ground and a lot of rope to pull her outta there…'it'll never run after that, Martin,' they said. But, a little starting fluid and a heavy foot on the gas blew all that durn water out that engine…I walked away with that Pickering boy's fifty dollars in my pocket; you betchya that. And, that engine ran until I married this one's mother, and I sold the truck."

Another story falls upon them about how he once found three jars full of silver dollars inside of a wall while tearing down a fishing camp on one of his leases. He kept those jars under his bed for years. Claiming that he is not exactly sure how they disappeared, he says that he would bet it was some boy who rode a motorcycle that Irene knew in high school. At which Irene, does not know whether to laugh, roll her eyes, or cry. She does the preceding two.

After an hour and a half and several attempts to wrap up the conversation, Irene and Andarus finally are on their feet in front of Martin, who also creaks to a standing position. Irene leads the way to the door with Andarus directly behind her and her father following last.

Martin says, "I watch those detective stories on TV. I always figure it out before you guys do," explains the old man with glee, as he stays close behind Andarus, "You detectives—always missing what's right in front of you."

Andarus turns his stare from the back of Irene's head to over his shoulder and at Martin. "I never watch them. Can't take watching it at home after going through it all day long at work. You know, 'No one has worse shoes than the shoemaker's son.'"

Martin smiles at the platitude, as it is one he uses frequently, and he grabs Andarus by the elbow in a manner to share a moment of discretion. Paul realizes it and stops walking.

"Paul," he whispers, "I know I'm not a detective, but this one you're working on is strange. I've got a sick feeling about it. Those kids. That family. You take care of yourself," he says as he nods toward Irene who has kept walking into the hallway, shaking his head, "Ya'll are dealing with something twisted here."

Irene turns outside the doorway looking at them with a strange curiosity. Tact and whispering have never been traits associated with her father. Her arm reaches out slightly, turning at the shoulder and elbow, twisting like a rose vine. Her hand is open, palm up, and waiting for Andarus.

Chapter XXII

She stands with her toes over the edge. The wind whips her hair wildly, flinging the black mass with the long white stripe as if it were a flag. Drops of water fly out of her drenched mane into the violent downpour that surrounds her. The rain and the wind encompass her, but she looks straight down. It is a long way. Her left hand reaches back and to her side grasping onto a long, metal ornament on the roof. A tall, thin stained glass window behind her illuminates with the lightning and seems alive with the water sliding over it. The roof is at a steep angle and is wickedly slick. She thinks she will let herself fall.

It was a difficult journey to travel across town in the pouring, pelting rain. But, her real obstacle was in forcing herself to move. Every step was weighted as if she were underwater. Every movement felt as if she were dragging and pulling the world along with her. No voice had come to her in the alleyway; no sign had given her insight. The aching and the inner pulling ate at her every second that she sat in the alley. She did not leave with a destination but to find some reprieve to get her thoughts together or at least make them coherent. She stumbled through the empty streets, one of the few defiantly challenging the thunderstorm and its rumbling and flashing warnings. Sitting trapped between two worlds, yet belonging in neither, she knew the end of the line could not be the brick walls of the alley. At least, she was not ready to accept that fate for herself. So, she wrestled the pull that was trying to turn her inward, pull her down, and make her give up on seeing her family. It wanted her to slink into an easy nothingness; to be able to stop the pain of being conscious in a world where they were not; to forget, to let go, to stop hurting, to stop caring, to stop being. So, she forced her body to move against its resistance. She walked down the same streets as she did a few days before, but they looked so much darker, drained of color. Maybe it was the blur of the rain, the loss of her concern for such things, or maybe something had changed. Nevertheless, the surroundings screamed unwelcome.

The thought of the church never came to her until her hands slid over its bricks and their rough edges. Her numb hands could not feel the roughness of them, but she could feel the strength and solidity of their construction. The touch stopped the swirling images in her head. No more gore splattered on walls, mangled bodies, and horrific screams pelting her consciousness like the rain beating her face. All she could see was her family. All she heard were their voices. All of it cut. All of it hurt. But, it was a focus on where she wanted to be. It may only have been like a breeze to one being roasted alive, but it was something. Her mind was her own, and the force of the pull trying to consume her was greatly diminished as she could barely detect its presence anymore. It hung on the outskirts of the wild, keeping its eyes upon her as she touched civilization, and it watched her, howling and crying out at her, letting her know it was near and stalking, waiting for an opening to pounce at her. But, for the moment, it was not upon her.

The climb was not thought out either. It started with reaching to the top of an iron gate, which closed in a side alleyway, and pulling herself to the top of it. She stood atop the gate, then grabbed onto the edge of the roof. She pulled herself quickly onto the slick black roof, bending the gutter slightly with her hands. She walked to the second tier of the roof, which was slightly higher than her waist, and pulled herself onto it. At the edge of this tier near the front of the church, she spotted the tall, pointy ornament that resembled a spear. She made her way to it, and crept to the edge at which she still stands. Waiting. Deliberating.

It is not fear, but indecision, a pure lack of direction. Are her children somewhere behind splattering herself onto the concrete below, or is this a mistake? She wants it so strongly to be her way out that she knows she wants to jump. To leap. To destroy. To be done with her torment. To end it all. She knows she wants this to be the right choice; she is aware that she is biased, and she does not want to make a decision that will keep her away from Gabe, Daniella, and Susanna. Anger fills her, as this is not what she thought she had asked for. This indecision, this race without an end, is not what she wanted. She had not thought or planned beyond her vengeance, but she certainly did not expect this, to be Hamlet in hell. As she lets her rage build over the decision, the pull draws nearer, and she is smacked in the face with flashes of her recent macabre activities. Her hatred allows the images and the sounds to enter her. With each passing vision and shriek, she becomes more enraged, and, as she becomes more enraged, she opens the door wider for more recollections to enter. It is like a whirlpool building speed. Like falling. She can almost hear the pull laughing from inside of her as she sways with the wind, just as angry as it is. It swells. It would feel so good to let go. To stop fighting. To stop worrying. To stop toiling over a decision that she never dreamed she would have to make.

Her feet slip, hand clings to the ornament, body slides and crashes to the roof; her mind goes blank.

Chapter XXIII

A newspaper sits atop the clutter on the desk with the banner headline, "Record Rainfall Drenches Riverview".

"We've got a forensics report with no fingerprints for our prime suspect found at either of the crime scenes. We've got a mother who has not been to work, who has not returned to her local residence, who is not registered at any local hotels, and who has attacked me twice—also leaving no fingerprints in my car or in the office."

"And, she knocked you out twice, sir," smiles Irene.

"Thank you."

"Anytime," still smiling.

"Can I continue?"

"Please do, detective, sir."

"Well, I'm wondering what in the hell am I going to tell the chief."

Irene's smile is taken in a fast inhalation, "Oh, shit, Paul."

"Yeah," says Andarus, surprised that his partner uttered even the most menial of curses, "I've been ducking his phone calls for days now. Apparently, the mayor's been screaming at the chief to bring him the killer. This one's been in the papers and on the news—he's gonna want some resolution. I don't even have any answers: just a fairy tale."

"And if the fairy tale is true?"

"Then the whole thing gets blamed on an inept and possibly unbalanced detective who will be demoted and replaced to guarantee public safety and…"

"And what?"

"And possibly secure the chief's reelection."

Chapter XXIV

Laura wakes to continued rain. She looks up; the sky is growing lighter as rays begin to break through the raindrops over a high pointed roof and onto angelic scenes of glass. If gravel were not stuck to the side of her face, she might conclude that she is dead and looking at the outskirts of heaven. As she stares upward, she can see the mangled gutter that she crushed some hours ago. She lies, back to the ground, inside the side alley of the church; behind her is the fence that she climbed earlier. She is quite unsure of how she arrived on the ground from the roof.

The rain has thoroughly drenched her hair, clothes, and body, but she does not shiver. The awareness that she still resides in our world scorches her soul. Instinctively, she reaches her arm and touches the brick of the church. The intensity of her torment eases, which both comforts and enrages her. The calm it delivers to her thoughts soothes her, but the same strength that soothes also provides a reminder that a power exists to ease her pain. It is proof that something exists to solve her problems. This same power could end her misery and reunite her with her family, but it has not. This sparks her anger. If it has the ability to take away her misery, why is she left to suffer? Has she not been through enough, seen enough hell on earth? Furthermore, she rationalizes that this power could have protected her family from their horror in the first place. This burns within her. She views this power and its reprieve much as she views the pull. She will use it because she needs it to accomplish her will, but she does not trust it. And, she has no love for it.

With a speck of gravel clinging to her left eyelash, she stares at a door that is rounded at its top. It is the church's side entrance from the alley, but its function does not interest her; it is its shape that enraptures her. She imagines the shape in stone jutting out of the green earth. A realization comes that there is something left to do. She is not happy or relieved, but at least she knows where to go next. It is not the cure but maybe an ingredient in it. She rises to her feet.

Chapter XXV

Teenagers in awkwardly fitting suits and dresses huddle together under umbrellas in a feeble attempt to gain shelter. The rain has not had the decency to lessen its downpour for the occasion, and the sun humbly sets a dim hue behind the rain clouds. The priest has a steeply curved umbrella sheltering both he and his book quite well; he has been through rainy funerals before. The green grass is spotted with brown puddles, which have been splashed onto the shoes, pant legs, and stocking-clad ankles of all those in attendance. Leaning on a tree, Laura stands forty-two yards outside of the circle of people around the graves. The trunk on which she leans is on the edge of a tiny mass of woods behind her, which could hardly be called a forest. The entire area was once a thriving woodland that has been cleared as space was required. Where she stands is its last remnant. When more ground is needed, her tree will be uprooted, and the earth under her feet will be graveyard too. Her gaze remains on the somber scene in front of her. She stares at the activity, watching from a distance that which she should be in the middle, absorbing all that is said and done like a scavenger eyeing a dying prey. She has spotted the detective and the woman that she saw walking with him back at the high school days before; her attention is not on them, but on the words of the priest and the reactions of the students. Glancing around the crowd in attendance, she sees parents of friends of her girls, although none of her girls' friends are there. Colleagues of Gabe are there, some shaking their heads in disbelief. She sees the numerous students; many of them are crying openly. Athletes stand next to burnouts, cheerleaders next to outcasts, honor students next to detention dwellers. The high school caste system cannot help the situation, so they have deemed it useless, at least for today. They all feel the same thing sharing their umbrellas, many burying a man who was kinder to them than their own parents. Everyone in attendance focuses on the priest and the three freshly made plots in the ground. No one looks in her direction. The rain and the words fall around them, usurping their attention.

Beyond the people, she focuses on the three coffins and the vacant, reserved space beside them, aching to be in it. Yearning to touch them, she feels as if she can no longer wait. She wants to be where her family resides. She has convinced herself that this is her way out; witnessing the funeral will be the end of her mission and the ceasing of her torment. What else could she be made to do? It would be pure sadism for her to exist one moment longer than the funeral. Once she sees her family into the earth, she believes the opening will come for her to exit. As the thought of obtaining peace taunts her, words from the eulogy bounce through the rain-cluttered air to her ears. All of it is too much to digest; the words describe what has entirely consumed her being. It is all she has been for days. She holds her stare to the coffins and waits. The images and the screaming returned to her as soon as she stepped away from the church this morning, and she has been struggling to keep them at bay since. Now, they not only flash memories of the past, but of the possible present. She could tear into the mass of people in front of her. She could scream for them to leave her with her family, and no one would dare utter a word. Or, she could wordlessly grab them one by one and shove them out of her way. The pull yanks at her to go forward, to do it, to release it upon them, but she holds it inside, not done for compassion but for fear of shackling herself to this nightmarish in-between state of being. Nothing the pull can offer, no matter how tantalizing or how much she aches to release the hell within her, is worth banishing herself from her family forever.

Inside Laura, deep appreciation swims with malevolence as she watches the people stand in the cloudburst to show their sorrow for the very tragedy that has become her anathema. But, they unknowingly stand between her and where she wants to be. Their respectful effort causes her waiting. Thinking. Agonizing. Tasting hellish images and feeling unnatural shrieks run over her skin. Not even her body's newly formed numbness can shelter her from the squall that whips and whirrs through her mind at a much stronger intensity than the downpour that beats at the crowd before her. The atrocities, which punish her from within, strike far more frequently than the falling raindrops. Reflex to the shuddersome phantasms blowing through her frazzled mind along with the pull's suggestive encouragement send her consciousness staggering with rage and urgency. She yearns to do anything but wait. Faintly breaking through the thunder and otherworldly flashes in her brain, soft voices whisper to her. And, Laura struggles with all of the little that is left of her to hold on, to fight the seductive desire to let go, to resist it until she can touch dirt, and desperately cling to wooden boxes of carrion to take her to her family.

Unlike the looming clouds above, the crowd begins to disperse. All turn toward the narrow cemetery road except for Andarus's partner. Detective Bauchan taps Andarus's elbow as she exclaims quietly, "I think I see her over there by the trees!"

"Oh, yeah?" he asks looking at Irene and not at the sparse, wooded area, slowly spinning the bottom of the umbrella handle around in his palm.

"Over there, Paul, by the trees. Look!"

Glancing nonchalantly at the mildly forested area, "Yeah, I think you're right. It's hard to see with the rain."

"Come on. Let's go!" she says stepping toward the lone woman on the outskirts of the field of the dead on which Andarus and she stand.

"Irene, wait. Do you really want to question her at her family's funeral?"

"Yes, Paul. We can't wait to track her down later; she's dangerous."

"We're all dangerous."

With eyes that throb with frustration, urgency, and curiosity, she prods, "What on earth are you talking about?"

"This isn't the time, Irene…"

Interrupting, "Then when is the time, Paul, after she's killed you?"

"That's just it; she could've killed me anytime she w…"

"We don't have time for this; I'm going," she says with more agitation than he has ever heard in her voice as her back is already to him.

He looks from her to Laura who stands head up and as rigid as the trees behind her. Knowing any words are useless at this point, he follows quickly. He has no idea what to do when they approach her, but he is painfully aware of what awaits them. And, she has still not moved, staring at them as if she were a shark watching unsuspecting swimmers dive into her waters.

Andarus steps beside Irene and puts the umbrella over her head. Its protection seems ridiculous, but there is not much else he can do. Irene's eyes are fixed on the visage of the lone woman leaning on the tree; she has not taken her sight off Laura since she started walking, not even to acknowledge Andarus when he caught up to her. With every step, the cold face becomes clearer, sad and hard as if she were time itself watching the end of man. Dynamic are the eyes as Irene steps closer, a pale blue that ripples like the ocean or a velvet curtain rustling in a draft. Irene feels like they are pulling her in, changing her from pursuer into hunted, and Laura is not turning away. Each step sloshes its way into the earth, trodding closer. Her ankles buckle and wiggle with uncertain step. Andarus taps the handle of the umbrella to the back of her hand. Without thought, a word, or a look in his direction, she grabs it. Ahead of them, Laura's legs move suddenly. Andarus quickens his pace and steps in front of Irene. She cannot see anything over his back. From behind, a hand grabs Irene's right shoulder firmly.

Irene spins quickly. Heels move choppily through the thick, sloppy earth. Ankles, knees, and hips bend to gain balance. As she steadies herself, she sees confusion. A past-middle-aged woman stands in the rain, sheltered by a pink umbrella and a purple bandana wrapped tightly around her head, covering short, curly, gray hairs. Her clothes are black, and her face is wrinkled with trouble.

"Detective," she wheezes, out of breath, "Daisy? Have you found out anything about Daisy? She hasn't come back to school."

Suddenly remembering the secretary who interloped into their meeting with the principal days before, “Mrs. Guess, no. We haven’t heard anything about Daisy yet. But, we’re still looking for her.”

Sloshy footsteps creep behind her. She looks over her shoulder and sees Andarus. Leaning around and past him, Irene glances to where Laura was standing. She sees nothing but trees.

“Paul, where did she go?”

“She was moving. I turned around to see what was happening with you, and I lost her.”

“You lost her? Why…”

The older woman speaks up, “Who were you looking for, detective? Everyone was down by the funeral. I only came up here to ask you about…”

The woman stops speaking as Irene glances around in all directions trying to spot Laura.

“Is it Daisy? Did you see her here?” asks the woman.

“No, it certainly wasn’t Daisy,” says Irene glancing at the woman’s face briefly between scanning the area repeatedly.

“Oh, was it Laura? Laura Bonney? Did you see her? My God, how is she dealing with all of this? No one has talked with…”

“Ma’am, we’re sorry, but you’re going to have to excuse us,” explains Irene.

“Of course, detective. Of course. I’m sorry to intrude,” says the older woman as she drops her eyes and turns to walk back to the thin cemetery road.

Irene’s eyes scan the area hungrily.

“Come on, let’s go,” offers Andarus as he touches her elbow gently.

“No. Where is she?”

Sighing, Paul continues, “Irene, this isn’t the time for this. Those are her children and husband in those caskets. They’ll be in the ground soon. Let this one lie.”

Catching her eyes onto his and moving her hands to accent her words, “*Let this one lie?* What the hell are you talking about? The bad guy is here. She was right here, Paul. *Right here.* Some woman taps me on the shoulder, and you lose sight of the killer? What is going on with you?”

“Irene, what were we going to do? Shoot her here in front of her friends at her family’s funeral? She sure as hell wasn’t going to come with us voluntarily. And, if you haven’t noticed, Irene,” he says pointing at his forehead which is still slightly swollen, “she isn’t easy to handle. Do you want her coming after you too?”

Irene exhales, completely exasperated. She glances around the area one more time, and still sees nothing, “So, what, did she just vanish?”

“No. She was turning away from us when I looked back to see why you stopped walking.”

Sighing again, “We’re not done with this, Paul.”

Looking away from her, he says, “I know,” then looking at her he repeats, “I know. Let’s go back to the office.”

She does not say a word but turns to walk back to the cemetery road on which the car is parked. As they walk, he stays to her left, which places him between her and the coffins on the burial site. They do not say a word, but Paul surveys the perimeter constantly. He sees a shape moving in the woods very close to the coffins. He quickly looks away and back to Irene as they step onto the road. They remain silent as they get into the car and drive off.

The mother lies in the shadows on the edge of the tree line just a short distance from her slain family. She has watched interminably long as the last of the crowd has slipped through the rain into their vehicles and moved on with their lives. All of her life lies in front of her, and now she can touch it. A part of her questions whether she will feel anything when she touches the coffins. It wonders if anything will happen at all; what if it is not the end? What if there is no way out for her, trapping her forever in her current miserable state? But, she has no answers for this voice, so she pushes it down. Her remaining faculties are taxed as she fights the pull that wants her to lie down, to quit, and to turn into herself. She disobeys the tremendous fatigue that urges her simply not to be, and pushes away the horrendous images that will not leave her alone. Forcing her legs to step requires all of these things to be smothered. She gains control of the screaming stimuli in her upperworks and commands herself to move to the remains of her kin.

She approaches the two tiny coffins, which are to the left of the larger one. Walking between them, she slides her hands over the smoothly stained wood. Her touch is numb; she cannot feel the slickness of the shiny clear coat, nor can she feel the moisture of the rain which constantly slides down the curved decline of the coffin from the center to the outer handles. When she presses her hands down firmly, she can feel the strength of the wood and know the reality of the boxes. Imaginings of what lies inside cause ghastly recollections of her hours in the morgue to fling to the surface of her awareness. The shock causes her eyes to wrench tightly and her mouth to tremble. The pull rises up and tries to take her under, to make her absorb so much of the wretched images that she will drown in them. Its insidious grasp invites her to slip away with it. For a flash, she could embrace the pull to forget the intense emotion that has exploded inside her. She could sink into its depths and stop the exhausting treading, but those little voices call out again, whispering to get past the thundering emotions that beat her. She hears them, and she shrugs off the pull’s grasp.

A sweet voice calls out in her head, “Mommy, why aren’t you crying?”

The sound hurts. The words cut. Then, she becomes aware that she is still tearless. She remembers that she has not cried since she awoke on the floor in her office. Her rage stirs up like a hurricane, and, dropping to her knees in the sloppy earth, she punches into ground with all of her strength. She sends earth and water exploding like the original breaking up of Pangaea. Instead of rearranging the world, she wishes it would all fade away into nothing. Eyes shut; fists pound again and again. Her jeans become caked with splatterings, slowly covering her bloody stains with liquid pieces of the earth. Her mind spins with illogical and innate force. It is a spinning frustration and anger. It is a self-loathing and a hatred for all that is the universe. How could she not cry? How can a tear not fall for the ones that lie in coffins before her? How can she be deprived of the natural expression of her sorrow? How can anything have the audacity to exist in a universe where she is bereft of tears for her children and her love? Swirls of curses and sorrow encompass her: pleas of forgiveness to her little ones for having no tears left to give, beggings for them to understand how much she bleeds for them inside, and a hoping that they will hear her urgings and be all right.

She hears soft tiny voices coming to her. Soothing is not the correct description, but stilling her dizzying thoughts is more accurate. It dawns on her that maybe the crippling question was posed by the pull to torment her. Something in its tone seemed different than the calming voices that come to her now. At this, she shakes the thoughts from her head, and flings mud and smashed blades of grass from her hands. With some smashed earth still on her palms and fingers, she stands up and places her hands back on the caskets.

Her fingers stretch out over the surface of the coffins. The numerous flowers around them are drenched and falling apart from the downpour. She stares at the petals, soaked and heavy and barely hanging onto their base, as she holds herself up precariously with a hand on each coffin, her shoes still sunken into the ground, jeans legs drenched, mud-stained on the outside, and blood-soaked underneath. One of the saturated petals falls to the muddy earth. She feels as if she could descend down with it. A flash of Daisy in the rain peering into the waiting car comes to her mind. It is quickly followed by an image of her gagging on her own blood with eyes full of terror. Laura's body stumbles back a step as if struck. She remembers the long, slender fingerprints on the framed photograph in the foyer of her former home. She shoves the images out, and looks over the two small coffins and then to the larger one past them. The weight of the larger one is too much for her to carry now, but she knows it is coming down on her soon.

Memories of her children flood her, and it becomes hard to stand. Days in the park, trips to the movies, and Christmas mornings tumble down on her like a waterfall. Each recollection is beautiful as it falls and glistens through the air, but they smack her as heavily as rocks when they reach her. She sways with the bombardment of past events. Still, the only wetness on her face comes from the hostile clouds above, and she is most aware of it. Her fingers stretch out as far as they can go over the tops of the two coffins, and her hands make small circular movements, as if she is rubbing their backs to put them to sleep as she did when they were younger. She whispers soft words of which she is unaware; some are the names of her daughters and others are synonyms for sorrow, regret, love, and sleep peacefully. Her mind still battles the pull, but she is in much more control now. The deepness of her emotions does not allow much room for any more torment to enter, so keeping the pull out is currently not so cumbersome. She drops to her knees again, but her hands remain touching the two caskets, singing her unconscious words to them.

Her dirge-like lullaby is interrupted by approaching voices, "Can you believe this rain, Jameson?"

"No, Whitley, never seen anything like this in my sixty-one years. And, I've never seen the boss give us the day off either, but this is a nasty day. He should've let this one lie 'till tomorrow."

"Yeah, I think the boss wants these in the ground soon. He's a spooky kind-of-a-guy for a rich fella; seems like he don't want these bodies above the ground long. He told me to be out here no less than an hour after the people leave, and he didn't care if it was flooding the field by then that we better be out here anyway."

"Sad thing burying children, Whitley. I've never gotten used to it."

Laura hears one of the shovels making a scraping sound as it slides over a rock. Her eyes shoot open, but she stays kneeling in the mire, muddy hands on the coffins.

"Yeah, it's 'specially sad when rumors are running 'round 'bout the mother going nuts and disappearing. Boss said they had to follow the plans laid out by the husband before he died that they couldn't even get in touch with the woma…"

Whitley stops in mid word as he approaches the two smaller coffins and can see between them. He stopped when he saw the hands clinging to the coffin; he certainly did not expect to see anyone there in this tempest. Following the hands down to their owner causes his heart to lunge in his chest as if it were trying to escape from him. The matted mess of black hair with a pale, white stripe hangs in her face. Eyes burn from between the matted locks, making her look much like a cornered animal.

Jameson says as he approaches, "What you looking at, Whitley?" His shovel drops to the drowning soil, and the blade slices into the ground as if it is tender flesh.

Whitley's hand is pressed against his chest as he stares at Laura who is still crouching down, knees in the mud. Jameson grabs Whitley by the shoulder, turning him away from Laura. Suddenly Laura's hands press hard on the caskets, and she pops up to her feet in one smooth, lightning motion.

Jameson wheezes, and tugging at his partner harder and turning him completely around, he says, "Come on, let's go, Whitley. We'll come back later."

Jameson throws his arm around Whitley's shoulders, and his cohort starts to step in stride with him. "Let's get some coffee in the lounge, and we'll both go home and relax. We'll come back tomorrow morning. Before the boss gets here. Maybe this storm will lighten up by then."

Whitley looks at his associate's face and says, "Not bloody likely, Jameson."

Jameson nods his head and continues to lead his friend toward the narrow cemetery road that will bring them back to the brick building in which they have spent many an early morning.

Returning her attention to the emotional grindstone that is the reflections of her children, her eyes turn inward again. Birthday parties and dancing classes haunt her. The pale sun drops slowly in the bleak sky. First days of preschool cause her to shudder. The sun drowns into a drenched night. And, from further back in her mind, she remembers lying in a hospital bed holding each one on each's special day with Gabe by her side. The recollection of Gabe beside her at their births sways her consciousness. It does not escape her that he is now at her side at their funerals, lying in his coffin mere feet away.

The longer coffin is something upon which she was trying not to focus while thinking of the girls. But, now as she finalizes her goodbyes to their bodies, Gabe's coffin is on her mind and will not leave. The thickness of the dark hours feels as if it is grasping her chin, forcing her to stare at it. Her feet slosh their course to the solemn box. It is as if the sea of twilight is pulling her in its current to the casket. Her tired eyes stare at it as if she expects the lid to open with Gabe's long, thin arm. Every second that it remains shut is a continual reminder that his body is never coming out of that box, and all that remains is his mutilated corpse inside.

The incessant droplets slide over the lacquer finish of the wood in an ever-dynamic, sheer, liquid surface. It gives the illusion of life to a box for the dead. She does not know if she hates it because of its false implication or if she appreciates its diversion from the stillness that is the box and her current desolate existence. Either way, she stares at it, and her exhausted delirious mind imagines his face in the slick water's moving shapes. Slowly it creeps on her. Inevitable as she knew it would be, but she still does not feel ready for it.

Memories saturate her while she stares at the grain of the wood. It reminds her of the park—the trees. Twelve years ago. She sat on a bench at the edge of the park. Lost. Dirty. Rageful. She was a rogue creature in the city then. Strangely, considering all that has happened since that desperate time, she is in much the same condition now as she was twelve years ago. Except for the intensity. The inhuman intensity of her emotions right now is much stronger than it was then. It was the same feelings on that day a dozen years before, but nowhere near as powerful or debilitating as they are presently. Back then, she was hopeless on the bench watching life, squirrels, and people as if she was not part of their world. Her last friend had been impounded and needed an oil change, and she was far away from any place that she had ever called home. That bench seemed like the end of the line for

Laura, but then he walked out of the door. It was a large door with intricate carvings and a beautiful, diamond-shaped pane of stained glass. An angry woman, yelling and cursing, stormed to a car named after a svelte cunning animal, a creature which quite resembled herself, her keys clanging out of her clenched fist as she stomped. Gabe called after, but it was not with all of the protest that his voice could muster. It was like he knew it was time for this to happen, but he had to call out and try to make sure that he had done all he could. Somehow watching it die with a small protest was more acceptable than letting it die right in front of him with no effort to save it. Harsh words flew, but they did not seem to cut him anew as much as they smacked upon wounds that had long been healing. He knew. He knew she would walk with this decision. He could have thought of a thousand indiscretions that she would ignore, but he knew this one would be fatal. Yet, he made it anyway. He had reasoned it out for quite some time, hashing and rehashing mental arguments in his head, playing his own devil's advocate. Logic led him nowhere. His feelings were what they were, and he had grown ill from missing his smile. Laura, watching it all from the park bench directly across the street, knew nothing, but she saw it all on his face. The anger of the woman's voice contrasted with the tone of his own. The woman clutching the keys sounded inordinately angry; angry with Gabe for not seeing things her way, angry with herself for not detecting it sooner, and further angry with herself because she did not like how her words sounded once they sliced the air. Gabe sounded like an old man who decided to put his sick dog to sleep. The contrast between the two told her a novel as she sat on the bench. And, she watched. Knowing nothing, but knowing this was something. That he was something, and that bench was there for her that morning. Something was coming, and she welcomed it with both hands. The woman tore down the street in her luxury cat car, and Gabe walked to his vehicle and took off down the street too. However, the elaborate door was sitting against its frame, but not shut, and certainly not locked. She thought a shower might change her perspective. Getting the grime off her body might wake up her soul.

The shower might change her perspective.

As her thoughts leave the green-tinted memory of the park of twelve years prior and her focus returns to the present, she thinks about the last line, letting it bounce around her head hoping for it to hit meaning. As she looks at the descending rain, she feels anything but hope. Loathes it because it is a mockery of her barren tear ducts. And, every crashing drop is a continuous reminder that she still remains, that she is an exile. She is quite sure nothing can come to her now—there will be no fancy door opening with a new life. Another's destruction will not give her a rebirth as it did twelve years ago. All she wants is out, to be with the three that are no more. The one lies in the long box. Still hard for her to believe that he's not coming out of it. Her hands slide across the liquid sheen. Her forearms fall to its surface followed by her upper arms, face, and chest. Her lips catch the surface and remain touching it. It is the closest thing that she has felt to an embrace since she came home to visit at Christmas. The morning of Christmas was a good time, a warming memory, but what aches her is not what Gabe said while she was there but the dozens of things that he did not bring up. The many questions that she had been posing to herself ever since she left them to go out of town. She already had some answers ready. The questions would have been almost welcomed. The fact that he let the issues lie only made her feel low. He had a right to protest his wife being away for so long. He was entitled to be frustrated with having to repeatedly tell his daughters stories of mommy, hiding his own hurt and concern while answering their questions, and surrogately reminding them of how much she loved them. But, he let it all go to have a nice day with her. Hearing Gabe's complaints and taking some venting words would have made her feel like she was paying for the pain of her absence, somehow alleviating the hurt that she had caused, draining a tank of anger. And, it reminded her of his tone on the morning that she first saw him while sitting on the park bench—tired and defeated, yet tender. She did not feel that he had given up on her yet. The thoughts cause her body to ache, and she pulls herself atop his coffin.

The drops cover and run over her like ants, but she does not feel their moist slithering blanket slide across her. Her hair clings to the shiny dead tree as if it is spilled, black paint with a smear of white in the middle.

She curses the sunlight as it confirms the reality of her frenzied fears; it is a brush painting her most horrid thoughts before her hopeless eyes. She stares at it as baffled as if it is the wind making only the shadows move; she knows well what it means. The world is her holding cell, and she has just heard the door slam shut. There will be no escape for her; no happy reunion. The sun's illumination breaks through the gray clouds and the rain, eventually hitting the branches in the nearby grove. The rays are broken and separated by the arms of the trees, and they resemble light falling through the binding bars of a dungeon onto its dank floor. The morning is the birth of a new nightmare, a confirmed hell. The morning is a debt and the devil. She wants neither, but both point out the futility of her lying on a cold, wet coffin that has not answered her, comforted her, or opened an opportunity for her to leave her current dismal state. No ferryman has appeared from out of the mist to guide her to her stolen family.

At that thought, she hears whispers emanating out of the dense, rain-filled air.

The sight of them intruding again is a sign to her that this is absolutely not her exit. If this were her way out, they or anything else would not be allowed to interfere. She holds her enraged head up, staring at them with the detest that she feels toward everything left in the world of which she no longer wants to be a part. Her eyes boil with rage. No tears have fallen, but none would have a chance to escape now, as the burning anger in her eyes would surely sizzle them away before they could form. The entire world entombs her as a layer of obsolete skin that she cannot shed.

Jameson and Whitley halt where they stand as soon as they see her raised head atop Gabe's casket. Her body is face down and flat on the coffin with her torso slightly raised and her head upright and daring them to come closer like an enticed cobra.

Whitley's voice stumbles, "Let's go back, Jameson. To hell with the boss being angry. I ain't going down by those coffins again…"

Jameson raises his hand, silencing his coworker, "No, Whitley, I think she's had enough."

Whitley looks on with the attentiveness of a young child watching the bedroom door open in the darkness. Is it a parent coming to tuck them in, or is it something of nightmares?

She leaves like the winter. Slow, smooth, and with an icy lingering.

"Yeah, see; she's not coming back," assures Jameson in a whisper.

Whitley asks, his eyes watching Laura's image disappear into the trees, "Jameson?" pausing, "Jameson, have you ever seen one freak out like that before?"

Thinking for a moment before answering, "Been doing this job since I got laid off from the refinery during the big oil bust. Been a long time. I've seen fights. I've seen fainting and fits. Swearing and wailing. I've even seen a heart attack at one of these. But, Whitley, I've never seen anything like that."

Their eyes rest on the thinly wooded area where Laura has slipped away, still cautiously wondering if she will return. But, her feet move away from them and the three fancy, planked boxes that hold the remnants of her life. Her focus is much more inward than it is on her dreary surroundings, but she continues to walk slowly. She does not even notice the words "we're always here for you" written on the sign as she passes it. Her despair is only matched by her anger and horror over being trapped in this world. The three emotions mesh into a turbulent, brackish mess inside of her. While on her path of blood and vengeance, she had been guided; even if it was only a faint illumination, her next step could always be felt out in the darkness. It has all led her here where darkness is no longer just a lack of light or a shadow on the world, but it is a primal vacancy, a void. There are no signs now. There is nothing for her to discover. The path has ended in the wild, exhausting her in the process. She can't go back to her former life; she has no desire for it, nor does she think she has the strength left in her drained limbs to retrace her steps. It has never before occurred to her that there is nothing more menacing than being in a total limbo. It is as if she has swum to the middle of the ocean to achieve retribution, she has accomplished her task, remains exhausted, the only three people whom she has ever truly loved have died savagely, yet she is not allowed to escape, not allowed to drown, and she is forced to tread water indefinitely. She stares with a questioning hatred at the emotionless, gray sky above. Her eyes tense as if crying, but they are not allowed release. Her throat strains and her mouth stretches as if to scream, but no sound is granted. The treading has gotten to her. The anger swells. Swallowing in the encompassing despair, she peers into it. Knowing that she can't drown, she swims into its chilling waters, a seductive release from treading, uncertain of whether she will be on the prowl or if she is trying to reach out and grab a shark.

Chapter XXVI

Yesterday evening hosted a brief conversation between Irene and Andarus following the funeral. Their dialogue was circular; the same lines were often repeated by the same pair of lips. The discussion was followed by a long silence. Individual conversations would only occur between Irene and Jackson & DiNardi and between Andarus and Jackson & DiNardi. These exclusive conversations were scattered about the remainder of the evening's work. Irene worked until 6:30pm, and left with telling Jackson & DiNardi goodnight. It was the first time in a long time that she did not ask Paul about what he was eating for dinner or encourage him to get a good night's sleep. As Andarus sat at his desk making phone calls, gathering data, and watching surveillance videos until 9:30pm, he certainly felt the rift between the two of them. All he hoped for was that it was not too deep. Eventually, he did leave for the night, but sleep apparently was not speaking to him either as he stared at insipid late night television, reclined uncomfortably on his couch, and sometimes thought of the case, but mostly thought about Irene and all that she had to say.

The nocturnal hours were extended, lingering, and restless, so much so that Paul welcomed the morning as an end to it. The futility of lying there without sleep only seemed to frustrate him more than being up and around in a groggy state. He arrived at the station forty-seven minutes early, and even piddled around his office for a spell without pouring his first cup of coffee. Anxious was the night before, and now, as he still remains in the dormant, vacant office, the feeling has become him. His ears tingle as he hears the sound of pumps stepping out of the elevator and smacking the floor. They tap gently but at a quick pace. Without looking, he is sure it is Irene. It is still a good fifteen minutes before anyone else should be arriving, even the early ones, and he has become familiar with the rhythm of her step. The rapping feet do not head toward the opened office door, which is the only light burning on the entire floor except for the subtle glowing of computers, power strips, and various other electronics in their hibernation modes waiting to be awakened from the still night. The feet enter the lunch/break room, and the noises of opening cabinets and drawers reverberate through the quiet air. He hears a very distinctive sound, one that has become quite soothing to him. It is the whirring ringing of a spoon making fast circles across the bottom of a coffee mug. It lasts longer than it should for one cup; Andarus is positive of that. Maybe, she is stalling. For that, he would not blame her. He surely does not have a solution to their current quandary, although he strongly wishes he did. Despite having no plan, new insight, or even a rested mind, he does not want their duologue to remain unrescued where it crashed last evening.

Trying to promote some image of himself working this morning and wanting to give his hands something to do besides shake from weariness and nervousness, he plays a video that he found to be vastly troubling the night before. He wonders if lack of sleep, distraction from the disturbance with Irene, or, possibly, something more sinister is the cause of his frustration with the video. Hoping the new morning will bring a solution, he stares at the screen waiting to scour a very familiar entryway to a building on Planeline. His inflamed eyes strain to focus. The monotony of the framed shot of the driveway further increases his difficulty in sticking his focus to the screen. As unsettling as the video remains, the sounds coming through the wall hold much more interest to him. Eyes on the screen, ears absorbing all that is audible from the break room, awareness weakened and fading: all comfort has abandoned him. No progress on the case; no peace at night; Irene feels betrayed, disillusioned; and there's still the lingering issue of Karen. His mind is all but conquered. The sounds from the next room stop. They are replaced with the patter of the pumps, but they are much more muffled than on their earlier walk from the elevator. The soft steps die away close to his office. Two thin knuckles held closely together create a gentle tap on his opened door. Forgetting his façade of being enraptured in work, his head jerks toward the tapping in the doorway. He sees the knuckles are wrapped around a coffee mug handle; he is slightly amazed at her grace in being able to knock so smoothly without spilling a drop of the steaming, aromatic liquid. It is his coffee mug, and her other hand holds hers. He smiles. His eyes still show his hurt.

She allows the slightest smirk to emerge, but she is not willing to let a smile form completely. The screen that he was so intently watching is out of her view, but she can see its reflective glare as it soaks the room.

"What are we watching, detective?"

His smile extends at hearing her tone, and he is momentarily dumfounded for a response. Her voice and the eerie anomaly of the video are hard for him to digest at once, as if they do not belong in the same headspace. He coughs, and lets the reality of the video flood his fleeting moment of happiness and security.

"It's the video from the No-Tell Motel. Been watching it over again since yesterday afternoon."

Handing him his coffee and noticing the slight trepidation in his voice, she asks, "So, have you found when she passes the office?"

Pausing, "Well, the motel owner said she walked right past the office, right?"

"Yeah."

"He said she walked right past and stared at him. Scared the hell out of him."

"Yeah, Paul, we've established that."

Looking directly in her eyes for the first time in the conversation, "Irene, I watched this surveillance recording five times last night. No one walks through the entrance during the entire thing."

Stares.

"Not one person, Irene. The rain starts about an hour into the video, and then it was pouring raining the whole night. No one walked through. Two cars drove in before the storm started. No one walks."

He elevates his mug to his face, and, breathing in the arousing scent, he takes his first sip. Irene remains gazing at him.

After swallowing his gulp, he raises his mug to her, "Thank you, Irene."

Her unmoved peering continues as she brings her lips to ask, "Are you sure?"

"Yes, really, thank you. This was really kind—I appreciate it," he answers still holding up his mug.

"No, Paul, the video. Are you sure?"

Shaking his head in negation, probably because he deeply wants the answer to be no, he says, "I've been pretty worn out—yesterday was not one of my better days. But, yeah, I'm pretty darn sure."

"Well, maybe he gave us the wrong tape."

"No, time and date are in the bottom right corner."

"Well, maybe you're just missing it. You are exhausted," creasing her brow as she looks at him, "You don't look good, Paul."

"Yeah, I'm sure I don't. But, the footage from the front of the station, the one that captures everyone who comes in and out of the lobby all the way to the elevators—I can't find her on there either."

"What?"

"Yeah, I can't see anyone who even resembles her on the night that she came up here and knocked me out. And, I'm positive she took the elevator."

Trembling vaguely, "*Paul, this is nuts*."

"Yeah," he whispers as he takes another dram of his coffee.

So focused on thought, her eyes are glossy, "Maybe, he lied—the motel owner."

"Yeah, but?"

"But, why would he lie? And even then, why wouldn't she be on the station surveillance?"

"Yep, that's the skinny of what I've been thinking about…Irene, I need you to look at this for me—an objective opinion. I'm too close to this one; I know it. I need for you to analyze what's the most logical explanation for all of this—all of these pieces that don't seem to fit together."

She bites her lip pensively. She feels more awkward with second-guessing Andarus than she does thinking of the newly-widowed Mrs. mysterious Bonney.

"You," she says stumbling, "you know what I'm going to say, don't you?"

He nods his head affirmatively.

"Well, the video from the motel could be inaccurate, or the motel owner may have been involved. I don't believe the latter for a second—no motive, he called us, and he was cooperative—he would have been implicating himself by telling us that he saw a woman at a certain time and then handing us a video proving that he was lying. He would either have not told us that he saw her or not given us the video so easily. It makes no sense to do both."

Andarus nods.

"So, possibly, the video is still the wrong video. Maybe the date and time were not set correctly. Despite the rain on the video coinciding with the rain that night and the fact that we picked it up the very next morning, maybe it is a mix-up. It doesn't seem likely that the video is of the wrong time or day, but it is the only conclusion that is logical…Or, maybe, possibly, he thought he saw something that wasn't there; it was raining heavily and lightning. But, I don't think I believe that either. Especially since he claims to have seen her before the heavy rain."

Andarus still nods.

"And, the video of the precinct," she exhales roughly, "it's only one of three things. One, she is in both of the videos, and you are just not seeing it. You are exhausted and could be missing it right in front of you. Two, you blacked out due to exhaustion and hit your head—she never was here. It was all some sort of a breakdown," she can see Paul's head drop to his chest as she speaks, "Or, we're dealing with a situation that is beyond logic, which I just don't know if I want to accept."

Slowly raising his gaze to her head level, but not looking in her eyes, he asks, "What do you think?"

"I don't know what to think, Paul…"

"Irene?"

"All right. I don't think you could have missed her that many times. Maybe once or twice you could've missed it, but not as many times as you've watched these two videos. I've seen you, even when you're tired—you're too good. Too good on details. We should still get Jackson or DiNardi to scan over them later just to be sure—don't think we should waste our time on it now."

"Okay, and?" he questions.

"And, I don't know what is going on with this woman and her interactions with you. Obviously, she needed to get information from you.

She hasn't popped up randomly—at least not yet. She has only shown up when she needed something from you. But, the videos don't back up your recollections. The doctor was very concerned about your insomnia—maybe what you think you see and hear are not reliable right now."

"Not real or not reliable? That's the question," interjects Andarus.

"From our perspective, it barely matters, Paul. If it happened, you saw it, and we can't document it; it might as well have never happened."

"Yeah, but, what do you think?"

"Paul, it doesn't really…"

"Matter? Matters to me, 'Rene. Matters to me."

"I think something bizarre is going on that we don't have all the facts on yet. There is too much that doesn't fit in this case. Likc, where the heck is Daisy? Plus, there's a lot that I found out right before I left yesterday."

"What'd you find out?"

"I've been doing some financial reconnaissance on Mrs. Bonney. She has not claimed the life insurance money; in fact, she hasn't even contacted the company, Perpetual Life. The neighbors haven't seen anyone coming in or out of her house. Also, she isn't registered at any of the hotels or even motels in town. Her credit cards have not been used since the day before her children were killed, and she has not accessed either her personal checking account or the business's checking account. So, the question rises, 'Where is she staying—where is she sleeping?' It has been confirmed that she still hasn't been back to her work in Houston. And, her car has been found in the parking lot at the morgue, so she is officially linked to the battery of the pathologist."

"We should try to talk with the pathologist again too."

"Yeah, it would be great if he could talk to us this time," she says. Realizing how self-serving her comment sounds, she adds sincerely, "I hope he's recovering well."

The elevator dings at the end of the floor, and Andarus leans in his chair to see who is arriving. A tiny part of him screams that it could be Laura, that talking about her may have brought her to them. But, the narrow slivers of daylight coming from the corners of his closed window blinds give a thin sense of security in that she does not belong there now. The thump and the tap mingled together should be enough to signify to Andarus that it is Jackson and DiNardi reporting for work, but he leans forward until he can see them coming toward the break room. The heavy clomps of DiNardi are interspersed with the quieter clomps of Jackson. Being partners for extended periods of time causes strange complementary idiosyncrasies. Her steps fall between his, creating a chugging rhythm like that of a horse's smacking feet falling in stride with the subtle creaking sounds of the wheels of the cart that it is pulling. They continue their partnered walk until they both stand in Andarus's open doorway.

"Mornin'," offers Jackson with as much enthusiasm as she can muster for having to work on an early Saturday.

DiNardi nods, his hands clutching both ends of his usual donut box.

"Morning," responds Andarus and Irene in unison.

A half an hour earlier, her head swung in circles creating an amalgam of stained glass windows, a bleak gray sky nearly smothering the morning sun, the black bars of the gate, and the brick wall in front of her. The journey back to the church had been one to which she did not pay much attention. Laura had drifted through the streets as if pulled by the storm's autumn-like wind. Her mind was the target of a four-front assault, being tormented by phantasms of her family in and out the closed caskets of the graveyard, choppy skewed recollections of the vengeance she enacted, her anger at the universe for unwillingly being banished in this world, and rageful imaginings of smashing her pain out onto the environment in which she is celled inside. Loss, anger begetting anger, hatred over being forced to continue to taste life, and the pull's whispering promises to bring about more destruction—all these thoughts swirled in her. If not for the emotion-soaked overload, she knew she would be acting; she surely would not be in the church alleyway. She didn't know exactly what she would be doing, but something—some venting, some destruction, some breaking down, some bloodletting, some release. Something so harsh that all creation would stand up and take notice of what it has done to her. Something. Feeling everything at once is a lot like feeling nothing; simultaneous everything is as equally indistinguishable as nothing. Inconsolable and drained, her head continued to rotate in small circles. The rage began to gain strength and swirl her anger into a powerful monsoon, which belittled the ongoing outside rain that continued to ping her body. Images of her desecrated family were flung to the top, and she felt as if her soul would bleed straight through her body, seeping from her pores. Control flashed for the tiniest moment, and she grabbed it with both hands. She cocked her head back and flung it forward against the bricks like a rainflash. As she fell to the ground, her consciousness slipped into dreams. The four-fronted attack consumed her before she ever touched the earth, sliding around her and absorbing her as if it was a marsh into which she was sinking, and it still is having its wicked way with her in the early morning.

"We can't find anyone walking in or out of the motel in this video," explains Jackson as she sets it roughly on Andarus's desk.

"Really?" asks the man in the tattered chair behind the worn, wooden, work table.

DiNardi chimes, "Yeah, we couldn't find anyone walking. At all. Watched it twice."

Jackson nods. Andarus's face does not change. Irene, who has said nothing, busies herself in the paperwork before her, opting to not pretend that she thought they could have possibly found something. Andarus is not one for interoffice secrets, but he decided that it was necessary in this situation to ensure an honest effort from Jackson and DiNardi. They did not need to know that they were only watching the video to double check their boss, who may or may not be mentally stable, nor did they need to know that they were watching a video that had already been screened five times.

"Okay," says Andarus, "I've got another one for you two to screen through."

"All right," answers Jackson trying to hide her lack of enthusiasm for the assignment.

"This one's a little bit different, guys," he explains as they listen curiously, "This one's of the station. Mrs. Bonney was said to have been seen here on the night of this surveillance. You guys know what she looks like, so there's no one better to screen this video for her. If you find her, I want to know right away."

"She came here? What happened? What did she do?" asks Jackson intently.

"Well, that's why you're screening the video; we need to find out."

Not satisfied with his answer, she nods her head and grabs the video. Both she and her partner disappear to a screening station down the hall. Andarus and Irene exchange a quick look expressing that neither are surprised to hear that Jackson and DiNardi found nothing in the stormy, lightning-filled footage.

They both continue to busy themselves in the paperwork of the investigation, looking for something that they've missed, some detail, some opening. Andarus glances over Irene's notes from her phone conversations from the day before. Her handwriting is a luxurious, curvy vine of clarity and femininity. Entwined with cursive lower case letters and budding with printed capital characters, the words of her hands are clear and certain, but there is enough softness and style in their design to cushion any harsh news that they may carry. Their meaning is definite and unmistakable, yet the roundness is there to add a soft shade to the blinding truth. The style is where the true content resides as she can't bring herself to say what she feels about him. The tenderness in the handwriting is her whispered invitation, a silent call, a closed-eyes outstretched hand in the dark hoping to grasp happiness. It doesn't escape his attention. Nor his emotions. But, neither does the lingering memory of his ex-wife's voice.

Andarus breaks the silence, "I called the hospital while you were checking in at Riverview High. The doc says that we can come by any day this week as long as we leave before nine p.m. He said Howard's doing significantly better, but he wants to be present when we go talk to him."

"No surprise there," offers Irene with a half-cocked smile.

"Yeah, we should drop in on Debbie too. Maybe we can get through this time without having to threaten anyone."

"It would be a miracle."

A dark miracle spawns inside of her mind, which rests slightly sunken into the soaked mud of the alley. Flashing memories of what was, what has become, and what terrors could be all raid her head. On the ground beside her skull, a roach creeps through the splashing droplets. It is on course to crawl directly over her face. Its wiggling antennae and its hinge-like method of locomotion pause as it inspects what is in front of it. Her hair is splattered before the roach like each strand is a stream leading to the lake of her head. The roach alters its path and works its way around her, deciding the streams of the rain are less dangerous than the streams of her hair. Wicked thoughts whip through her brain mercilessly, turning what feeble lights that still dare to burn inside her into ash.

"Detective! Andarus!" the shouts come from down the hall.

"Yes?" he responds from within his office.

He can hear the urgency in the approaching feet; comforting, it is not.

"We found it!"

"What?" asks Andarus toward the empty and opened office door.

Irene looks at Andarus with wide eyes, and he responds in kind. Could they have found Mrs. Bonney in the video? Irene hopes with her entire being that they have. A return to logic would certainly be welcome. Her partner would also like to know that his senses can be trusted.

Uniforms appear in the door, somewhat disheveled from the hectic dash to the doorway. The unkempt appearance matches the excited looks on their faces, which are normally set to neutral.

"We found it! The car. It's at 391 Sanctuary. Neighbors reported it—no one's living in the house, but the car's been there for three days."

Without a word, Andarus is on his feet with his keys in his right hand. Irene is already around the desk. Jackson and DiNardi step out of the way allowing them to pass through the doorway, and then they follow close behind.

Without looking over his shoulder, Andarus says, "Jackson, get us backup. We're liable to need it."

She needs it more than she ever dreamed she would. The blackness. Her eyes have opened to an approaching evening; the sun fades in the constant rain clouds. She sees each falling drop as if it were one of the horrific images bombarding her mind during the time her eyes were shut tightly. All she wants is to black them out. All of it. Anything has become too much to see. Laura gathers her resolve to do just that even if she has to take the whole world out with her.

The car was the least of their worries. It checked out to be Jeff Koye's vehicle that was carjacked by a woman matching Laura's description: long, pale streak and all. As expected, nothing was missing; there was no damage to the car at all. But, then there was the house. Neighbors said it was abandoned; it was a likely place for Laura to be holed up. It was a likely place to find a teenage corpse. Entering the house proved easy as the back door was not only unlocked but ajar. Stepping into the house with guns drawn proved much more difficult as the pungent air stung their nostrils like venom.

All of this seems like thoughts from a previous day as Andarus now rubs both of Irene's shoulders standing behind her, her body leaning on him. They had found Daisy. Pieces of her. Somehow the experience at the motel did not prepare them any better for this scene. It is like the smell of an alcohol on which one has gorged oneself to the point of chemical poisoning; upon smelling it again one becomes quickly sick, or, more aptly, the sickness becomes a quickening, and one is certainly no stronger from having experienced it prior. The recollection of the previous experience only adds to the devastating effects of digesting it again. Trying to shoulder much of the first hand labor that he did not cover at the motel, DiNardi is the worst for wear out of the bunch. He steadied his unsteady hands every time he needed them to work, to handle evidence. But, his stomach, a source of strength for him, proved to be not so stable as he trudged through the vile mess of a teenage girl. More disheartening to him are the tiny details. The smeared, bloody hand streaks across the walls of the hallway; something about these markings reminds him of his own reaching out to the world for an end to his loneliness. The carpet smashed into her broken and bleeding fingernails. And, of all the blood, the dried streams that ran from her mouth and eyes are the ones that he can't hold his sight upon. The carnage that is her torso and limbs is monstrous, but it does not poison him quite as much as the other details. He is not sure if his tears are for Daisy, himself, or the world, but he is sure that he doesn't want anyone else to see them. Since no one is in a hurry to enter that hallway again, he is in luck. The one amenity that the hallway provides is solitude.

Everyone has known that he had it in him, although this is the first event that they can point to that proves it. Typically, DiNardi will do all that is asked, often more than is asked, especially when it involves assisting Jackson. But, he has always been squeamish at both confrontation and murder scenes. Wit and courage have never come to him as easily as compassion and patience. But, this is a rare opportunity for him to have a second chance at the same situation. He missed his chance to be the daring one inside the room at the motel. He simply tended to those who were suffering from having been in there. Now, after days of beating himself up for not usurping the opportunity to excel at his job, help his friends, and confront his fears, he is in the same situation, doing that which he never thought he could. They all see it, and he sees it. But, they don't have to continually witness what he is viewing inside that hallway. And that, at the moment is his only hint of comfort. Glancing at the torn body on the floor of the hallway, comfort itself feels alien and inappropriate. A line from one of Daisy's favorite songs fits her now more than ever, "Even in death she still looks sad." As he works, he ignores the gargling that he swears he hears. It seems to get louder when his eyes hit Daisy's crimson-coated mouth that is opened widely, frozen in a terminal gasp. There are few more haunting things in creation than beholding violently shaped rigor mortis. The shapes of slender fingers are crushed deeply into her neck. As his eyes drag along the ghastly contours, he swears he can hear the flesh crushing. While he continues to work, he tells himself that he is not hearing choking or flesh crushing and that the hideous grooves upon which he is looking are not a piece of fossilized hell.

The fossil of her fall to the alleyway consumes her focus as she stands in the faint, pale moonlight that is granted passage through the dense rain clouds. It is full of water that is routinely pelted with rapid raindrops. The constant precipitous beating makes the pool of water look like it is boiling. She slides her vision over all that she can see from her perch on the slippery rooftop: the street, the tops of all the buildings, the sidewalk below. In fact, the downpour is so fierce, so thorough, that its drops shatter harshly upon landing. The popping raindrops give the illusion that everything is boiling as if in hell itself. Returning her stare to the indentation that she left after her fall before the funeral, she decides that she needs to climb higher. Even though she landed on a softer earthen surface in the alleyway than where she soon plans to crash, she decides that climbing up to the next stratum on the multilayered roof is necessary.

As she steps along the slick, slanted roof, the moving sheet of rain tries to grab hold of her feet and send them crashing back to the pen of the alley. The wind shoots at her violently, an eager partner to the rain, but it even seems to bring the maniacal laughter of the pull to her ears. Since stepping away from the funeral, the pull has been relentlessly upon her; dynamic in its attack but constant in its ferocity. Even when her consciousness waned, it was there; graphic, taunting, and slicing in its creation of nightmares beyond imagination. Her tolerance has died in waiting for an opening to appear through which she can exit this world. Her patience has been burned in waiting for future guidance. Her strength for listening to the pull's seductive words has abandoned her. And, she has willingly extinguished her respect for life, especially that of her own. All that she remains is a desire to rip out of this world. She cares not what she has to destroy to create this rift, nor does she care if this tear remains open after she passes through it as a scar upon all mankind. Mankind has killed her family;

providence would seem to be the culprit that has chained her here. Exit is imperative. Life has become expendable.

"Right, I'm expendable. Got it," Andarus says into his phone as he ends the conversation that has dragged for the better part of five minutes.

Irene's eyebrows emit more than she can say as she stares at Andarus from the opened back door of the house. The yard has grown dark with the evening, but the smell has not lessened its claim on the domicile, and neither has the swarm of flies that plague the home. If not for their hovering presence and the weight of the stench, the back door would have been closed long ago for fear of something contaminating the scene.

Andarus sees the emotion emanating from her eyebrows. He forces a feigned smile to which she does not respond. Speech is not an activity in which he has any interest at the moment, but he sees no way around it.

"Don't worry about it, 'Rene. It's gonna be all right."

She bites her lip, and her eyes scream for him to drop the thin illusion.

Sighing, he surrenders, "He wants a head for this one. Needs someone in a cell, or a body in the morgue. He doesn't care."

Eyes watering up, she adds, "He needs someone's body to fill the hole that fear has ripped into this town. Is that right?"

"Yeah."

"Does he even care if it's the right one?"

"Don't think so, darling. Especially if it's a body in the morgue. Bodies don't hire lawyers to prove that they're innocent. Bodies take the rap."

"It's never been like this before, Paul. Was it like this before I got here?"

Scratching his head, "Different chiefs, different methods, but it's all the same. They never want the public to feel unsafe. Can't blame them for that, really. Even if they are only caring about themselves and their public image; it still is a legitimate concern. This case is just a creepy headline, a never-ending whispering among everyone in town. That's why he's riled up; people talking changes elections. Too much people talking leads to the public being so freaked out that they do stupid things too. Stupid things mean people get hurt—sometimes really good people, and that leads to more talk and more chaos."

He pauses as he quickly and repeatedly swings his leg in a short, back and forth motion in front of him, tapping the heel of his right shoe against the tip of his left shoe. It is a habit of which he is unaware, but one to which Irene has long been privy. Had he been more self-observant, his shoe buffer Christmas present from her would have made a lot more sense last year. None of his words comfort her, but she listens intently anyway.

"And, there are other concerns. Anytime some rampage hits the papers with some type of notoriety, it's encouragement to other psychos that they can make their mark on society, that they can achieve some twisted piece of fame. He's not entirely wrong—he's a jackass, but he does have a point: someone has to hang."

Her legs hang over the edge of the second tier of the roof as she struggles to pull herself up. The wind beats against her limbs as if deliberately trying to shove her down. The pull infects her mind with the same barrage of horrible thoughts, sights, and remembrances. It fights with intensity, trying to prevent her from climbing up to the next level. The ruminations of the pull's cruel fancy make it hard for her to focus on scaling the lubricious rooftop. Its strength is within distraction and frustration, of which Laura is cognizant but remains powerless to rid herself of it or to not feel despair at its painful portraits. Finally, her legs are on the second echelon, but she is not finished there. She takes a few steps and grabs onto the next level of the roof; each one runs longways from the front to the back of the church. Each angles upward toward the center of the roof until it is interrupted by a small, shoulder-high wall with a new level on top of it. It takes six tiers to get to the uppermost point, which makes the entire roof resemble a set of stairs with angled steps on both sides of the church meeting at a steep point in the exact center of the building.

Besides the chilling tone of the pull, the wind carries two tiny voices to her ears like a distant children's choir. Suddenly, their drone becomes louder, clearer, and she finds her body immobile and stiff. The voices whisper, giggle, and wail in unpredictable intervals, keeping her unprepared and vulnerable.

"Hello, mommy…hi, mommy…love you, mommy…hee hee hee…why aren't you here with us, mommy?…why did you leave us? Didn't you love us anymore?…hee hee hee…mommy, do you wanna play?…we're too big now for the games you know; you've been away too long…we'll teach you new ones…what are you doing on the roof, mommy?…careful…you might fall…hee hee hee…"

Her eyes feel as if they will explode, but, even now, she is still granted no release.

"Mommy, don't you love us?…Why don't you join us?…Daddy's here too…hee hee…he misses you…hee hee hee…you better hurry before he forgets you…"

Another voice calls sternly, "Girls, leave your mother alone!" silence is there briefly, then the voice continues, "Laura, why did you leave me alone with them? Why did you…"

She shakes her head as if she could make the voice fly out of it. She knows it is nothing more than one of the pull's machinations, as Gabe would never speak to his children that way, nor would he lay so much guilt on her so easily. She pushes the voice to the background. In being so certain that it was not her Gabe talking to her, the voice lost its power despite its perfectly replicated tone. If the pull has a weakness, it is in its relentless cruelty. With a little more subtlety, the voices may have been more believable and taken her completely. But, maybe it knows what it is doing; maybe it is all part of its treachery. Either way, Laura does not think of it; the pain of the voices only made it more urgent for her to shut them down—to destroy herself and all of her torment with it. So, she looks at where she needs to climb.

Staring at the most paramount part of the roof, she can see the raindrops slamming into it and splattering violently. This activity creates a mist over its surface, making it appear mysterious and otherworldly. With the temporary relief from the voices, she rushes forward, nearly losing her footing, and she grasps the edge of the roof's next slanted platform and drags her body onto it. Uneasily, she stands. She quickly lunges at the next level, climbs, and stands on it. From her new vantage point on the fourth tier, she can see the courtyard behind the church. Flowers sag toward the ground looking violated and defeated by the onslaught of the rain. It has been days without relief, and Laura sees her worn soul reflected in them. A concrete fountain overflows with excess and is polluted with fallen leaves, flowers, and branches. There is an oak tree in the courtyard, tall and outstretched with age. It is bent backward at the upper trunk, pushed by the storm. Its branches are all held upward and back by the wind as if in surrender. There is an uneven gurgling sound that reaches her ears between the roars of thunder. It is the choppy gasping of the gutters expelling rainwater. The spurts resemble the desperate breathing of one sitting in the defendant's chair waiting to have their fate handed down to them. But, she pays no more thought to the surrounding activity and pulls herself onto the next level of the roof; observation holds no flavor for her anymore.

As she spreads her hands onto the brink of the final tier, she is aware that the pull has not returned since she rejected its impersonation of Gabe. Its absence does not provide comfort; she would prefer to have it where she can see it, much rathering to hold the knife by the blade than to fall upon it in the dark. Her arms drag her torso across the edge of the partition. Her soaked dark blue shirt stretches and wears against the angled edge, embedding miniscule black bits of roof into the fabric. Her flesh should feel great discomfort at the friction, yet she feels nothing but pressure—no scraping, pulling, or scratching.

Her waist and then hips reach the edge, and the thickness of her black jeans holds up much better to the adverse shingled surface. Her legs feel nothing, and then the pull comes sliding over her. It comes fast, smoothly, and giantly like an iceberg out of the mist in front of an unsuspecting vessel. It encompasses her with ease. She is on the last tier; it must strike concisely. It must be a quickening, or she'll be descending in the damp wind before it takes effect.

Images of stains on two tiny beds. They knock all thoughts of the rooftop out of the hands of her attention and replace them with horrific sadness. The stains shake in her mind. Pulse and quiver. Then bubbles form in the crimson spots like the puddles below her as they are disrupted with raindrops. Something writhes in the stains. She doesn't know what it is, but its motion telegraphs malice. In the unholy mess of sheets, it metamorphoses. Wriggling, in each pool of premature blood, something begins to crawl to the puddle's edge threatening to lunge out of its sanguine cell onto the sheets. Her mind focuses entirely inward, unwillingly glued to the horror in her head. Her only thought of self-awareness is why is she letting this spawn of dark imagination incubate inside her. Why is she allowing this odious fantasy to play out within her head? The unsettling answer is that she has no control over the unfolding performance while it clings to her with parasitic fingers, rowing her through sulfuric rivers in her mind. As if time is twirling in reverse, the bubbling beings crawl out of the bloody ooze and transform into the likenesses of her daughters. They face each other on their tiny, identical beds, each holding their teddy bear; Daniella's brown with a pink bow tie, and Susanna's fluffy, collarless, and white as a blank, unspoiled piece of paper—one that could contain the perfect words, the ideal story, something of purity to uplift the entire world. Soon, little eyes close, and sleep slides its thin black veil over them. The door juts open, and a foul light penetrates the naïve darkness. A beast stands in the doorway grinning like a wolf in its bloodlust. It is the alpha male of a sickly tribe, a pathetic demi-leader of an unholy troika. His smile gleams in the artificial hallway light while he stares prospectingly at the unprotected prey before him. Humans are one of few creatures who have the ability to not delight in devouring another's young. However, humanity is something that this one has long rejected, and, to his recollection, humanity seems to have rejected him equally in return.

Soon another one, one with a similarly disturbed look in his eyes but without the certainty of the first, pops up behind him in the doorway, glaring over his shoulder into the parentless, sleeping den. She views every inch of their faces; they are nearly identical to when she saw them at the motel. Except, their features seem slightly more exaggerated than when she looked upon them in the flesh. They are definitely the same two, but it is as if they have been tempered in some mal-forming heat or dipped in something rancid—something that would leave them slightly askew in appearance. Their features are hideously cartoonish, animalistic. Maybe, they are just basking in the glow of the atrocity that they are about to ignite. With speed as unnatural as their faces, they tear toward the beds. The tiny ones dreaming under their sheets wake far too slowly to scream before dirty hands muffle their mouths; their eyes bulge and squirm, wide and pulsing. Youthful pupils cannot comprehend the changing faces of their attackers, which vacillate from grinning fiendishly to contorted anger. The ripping of clothes, the slapping of rosy cheeks, filthy muttered curses, the digging in of pink nails, the kicking of small, bare, feeble feet, it is all far too much for Laura. Her chest is a twirling void that seems to get wider as it spins. But, she cannot shut down the nightmare. Bloody tears run down curvy little cheeks. Sniffles and gasping spatter deep red spots of tainted innocence. The desecrating thrusting continues. Daniella's eyes are an unmoving, frozen atrocity like the eyes of Lot's wife as she turned back to catch one last glimpse. Her thin nostrils no longer move, and her chilling whimpering has faded away. Yet, the thrusting continues. Laura's feet stumble at the vision, trying to regain her balance. Feeling as if soon she will be voided away, an urgency shoots through her. It is the first reminder that she still exists outside of the demonic theatre in her mind; she had almost forgotten where she was and indeed that she still was in our world. The rain and wind mean nothing to her, except that the pull is near. The roof means something. Escape. An end. She can still hear the unholy rhythm of her children's pounding desecration stinging her like the shrillness of a bat echoing in the caverns of hell. The wind smacks her face, and her awakened, gray eyes fling open. The gust reminds her that the pull is on her, conjuring the tormenting scenes of her children, but something in the vision makes her believe that all of its atrocities are true. An overwhelming urge to be rid of her torment rushes through her. She shakes her head, rejecting the vision but still feeling repulsion from it. Her body rocks in the wind, and her feet slide several inches down the slick incline. Her right foot barely grips enough of the roof to cease her unwanted decline. Her body tightens, and she regains relative balance.

She looks over the town in a slow, panoramic scan. From the height of the topmost part of the church roof, she can see more of the area than she ever has at once. The windows of all the buildings are fogged over and opaque. They look as if the weather has choked the life out of them all. The end of the roof juts into the darkness of the night; the rain pouring down provides a thin link between the roof and the air beyond it. She steps toward it. The first step feels as if the pull has grabbed her foot with all of its strength, but the edge looks far too much like relief for it to hold her back now. With the second step, it seems to have retreated altogether. Walking freely, she moves faster toward the edge. A light, from far below in front of the door to the church, basks the edge of the roof several feet in front of her, lighting her way to it. She yearns to touch it, to reach it, to fall through it, to send herself crashing to her husband and children.

The terrible thoughts seem to have floated further away from her, not gone, but no longer directly upon her. She does not trust the momentary peace, but it is an opening, a break in the storm. All she needs is a second, one leap, and she will be out of the pull's reach forever. Her mind is focused; the images of her family are her own and the ones that she wants to remember. They are as painful as they are comforting, but they are a reminder to keep moving. As she steps to the edge, she has more control of her mind and her feelings than she has since she arose from the floor of her office. The rain descends at a steady pace, and her mind remains focused and clear. Her feet inch up to the dim golden light that subtly touches the edge of the rooftop. She sees what she has been looking for: the cold, drenched, hard sidewalk. She peers down at the concrete walkway far below and the drops that splatter puddles and coat all that she can see on the pavement. The coating water appears much like a layer of skin over the entire street, covering her visible world. She hopes to fall with enough force to punch through all of it and that the rain will lubricate her way.

She lunges with her legs, her torso falling forward. Her body plummets toward the earth, her head leading the way. The last wave of falling rain is just ahead of her; the six-day-long downpour stopped an instant before she left the roof. The sidewalk zooms in rapidly as she falls toward it. The stained glass windows, the streetlight, the bars of the gate on side of the church, and the awaiting sidewalk are all a fast blur as she falls. From out of the blur, a primordial cackling howls. She knows its call well after all the torment that it has thrust upon her. But, the question arises; is it chasing her and trying to get its grip upon her one last time, or is it already upon her enjoying every second of her descent? Having no time for thoughts about the pull, she holds her face pointing toward the concrete below. An image of her family surfaces in her mind, and she aches to reach the ground. Yards. Feet. Inches. Her face crashes into it. Pressure explodes into her head, neck, and chest. The sidewalk itself buckles. The sound of the collision cracks like the thunder that has been bombarding the neighborhood for some time. Her body bounces in a sickening flop off the sidewalk, back into the air. Her hand flings out and smacks the brick of the church. Her mind goes blank, and her body slams backward to the ground.

Chapter XXVII

"Remember, Andarus, when we go to talk to the pathologist again tomorrow, try to make this thing with the doctor work out better."

"Now, whatever do you mean?" he says into the receiver as Irene, miles away, looks at her phone with humorous suspicion.

"Well, I think it would be more beneficial for us to have a jovial interaction with the doctor instead of you grabbing him by his shoulders, pushing him against the wall, telling me to keep asking questions, and informing him that a young girl may die if he didn't stay the hell out of the way."

"Well, it seemed like it was appropriate at the time; he wasn't cooperating with us."

"Maybe, he was trying to protect his patient, Paul."

"So was I, Irene," he sighs and continues, "Didn't do Daisy any good anyway. Had to try."

"I know, Paul, I didn't try to stop you. I didn't like it, but it was the only thing to do to try and help Daisy. Don't blame you; I just want all of that behind us before we go back tomorrow."

"Well, I've let it go."

"But, what if the doctor hasn't? Doctors don't adjust well to being forced to do anything, much less forcefully holding them against a wall."

"Well, that don't confront me none."

"Paul, you can't use 'confront' like that."

"Why not?"

"Are you deliberately trying to frustrate me tonight?"

"Not particularly."

"You know that's not correct English—confront is not meant to be used that way."

"Well, that don't confront me either," he says with a chuckle.

Playfully, she adds, "Don't make me come over there and smack that word out of your vocabulary."

"That don't confront me either, ma'am. I think it'd be fun to see you try."

"Paul! I swear I'm gonna get you if you keep it up. You c-a-n-n-o-t u-s-e that w-o-r-d that w-a-y."

"Well, my friend George Thorogood and I disagree with you."

"Well, all right, Andarus. You and your friend Mr. Thorogood get some sleep tonight, so you'll be on your game tomorrow."

"Sleep don't confr-"

Cutting him off, "Good night, Paul, see you in the morning."

"Wait, Irene! There's one more thing," thick silence, then he continues, "I don't need sleep; I'll sleep when I'm dead. It don't really confront me at all."

Tired snickering is all he can hear on the other end.

Not asleep and surely not dead, Laura's eyes open. The rain has indeed stopped. Her body landed against the step of the church after bouncing off the concrete—the point of the first step digging into her lower back, her legs sprawled before her on the sidewalk.

The sidewalk buckled angrily upon her arrival, leaving cracks in it that were not there before, and its overall shape is like a V. The spot where her body crashed formed the lower point of the V, and the sidewalk on each side buckled upward forming the two long lines. Her vague vision is set on its shape as her eyes struggle to focus and her mind slowly comprehends that she still is in our world and somehow still alive. The stinging runs through her head and into her torso. Nothing feels broken or missing, but tremendous pressure is upon her entire body. It is too much for her to move yet.

A din grows louder and louder in her head as she regains cognizance. As the mangled sidewalk comes into focus, the growing noises in the background become clearer. She knows its call, and dread fills her as she also knows that she is in no condition to fight it. Instead of attacking her with the familiar images and voices of her family, it laughs. It mocks her situation with fervor, the laughter of the mad. Laura feels as if its crazed mirth and her mind are not so different anymore. If she would let go for just a moment, both the pull and she might join in a twisted merriment, losing herself forever, never to return to her consciousness. With her vision still flashing, she shoves off the steps bringing her torso up to a sitting position. With one more heave, she jerks herself onto unsteady feet.

The street itself is still drowsy from the storm's onslaught; tree branches incessantly dribble residual water, and the drains gargle and choke on its remains. The sewers gasp as the quietus of the rain slithers its way into its subterranean depths. Her vision still lacks refinement, pulsing from the collision with the concrete. Her thoughts are too scattered to build into anything signifying a plan or even a reflection on what has happened. She is only distinctly aware of three things as her feet clod along the sidewalk: her family is dead, she should not be here—definitely not alive, and the pull is celebrating. At the moment, the last is the most troublesome. Even before her vision clears, the wrath swells inside her. She can taste it at the back of her throat, both nauseating and enticing her in unison.

Most lights along the street have been extinguished as nearly all are sleeping. The rain, even violent rain, is trancelike in its ability to lure one to sleep. Streetlights burn giving off odd light that refracts through the drops of water which still cling to them. Even stranger does it look in her unfocused sight as she strains to see a setting in which she does not want to reside. The remaining light blurs the surroundings, causing a disdain to grow inside of her for its presence. Looking down from the streetlights and staring straight ahead, she sees a stronger, more audacious light slicing into the night's shadow. It is a block down, and her feet move toward it.

With each step, a small amount of balance returns to her. Dizzy she still is and will remain for a while, but the tiny improvements bring her dangerously closer to cognition. Her mind begins to awaken. She remembers the roof and the difficult climb to the top, the pull's hideous visions that tortured her, and the storm that tried to blow her away. Then, the fall flashes through her head, ending with her face crashing into the ground, which only further taunts the pulsing of her skull. Cheated out of death—that is the thought that formulates inside her as the scattered fragments of idea finally mesh together inside the earthquake of her brain. A bile-inducing loathing courses through her, leaving her completely inconsolable and irascible. The pull, smelling the hatred, pounces upon her, filling her ears with its mocking laughter and her mind with its thorned thoughts. It feasts upon her discomfort and drinks from her flowing hostility. The violating light ahead is still unclear to her, but she targets her hatred upon the bleary image of it.

She reaches the corner, and her foot slides down the curb's incline to the recessed level of the street. Her balance has improved some along with her sight. The light of the all-night breakfast restaurant/café ahead of her slowly becomes clearer to her vision, and her mind builds angry thoughts. Precarious is what she is, and the pull thrives in her unrestrained and unpredictable presence, enthralled in her potential for destruction. Bad things step toward the café on the heels of a long downpour.

The large window that makes up the front wall of the café is hazy and spotted with raindrops. Immediately past the window, sits a couple at a tiny two-person table. Beyond them, is a bored server leaning with her elbows on a shiny countertop, resting her chin on her two overturned palms. An opened *Biology: The Cycle of Life* textbook is sprawled before her on the counter, but the last tears of the rain are far more interesting at the moment as they trickle their way down to earth through branches, buildings, and drainpipes.

The couple, sitting in discomfort at the table, stammers through a conversation that is fast losing its civility, which is a new and feared territory for both of them.

With her brown eyes maneuvering between compassion and frustration, she asks, "I just don't understand why you don't trust me? Why is this such an issue for you?"

"Because he'll be staying in your apartment, Jamie. An ex-boyfriend staying in the apartment easily turns into a revival of old affections. He'll be in the same situation as when you guys were intimate. It's not that I don't trust you; it bothers me that you would so willingly invite trouble into our relationship—into your apartment."

"If you think that something would happen, then you don't trust me," frustration taking over.

"No, that's not true. I don't know how to explain it to you; it's just that you're precariously placing yourself and my emotions over something that is not necessary at all." At this he pauses, and she shakes her head staring toward the counter as if the server could offer some female support to her argument. His head drops toward his half-eaten steak and eggs combo, and then something occurs to him.

"Jamie," he says, seeing that she is still looking at the counter, "Jamie, please, look at me."

Sincerity in his voice relaxes the thin lines in her face, and she complies. He gently grabs her hand for the first time since this topic was brought up three hours ago when it was still storming outside.

"Jamie, what if it was Tiffany staying at my house for a week?"

As soon as the name of his long-time ex is mentioned, the lines retighten on her face. She knows what is coming, and she does not like it.

"She lives here, Brad; there's no reason for her to come and stay with you."

"For the sake of argument, baby, pretend that she doesn't live here anymore and that she's coming to stay with me for a visit. How would you feel?"

Her face crumples. He has always found her to be the most stunning girl that he has ever been allowed to touch, but at this brief moment he can't see any beauty in the face across from him.

"It's different, Brad. You were dating her when you met me."

"You know that doesn't matter—it's the same thing. He has other friends here, Jamie. He asked to stay with you for a reason. Trust me. It's no different than Tiffany wanting to stay with me."

With fervor, "That little slut could stay on Planeline Highway for all I care," then looking back toward the counter, she adds, "Besides, he didn't ask."

"What?"

"He didn't ask. When he called he just said he was coming to town—I asked him."

A feeble sound crawls from his opened mouth. His heart feels as if it has been punched. His eyes gloss over, and, for the first time in his life, he doesn't care if the girl sees it. He looks up to see her staring away from him at the counter. Nothing but sting and defeat are inside of him. Feeling that everything before him is lost, he glances out the opaque window. Through the window's haze and droplets and the dankness of the night, it looks as if a shadow moves. His mind remains on Jamie and on the emptiness that has so unexpectedly come over him as a result of her, but his eyes follow the moving darkness as it crosses the street. It is in the form of a person, but something seems askew in its movement like it is only halfway there, like the opposite of a moving beam of light—it has shape but no perceivable mass; it can be seen, but it does not look like it can be touched. The approaching being certainly resembles a moving shadow. As it reaches out for the handle of the door, he feels as if it is already sliding its way up the back of his neck.

The light hits her soaked body as she steps into the tiny restaurant. Her face glistens with droplets of rain that blew onto her from the branches swaying in the stinging wind. The droplets that swirled in the breeze created an illusion that the rain would never end. It was a feeling that weighed heavily on her as she walked from the church to the café. Her eyes look as the eyes of one who had been ridiculed and cast aside, only to be the lone correct one and then to face nonstop rain for forty days. The eyes of Noah know isolation.

She glances to her immediate left and sees Brad and Jamie. Brad stares open-mouthed; his mind was already drained before she came through the door. Jamie still looks to the counter at the server, and she sees the server's quizzical expression at whatever just walked in the door. Quickly turning her head toward the entrance behind her, she sees a woman with a long, white streak in her hair and bits of dirt and grime dangling from it. Involuntarily, she gasps while the woman fleetly moves to the edge of their table.

Laura stares at Brad and then at the table directly in front of him. In a flash, she grasps his steak knife from his plate and yanks it to her side. Dumbfounded, the couple stares at her. Brad's mind is bogged down heavily, but he knows danger is before him. Glancing across the table he sees Jamie's face, which is devoid of comfort, hope, and confidence. Laura turns suddenly facing both Jamie and the door just past her. She stares over the girl's shoulder, focusing on the exit, but it appears to Brad that she is glaring at Jamie. Surprising even to himself, he finds himself on his feet shoving his arm between Laura and Jamie, holding onto the top of her chair.

Laura turns to face his advance much faster than he imagined, as he slides his body in front of his girlfriend and uncomfortably close to the woman with the stolen knife. He looks down at the sharp utensil and sees that two of her fingers grab the handle and two of them grasp the edge of the blade tightly. Wordless she stares at him, and his gaze slides up from the blade to her face. Silently, she dares him to move, to stand in her way, to try to take the knife from her. The pull bellows within her to attack, to stab, to push her tormented feelings out onto him. Part of her yearns for the release and a reprieve from the pull. But, he stands still and moves not. The rain is still ceased outside, but foul little streams of liquid shoot down his legs and spew onto the restaurant floor. Laura turns from him and rushes toward the exit and the darkness beyond it. His eyes shut before she touches the handle. Female fingers slide over his upper arm, and his eyes jolt open. The door to the café swings closed with no one standing near it. Looking to his arm, he sees Jamie's hand on it. He looks to her, unsure of what to expect or what is even real.

Her face looks more like the one he has adored and less of the one she has created this evening. Lips move and say, "I'm sorry, Brad."

Moving to another place without reason or direction. Not that any place would be appropriate, but, she knows the café is not the right setting. The knife is still gripped tightly in her hand. The blade causes a faint pressure on two of her fingers, but she ignores it. The pull is not hindering her as she walks. Its approval of her actions leaves her unsteady. She knows something terrible is brewing ahead if the pull is allowing her to approach it without torment.

Without having to fight off the ill thoughts, her imagination creates a vision of Gabe, Daniella, and Susanna smiling in the afterlife. It is only the second image of them being peaceful after death that she has been allowed. She aches to be where she dreams, and she squeezes the knife a little harder. So absorbed in her fancy, she is not aware that she is retracing her steps. Nothing seems familiar until she finds her left hand upon the iron gate to the alley beside the church. Looking to her right, she sees the massive scar left from where she struck the ground. Long pieces of sidewalk jut out of the earth as if trying to reach heaven and escape what lies beneath the surface. Thinking of the knife in her hand, she decides that she will have to be more forceful this time.

Scaling the gate is a simple task for her, even with only one free hand. Most of her mental and physical control has returned. Her feet hit the slushy dirt ground of the alley, and they slide into it about two inches deep. The grass never grows there because it is in the shadow of the high wall of the church. So, it remains slippery, slushy, and entrapping. Bringing the point of the blade to her stomach, she winces her eyes tightly together and thinks of her family waiting for her. Praying that destruction leads to rebirth, she falls forward, holding the blade to her and the handle at the ground. The handle meets the mud first, sinking into it nearly three inches before it finds stability. Her body crashes down upon it. Pressure shoots through her torso stemming from the epicenter of her stomach. She feels no penetration, but her thin, dark blue t-shirt tears at the contact. Her body falls to its side, sliding in the mush. Lifting her shirt to reveal her midsection, she sees no blood. There are no scratches and no signs of entry. The pressure inside of her remains strong, but there is no evidence of the injury on the outside. She flings mud from her left hand, and then slides it over her stomach searching for a sign of friction. There is none.

The laughter returns. The pull that had left her alone for a few minutes has returned with full intensity to enjoy her failing effort to escape. The volume of its cackling rattles her eardrums, and she knows she cannot stand it for much longer—she has to move quickly, although quickly is not something that her aching stomach wants to acknowledge. She struggles to get back to her feet and faces the side of the church. Staring at the brick wall in front of her, she brings the blade back to her abdomen.

She closes her eyes again and tries to cling to her earlier images of her family in a peaceful setting, but they soon melt into horrific caricatures of themselves in the presence of the pull's sickening celebration. Smiles turn to writhing, twinkling eyes morph to weeping, and hands held in affection now squeeze with anguish. Her mind feels as if it will tear in half at the sight. Shaking her head defiantly, she clutches the knife with all her strength and runs directly at the wall. The handle slams into the brick, her hands holding it straight. The handle remains perpendicular to the wall as her body smashes onto the point of its blade. Pressure stings through her. Her head swings forward and smacks the brick of the church. Her lights go out. Hands grasp the blade in front of her abdomen tightly. Body falls to the ground. Consciousness leaves; dreams begin before she hits the ground. Her mind is but that of a viewer as the pull flings open the flamed curtains, starts up its ominous orchestra, and begins its wicked play before her helpless soul.

Chapter XXVIII

"Andarus, I know you're hyper from your coffee, but, if you say it again, I swear I'm gonna shoot my first person today."

Grinning as much as he can before seven a.m., he responds, "Irene, I understand that you have some anger issues—some that may need the assistance of a professional psychiatrist. Maybe we can get a referral while we're at the hospital from that wonderful doctor friend of yours that was so willing to diagnose me."

She glances away from the road and the upper rim of her steering wheel to throw an annoyed look at him. He pauses slightly, then continues, "I'm sorry but others' personality issues do not confront me, nor do they shape my decision making process. Nope, don't confront me at all."

Having said it again, he can see her teeth pressing together, and he decides that running two recent jokes into the ground is more than enough playful agitation for one morning, at least for a while.

Making an attempt to relieve the weight that he has placed on her, he says, "Hey, at least the rain has stopped. Could you imagine dealing with me this morning with the pouring rain too?"

Smiling at the opening, she says, "What are you talking about, boss man? I've been dealing with your insanity throughout the longest rain spell in city history. You're equally annoying, rain or shine."

He looks out his side window, so she can't see him smiling as they pull into the hospital parking lot. The hospital entrance starts with a short four-lane entrance from the street, two in each direction. Then, it leads to two traffic circles that intersect along the outer rim, creating a figure eight shape. The circles lead to various parking garages and medical buildings. At the far end of the second circle is the main entrance to the hospital. Andarus wonders what deranged engineer designed two intersecting traffic circles, with yield signs abound and merging traffic from multiple buildings, through which nervous people are to navigate when they are anxiously and desperately seeking medical attention. The possibility for injury is so great that it is hard to believe anyone could make such an oversight without a deviant sense of humor or a taste for tragedy.

She awakens and feels as if her veins are full of the heavy, sodden ground below her. Her thoughts are as sluggish as her body, but a general feeling of despair and an overtone of miserableness ring out. The sun has risen high enough to peek over the tall points of the church roof, and small amounts of light hit the far edge of the alley. Her body is sunken into the earth nearly two and a half inches, which puts the surface of the mud nearly even with her shoulders and just past her ears. An occasional car can be heard passing from the street, but most of the city has not come alive just yet. In the dim alley and through the bars of the gate, it is quite unlikely that anyone would see her lying down, especially since she is ncarly completely sunken into the slush from having landed back first and relatively straight when she fell last night. The bent knife lies beside her in the mud.

Her dreams had been fierce during her body's shutdown. The pull truly exhausted itself with its torturous creations during the night. Upon just awakening, the decorative points in the church's roof resemble that of torture devices. It takes her a moment to realize that she is no longer witnessing the work of the pull. But, being made aware that she is still here in our world is also no measure of relief. The light of day only reminds her of all that cannot be that should be, of all that she has lost, and how she still remains in a place that beckons one to live, to feel, to interact—all of the things that seem deeply inappropriate and profane. How can she touch something and feel again, knowing her children cannot experience it? How can she feel anything knowing that it is something she'll never be able to share with Gabe? How can she go on with anything when it would be an acceptance of being away from them? She wants to tear it all apart—to leave it all and join them. If she could black out the sun, the strongest sign of warmth, rebirth, and moving on, she would. Surely that would demand the attention of the creator and force a hand to remove her from this world. It angers her in its bright opposition, and its presence discourages her to move at all. After all, she is two and half inches in the ground. Another five feet and nine and a half inches, and she would be where her family lies. It dawns on her that it is nearly the distance of the height of an average man. Maybe there's one person standing in her way; maybe there is still more for her to do. She stares at the overhanging, shingled roof above and the thin amount of light that is being allowed to pass and disturb her, and she wonders if all that we put up to protect us from the elements also blocks heaven out.

"Andarus, I have to say that I'm happy with the way you got along with the doctor today."

"No problem. I told you it didn't con—"

"Paul!" she interrupts involuntarily louder than what she deems appropriate for a hospital corridor.

"Well, at least he changed his mind and didn't feel the need to follow us in this time."

"Yeah, really. It's nice to be unescorted."

They step into the colorless room. In its center, the pathologist lies in the bed, almost exactly where they left him upon their last visit. Not much has changed, except he is calmer and more relaxed as he sleeps than when they saw him last. His left arm is in a cast and sling, and his shoulder is wrapped tightly. To Irene and Andarus's immediate right is a man with a young face and a fresh haircut. His thin-frame glasses look very stylish as he sits in the hard, plastic hospital chair. Andarus would have sized him up as a high school senior if not for the beginnings of a receding hairline and the copy of *As I Lay Dying* in his hand. It is not so much the book selection as it is its immaculate condition. The corners of the book are pointy and straight, and, although his bookmark is three quarters of its way through the text, the spine is only faintly creased.

The young man with nearly twenty years of weight on him stands up and gently places his book on the seat.

He says quietly, "Hi, I'm Tim," pointing to the man sleeping in the bed, "I'm Howard's son."

Irene offers, "I'm Detective Bauchan, and this is Detective Andarus."

Andarus sticks out his hand to greet Tim.

Shaking firmly, Tim says, "Yeah, the doctor told me you guys came by before."

"Yeah," says Andarus gruffly.

"He said it was pretty intense."

"We're sorry about that, Tim," says Irene.

"The information that we were trying to get from your father might have saved someone's life," finishes Andarus.

There is a silent, staring pause between them.

"Did it?" asks Tim.

Andarus's face drops as he says, "We're not supposed to talk about it."

"I guess that means no," concludes Tim.

Irene is surprised that Andarus allowed any emotion to surface while on the job, especially as much as was just on his face. Having never before seen that, she knows something is changing in him. And, she is unsure if it is for the better.

"Well, please, do whatever you have to do if it is urgent. He slept through most of the night; waking him now should be okay."

"Thank you, Tim," says Irene with Andarus nodding at the sentiment.

Tim steps toward the edge of the bed and gently nudges his father's left leg. Eyes flutter as if frightened and then settle on his son and relax there. A smile overcomes him.

"Dad, some detectives are here to see you. Are you up to talking to them?"

His face grows troubled, but he nods his head in affirmation, even though he briefly closes his eyes to do so.

Andarus starts, "Howard, it's Bauchan and Andarus. How are you holding up?"

Coughing before responding, "Well, the doc says the internal bleeding's stopped, but the shoulder still hurts like hell. Feel like I'm bruised all over the place."

"Glad to hear the bleeding's under control, Howard," adds Irene.

"Yeah, yeah," says the man lying in the bed, "Things are better—Tim's here to take care of his old man, but I'd bet you've got some other stuff to talk to me about. Am I right?"

"Yeah, Howard, you know we do."

His face grows uncomfortable with Andarus's words even though he knew that would be the answer. "Well, let's get to it," he offers.

Irene asks the first question as Andarus takes out his notebook and pen from his pocket, "What do you remember of the woman who attacked you?"

Howard looks as if he will break down and sob. He squirms under the paper-like hospital sheets, and his face contorts with physical discomfort from the movement. His eyes well up, and he looks to his son, who has worked his way around the other side of the bed as the detectives. Tim is holding his father's right hand. Howard smiles at the gesture and looks back to the detectives.

"Now, that's something that I don't think I can help you much on," says Howard.

"I know this is painful, Howard, but we're still looking for her. Anything that you can give us could be immensely helpful," guides Andarus.

"It's not that, Andarus; I didn't get much of a look at her. It was all so…it was all so fast."

Irene asks, "How did it start?"

"Well, I was in the autopsy suite. She caught me just as I was about to start the post mortem exam on Mr. Bonney."

Scribbling away in his notebook, Andarus offers the automatic, "Uh-huh."

"I swore I heard the door open, but I didn't hear any footsteps. No sounds of anyone walking or moving. So, I assumed it was nothing—sometimes your mind plays tricks on you in the auto-suite."

He pauses to absorb their reactions, and Irene nods for him to keep going. The pathologist is much stronger and coherent than when the detectives last visited him, but in all of Tim's childhood he has never seen his father so fragile and trepid. The closest he ever saw his father to his current condition was when he told Tim at fourteen that he and his mother were divorcing.

With his breaths coming faster and choppily, he proceeds, "Then, without hearing a sound, I felt something was there. I turned. I turned and I saw her staring at me. She didn't say a word, but I knew she wanted me to leave. I can't leave—there's a responsibility to protect the cadavers. I asked if I could help her. She only said one word. 'Leave,' she told me. Her voice sounded like the wind through the trees. It was smooth but creepy. Her stare was something that was hard for me to focus on. Couldn't tell the color of her eyes—I could've sworn that they were gray, but they looked like they were moving. Swirling or twitching or something. I couldn't move. I was mesmerized, trying to figure her out. Her hair had a long, white streak in it—a little off from the center—never seen anything like that before. All I could say was 'No.' Her face turned angry, and, before I knew it, she was upon me. It was more of a blur than like I was looking at a person. So fast. She was so fast; it didn't seem human. As soon as I noticed that she was moving, she had knocked me into the wall with a kick to my chest. That's when I hurt my shoulder—it got slammed into the wall. I swear it seemed that she was on top of me before I even hit the floor. Punches, squeezing and attacking all came together—had no idea what to do. It was too fast to take it all in. Too fast to think. The last thing I remember was her lifting me off the ground and tossing me half way across the room. My head hit a table or the ground or something hard along the way. That's the last thing I remember before waking up here."

Irene asks, "The report said you were found by an intern. Is this correct?"

"Well, I don't exactly know. Don't remember any of that. The intern's name is Jenny Babin. She's a pathology resident—been working as a diener mostly, helping me get the bodies ready before the exam. But, she's been assisting more in the actual exams lately. Oh, she's been here since then to see how I was doing. She hasn't mentioned finding me, but I assume it had to be her since nobody else was supposed to be there. You'd have to ask her. She's a bit shy—a bit strange, but she's a good looking kid," he says smiling at his son, "Don't you think so, Tim?"

Tim grins and turns slightly red.

Andarus asks, "So, Laura, emm, Mrs. Bonney, didn't say anything to you while this was going on? Except for telling you to leave. Did she ask you anything at all?"

"No, nothing."

Andarus scribbles and Irene looks on with more empathy than anyone else that has come to visit him. He wonders if she knows something. Has she seen the woman? Could she possibly know what it was like? Andarus seems uncomfortable as he writes in his notebook, but Howard has always known Andarus to be focused on his work. The pathologist thinks that maybe the detective feels awkward because he knows him personally and has to question him in a hospital bed.

"You guys must think I'm crazy telling you all these things about this woman."

"No," Andarus says quickly, "You'd be surprised how common these descriptions are getting."

Relief seems to course over the man's face, "At least, I gave you more information than last time, huh?"

Irene smiles, "We weren't sure that you remembered that at all."

"Yeah, I remember that. Kinda wish I didn't. Embarrassing."

"No," says Andarus, "You went through a pretty tough ordeal, Howard. Nothing to be embarrassed about."

"Yeah," adds Irene, "We're just glad you're getting better."

"The boy's got a lot to do with that. He's been keeping my spirits up."

Andarus says, "Well, hopefully we'll see you back at work soon."

Scratching his head with his free hand, "Well, I don't know about that. Been thinking about retiring, maybe doing some traveling. Go somewhere warm with Tim. Do some family activities."

Irene asks, "Do you really think you could give it up?"

He says, "Taceant colloquia. Effugiat risus. Hic locus est ubi mors gaudet succurrere vitae."

Her Latin being a bit rusty, Irene's eyebrows crinkle at the words.

Tim translates, "Let conversations cease. Let laughter depart. This is the place where death delights to help the living."

Now, Andarus also looks puzzled.

Howard laughs, "That's my boy."

Tim explains, "He told me that every time I was at the morgue with him."

Howard continues, "It's the motto of Dr. Helpern, an old New York examiner. I always thought it was neat. Nerdy pathologist interest."

"I guess we better let you get back to resting, Howard," says Andarus.

"Yeah, I suppose so," returns Howard.

Irene leans forward and kisses his cheek. Andarus shakes his right hand gently. As they turn to walk toward the door, Tim stands and follows them to the hallway.

Once they are out of the room, Tim says, "I have some questions for you guys."

Andarus looks at him neutrally and says, "I thought that you might. With what can we help you?"

"I'm curious about what happened at the morgue."

"Yeah?" asks Andarus, fully expecting this subject to be discussed.

"I'm curious about security and what can be done to prevent this from happening again."

This specific aspect of the topic is not what Andarus was expecting.

"What now?" asks a surprised Andarus.

"Dad's not completely set on retirement. He's set on taking a break, but he's still deciding if he wants to go back after that."

"And you wanna know if this could happen again?" asks Irene.

"Yes. How it can be prevented in the future."

Andarus adds, "So, you'd say that you want to make sure this doesn't *confront* your dad again?"

Irene's pupils wiggle slightly in his direction as she hears the word he keeps prodding her with, but she maintains the element of concern for Tim in them.

"Yes, definitely," answers Tim.

Andarus explains, "Better locks on doors. Maybe a keyed entry system into every room. A silent alarm button might be useful. Don't think the city would pay for more armed security."

Looking at Andarus's face closely, Tim asks, "Do you think that would've made a difference?"

"It's hard to say, Tim."

"Just tell me what you think, detective. Please."

"Most of the time, yes, it would've helped. Hell, your dad's never been in danger before, and he's been working this job since before you were born."

"You said 'most of the time'. What about this time, Detective Andarus? What do you think?"

"I'm really not supposed to talk about this. But, no, Tim. I think this woman would've found a way. She's proven herself to be quite capable of getting in wherever she wants."

Tim's face looks deeply troubled.

Irene adds, "But, we're after her, Tim. We're trying to catch her."

Tim nods his head and whispers, "I really don't care if you catch her. I mean, of course, it would be great. But, I just want to be sure this doesn't happen again."

"Let us know if you need anything, Tim."

"I know this sounds crazy, but it's been kinda nice being here with dad. We haven't talked this much in years," looking down, "In fact, I hadn't spoken to him since the divorce. Not more than a sentence or two at a time." He completely stops, pondering if he should go any farther. "It's like this has brought us together somehow. Made me think how I would feel if he were gone." Sad pause. "I didn't want it to end that way."

She wishes it would just end, for the curtain to fall, allowing her to take off this macabre costume. The distance of one man, an average man, would put her six feet under. She is already a few inches in the ground; she is surely not alive as she once was and not like anyone else. Maybe, she has dug a few toes into the grave, but she can't push her body into it any further. Not like her family and not like the world, she feels as if she has fallen outside of the physical universe, banished in an otherworldly crawlspace, somewhere forgotten. She is held in a place that causes her torment and is a constant reminder of all that has been taken from her. But, she is severed from her surroundings just enough to prevent her from receiving its empathy. And, she is just far enough outside of our world to catch flashes of hearing her children and seeing her husband in the after. She is so far from happiness, but her family seems to be a short distance away. After all, she has already found a rift between the two worlds, but she can't push herself any deeper into the passageway. Such a short travel to be six feet down. Just the distance of one man. A glimmer sparks far off in her brain. As it increases in intensity, she is unsure if it is her own thought or the pull. The thought is a handle in the void, something upon which to grasp, and she grabs it, not caring to what it is connected. The thought is something; seize the distance of one man. Take it. Steal it. Consume it. The amount of one man will push her through.

One man sits at his desk, his feet atop his fate. Six days of headlines are under his boots and on top of his head. They proclaim murder is harder to reach than his long arm is capable; chaos rules over order. Those words are never said directly, but the town absorbed them from the atmosphere of the articles. Andarus knows it; he sees it in the town, and he can sense the uneasiness in his coworkers. But, as aware of it as he is, it is but one of the burdens on his brain. His mind's priority remains on two women: one who has gone to visit her father and one who has remained as elusive as if she has vanished into the shadows of the city. One question echoes in his mind over the latter, "Is it over?" Her husband and children are in the ground. Her family's murderers have been killed. Is she done now? Can she turn away from what she has become, or has she completely drowned in the madness that she created? He wants it to be over. Despite what he saw of the mortician at the hospital today, he wishes that she is done and will slip away. He just hopes that if he is wrong Irene will not become involved. He wonders what Irene would think of him pondering at his desk, as he is defiantly breaking her orders to go home and sleep. But, much like the paper underneath his feet says of him catching the murderer, sleep has been residing slightly outside of his reach.

Part of his defiance to sleep has not been his fault. Earlier in the evening, he had set the alarm clock that resides atop a file cabinet across the room to remind him when it was 10pm. He had every intention of leaving work at that time with the sound of its buzzing. The time rolled around, and he couldn't bring himself to head home yet, knowing that he was not enough at peace to be capable of falling asleep and that he had not accomplished much on the case. So, he rose from his chair and turned the alarm off. In his weary state, he nudged the clock halfway over the edge of the file cabinet. As he returned to his chair, he eventually became comfortable and tired. Just when his eyes began to grow heavy and sleep seemed a possibility, the clock fell off the file cabinet onto the floor. It landed upside down and still remains that way. The loud jolt of the clock crashing to the ground in the silent office during the quiet hours of the night startled his fatigued body, leaving him uneasy and agitated, and he decided he should not let his guard down again. That is when he began pondering over the two women that occupy the majority of his thinking hours. He focuses on a bizarre vigilante and on another who is close to his heart but far from his fingertips. But, eventually, his mind betrays his will. His chin falls upon his chest, and sleep envelopes him. His dreams are of better days, but they are still not happy. They're nearly happy. The quiet snoring is almost constant, but irregular breaks in its rhythm occur every so often. The white noise that he creates blankets the otherwise silent office with the whisper of life. She heard its taunting rhythm before she set foot in his office, grimacing in disdain. His eyes flutter, sending jumbled images to his mind that chugs itself awake. The white streak dangling a half an inch from his face and the cold, pained eyes behind the hanging hair; something is shining. He swims quickly trying to pull himself out of the dreamworld. His eyes are open, but he still drips with the fluid of dreams.

The shining object has a red hue glowing along its sharp edge. He recognizes the reflected red glow as being the numbers on the overturned alarm clock/radio across the room. He sees the blade reflected in her eyes, but not her reflected in the blade. He has lost the ability to discern dream from reality, as fear remains constant across both planes of existence.

The black handle that is clutched tightly in her hand is connected to the rent and mangled blade that would not penetrate her skin the night before, unable to send her away to where she longs to be. But, it can easily slice through Andarus.

A second seems like seven. Vulnerable he is in her shadow. His eyes are wide and frozenly unmoving as those of a desert vagabond struggling to decipher if it is a mirage before him or if it is truly an unnatural wasteland spring on which he gazes. Juxtaposed to his frozen state is her body, which is a war of serotonin, firing off like canons, stirring horrible machinations and pulsing the anger through her.

The red glare catches his attention again. It looks like letters instead of numbers, and his focus is on the word it seems to spell. Time is backwards and talking to him. He turns his head from Laura to glance at the clock across the room, and he wonders if his sanity has slipped away. Twenty-six minutes to twelve. A four, a three, and two ones. Flipped upside down it burns the world hell in scalding, red letters. They burn into the air and into Andarus, but Laura notices them not. She remains focused on him before her as if he is the last lifeboat on a rapidly sinking vessel. Her eyes pulse and race, and nothing else moves except for her slender, little fingers as they turn the blade by its handle.

Andarus's breathing is all that moves quickly on him. He turns his vision in disbelief from the red letters of the clock to the knife that reflects its glow. Then raising his sight to Laura's face, he is convinced that she is real because the terror of her eyes is too much for even his nightmares to create.

She looms over him as he stirs slightly in his desk chair. It is the first time he has managed to gain control of his neurology to move anything besides his eyes while in her shadow. The knife gleams in the dim light of the office. It is warped, reflecting the light unevenly, despite her attempt to straighten it out. His hand moves slowly like a rattlesnake across desert sand.

Intense stillness grows out of a clear decision that he does not want to take. The body struggles to hold strong and rigid in prideful and desperate resolution while the inside melts, sobs, prays, and shrivels. He watches her eyes as they quiver; the borders of her electric pupils quake as they rapidly and unevenly expand and retract like the edge of the ocean crashing onto the frayed outskirts of mankind. His mind swims back to the eyes of years past as his ex-wife stood mere feet before him, having verbally backed herself to the edge of a plank but desperately and secretly looking for a way out of it. He always felt that she didn't want to leave but had said too much to pull herself back and he didn't offer a new path. As Laura stands with menacing, unevenly gleaming blade, Andarus tells himself she doesn't really want to do what her body is threatening. He reasons that had she completely wanted to attack him she would have been upon him by now. She would not afford him this brief opportunity to act if she did not hope there would be something for him to accomplish. All her doors are closed. Instead of opening fire, he decides to grasp at a handle in the dark.

His fingers remain outstretched over his gun holster on the left side of his chest, knuckles bent, ready to strike. Her head and body hold like a statue; her eyes remain frenzied. His mostly certain index finger flicks open the leather strap holding the gun in place. The click of the strap unsnapping accelerates the animation in her eyes; they glimmer excitedly, untouched by caution or fear. His fingers and his gaze remain still. His mouth moves.

"You want me to shoot you," says Andarus in eureka fashion, slightly louder than a whisper.

"I don't care what you do," shuffling the knife's handle in her fingers.

"No, you *want* me to shoot you, to end all of this."

"Better do it while you can."

Stares lock onto each other's eyes. For the first time Laura looks uncomfortable. The moment rests on them like a weight. She lunges, knife flashing like an ember, elbow bent furiously, knife by her head, ready to come down onto him. Into him.

An explosion tears through the space between the open doorway and the desk. The searing metal projectile slams against the back of Laura's head. Her feet lift slightly, and her body crashes to the ground behind the desk. Her right hand smacks the tightly closed blinds blocking the window.

Andarus looks from the fallen Laura to the doorway. Irene stands with smoking gun in hand and her face a slew of emotions.

Laura's consciousness is limited, but she is quite aware that she should not be yet still remains. Vision is bouncy and smeared. Thoughts are a seismic anomaly. Despair is clear. As she tries to force focus on the swirling office, she sees the fuzzy red outline of the overturned digital timekeeper. She deciphers the shapes of the ominous letters, and she wonders if her intrusion into Andarus's world is his hell or if the entire earth has become Hades for her, an elm of false dreams, entombing her indefinitely away from her family. An all-too-familiar cackling slaps the thought out of her slick hands. It had left her just long enough to get into Andarus's office and to be surprised at its return.

The back of her head tingles. Countless pricks sting the rear of her mind. She sees the room in the way a sea creature views the sky. Blurry, wavy vision obscured by current and refracted, invasive sunlight. Her thoughts that sting around her external occipital protuberance are fragmented into a thousand miniscule bubbles that are sucked away from her and glided toward the surface. As the thoughts rise away in a continuous, fragmented stream, they obscure her vision further as they reflect just enough light to grotesquely smear her sight but not enough to help her peer into the murk of her mind's waters.

She would love to hear another shot. One took her vision, even if only part of it and for the brief present; a second could possibly take away more of her unwanted consciousness. The smell of gunpowder and the blast of a bullet would be a happy end to two senses for which she no longer has any use or joy. The echoing cackling reverberates between her ears. The devilish laughter lights a fire of intensity at the back of her head. This fire heats up her thoughts, causing the bubbles to split into smaller spheres and accelerate their pace as they flee from her. Unable to grasp a thought in her head's icy waters, the pull keeps Laura from seeing the room and remembering that her existence is sevenfold sped up over the world around her. What feels like more than six minutes has been less than one, yet she is entirely unaware of the gap in perceived experience and wonders why there has been no follow up to the initial volley. The pull shocks her with disjointed, disturbing flashes that pass before her eyes and are replaced by another twisted vision as soon as it is speedily swept away from her in the unholy current. A flicker of Daisy's mangled throat; a flash of the screaming wounds in Gabe's flesh; a shock of dismembered, chemical-filled bodies in a crimson-stained motel room; and her violated angels looking as desecrated as ravaged cherubim. Gorging on its torturous, phantasmic feast, the pull's vaulting hatred overleaps itself as the last hellish incarnation jolts Laura to attention.

Her eyes gain clarity; pupils narrow, worldly vision comes. The memory of her violated girls, the worst thing she has ever beheld on earth, brings her vision back to the physical world. She sees the one she came to shove. His gun still in its holster, his face a confused façade of one who has been awakened from a deeply demonic nightmare only to be anxiously unsure if it has ended or if the dream has spilled over into reality. Instinctively, she creaks her head to the doorway and upon the hot, short barrel that is still pointed at her and the twitching lips on the face that is soaked in disbelief two feet behind it.

Irene struggles to tighten her right index finger on the trigger. She squeezed it with such ease a short several dozen seconds before, but now it is as if the finger is no longer connected to her.

Wild are Laura's eyes, much to Irene's mesmerization. Her pupils rage and spin like saw blades. Thankful for the shot, but inconsolable over its failure, Laura imagines digging her fingernails into Irene's chest and ripping it open. The screaming of the pull overtakes her; the lust to make the world bleed for her tragedy swells in her, each second spawning more inhuman thought. She steps toward Irene, angling herself around the corner of the desk. Irene's face is full of emotion, but it is not predominantly fear; it is hopelessness. If she falls, she can't protect Andarus. Her face is dripping with desperation, begging to the universe for the impossible. It is a horrible expression to behold, and Laura knows it well.

The pull kicks into overdrive as she connects where she knows Irene's visage. It screams for her to stop thinking. To lunge. To tear. To destroy. To cut a hole into the world for all it has done to her. But, the remembrance which she has unleashed is too heavy for even the pull to float it away from her. Irene's face matches Laura's emotions as she gazed in terror without hope upon Gabe's lifeless corpse. Her face in the morgue matches that of Irene's before her now.

Thrusting her head side to side, Laura struggles to silence the increasing demands of the pull. She feels her insides starting to lose their resolve. The pull is beginning to move the seemingly too heavy memory away from her. Irene still stares with quivering lips as the only parts of her that move. Laura knows the pull is coming full force to drag her into creating more carnage. Her teeth gleam white in gluttonous lust complementing the shimmering streak of white in the blackness of her hair.

But, Irene's face is unchanged. Laura knows that pain. She *is* that pain. Shaking her head harder, she turns from Irene, stumbles two steps toward the tightly shut blinds. She pushes her feet off the ground, jumping to the arm of Andarus's chair and springing herself directly at the concealed window. Crash and flying glass. Mangled, bent, flapping blinds dangle in pieces. Moonlight creeps into the room upon the two detectives who have drunk in more with their eyes than their minds can taste.

A sound causes Andarus's mind to start moving independently. Approaching footsteps remind him of what has happened. The loud gunshot, shattered window, a string of unsolved murders, a discontented police chief, broken blinds, and no culprit. Irene moves toward the window to gaze through the hole that was just smashed through it to the night outside. He knows what she'll see when she peers down to the sidewalk below. He knows reality and logic will cease to exist. He also hears reality coming to him in a dozen or so rushing footsteps, getting closer and closer to his office door. What he does not know is how could he ever explain what has happened. How can he explain what has happened to the missing bullet from Irene's warm gun?

Moonlight filters through a screen of clouds like a scream; each reflection on a drifting thunderhead is an echo of the original shriek.

The driver's window goes from black, to brief light, and a return to black. Out of her car, she walks toward the front door. Her steps are quiet, an unconscious reaction to it being so deep into the night, for she cares not if anyone hears her coming. The lawn is cut, but the edges run over onto the sidewalk. The mail still sticks out of his small, black receptacle beside the door, and yesterday's newspaper lies tangled in the bushes of his garden where it was so delicately thrown. All are signs of one who lives in his mind more than the physical world. Even more so, she turns the handle, and it is unlocked.

She flings the door open.

"It was a nice shot," he says as he lies on the couch gazing at the TV as if he were interested in it, "You know that, don't you?"

"What?"

"Well, you did shoot a woman in the head tonight, Irene. How many other shots were there in the last few hours?" he asks in a tone softer than the words imply.

"Oh," she says reaching for the door handle, feeling uncomfortable shutting it behind her and enclosing Andarus and herself in a dimly lit room in the middle of the night, especially as she has not yet been verbally invited inside. Her lecture about staying awake all night when he promised to go to sleep has disintegrated in the darkness.

"I'm always pressuring you to go to the shooting range. But, that shot was perfect. Dead on," uncomfortable with the last two words as soon as they escape from him, "I wanted to tell you that you're a great shot, and I'm sorry for worrying about you."

Her smile creeps up on her as she says, "I'm a great shot because you always tell me to go to the firing range."

"Well, either way, I wanted you to know that no one else could have done it better," he says sitting up and providing Irene with a place to sit.

"It's not that hard, boss. When I'm at the shooting range, I just picture your head at the center of the target, and blam!"

Causing his stubble to shift like a current, he smiles, "You wouldn't be the first."

Smacking his shoulder, "Only teasing you, Andarus."

Silence creeps in at the touch.

Breaking, “You know,” she starts, pausing, “You know, Paul, you shouldn’t be so negative. You are a great person; I don’t think you see that.”

“There’s a line of people who would beg to disagree with you on that, lady.”

“Like who? Karen? So what if she would? That wouldn’t…” catching herself, “I’m sorry, Paul. I didn’t mean…I didn’t mean to overstep my bounds.”

“Irene, as much time as we spend in the same room or car together, you are allowed to have an opinion every now and then.”

“Well, you don’t look that comfortable with it,” she says, scaling over his face.

“Whether I am or not, this is one of those times when you can say it.”

Breathing deeply and pressing her lips tightly together before starting, she says, “Paul, she hasn’t called. She’s not coming home. You make yourself miserable; you close yourself off from the rest of the world.” Looking around the dim room, she continues, “This is no way to live, Paul. You deserve so much better, and I just don’t think you see it.”

“This is my life, Irene. The thing is it wouldn’t be me leaving this for a new life; it would be someone else giving up their normal, cheery life to come into my world: fatigue, catching the bad guys in the middle of the night, being awake in the darkness and halfway out of it during the day. It would be me pulling someone else into this,” Irene’s mouth starts to move to protest, but he continues, “And, what kind of life would this be for them always wondering, *will I come home that night, or is it the end for me? Did I really have to work that late, or did I want to miss our anniversary? Is that woman, that I work with so many more hours than I see her, an affair or just a partner?*”

The last three words bother her in a way that he did not intend. But, she responds anyway, even if a little defeated, “But, if you were happy, Paul. If you were happy, you’d be able to sleep. I know it; I can feel it.”

Their eyes turn to random objects around them as the emotion of her words hovers in the room and hints at feelings that neither wants to acknowledge. The flashing images of late night TV seem to mock the seriousness of the conversation, but they do provide a distraction.

“Paul, after all that we’ve been through in the past week, do I really need to tell you that you should lock your door?”

“Well, I figured if I left the door open, it would keep her from crashing through the window.”

Irene is a little surprised that there was some rhyme to his crazy, exhausted, midnight song.

“Figured I’d hear the door handle turn a second or two before she was upon me. But, I think she’s figured it out like every other woman I’ve ever known,” exhaling softly, “I don’t have anything to offer her.”

“What?” she asks befuddled.

"She wanted me to kill her, 'Rene," he sighs, "Right there in the office."

Shaking her head, "Uh, Paul, she was coming at you with a knife. I think she was trying to kill you."

"No. If she would've wanted to kill me, she would've done it. She would've done it before I even knew she was there," pause, "Hell, she could've killed me after you shot her too. Think about it, Irene. She could've had me."

"Me too," she mumbles.

"She did fall three floors to the sidewalk and walk away undetected right in front of a police station. And, after a shot was fired."

"Yeah," she asks, "So, what do we do now?"

"I don't know if we can do anything. Don't know if I want to do anything. Don't you think…"

"Paul, don't start that. She's killed three people and has attacked you three times."

"Then she left me and walked away from you," hesitation, "The only three people that she has murdered raped her daughters and killed her family, took away everything from her. Do you blame her?"

Irene drops her head to avoid looking at Paul's eyes, "Damn it, Paul. This is our job. We're not supposed to…"

"To what? Think?"

"No, feel sympathy for the suspect. You know this."

"Irene, you shot her in the head to protect me. In the head, Irene."

"That was to protect you, Paul. Not for revenge."

Paul stands up in front of her, and her eyes meet his face.

"What if you would've gotten there thirty seconds later? And, say for the sake of argument that she had killed me. Tell me you wouldn't have shot her right then."

No answer. Eyes quiver.

"Tell me."

"Paul, you know the answer to that. Don't make me say it."

He nods.

"This isn't our job, Paul. We're supposed to bring in the bad guys and let a jury figure the rest out. It's not our job to feel for her."

"Well, maybe it should be."

"Paul, no…"

"It might not be my job much longer anyway."

She pauses, feeling the weight of the previous comment, "Not if you bring her in."

Andarus smiles an exhausted smile, "And, how do you propose we do that?"

Every passing second to the world remains sevenfold to her. She is possibly the only creature that would think it torture to increase its short life seven times over. Every day would be a week, every moment could be more properly absorbed before it faded away, and time would be ample to deliberate and never miss an opportunity. All that is around her moves in slow motion, and it vexes her. It's not the burden of her loss that makes all that she senses become so revolting to her taste and hideous to her eyes. Her loss accounts for her melancholy and her complete despair, but it is what she has become that stirs her disdain. She put on this costume to right an atrocity, and she did it with no restraint. Now, her role is seemingly done, and the costume has become her skin. In her dark metamorphosis, all that she was originally seems to have been discarded in a dried cocoon shell. Sitting in the shadow of a silent church, she feels like a noir Maslenitsa Doll waiting to be burned, marking the end of winter. But, the cold weather is just beginning to come this year, and it is a long way off before she'll be able to burn herself away from it. Pure Monday is forever away. A pure anything seems like a lie.

Chapter XXIX

The light of day angles into the church alleyway and falls upon a body lying in a wretched position. A slender forearm rises toward the heavens from a bent elbow that is mashed in mire. The hand remains open and flopped forward as if reaching. Its shadow on the damp ground looks like a withered tree in winter waiting for nature to break it back down to the earth. Her eyelids are open but detect nothing in front of her. Her focus is on an internal play. Curtains of fire. Scenes of loss. A chorus of misery. But, the eyes that look upon her are wide open and unsure of what they see before them.

A man of forty-one stares down at the crash of a human being before him. He has gazed upon vagrants, the forgotten, and the unstable for much of his career. He has spoken words over the dead, but something about this woman gives him a strong mix of compassion and unease. Her body has a light smell to it, but it is not the urinary reek of the insane or the earthy scent of the homeless. He leans forward to see if her chest is moving; to verify if she is breathing. His knee creaks slightly and his frame blocks the sun from reaching her face. Her body awakens at the change, and her eyes are switched on. Glowing, spinning. Opening her eyes to see the black iron fence before her, she instantly realizes she's in the church alley.

She looks upward to see what has blocked the sun and has caused her to stir awake. She sees a startled man with a white collar around his neck. Looking upward at squinty sunbeams, it appears that his collar is hooked to a beam like a noose, connecting him to the sky. The pull cannot be heard, and no visions are haunting her inner halls. She does not know what to do; it has been so long since she had to act without fighting or giving in to the pull's persuasion, so long since she had to think about herself, about her current existence. Now, she has nothing against which to fight or to follow. She is certain that she does not want to be, and she already resents the one standing over her for forcing her to act.

Surprising to Laura, the man's face regains some stability, and he says, "I'm sorry to startle you. How can I help you?

Those words lie on top of her for a moment. They sound ludicrous yet inviting. How can anyone help her without raising the dead or doing more damage to her than a headfirst swan dive to the concrete or a bullet to the head at close range? What could he possibly do? Part of her wants to laugh maniacally; part of her wants to rip him apart for making such a useless and insulting offer; and part of her would like to believe that someone, anyone, could help her now. The pull is no doubt planning some new torture for her and will return soon to inflict it. She certainly wouldn't mind a reprieve from the pull, but she wonders what could the man over her possibly do to stall its insidious machinations. Still, she remains wary of help, as her insides burn to be with her family. Everything that she witnesses around her is perverse, because she doesn't want to experience anything past her lost ones. She wants no part of a selfish joy or a new life, and this is the same part of her that wants to squash any thought that someone could help her. Help might mean coping, and she has no interest in adapting or moving on. She only wants counsel on exiting this nightmare. For that, she believes no one can assist.

"Andarus, are you sure this is going to work?"

He thinks over the probability for success of his proposed scheme, quickly analyzing the possible outcomes and likely responses, "No, 'Rene, I don't think we've got a shot."

She notices the carefree smirk has not left his face as he speaks. He certainly is not entirely happy, but she is sure something has changed in him through recent events. The last seven years of his life are in jeopardy. All of the long hours are in danger of being filed into a worthless cabinet and marked as unprofessional and inadequate. The same lengthy, costly hours that spent his marriage, that cost his happiness, are all likely to be deemed worthless. His career is about to be archaic currency, and he smiles. She has never seen him like this, and she has noticed a hundred subtleties that no one else would; something is certainly going on inside of his sleep-deprived mind. Although there are a thousand pressing details upon her, this is the one that flashes the brightest in her mind's sight.

Thirty-five minutes later.

"Gang violence?!" the question bellows out of the speakerphone atop Andarus's desk.

The voice peaked out the feeble phone speaker with its loud roar and hefty bass. Irene strains to hold back laughter at the voice's cartoonish response despite the rising potential for disaster. The corners of Andarus's lips are thinly pointed and ever-so-slightly raised as he responds, "Yes, sir, gang violence."

"Gang violence?" again asks the harsh voice stripped of any aesthetic appeal, "What in the name of all that's holy makes you think it's gang violence?"

Irene's silent giggling is extinguished. Andarus sends her a look of reassurance, which she only responds to with a forced twitch of her cheek muscles. He looks at her as he begins to speak, and, even though it makes no sense to her, she thinks he should be looking at the speaker phone when he talks.

"Revenge killing of a teacher who was responsible for their expulsion. Drugs were found at the scene of their death, enough to constitute intent to sell. Their deaths could easily have been a bad drug deal or a turf hit to eliminate competition."

"Come on, Andarus. A turf hit?"

Irene's voice throws color into the black and white conversation, "Planeline is riddled with drugs, sir."

"Thanks for the update, Bauchan," flutters the speaker.

Andarus's smile is replaced with tight, tense, level lips, and his voice carries a hue of annoyance, "Gang violence and a turf hit. That's what the evidence suggests."

The speaker warbles, "What about the statement from the motel owner? Didn't he claim to have seen a woman walk in who matched the description of the teacher's wife?"

"Yes, he did, but the security video doesn't support his claim."

"Well, what does it support?"

He coughs and says, "No one came in or out of the motel; it was storming."

"What the hell, Andarus? What are you trying to have me believe? A witness who reported the murder is lying to us? Those two boys were killed by an invisible assailant? Someone had to have murdered those two boys."

"Maybe they were already there. The No-Tell never has a shortage of miscreants. Maybe they were still there in another motel room when we were on the scene," explains Irene, "And as for the motel owner; it was raining horribly, low visibility, long hours; he obviously doesn't know what he saw. The video proves that much."

The tiny speaker blurbs, "And what about the high school girl who was torn apart?"

"She was living in a vacant house, and she was friends with the other two, romantically involved with one; she could've been in the same trouble as the other two."

"Even if all of that is true, what the hell happened with the broken window and the gunshot in your office?"

"Weapon malfunction."

"For the love of God, a weapons malfunction?"

"Yes. Complete accident. Lucky no one was injured."

The speaker burps, "Andarus, I'm growing tired of this conversation."

"You're not alone on that one," whisper-grumbles Andarus.

Irene half-smiles. The speaker's silence is more disturbing than its unsettling garble. Many times in life Andarus has found himself bailing out water that his mouth has let in, frantically reeling in line that his words let run out with a current of emotion, but this time he's filled his cup with exactly what he wants to drink, not caring in the least how it's going to taste.

The little cone of the speaker bounces in its recessed cavity, pushing ugly, distorted sound waves through the pinholes of the grill above it and into the awkward-filled air of the office.

"My boy, you've got enough to worry about without starting a war with me."

His smirk returning, he responds, "Well, you know what they say about idle hands…"

Irene wants to cry but a soft snort that is more feminine and attractive than she knows escapes from her. It's the first time all morning that Andarus's smirk has evolved into a legitimate smile.

"Damnit, Andarus, have it your way; gang violence, spontaneous combustion, or the boogeyman—I don't give a damn! But, you better capture your mystery suspects and give this town peace. And, you better find this estranged wife—Mrs. Houdini, and show this damn local paper that we're not all being stalked by some deranged vigilante. We're being picked up by national news now, for God's sake. World's worst newspaper we've got here, written at a third grade level, and people all over the country can't get enough of this story. Idiots…"

"Sounds like good words for a reelection speech, chief," interjects Andarus.

Irene bites into the knuckle of an extended index finger.

The undersized speaker spits, "Enough! These people are demanding an end to this, and they're looking to me. You bring me the killer or his corpse, or I'm throwing you to the people as the one who let all of this happen."

A loud, sharp metallic ring chimes from the speaker, followed by a dial tone.

Eyes are closed. The sound of crinkling rustles over her eardrums. Eyes open. Twilight lands on her vision. A single word spins in the posterior of her mind, but she can't decipher it. Realization slides over her, and she rolls off her back and onto her knees. She doesn't see the man who was standing over her earlier. If not for the sandwich wrapped in cellophane and the bottled water next to where she was sleeping, she would think he was a character in a fever dream.

She remembers her last glance of him. She was so dizzy. She remembers his one question and her unease over it. And, there was one word. Her last conscious effort before the black. It stays just out of reach, and she hears the clamor of the pull approaching again. She looks to the moon hung low, sees horrendous images of her family, and knows it's going to be a long night.

Four long hours later. She ambles on streets that she has not stumbled down since she was a wandering teen. Only the grim images in her mind could have dragged her back here again. Every filth-covered block has a memory from her sad youth that she had gladly replaced with Gabe and the girls. She had been long content to scrape thoughts of these streets and that part of her life from her mind to focus on family. But, these morose memories from her past are no match for the dreadful dreams that shoved her here. As much as she never wanted to retrace these misled steps, she followed the pull's persuasion to return, as it is a slight reprieve from the twisted scenes that it was playing in her head. As on her previous ventures, she remembers the pull's taunting offerings much more than her specific path back to Cellar Street.

Every graffiti-spattered building and post, covered with new and old flyers for local music shows which wrap around them like a shedding serpent's skin, marks some past disgrace turning her insides even further sour. Distant memories and current torments ignite into a dark illumination; misery blooms in the rays of her black sunshine.

Her mood is so foul that she can taste its bitterness at the back of her throat. Kids are standing outside a familiar building as the sounds of a band playing aggressive tones creep out the opened door to the side courtyard. The courtyard is caged in by an eight-foot chain link fence. She always remembered the undeniable feeling of being cooped up like an animal or caged in like a criminal when she was there. Yet, it always seemed better than home.

It's 11:58 on a Monday night, and curfew is as ignored as subtlety and understatement. These are the kids who make the rest of the school laugh with bawdy comments in class, many of them routinely increase the bell curve, they speak slowly to imply a chemical haze which grants them the badge of a burnout and a ticket to the second highest level in the popularity pyramid, and several of them are usually nursing some type of injury from crazy stunts like homemade bungee chords, roof surfing with pieces of sheet metal, or jumping on the hood of a friend's car as it pulls into a parking lot. None of them are stupid, but they often go to extreme lengths to keep anyone else from finding out. Years have passed since she was among their ranks, hairstyles have shifted, clothing has evolved, but she recognizes their demeanor in how they stand. She did not exhibit most of their characteristics, but she did enjoy their lack of respect for convention, tradition, and other things for which she had no tolerance. The pulse of the music is still the same. It's not the music that bothers her, but the remembrances of what she was going through when she would feel its melodic surge shooting through her young body. The aggressive tones would compliment her present mood if feeling anything had not become an unwanted and burdensome gift to her now.

She sees an alleyway where she saw the first dead body in her young life. A girl with a needle in her arm, pale as a winter in hell, was face down and alone, a colorless flower in a concrete garden. The girl's friends ran when they saw she was not breathing. Laura found her when she walked out of the music show to go home. She ran back in and found people who were more interested in the excitement than who felt compassion. She called the police from the phone inside, which cleared the place out once everyone heard the law was coming. All the call got her was the reinforcement that the girl had overdosed beyond help, and she was given the riot act from local police who insisted she knew more about it than she did. Drugs were never a vice of Laura's, just a part of the scenery around her as it eroded people she knew. But, she had no argument that could keep her out of handcuffs and the back seat of a cop car. That was the first time that she seriously thought about getting the hell out of Riverview. Little did she know then that the girl in the alley would be a cartoonish, censored version of death compared to what she has seen lately. On this street, her blood-spattered, dirty clothes will not draw much attention. Junkies are often dirty, and the bloodstains, while considered a bit over the top, can be written off as fake—merely a fashion statement.

A loud whistle cuts through the moonlit evening, with the orange-yellow celestial body still looming low in the night sky, and it is followed by, "Hey baby, where you going?"

It's a familiar call on this street, usually ignored or returned with a single finger in the air to let the caller know that he is number one or another, more uncomfortable sentiment. Her pupils twist and the pull swells inside her. Rage is her driver as her focus races to where the voice came. A quiet, teenage squeal escapes the body in the caged courtyard as her eyes land upon him. His foot stumbles back a step, nearly losing his balance. He wears a worn, black t-shirt not displaying his favorite band but the one with the most provocative name. The overconfident, waiting-to-shove-a-word-in-any-discussion demeanor has left him, yet he cannot pull himself away from the woman staring at him, although he would much rather slink back into the crowd and disappear as one of the ants on the bustling mound. His mouth stays open. She stares at it, watching for another word to fall out, anxiously waiting to pounce. The pull is on her back like a crazed, frenzied primate, swinging a bone over its head, screaming for violence. Screeching for sanguinity. His eyes well and his Adam's apple quivers. She turns from him as he is not what the pull has sent her here for, although it would love for her to fray apart the overzealous, speechless boy in front of the young ones behind the diamond-shaped, aluminum-rimmed holes of the fence. However, her ears remain open as she steps away toward the rougher end of the street.

A much larger friend, who gleefully witnessed the entire exchange, slaps the outspoken one on the shoulder and says, "Great job, Johnny. *She really wanted you, man.* Now, go change your underwear, and we'll go back inside."

Several people standing around the courtyard snicker at the comment. Johnny looks at his friend with a disheveled expression that seems to scream, *Brian, help me* and *go to hell* at the same time.

She felt every sound touch against her eardrums, but she keeps walking toward the louder, stickier end of the street, the end that the pull is intent on visiting. The sound of peeling off a piece of plastic wrap is heard with every step as her shoes extricate off the ground covered in garbage water, spilled alcohol, and unmentionable fluids. The liquids are spread and tread upon by boots during the busy night, and the sun bakes them into the sidewalk and street during the tamer day. The street has cooked in its own rank juices for longer than Laura can testify, being absorbed through the roots of a suburban subculture for generations.

The air used to smell like freedom and adulthood. Choosing how one acted without parental guidance in a tinted microcosm of the grownup social order, the sounds of the street were energy, a chance to change the world, a rebellion against all that caused her rage inside. The street was its own world; amazing freedoms, the thrill of expression, sharing a conversation on the curb with another soul from a sad home, tasting waters of the forbidden adult world which could be sometimes thrilling but mostly disillusioning, feeling utter rejection and loneliness within the refuge of the dismissed, depression and conceit circling in the same chamber, depravity and morals wrestling in the filth puddles harboring every curb. Even though it proved to be the happiest times of that period of her life, she was all too happy to forget it when she found Gabe. It is anything but amelioration that she feels now.

A parked car, with a girl leaning her dyed, multi-colored head into an opened window, spews out a familiar sound. The engine still runs as the exhaust adds one more toxin to the street, but all that can be heard is the stereo. The song is one she knows well.

"…My reflection's got bloodshot eyes…Blood and lies make a busy hive…"

Music has been the only constant resident of the street since live bands began performing there four decades before, but now she wishes it would silence itself. She used to love music; it was her poetry, her bedtime stories that she never received, her source of strength. Now, it just sparks unwelcome emotions.

"…Dripping soul poisons the mind…Soul slips away all the time…"

The words are in her head, deeply recessed, and have been starved of the light of thought for many years, yet they have remained. She always had a close affection for songs expressing her discontent. Especially this one. Its volume reaches its peak as she passes directly on side of the car. The girl leaning against the vehicle offers a clear view of her attention-demanding stockings and high heels.

"…A black day meets a black night…Silence keeps it from the light…"

She steps toward a bustling bar. People smoking cigarettes outside the front door. Bouncer with more cellulite than brains guards the entrance. And, faintly she can hear the loud short bursts of individual instruments as a local band inside is wrapping up a quick sound check.

A brief silence from the local music allows the familiar song to reach her ears again, "…Too tired to move with the flow…Luck sold me out a long time ago…"

She passes a dark alleyway in which she sees a tiny bag exchange hands. She keeps straight for the door. The bouncer has a small line hanging to the far side of the entrance. He checks their ID's with the determination of a radiologist inspecting a suspicious blotch on an x-ray. He holds his meaty forearm in front of the line as a fleshy drawbridge.

She can hear him say as he slaps the card back into the hand of the awaiting patron, "Three bucks at the table; no fighting."

Laura keeps her steady pace as she approaches him. When he sees a body nearing his doorway so rapidly, he feels both appalled and excited. He gives the young guy in front of him a slight nudge at his chest to warn him not to move forward. Then, he turns his full attention to the approaching Laura.

The words float from the car to her ears, "In a world that constantly denies…we shed ourselves, but ourselves are always growing dim…growing dim…"

Her body is three steps from invading the protected entrance.

Meaty says with his lips turned entirely downward in a hairless, menacing natural goatee, "Where in the fu—"

His tongue stops flapping in his mouth. His mean face leaves him. Typically, he only loses his angry face after having thrown someone out of the bar or having knocked one unconscious. On a few occasions during his rare evenings with a female, he has let the mean face disintegrate for a moment, but none of them have ever noticed, only giving him more fuel to keep the façade running. His sight scales over her with nostalgic affection.

Almost grinning, he says, "Haven't seen you in years, girl. Where the hell've—"

Laura steps right past him through the opened doorway before he can finish. His eyes are wider than the normal thin slits through which he sees the world. The guy standing in the front of the line, who recently had his chest pelted, chuckles at the event. Meaty snaps his head to attention mere inches from the hopeful patron's head. His breath is heavy and blown directly in the customer's face.

"Think something's funny, tough guy?" he asks the one awaiting entry.

Looking to his three friends standing in line directly behind him, one of which is a female, he responds, “Yeah, that girl walked right past you. You must be getting old.”

Meaty stares at him. His face is hard; his eyes are lost.

“She’s been here before, kid. Long time ago,” snapping the card against the patron’s chest, “Three dollars at the table; no fighting or I’ll come looking for y—”

Inside the doorway, a girl sitting at a raggedy folding table with dark makeup and a bashful yet irritated expression watches Laura saunter past her quiet and aloof demands for three dollars. Normally, she would make a scene and scream for Meaty to assist, but something in Laura’s face exudes danger and convinces her that this one would be far too much trouble. The girl glances around to see if anyone saw her get stiffed and ignored; no one noticed, so she looks at the guy walking past Meaty through the doorway and repeats her demand to a new set of ears.

The bar is decorated in a black and white checkered floor, black unadorned walls, and a three feet high wooden stage with dark red curtains as a backdrop. The curtains send a prickling feeling at the back of her head. Her mind envisions them flinging open to reveal some twisted torment of the pull. But, a four piece band talks amongst itself near the drum riser. It is a familiar sight for her, as she has seen more local shows than she can recall. It always seems that the drummer wants to open with a song that starts with a cool drum roll, the guitar player wants the song with the best solo, the bass player wants the song with the heaviest groove, and the singer wants the tune that is the easiest on his voice as his vocal chords struggle to throw off the alcohol that he has dumped on them while waiting for the show to start. Sure, the set list was discussed previously in a tiny practice room before the show, but it all goes out the window when the venue is packed and the mumblings of the crowd morph into excitement and the feeling that this could be the beginning of something bigger if only they played their best song first.

Laura glances over the crowd. She sees a grizzled face. A memory of a faded dream. He leans over a girl younger than his daughter, whom he hasn’t seen in days, with his left arm propped behind her on the edge of the bar and his right arm holding his drink.

The pull’s insidious magnetism strains to bring her to an empty stool, two seats away from the grizzled memory who is whispering in a young girl’s ear. The bar itself is shaped like a long rectangle, but within it is a recessed area in the form of a hexagon in front of the stage. This pit places even the tallest member of the crowd at the ankle level of the band. Not the best thing for the sound to flow over the heads of the crowd, but, it does make a local band look much larger than they are. The recessed area has a three foot wall enclosing it with a four-foot rail on top of it on which patrons lean who want to see the show closely but not participate in the violent carnage that always takes place in the area directly in front of the stage. The stage is three feet higher than the wall of the pit, and the rail meets it on each side, enclosing the hexagon.

The door through which Laura just walked is to the far end of the building as the stage. She currently weaves through busy pool tables, which provide a constant clanking between songs. For most in this place, hitting the ball hard is equally important as making the shot. Usually, someone drinking slowly and hitting the cue ball softly will leave with a pocketful of crumpled bills. To the immediate left past the billiards tables is the long bar that nearly stretches the length of the building. It ends with a narrow wall that creates a dimly lit hallway to a pair of grungy bathrooms, both devoid of an official sign but with the words “sacks” on one door and “slits” on the other, carved deeply into the wood in the fashion of a struggling third grader.

She grabs a bottle that is seven tenths of the way empty from the edge of a pool table. No one notices as the shot was at the other end of the table. She steps in stride toward the open stool at the bar. Sliding herself onto it, it feels odd to sit. For most of the past week and a half, she has been either standing, walking, or lying down. Somehow this feels recreational, and it causes her eyebrows to furrow downward and guilt to flow through her. The pull is content and sends no more disturbing images or thoughts her way; it sits in its excitement and anticipation. She looks straight ahead; there is a mirror that runs the length of the back wall of the bar above the sinks, coolers, cabinets and other bar supplies. As she stares at the mirror, she looks at the reflection of the grizzly and the girl. She is quite tempted to pull her hair entirely out of her face and gaze upon her own eyes in the mirror, retesting the events at the house with Daisy. She wants to challenge whatever was knocking her out before. She would almost welcome its pain as a distraction, but she has another matter to attend. One in which the pull is quite interested. Reluctantly, she keeps her sight on the reflection of the people next to her and not on herself. She can hear pieces of the conversation taking place about two and a half feet from her.

“Come on; let’s get out of here,” the gruff voice prods.

An uneven, softer voice responds, “I don’t know. I came with my friends. I don’t think I should leave them here.”

The gruffness pleads, “They’re out there waiting for the band to start. They haven’t come to check on you in over a half an hour. They ain’t concerned with what you’re doin’, so why are—why are you worried bout them?”

His voice smells like the staleness of alcohol, and over the course of the evening he has said to her some of the words that her father has never told her. He should know this, because they are words that he never told his own daughter: beautiful, smart, adult, princess, flower, pretty, angel. The words “ain’t concerned with what you’re doing” touch a deep-rooted fear that has been kept inside the unaged girl next to him. For her entire life, her responses in group conversation have always been several seconds late so she could double-check her thoughts before expressing them, and oftentimes it has prevented her from speaking at all. When someone else would speak exactly what she was deliberating to say, she would feel cheated and cowardly, which only made her doubt herself further. The weight of the idea that her friends truly do not care about her sits heavily upon her chest, smothering her defenses against what she feels to be a potentially dangerous situation in the grizzly man sitting far too close to her. She wants to embrace something. Maybe they don't really care about her; she is underage and getting drunk at a bar with a man who is a lot older than she, and her friends are more interested in the music and the show than in seeing if she is okay. As she stares at his unkempt face, she thinks of the beers that he has bought her, of the compliments that he has thrown at her, and of his persistence in getting her to leave with him. Maybe he does care about her. Maybe she is pretty. Maybe he does really like her. Maybe she is not a reject. Maybe, somehow, this means her daddy loves her too.

Feeling out of sorts is nothing new for the young girl. She is the only Asian among her group of friends, and Asian boys have never held her interest. Neither of these things should make one feel out of place as they are frivolous details, but both have caused her a great deal of self-imposed doubt. Maybe she simply is not attracted to Asian boys because they remind her of her father. And, maybe she has no Asian friends because she has never met one with the same taste in music and clothing. But, these logical reasons have never helped her as she has always thought of herself as an outcast and a poseur, even among her group of friends. Part of her feels like a traitor for not having any interest in her culture, but most of her wants nothing to do with her father's beliefs and background. Her name is Meelynn, and right now she is embracing danger in place of lonliness.

Meelynn's head spins like the drumstick in the impatient drummer's hand perched on the throne behind his set on the rear center of the stage. The debate over the band's initial volley of sound has been narrowed to a bandy between the bass player and the singer. There were four egos preventing the start of the show; now they are two people closer to music. Soon, his drumstick will stop twirling, and he will be banging out his own brand of noise into the crowded room. But, Meelynn's head at the bar is still spinning, far away from seeing clearly, and she is so unsure of what kind of noise she wants to make. The man stares at her, awaiting a response. His lips shake in an awkward smile, but his eyebrows form two angry downward slopes. The gray strands in the hairs speckle the slopes with a slight frost. As she looks over his face, she gains no assistance in making her decision. She knows she wants to believe the good stuff, and she tries not to think about the crude comments or the other girl to whom grizzly was talking before he started in on her. She knows his name is Chris; for the moment that name belongs to her, and it is something to hold.

The bartender steps forward and blocks Laura's view of their reflection. The woman looks over Laura with a plain and emotionless expression. Laura's hair shields most of her face from the barkeep.

The barmaid rubs a stained white rag across the bar in front of Laura and says, "If you're gonna sit at the bar, you need to buy a drink. Stools are for drinkers."

Laura shakes some of the hair from her face and raises her hand with the stolen bottle of libation above the bar for the bartender to view. The bartender's nose wrinkles at the sight. Most of the girls in this bar don't seem to buy their own drinks, and they certainly don't tip her as well when they are buying. She is pretty, but she has an impossible time seeing it when the words only come from the drunks at this miscreants' watering hole. Her life is a series of regional bands, promising musicians who seem to fade into the local scene, and every few months realizing how much more of her life she has spent in this bar—how many hours her medically enhanced body has spent leaning over an abused, wooden counter taking alcohol orders that beget more alcohol. Sometimes, she worries that she will never leave, and some nights when she is treated like the proprietor of the local rock music scene and the dispenser of wild and crazy times to everyone in it, she feels content with her little personalized corner of the street that she used to wander down as a teen, sneaking into the very bar that she now manages. But, the latter times have been coming fewer and fewer as of late. She wonders how long she will be able to look attractive enough for the tips to justify the job. The lines on her face have slowly deepened. Not enough for anyone that she knows to notice, but she can see them. If she still talked to her family, they would notice. Her hair has thinned at her bangs ever so slightly. And, once again, her eyes are the only ones to notice their subtle erosion. She frequently ponders how long does she have before the ocean of her fears washes away the rest of her hair. Or, at least enough to cut into her tips. The only male to have held his stare at her face while talking to her all night is the guitar player in the band on the stage. For a moment while he talked to her, she started thinking about getting out of the bar. Moving on to something else. The guitarist certainly seemed like this place was but a stop on his long road to where he wants to be. At the same time, she even thought that still working in this bar with people like him in it was not such a bad way to earn some dollars. Either telling the owner that she was leaving or staying at the bar—both appeared to be exciting and viable choices. All of the life decisions ahead of her seemed full of promise and new life. But, soon after, she saw the guitarist kiss a girl before sound check, and all of her hopes drowned under the alcohol that she was serving. Another light burned out before her, only giving her a brief glimpse of the direction in which she seeks, much more of a blinding tease than a help. She has spent most of her life chasing after these flashes, only to be left with stunned eyes and empty hands. She had just about given up on ever finding a light again, but then she saw him earlier tonight. He seemed to be the culmination of all that she had been chasing after; a validation that her meandering search was not in vain. All of her romantic exploits seem to her like the menial antics of a dog trying to be let inside the right house. It is an image that she would gladly drop from her mind, but it is imbedded there. For a while this evening, she thought maybe it all was not for naught, as it could have led her to him. The wandering path would not be pointless if it led her somewhere besides more turns and false hopes. And, this created the morose look on her face. Years of memories surround her in this bar; living in one's own nostalgia creates a unique relationship. Comfort and stagnation. She is the legendary queen of the bar, a fixture in this scene. A title of which she hates as much as she loves the notoriety.

She tells everyone that her name is Demure, and she is at heart. But, not in this bar. And, unfortunately, this is where she spends most of her time. Her intensely dyed red hair is unnatural yet uniquely appealing and fitting in her surroundings. She is five foot four, but her spiked heels place her closer to five foot eight. She has never been to work without wearing them or one of their stiletto counterparts, but they could never lift her quite high enough off the grungy floor. Her clothes are slightly revealing yet stylish. Her life has often been a wreck, but her wardrobe has been exactly on the course that she has desired. Tattoos run the length of her thin forearms. These markings are perennially vexing to her as they remind her of whom she was with at the time, or even how long it has been since she had it done and how little has changed in the interim. They are ink and skin hieroglyphics documenting years of regret, changing styles of music and aesthetics, and even some shame somewhere between the skin and the ink. While working, she keeps her hair tied tightly in the back of her head with a carefully selected ribbon to match the outfit of the evening. Her bangs hang on the sides of her face in two wavy tendrils framing her high cheekbones. There is a regal quality to the lines of her face that makes her look classically stunning, like a face from a Grecian bust. But, she would become irritated if someone told her that, wondering where was the joke and why someone would tease her so cruelly. Her appearance is that of a delicate knife; beautiful, slender, but with a menacing edge reflecting the meager light in the dingy bar, daring anyone to try and grasp it.

Laura came close to getting a tattoo a few times before she met Gabe. But, it seemed that everyone else had one as a membership card into the subculture just as the well-to-do crowd had their tiny emblems sewn onto the chest of their overpriced shirts. Besides, she never came across a design that she was convinced she would still like nine months down the line.

The bartender turns her focus from Laura to the young girl two stools over. Meelynn does not resemble Demure very much at all; she is of a different race, four feet ten inches in height, or four-ten, which she loves to point out to everyone that it is just like the shotgun, and jet black hair that shines in a way the bartender's never has. Despite their physical differences, the barkeep views the girl sitting on the stool before her as herself minus fifteen years of drinks, music, and failed adventures. She wants to say something to her. Tell her to run, to get away from the urchin in front of her, to think of the rest of her life. That just one day, just one night, can turn into years. Every diversion taking a little more from her, making her feel like there's not much left of herself. She wants to point Meelynn in another direction, but she doesn't even know where to direct herself. She wishes she could go back to that age and find a different path, a path that would make her feel something else.

As the seventeen-year-old looks at the inebriated man in front of her, she wants to feel something, but she doesn't want the hand reaching out for her elbow to touch her. At least not yet.

A guitar rips through the air of the building like a demon screeching into the void. The sound is fast and energetic, melodic yet forceful. It's like a raucous orchestra as the band joins in on the second round. The bartender's face lights up briefly as she looks to the guitar player moving around the stage as his fingers slide up and down the guitar in a blur. Girlfriend or not, watching him playing sparks something in her, and, as the crowd awakens with an inordinate amount of energy for a local show, it sparks something in the whole building. Pool cues are held motionless as players watch the stage instead of the eight ball. Conversations come to a stop. And, for a small fraction of time, even drinks are held still and away from awaiting lips as the crowd collectively watches the performance. The only three people without any sign of a grin on their faces are Laura, Meelynn, and the drunk. In fact, he is scowling in his impatience.

His face contorts as it struggles to go in the opposite direction of the vigor and pulse of the energetic songs. He has come here for years, but he has never been fond of the music; indirectly, he has only appreciated the decadence that has surrounded it. He has not looked this upset since the one night he saw his daughter sneak inside. He was more offended that she had invaded his private getaway than he was at her sneaking into a bar. He reaches his fingers out closer to touch the youthful elbow of the minor perched on the edge of an adult stool.

The juvenile girl looks to the black and white checkered floor and says, "I've gotta pop a squat, I'll be back."

"No, wait, Mee-, Mee-, sweetheart," he says leaning forward making certain that she can hear him over the music, "You can piss when we get outta here. Let's go now."

His fingers slide roughly over her elbow. Still watching the two of them, Demure bites her lip. Laura watches in the mirror. The teenage girl seated at the bar shakes her head, quickly spins around on the stool away from him, hops off the vinyl perch and onto her shaky legs, and walks briskly toward the bathroom. Meelynn does not look back as she moves through the crowd to the door labeled with a coarse word. Laura can see his face as it contorts into a mess of enraged frustration. There is something about him, something to do with the pull, but she hasn't figured it out. She thinks he may be something out of a dream, but the context escapes her. Running through her memories of the pull's torments, she tries to find him. Bricks. Water running over bricks.

He slams his beer down on the bar. Fizz flows over the rim and runs down the length of the bottle. He has torn the label off the glass vessel in a clumsy fashion, as is his habit.

Watching the erupting alcohol ooze onto her bar, Demure shouts over the music, “Chris, cut that shit out! Don’t make me go get Gino; you know he doesn’t like you anyway.”

Chris grunts, slides off his stool onto a standing position, and grabs his sloppy bottle off the bar with his thumb and first two fingers. His digits do not have the stability that he assumes, and the bottle goes crooked, sending a stream of fizz and transparent yellowish brown liquid falling to the floor, a tainted little waterfall soaking the black and white checks with its chaos-inducing nutrients.

Demure huffs in exasperation, just one more reminder of exactly what her job and her life entails. The word Gino is on her lips, but she doesn’t feel like dealing with the situation. Bottling up the frustration seems easier than pouring it out.

The same word connects with something in Laura’s mind. Gino. She remembers the name from years past. It goes to a far enough place in her mind, where the robust door muscle was but a skinny teenager devoid of warpaint-like tattoes, whose deepest fear was having anyone find out about his various learning disabilities. She remembers hours of sitting with him and a few other people in a friend’s first car that smelled of mildew and cigarettes and listening to early era Metallica at a volume that peaked the enervated speakers far beyond their capacity. It was a dank, mobile clubhouse that was filled with the energy of youth and the drug of hope for their futures and for changing the world. Without the dreams that started in that dilapidated car, she may never have found her way to Gabe. The last time that she saw Gino he was just beginning to put on some weight, though he was not quite meaty yet. They must have been about fifteen then. It wasn’t much longer that she left Riverview and Cellar Street to deal with her wounds under different skies.

Laura’s thoughts abandon past memories that are devoid of comfort to focus on the unpleasant happenings of the present. The pull twirls inside of her like a shark circling an unsuspecting seal, unseen under the icy shadows of arctic waters. Jabbing its fin out of the surface, it forces her attention on Chris as his worn and stained shoes stomp at the ground underneath him and as his hot, impatient breath singes the air. The harsh lines of his frown are deep, and people quickly step out of his way as to not have to look at him any longer. He is stumbling on an awkward path toward the bathroom.

People still smile, focused on the stage, all sharing a common pulse, a unifying and leveling emotion. Roles within the scene are tossed aside, and all are part of the show. As the guitar solo starts, a soft gasp can be heard as sound pyrotechnics scream off the fretboard. Blur, bend, shred, wail, and melody coexist in the sound that is equally part Niccolo Paganini and hard rock.

Despite the depth of the music, the only thing pulsing through Laura is the pull. It screams for her to follow the careening drunk toward the dim hallway. At this juncture, Laura simply would rather not do anything. It is not that she wouldn't normally want to help; it's more that she's had enough and would rather experience nothing else in this world. If she is going to focus on anything around her, she would much rather wonder what is going on with her. Why can't she die? Why is she trapped here? And more specifically, how can she get out of this and return to her family? Besides her desire to focus on an escape, there is something sickening about being the pull's errand girl. It will not let her sleep; it taunts her at every failed attempt to reach her family. It completely revels in her despair, constantly playing horrible scenes behind her eyelids. Even when her eyes are closed, there is no sleep. It is a restless, personalized hell created specifically for her, as the pull would never allow her a true reprieve. Words of a cliché come to her mind about a lack of rest for the wicked. The pull cackles at her irritation and urges her once again to the hallway. Her hand clenches around the dark bottle in her hand, and it explodes into shards like a shattered stained-glass window.

The familiar sound of glass breaking pulls the bartender's attention from Chris entering the bathroom hallway to Laura. Demure says something, but the music is far too loud for Laura to hear it from several feet away. The bartender turns her back to her as she grabs at a broom and searches for a dustpan. Laura is bombarded with a blitzkrieg of flashes of horrible images and sounds. Her daughters weeping, choking, and bleeding. Gabe coughing up blood. She shakes her head hard, and the pull shows her the hallway again, beckoning her to move toward it. Laura wants to fight it, searching for another way to rid herself of the dirt that the pull flings in her face. Following the pull to stop the images is a tempting relief, but freedom from its treachery is currently more appealing. More images smack her mind of Gabe lacerated and in a bag and two smaller bags with their own atrocities inside. Then, the play begins. Her girls are naked, pleading, and whimpering.

"Why did you leave us, mommy? If you were there, you could've helped us," holding up their arms to clearly reveal their beaten bodies, "Look at what they did to us. Look, mommy! Why didn't you care?"

The words sting, and her stomach tightens. Her chest leans forward, and her neck throbs as if she will vomit. Her eyes are rolled backward, only showing the very bottom of her irises. Everyone around her is still focused on the stage and the music. Demure is making her way around the bar with the dustpan and broom. She notices Laura's peculiar position and immediately assumes that it is of a person who is about to purge herself of the abundance of alcohol that she has consumed. She quickens her step in the direction of Laura. A shove to the bathroom can save her a terrible mess.

The pull flashes the image of the hallway once again. Having no desire to hear her children say things far worse than anything they said during their lives, she concedes to go to the hallway. Her eyes open, and she sees the dreaded doorway as an escape from the nightmares and images.

Demure glances to the stage as she walks toward Laura and the broken bottle. The guitarist and the bass player exchange smirks and glancing kicks at each other as they speed through the song's bridge into the final chorus. The smirking is contagious as the crowd is elated in watching the performance. When she looks back to Laura, she is gone.

Laura can smell the stench of an unsanitary bathroom as she enters the hallway. The first door that she passes is the one labeled 'sacks'. Spilled beer, bodily fluids, or an overflowing toilet fuel a thin stream that creeps under the door and into the hallway. Laura quickly steps past it to the next door. Opening it, she recognizes that the bathroom is exactly the same, except the stalls have been painted black, and the walls are now purple. In her day, everything was off-white. The grime around the sink and mirrors appears to be the same. There are two stalls. She sees two pairs of feet under the panel of one stall. The two pairs of shoes are facing each other. The pull immediately screams for her to rush toward it. With the shrill sound of her daughters' cries still fresh in her eardrums, she steps toward the stall. A mirror is to her left on the wall above the sink. One of the faucets still runs. Possibly, it was left running when someone was abruptly pulled away from it while washing her hands. The temptation remains for her to stare at the mirror and see if she can knock herself out again. Maybe if she can hold her stare long enough, it will knock her out of this world altogether. The curiosity is intriguing; the thought of possible escape is tantalizing, but the desire to spare herself more cutting images of her family is more immediately pressing.

There is little sound in the bathroom save the running water and the echo of the live music filtering its way through the opening to the hallway, down the hall itself, and through the closed door to the bathroom. Laura keeps her steps quiet, and there is no one else in the small lavatory except for the two in the stall. She can hear some movement, and a soft sound that could be crying or moaning. The pull jumps up and down on her back, practically shoving her toward the stall door. Her hand slips over the top of the door, and she shoves it forcefully inward. A slide lock and its screws rip out of the stall and clang to the decrepit tile floor. The door smacks firmly into the back of a body.

"What the—" screeches a voice squealing in discomfort from within the stall.

Laura's hand wraps around his mouth before he can reach the profane portion of his sentence. She drags him roughly out of the stall, ripping the door off its top hinge. His heels are the only part of him touching the floor as they move. His arms begin to swing wildly behind him. A few blows glance at her legs, but she feels nothing more than a slight pressure. Looking to the other body in the stall, Laura sees streaks of eye makeup running down both cheeks, smeared lipstick, and a shirt that has been stretched and torn. Passionate moaning is no longer a possible answer for the unexplained sound.

Grabbing his jaw tightly, she smacks his forehead down on the rim of the sink. The sink is not attached firmly to the wall, and it wobbles from the pressure. She holds his head down tightly enough so he cannot move. He struggles to speak, and saliva pops out of his mouth and onto his face. Rabid is his mind and his appearance. He cannot see his attacker, but nails dig into the side of his face, causing him to assume it is female, which increases his rage. Meelynn's eyes in the stall grow wide in confusion and relief, unsure if it is Deus ex Machina or simply a larger predator nabbing the shark that was upon her. Is she safe from what has attacked her attacker? She is completely uncertain. But, relief is inside her, even if temporarily.

Mutters and curses slop out of his mouth between his gasps for breath. As she holds his head to the porcelain, she is unsure of what she is supposed to do next. The previous urge to shove the stall door open and drag him out was strong and clear. She feels as if the pull wants her to kill him. To spill more blood. To unleash more carnage. But, she has no desire to do anything, much less kill someone, and she does not feel enough pressure for her to move further in this attack. She considers looking now into the mirror just above the sink and trying to knock herself out again. The pull flashes a vision of Gabe into her mind. He is sitting on the couch smiling at her. It is an image that she would frequently see after dinner in the late evening. His smile is slightly exaggerated, not quite natural; the peaks of the corners of his mouth are just a bit too high and too pointy. She tries to brace herself for whatever is about to happen, since she cannot get away from something that is inside her. As the image of Gabe smiles, blood patterns begin oozing through his clothing. A bloody fingernail impression is the first to emerge as its crimson outline soaks through his shirtsleeve. A stream of blood runs out of the corner of his mouth, down to his slightly pointed chin, and slides down his neck. His pupils swim around his eyes as if no longer connected. This image causes her own eyes to roll backward again, and her hand slips off the inebriated mandible that she was holding to the sink. Drunken knees smack the tile floor, and it takes a moment for him to realize that he is no longer bound.

Laura stumbles as she sees knife wounds forming and draining her husband of his life. Meelynn panics in the stall, as she knows what type of beast is loose and that he has a taste for her. Furthermore, her mysterious buffer is now meandering and looking like she will drift into a seizure or completely black out. The face of the grizzled beast turns from panic and surprise to fury and hatred.

The sounds of the band come to a screeching halt as the song ends on a fast, harshly bent note on the guitar and bass, accented by a vocal growl and a hard cymbal hit. The quieter yet whooshing sound of the crowd cheering heartily washes over the room. The change in sound reminds Chris that he is free and can act to change his own situation. A choppy rise to unsteady feet. A push off the sink toward Laura. A grunt is followed by movement. Something whizzes past the side of Laura's head, sending a brush of wind into her ear. Her focus is still inward, and she clumsily shifts her weight from one foot to the other trying to remain standing as the horror show continues inside of her. Another rush of movement is followed by a reverberating thud. The sickening sound of bone crashing upon bone only sounds like part of the soundtrack to the nightmare playing in her mind, but it echoes through the small bathroom and not just inside of her. She feels pressure upon her head, but her eyes remain rolled backward.

The drunk hops around holding his right fist in his left hand. Recoiling, he wheezes as if someone had knocked the wind out of him or if he had stuck his hand into an arctic lake. Meelynn, who has sunken down to sitting on the toilet seat and is watching on intently, would have laughed at his lumbering misfortune if she were not so desperately afraid that her protector might fall. Meelynn has lived her young adult life as a pacifist, but right now she wishes for nothing less than Laura to beat Chris unconscious so she can escape the abuse that started a minute or two before her defender broke into the over-occupied stall.

Chris sees Meelynn eagerly looking on as he spins in circles, clutching his fist in pain and frustration. The band kicks into a new song with a heavy, fast, deep-sounding groove. He points his uninjured hand at the girl in the broken stall as if to say he'll be coming for her soon enough.

Lyrics from the song find their way into the air of the tiny, tiled room.

"I feel like my soul's bleeding to gray…Nighttime looks like day…"

Light begins to fire in Laura's head, bringing an end to the pull's sadistic scene of her suffering husband.

"…Wish I could make my choice…If I could only hear one voice…"

Her eyes open and the room comes into focus. A fist flies at high velocity toward her face. Her hand flings upward, quickly catching the fist and stopping its motion three inches before her left eye. Chris stares at her, shocked at the powerful action. Laura has always had speed, but this was fast even for her. Her aerobics classes and her years of Jujitsu in her teens made her quick, but she has never had the strength to cleanly catch the fist of a man outweighing her by eighty-seven pounds. She squeezes his hand with all of the anger that she has felt during the pull's most recent movie.

More lyrics push their way into the room, "…Owe one more but got none left…Wait for me, I'll come out soon…If you run, it'll chase after you…"

Chris drops to his knees as she clenches more tightly on his fist, sending shocks of pain up his forearm. Meelynn stares on silently from the toilet. The rage rushing through Laura's eyes is a pulse being shot out by the pull. The most recent memory was a surefire way to boil Laura's temperature up to a murderous high. Injecting her full of the desire to kill, the pull knew she would be aching to unleash it on anyone attacking her, even if her real desire is to tear apart the pull itself. The song's chorus is heard in the bathroom.

"Can't you see…you're pulling me…down…down…down?
Can't you see…you're falling with me…down…down…down?"

Drunken tears roll out of bloodshot eyes, and indecipherable high-pitched jumble streams out of his mouth. Laura is aware that she has been pushed into doing exactly what the pull wants her to do. She can't overcome the ravenous rage that has been stirred up inside her, yet she does not want to go where it is dragging her. If she does not do the pull's will, the haunting, terrorizing images will no doubt become worse. But, she cannot stomach the idea of being the pull's executioner for the foreseeable future. She knows she is in for torment on either path. As she watches the excruciating expressions on Chris's face, she has an idea. One that she embraces quickly.

She grabs Chris's shirt with her right hand and yanks him onto his feet, still holding his right fist in her left hand. She slams her forehead onto his face with all the force that she can muster. Cartilage crushes and sanguine runs out of his nose. She immediately glances to the mirror as his unconscious body drops to the ground. Flipping her hair out of her face, she stares at her reflection. The swirling pupils speed up exponentially and swell from the excitement. She feels faint and strains to keep herself upright and conscious.

Lyrics intrude again, "No one said 'love's an easy ride'
Are you sure you'll last the night?"

To escape the rage tonight, she has to take one powerful hit from the mirror before the pull can concoct some other torture for her to endure. Images of her daughters swirl around her mind as she struggles to hold her focus on her own reflected eyes. The pull's screaming is enough to deafen her. Her hands grasp at the unstable sink trying to hold herself upright. The sink bends further and further downward as she holds herself longer. Her knees quiver, and her mind frosts over as her consciousness starts to slip away. Her pupils twirl and flash. The pull flings images to her that are too vile to describe outside of hell. She lets the sights burn into her, and she holds to the mirror for a moment longer. The spinning of her pupils is more intense than it has been since she was atop Daisy. A harsh flash flickers in her eyes, and they close as she falls to the ground. The back of her head smacks Chris's mouth, striking blood and sending three of his teeth down his throat with a cough and a grunt. After the grunt, his body does not move except for the subtle rising and falling of his chest in respiration. Laura's mind flows through unholy rivers navigated by the pull, who is now completely furious. One side of her lips is held downward in suffering and the other half smirks in belligerence. Within two minutes of the pull's show time, the smirk fades away, and all of her mouth appears to be in discomfort.

The music continues, "So much of me they misunderstand,
The whole world tries to tie two hands."

Meelynn has stared at Chris's still body since he fell to the ground. She still stares over the two of them. A hideous pile. Some of Chris's blood spattered Laura's face upon the earlier contact. It is more of a morbid sight than Meelynn has ever wanted to see despite her fascination with horror movies. Seeing gore outside of the enclosed TV screen gives it an entirely different feeling. Flee instinct builds. Finally, she feels that she can safely get away. She has been awaiting this moment since the stall door was broken open by the woman who now lies on the floor with her head atop the monster with a grizzled face.

As she steps toward the exit, she glances at Laura, motionless on the floor. Guilt and gratitude pour over Meelynn as she looks at her fallen intercessor. She thinks of how the beast will respond when he wakes up, and she knows she has to do something. She runs out of the bathroom as fast as she can and down the hallway. She almost slips when she hits the unclean stream coming from under the other door. She sees a red that is as unnatural as hellfire, and that is exactly for what she was searching.

"Hey!" screams Meelynn, trying to be heard over the loud music and searching for the name of the bartender. She knows she has heard it before; everyone knows her. She leans over the bar directly in front of the master of libations. "Demure! Demure! Help! Quick!"

Each of Meelynn's words was said with unintentional rhythm as she took in a deep breath between each. The bartender puts down the bottle of rum that she was pouring into a small glass. She turns and sees the running eye makeup, the lipstick, and the mangled clothing.

"Bathroom. Now! Please," insists Meelynn.

Demure nods and climbs directly over the bar to get to her. Her knees are moistened by spilled alcohol as she slides herself across it. Her heels cause her ankles to buckle as they land on the floor. Demure grabs Meelynn's hand, and they rush to the bathroom.

Meelynn steps over the unclean stream at the beginning of the hallway, but Demure slides a few inches when she crosses the slick. The crudely labeled door is flung open, and Laura still lies with her head atop Chris. Meelynn wants to explain the unbelievable things that she has witnessed, especially the eyes of the woman lying on the floor, but she has no idea what words contain that much power or where one even begins to explain something like what she has seen.

Demure says, turning to the girl whose hand is now trembling, "I'll stay here and watch him; you go get Gino—big guy at the door. Go! Fast!"

Meelynn almost smiles at the direction, and she darts out the door and out of Demure's sight. Glancing over the bodies on the ground, Demure thinks of all the times she has seen people carried out of this place. Some were drunk, some had overdosed, some were knocked out, some didn't have enough money to pay for their drink order, and some were dragged out for being too rowdy. None of the memories are pleasant, not even the ones of people whom she was glad to see leave. This is not even the first time that a guy has had to be dragged out of the wrong bathroom. Drifting back to her earlier thoughts on her place in life, she wonders why she has stayed here through all of these memories.

She steps toward the sink quietly and looks over the two bodies. Chris's face is a mess, and she is sure that he deserves it. But, she is not finding any pleasure in looking at it. Moving her eyes over Laura, she cannot see any signs of damage. Her skin looks pale. She glances over the white streak in Laura's hair and marvels at it for a moment. She has taken many fashion adventures in her time, but a white streak down the just-to-the-side-of-center of her hair is one that she has never even considered. Suddenly, Laura's face twitches as if having a dreadful dream. It startles Demure. Laura's eyebrows wriggle in discomfort, and Demure wonders what could be running through her head. There are Chris's blood spatters on her face from her contact with his nose, but there are no wounds, no red spots. An eerie feeling slinks down the back of Demure's neck, as she still cannot see any damage on the woman on the floor. She looks at Laura's knuckles, and they appear to be unharmed. Looking back to Chris's face and his busted right hand, she knows something is missing. People don't get knocked out without having the bump to prove it, and people don't knock other people out with their bare hands without at least having a sore fist from delivering the blow. Chris has his marks, but there is something about Laura that she just cannot see.

Laura's leg kicks. It touches the top of Demure's foot at an uncovered part of her heeled shoes. Cold shoots through her foot. Disturbing. Chilling. Laura's other leg kicks in a quick, jerking motion. Demure wants for Gino to enter the room more than she ever has before. Laura's eyes begin to flicker, and she sees flames reaching down toward her face. Straining her vision to focus, she sees two long, curly, red bangs hanging down at her and a face that she recognizes as the bartender. Laura feels that her head is propped up on something of which she has a strong urge to remove herself. She slides her body onto its side, and her head moves off Chris and smacks the floor. Demure flinches; Laura does not blink.

Rolling her head backward to see on what she was resting, she sees Chris, bloody and beaten. She glances upward toward the mirror on the wall, and the events leading up to her position on the floor all come back to her. She grabs the sink and pulls herself up to a standing position. She looks at Demure standing two feet from her, open-mouthed and silent. Past the fire-haired drink mixer, she sees the broken stall door hanging crookedly in its opening. Memories of the inside of the stall come back to her. She kicks Chris with force in his ribs. The blow stirs up the pull. The injured drunk coughs at the strike, and the pull howls for more. Laura shuts her eyes, trying to silence the pleading for violence. Her kick was about an abused girl, not gluttonous bloodlust. Her brows beat down at her eyes in anguish as the familiar parade of the pull's images beleaguer her.

Demure watches the woman struggle with something that she cannot see. Pity breeds in her. Yet, she cannot think of a thing to say. The cold, accidental brush of Laura's leg across the top of her foot is still too much for her to consider reaching out to touch her. Laura's internal struggle seems to be enough to knock her unconscious again. Demure can see it on her face and knows she has to interrupt in some way.

"Hey, did you break that bottle because of him?"

Laura's eyes open and stare at Demure.

Demure looks to the ground and back at Laura, "The bottle at the bar—did you break it because of him?"

Laura continues to stare, but hoarsely whispers, "It was another nightmare, red."

Demure nods her head in acknowledgement. Laura glances down at the human wreckage by her feet. Her nose wrinkles in disgust, and the pull's demands wail within her. As the painful pictures fly around her head, she decides she had better make her way out of the bar while she still can. She steps over the sad, still body below her and toward the door. As her hand grabs the handle, she looks back to the bartender who has been watching her every move.

Laura glances to Chris on the floor and then back to the woman, and says, "Get out of this place."

The door opens, Laura disappears into the dank hallway, and the bartender is alone in the bathroom with a beaten animal lying on the floor of a room in which he does not belong. Her question has been answered. Granted, it is not through a medium in which she was expecting or even would have wanted, but her query has been specifically answered by one who had no idea that she even posed a question earlier in the evening.

The night spreads the disease of bad recollections as Demure thinks of times in the past when she has had to deal with ill-tempered drunks, particularly the ones with sex on the mind. Just as her fears start to rise, the door swings open, and in its passageway is a doorfull of Gino, who completely blocks the view of Meelynn following closely behind him.

"Did he hurt Laura?" Gino asks with an uncertain and troubled expression.

"Not exactly."

Gino thinks about her response for a moment and then smiles, "Laura took him down?" He grins widely, "She always was a tough one."

He slowly looks over Meelynn's disheveled appearance, and the reality dawns late on him.

Placing his hand on her tiny shoulder, he asks, "Are you okay?"

Meelynn's eyes run, but she nods her head in affirmation. Demure steps closer to the girl and rests the damp little face on her shoulder. Gino pushes out his bottom lip and looks at the lump of flesh on the ground that is now wheezing unevenly in his sleep.

Speaking softly as he always does to Demure, he offers, "Why don't you take her in the back, Dem? Call the police. And, I'll drag this piece a garbage outside."

A block away on streets that are far too chilly for this time of year, Laura tries to mind where she is walking, but the pull provides a constant, agonizing distraction. Its anger has grown over her refusal to excise Chris's life from his body. As she walks, her insides are scorched. Her mind festers amidst familiar troubling sights. She becomes irate with Chris for being a drunken idiot. Were he not such an abusive and horrible human being, the pull could not have pushed her so hard. She is not sure if she could restrain herself any longer if she were looking at him presently. Yet, part of her still finds a small strength in the fact that she defied the pull, although she is being made to pay for it now.

It seems to take her far too long to cover the distance of another block. She wonders what kind of existence she has been pushed into. What will her life be like if she is going to be made to suffer this much every time she fights the pull? And, what would be her alternative? Follow the guidance of the pull. Commit an unnumbered amount of terrible deeds for eternity. She can't die, but she can be made to suffer. She thinks of her family in the after, and she wishes deeply to join them. At this level of misery, she would accept nearly any offer to leave this life and fly to them. She wonders if the pull knows of her desperation, and if it will offer her some tremendously cruel task to complete in order to reach her family. Or, maybe for all of its torturous powers, it has no authority to send her there. Possibly, all of its powers lie in worldly temptation, and her desire resides outside of its domain. But, even then, it has proven to be treacherous, and maybe it will lie and offer a promise that it has no power to fulfill in order to make her do its bidding.

Her feet become heavier with every passed building. She has become momentarily deaf to all outside sounds; the screeching of the pull has consumed her auditory abilities. She struggles to keep her eyes open to see where she is headed. She walks on instinct, not entirely knowing her destination. She knows she is walking away from the bar and the person the pull wants her to destroy, and that is good enough for now. She has the feeling that she is headed to more peaceful surroundings, but she is unaware of exactly where she is going or why she even believes it will offer any relief.

She sees Gabe, Daniella, and Susanna, but she also sees three teenagers who all die in her hands. Even the last three bring her little relief. Her feeling of justice and retribution is smothered by the terrible reality of her current existence. She has killed her family's killers, but in the process she may have removed herself from her loved ones for all of the afterlife. In essence, they took her family away for this short life, but maybe she has taken them away from herself for all eternity. The thought sickens her. Remembering her failed attempts to leave this world pulls her further down into despair, as she realizes she is helplessly trapped. Hope seems naïve.

Her eyes close at the pull's increasing attacks, and she stumbles along blindly. When she opens her eyes, she is further away; her pace has quickened in response to the escalating inner torment. She is so tired of fighting the visions that she considers dropping to the ground in an alleyway and allowing the pull to consume her, even if she would lose herself in the process. But, a need to keep going, a desire to still look for a way to get to her family, and a survival instinct keep her trudging on, despite her fatigue and bleak future.

The church is in sight. She has had no idea this was where her feet were leading her, but it feels like the finish line. She approaches with heavy tread. The tumult inside of her is clamoring for her to pass out before she reaches the building. She remembers the man that she saw briefly during the daylight hours. The refuge of the church alley seems less safe, but she knows she will be lucky to reach it, much less venture to another location. Her foot catches the curb in front of the church, almost making her crash to the sidewalk. Her vision catches the mangled earth that broke her fall two nights before. Even the sidewalk rejected her being a part of it when it flung her to the church step. This thought slips through the battlefront of her mind, and, even though she wants no part of this world, it is not a comforting sentiment.

The pull lunges at her, noticing the momentary weakness. It places Susanna, her youngest, screaming and crying just out of her reach. The little voice pleads for her mother to hold her. In her mind, Laura stretches her arms until they ache, but she can't touch her suffering girl. The pleading escalates, and she feels that she can fight no longer. Allowing herself to fall into the abyss sounds like relief. Her eyes open; she is at the top of the fence to the alley. Lost within the pull's performance, she had no idea that she was in such a position. She can see her imprint in the mud reflected very slightly in the moonlight. She would love to fall back into that earthy mold of her body. Whether the pull tortures her incessantly or if she is given some reprieve by her proximity to the church, she does not care. Her resistance is taxed, and her emotions are charred; either situation will not require her to travail defiantly. So, she is willing to accept either. Her mind pulls her back to introspection with the screeching of Susanna. Laura catches a glimpse of a teenage body sliding atop her child. Her jaw clenches, eyes roll back, legs lose their rigidity, and she falls sideways and forward toward the side church wall. Her head smacks the brick; one corner of her mouth resumes its smile while its counterpart still dives downward at the piercing cries of her daughter. Her body smashes into the soft earth in a tangled mess. An arm is bent backwards, her neck is at a dangerous angle, and a knee is impossibly twisted with its attached foot touching the wall of the church. Her face is as expressionless as the brick.

Chapter XXX

Walking up to the building with palm trees along its entrance, he notices how out of place the tropical timber is in Riverview. Then he thinks of the girl that lounges beyond the long, narrow window on the second floor; exotic yet welcoming, eloquent yet free of pretense, soft yet determined, beautiful yet smart, discerning yet loving—she is far more out of her environment being in this bleak city than the palm trees growing in a former marshland.

He makes his way up the staircase. The wooden steps bend in the middle at each footfall, having been weakened by a persistent ceiling leak. He has nudged her on several occasions to move to a different area of town, one with a lower crime rate, better-kept apartments, and trees that are indigenous to the region. But, this is the neighborhood in which she grew up, and it would take an amazing offer to get her to leave it.

The window at the top of the stairwell has no covering, and the rising sun can be seen breaking over the buildings across the street and highlighting the derisory palm limbs with a pinkish pre-rooster hue. It is normally a sight that would only grate on him as a sign that he has missed one more night of sleep and has a long day ahead, but, on this morning, it makes him smile, despite the unpleasant task before him.

It is just like the city to lump three welfare funerals into one day. Taking into account that these three teenagers were friends, it is very inconsiderate to anyone who knew them for the city to schedule all three services on the same day. But, having been to government paid funerals in the past, Andarus is well aware that there may not be many attending any of the services anyway.

The pink breaking over the top of the church and invading her alley warms her eyes awake. Her foot is still bent awkwardly against the brick of the modern basilica. And, as she takes in the rising faded fuchsia that she does not want to see, her only thought revolves around the absence of the pull. She remembers the night before, and its rage at her defiance. How it could have left her alone for a night is beyond her. Not that her dreams were anything nice, but at least they were her own fears and regrets in her head, not those of a twisted force bent on singeing her sadistically. She feels just as tired and drained of energy and life as she had when she fell from the top of the iron gate, but her mind is clearer, full of her own emotions and free of the clutter of an outside presence. Although she knows it will be brief and she cannot relax, she wonders what has kept it away from her at all. When she fell, she had no strength left to fight; she surely thought the pull would finally wind her back inside of herself, imploding her body into a nothing, yanking her into hell.

She lowers her vision from the ascending light to the door at the end of the alley. It is ajar. It is true that she has not paid much attention to her surroundings during most of her recent bizarre occurrences, focused far more on the dissonance in her head than on her environs, but she is quite certain that that door has never before been left open. The urge for her to get up and investigate the unclosed entrance makes her aware of her contorted body position. Although instances of it are becoming more and more common, she is amazed that her body is in such a shape yet she feels no pain, but only heavy pressure. She should be unable to move, possibly paralyzed, and likely to have brain damage from the head trauma on the bricks, yet she slowly untwists herself into a standing homo sapien position. As she nears the door, the immediate space behind it is dark, but she sees a light has been left on not far past it.

Her internal tormentor has awoken itself and whirrs around her mind, pleading with her not to enter the doorway. *You don't belong in there. This is the house of the one who has done this to you. As if you would be welcome there anyway. You're too stained to walk through this door. You are not welcome.*

She looks to the handle of the door, and there is a tiny note attached. It reads, "Welcome."

At this, the pull's tone hisses much like a snake, and its attack is so intense that it is a jumbled mess, completely indecipherable to Laura. She nudges the door with two knuckles on her right hand, and she steps into the darkness with her eyes on the light not far ahead. The tiny, dark room just past the door appears to be some type of a supply room. She can make out the vague shapes of a mop and broom leaning against the wall near a shelf with cleaning supplies. There is a doorway that leads to another room; this is from where the light is entering the small chamber. She walks toward it, and sees another note attached to the wall by the opening.

Her eyes strain to read the letters in the darkness before she is quite close enough to see it clearly. It says, "Glad you came inside. There is a shower in the bathroom in the next room. Feel free to use it. PS—There are bags of donated clothing near the door to the bathroom."

He has been on the job a long time, but three closed-casket funerals are a daunting burden for even Andarus. At least this is one discomfort that he will not have to endure alone. The woman in the bedroom, which is down a short hall from the living room in which he sits, finishes readying herself for the day. He is not used to waiting for her; she has always been prepared, professional, and prompt. But after all, his arrival this morning was earlier than expected by at least a quarter of an hour, so she is not truly tardy.

He sits on her futon and rests his arm on the cool, shiny, black metal of the armrest. Scanning over scenery as one waiting inevitably does, he becomes inordinately interested in every element of the décor. Each choice and placement reflects elements of her personality, and his mind roams over them. For Andarus, it is much like an archeologist venturing into a lost temple of which he has studied its history in great detail but has never seen in person. Every corner validates or disproves a theory. The apartment is adorned modestly but stylishly; given her meager salary and flare for fashion, this is no surprise to him. There are prints of classical artwork next to illustrations that she no doubt found at a local art show. A floor furnace is near the wall opposite him. Its gas pipe juts out of an unevenly cut hole in the wooden floor. There is a pair of pliers on the ground near the antique heating unit, no doubt for turning the ancient gas knob on and off. A small hole on the side of the unit has some flame scarring surrounding it from years of use. Watching with dried and burning eyes, he feels an attachment to the archaic floor furnace.

Perpendicular to the sofa is a wall that consists mostly of large windows with a long, narrow desk in front of it. After noticing a slight flicker in the blinds, he discovers that a small piece of one of the windowpanes is missing, allowing wisps of outside breeze to invade her domain and rattle her Venetian visors that shield her from the world. Upon her desk is her sleek computer. Near the computer is an empty vase with a thin, shiny rim of reflected sunlight around its tip, and the rest of the flower receptacle is filled with shadow and a thin layer of dust.

Most of the room's color comes from the hundreds of books that line her walls. Bookcases cover a large portion of the wall space, and a simple shelf that she made herself lines the top of the wall where it meets the ceiling, holding mostly books that she has read long ago. The spines of the books are of various colors and differing degrees of creasing, and the evolving styles of type font define in what time period the book was pressed. He scales over the titles that range in genre from literary to fantasy to detective. There are a few classics, but most of the books seem to be stories that she sought out for herself—ones that could form her own unique base of reference and create an uncommon environment in which her imagination could live. He would like to read them all to better understand the world underneath her eyes, but he knows he does not have the time. Despite his double major in English and criminology, the depth of her reading catalogue is quite intimidating. Even if he tried to read one of the books when a bout with insomnia would threaten to consume an entire night's sleep, he knows his mind would not let him focus enough to absorb the text or even to enjoy it.

Gentle sounds of a brush tapping a dresser, the closing of a canister of makeup, and other rustles of preparation sway from around her nearly shut door, through the hallway that he dares not step inside, and into the living room in which he waits. He notices there are no pictures in the room, save for one old frame. He knows who the woman must be, but the woman in the picture is a subject about which the girl in the room has sparsely spoken. He hears the old hinges on the bedroom door creak, and he knows she must be ready for him.

Outside the bathroom in the rear of a sanctuary, a man knows that she is nearly finished when he hears the squeak of the two knobs and the ceasing of the spatter of water that has been constant for about twelve minutes. As soon as he heard the water running, he came into the room that is used to store the collected supplies for the homeless, which also contains the door to bathroom, a door to the back rooms of the church, and the opening to the supply room and side alley exit. Now as the drone of droplets has ended, he is aware that his proximity has become very important. If he stands too close to the bathroom when she exits, he may appear to be perverse or intrusive. If he stands too far away in the building, she just might slip back outside before he can get her.

The shower door chirps as Laura pulls it open. Washing the blood and dirt from her body was not as refreshing as one might think. It was a layer of her experiences. Even though she did not want them, they were a proof that she had done what she set out to do; they were a receipt, a redemption voucher. The grime was what she thought would be her ticket out. Now it has run down tiny holes at the bottom of the shower, trickling onto a smaller world in the same way the rain fell upon and drenched her every move soon after she stepped into a grungy motel parking lot.

The tiny bathroom is decorated in a very minimalist, utilitarian fashion. The walls are plain white with no pictures or adornments except for a solitary crucifix near the door. The towels underneath the sink are white cotton, and there are only two sets of washcloths and towels. Above the sink is a small, rectangular mirror. She is tempted to grapple with her reflection again, but she thinks better of it and decides to leave the sanctuary as fast as possible. Despite how insistently the pull was trying to keep her out of here earlier, she does not feel comfortable inside the back rooms of the church. Even though it is the opposite of where her tormentor wants her to be, she does not view it as the reverse of torment.

Except for the despair in her eyes and in the expression on her face, her body looks clean. Her clothes, however, are hopelessly stained. She holds her jeans in her hands, remembering well where she pressed the deep crimson stains into the knees of the black denim. She recalls the imprint of the jeans on the carpet below them in her former home and how they looked like wing prints, blood angels. Her eyes scale the walls of the tiny room. She feels even more out of place knowing that she is in the rear of a church and thinking of the impressions that she has pushed into the world. Looking at the sweatpants and faded t-shirt, which she had earlier pulled out of the bags near the door to the bathroom, she now does not think she can put them on.

Outside of the door, the man hears a sound coming from inside of the church itself. It is the familiar thud of the heavy door at the front of the building pulling itself shut. He raises his hand to knock at the bathroom door and opens his mouth to speak, but he turns from it and makes his way through the back of the church and the sacristy to the front of the altar. At which, he sees Mrs. Simmons, one of his parishioners, whose face pleads for counsel.

Andarus stares down at a man with his hand wrapped in gauze, and a bandage over the left side of his face. His nose is raw and has been busted recently, and his lips have both been split open. This pathetic image is symbolic of the day for Andarus. The first funeral was attended by the immediate family and some cousins of Simon Murdstone, no more than eleven or twelve people. Mrs. Andrews and Mrs. Guess arrived and paid their respects at the wake of both boys, but they did not stay long. A loud comment about how did they have the nerve to show up after they kicked the boys out of school prompted the two ladies to exit before the morbid scene turned uglier. Edward Legree's funeral followed second with no one present at his burial except for Andarus and Irene. Earlier at Edward's wake, his mother and a few relatives were present, but none of them stayed for the actual funeral. They were discussing going out to eat at a local buffet when they walked out of the building. Andarus heard Ed's mother saying something along the lines of "This's all been so horrible I jus' cain't bring mahself to see 'im lowered inta tha earth." Whether those were the exact words or not, those are the ones that are going to live in his head, festering there for far longer than he would like. The current funeral for one Daisy Slykovsky is an equally sad affair. Her father is the beaten mess sitting in a folding chair not far from her coffin. He smells of alcohol and a long night. The knot of his tie does not reach the top of his collar, which is unbuttoned, by several inches, and it hangs crookedly to the left side of his shirt. Mrs. Andrews and Mrs. Guess have reappeared from their retreat to be present at Daisy's funeral, with the secretary sobbing incessantly. The only other two people at her funeral are Jeff, the guy whose car was stolen by Laura, and a girl whose hand he holds tightly in his.

Her funeral service started on time but was stopped quickly and delayed as her father excused himself to vomit. Upon his return, he demanded the folding chair in which he now sits. As the minister speaks, Mr.

Slykovsky's head bounces up and down, struggling to keep his eyes open. As Andarus watches the man in the chair, pity and disgust wrestle inside of him, each grappling for supremacy. As the man belches aloud, pity's shoulders are pinned to the ground.

Seventeen minutes later, as they are driving out of the funeral home/cemetery, Andarus sees a sign with the name of the funeral parlor and a slogan beneath it that reads "We're Always Here for You". His mind stays with that slogan for a spell.

"Irene, don't you think that that sign is a bit strange?"

"Which one, boss man, the one that said 'We'll Always Be Here for You?'"

"Yeah, something like that. Don't you think that it is an awkward thing for people to read as they're leaving a funeral—after having just buried a loved one?"

"Hmm," she hums in response, "Hadn't really thought about it, but, yeah, it is kind of a creepy sentiment to think that they're waiting for you, isn't it?"

"Irene, we need to talk with Jeff and find out what he was doing here. Besides, forensics should be nearly finished with his car soon; I'm sure he's dying to get it back."

"Yeah, sounds reasonable. Should find out what is his connection to Daisy. Friends? Relatives? Ex-girlfriend? Could somehow be relevant...He could easily have been the last person to see Laura before the murder. He was interviewed the evening of the carjacking, but not by us."

"And, Daisy's dad's been in a fight recently. Obviously. We need to find out what happened to him."

"Yeah, we do. I don't think he had anything to do with Daisy's death, but it is awfully suspicious. He does have a history of abusing her, albeit documented only by the opinion of Mrs. Andrews and his landlord. But, technically, we need to consider him a suspect."

The car bounces as they roll down the curb and onto the street. A question bounces inside Irene too, although she has refrained from asking it thus far.

"Andarus?"

"Yeah."

"I-uh, have to ask you something."

"Okay, shoot," with trepidation at her easing into the question.

"Did you see Mrs. Bonney there today?"

Andarus smirks bashfully, "You saw me looking over my shoulder, didn't you?"

"Only because I was looking over mine," she explains, and then pushing the question, "So, did you see her, Paul?"

Glancing from the road to her, "No, of course not. You didn't see her, did you?"

"No, I didn't see her, although I was looking. I mean, we both knew it would be a possibility that she might show up."

"And, you didn't think I'd tell you?"

"Well," Irene starts, "I just wanted to make sure. You know, a lot has been going on lately…and there was the incident at her family's funeral."

"Irene, I wouldn't withhold anything that would put you in danger. Laura being around would have been dangerous. I'm onboard with trying to find her whether I think she is justified or not; we still need to make sure this thing is over and give people some closure if we can. But, no, I haven't seen Laura anywhere outside of my head since she was in the office the night that you—the night that you saw her."

Her hand slides into her jeans pocket as her eyes squint at the noon sun beaming into the alley. The roughness of the jeans does not register on her knuckles, but her distain for the brilliance of midday does score in her brain. Her irritation for the light might be its brightness against her eyes that do not want to see, or it might be that the taunting returned to her as soon as she stepped out of the sanctuary and into the illuminated alley.

The day has been like the others, miserable. The only variance is that she wandered the streets with the voice battering her mind the entire time, instead of holing away in the alley until the sun was gone. She was as lost as a child exploring the unknown in the midst of the night. Her lifeless appearance mocked the daylight as much as its intrusive rays vexed her, but the sunlight surrounded her like water around a creature in the ocean; she was but one, and it was a legion of innumerable particles.

Her daily torment had one new facet. She repeatedly saw the beaten face on the floor of the bathroom waking up, snarling at her, and glaring at the trembling girl in the stall. The pull tried to plant hatred into her toxic soul hoping for it to take root. If nothing was going to penetrate her skin from the outside, it decided to focus its efforts on piercing her from the inside out. She struggled to dispose of the thoughts as they would arrive, visions of silencing his repugnant, grunting mouth, smashing his unwelcome and probing fingers, and shutting his eyes that only see malice. The bitter taste of the violent thoughts made her feel sour, yet it tugged at her like an addiction, infecting her with the cruel desire, pushing her to answer the call, scratch the itch, and rid herself of its needful beckoning for at least a little while. But, she held it as far from herself as she could. Thinking of anything except her family still seemed deviant to her. So, she shoved the thoughts of everything else away as fast as she was able and tried to focus on the faces of the three she missed.

The movements of the people glancing in store windows or looking down at the sidewalk just ahead of their feet; cars humming, exhaling, and passing in a blur in the street; and random, busy sounds surrounding her were a wind that she could not feel. The energy of the street movement was the marrow of the street. Bags in hurried hands, the smell of food drifting out opening doors, feet stomping the sidewalk; it energizes everything within her sight. But, none of it touched her in her hours of walking; all of the world's actions amount to little more than an undetectable breeze in a wasteland, except for two small particles in its stream that caught her attention. The first was a woman holding her daughter's hand with shared excitement as they moved in a gait close to a skip down the sidewalk and into a dress shop. The only other speck of dust to strike her eye as it swirled in the wind was a creature in a pickup truck. The truck was burly and loud. Dents spotted its side and caused an aberration in the stream of light shining off it. The dents were isolated spots, most of them too pinpoint and far too high up for another vehicle to have caused the damage. But, the face grimacing behind the wheel was what struck her. Behind bandages and bruises she saw a face from the previous night and a fragment from what seemed to be a rainy alley dream ten evenings before. It was a face that had been appearing before her repulsed mind all afternoon. She wondered if it was him, or if it was an innocent man who had done no wrong except having a doppelganger who preys on the inexperienced at local dives. However, the pull screamed inside her at the sight of him, urging her to lunge at the window of the battered truck paused at the intersection. The density of its demanding voice made her vision bounce. Then, the truck chugged forward, and it slowly disappeared from her sight. The pull's initial rage lessened, yet it held a steady flow of variations on its familiar flammable images.

Unlike the concert to catch Daisy or the raucous night on Cellar Street, many people noticed the blood stains on her clothes. Bent necks and bewildered eyebrows scanned over her suspicious spots, but they soon returned to the errand at hand, thinking it couldn't have been what it appeared to be.

"Andarus, what are we going to tell the chief to keep your job?"

Smirkingly, he says, "So, how are things with your dad?" throwing delirious eyes full of mischief at her in the seat next to him.

"That's not what I asked you."

"No, but, it's a topic that might result in a productive conversation."

"Seriously, Paul, we need to figure this out. Our last stunt bought us some time, but it also got the chief angry. We're not uncovering anything to help us catch Mrs. Bonney, and we don't have much time to fix this."

"Irene, we've hashed over this all day, well, in between burying juveniles; it's all I'll see when I try to sleep tonight. I assure you I'll spend my hours thinking over it; it is unavoidable," he pauses, and he sighs before he continues, "Let's talk about something else."

"All right," she says in an accepting whisper.

"So, how have things been since we went to see your dad?"

"Well, kinda strange, kinda the same old. He is still pretty grumpy with me, especially when I'm there by myself, which is the same as always.

But, lately he seems to be more irritable than usual. He'll be in a bad mood and picking at me with little comments, but then, when I go to leave, he'll get really quiet and fidgety." She hesitates, and Paul gives her space to choose the words to describe the conclusion that he has already drawn. "It's like when I was in high school choosing my own electives and activities, driving myself where I wanted to go, and working at a job for my own money. Before that, things weren't quite as strained between us. I think he felt like he had lost some control, and he resented me for it. He couldn't tell me not to do things for myself, or he would've been supporting me forever—which he didn't want either, but he sure didn't like losing his say-so over some things."

"Uh huh," interjects Andarus holding the conversational door open for her to continue.

"I think he is acting the same way now. He devours the paper every day; he has to know what's going on in this case—at least what the paper is reporting, and he can't tell me what to do. He can't dictate police procedure, but his daughter is in danger. He feels helpless. And…and, I think he's worried about me."

"I'm sure he is," he explains, "'Rene, he did tell me for us to be extra careful when we were leaving him the last time I went with you. He grabbed my arm as we were walking out and said it quietly. He must have told me because he didn't feel comfortable saying it to you."

Speaking meekly, she says, "He's always been that way. Could always tell me the harshest of things but never the important ones."

Andarus's head nods, wishing that he could think of something useful to say. Even more, he wishes that he felt free enough to reach out and grab her hand. The car shakes, absorbing shocks as it hits the partitions in the street, creating sounds at a repeating rhythm, counting the length of the void in conversation. It tolls the death of a missed opportunity.

Looking away from the road to her face, he sees her lower jaw sliding around in her mouth feeling for the right words.

"Do I…," creaks her timid voice, "Do I do that to you?"

His face squirms as he struggles to connect her question to the preceding conversation, "Do you do what, 'Rene?"

"When I fuss at you for not getting enough sleep or if I make sure that you're eating right, am I trying to control you? Do I make you feel like he makes me feel?"

"No."

"If I am, I really need to know, Paul. I'm afraid of turning out like him. He's my father, and I love him; but, I don't ever want to treat people the way that he treats me. Are you sure that I don't make you feel that way?"

"Never. It's…" The first two words flew out of his mouth quickly. Many words come to fill the space that he has left open, but he can't bring himself to say any of them, no matter how much he'd like to. "…okay. It's…okay, 'Rene."

His insides burn and twist, unhappy with his response. Irene's breathing becomes more stable, and her mouth no longer frowns. But, she could be smiling, and they both know it.

A smile is something that she could not find on any of the faces appraising her somber appearance while on her second destinationless meandering of the day. After her first venture and midday return to the alley, she could not be still for long. Within an hour, she was wandering again. Now, as she has returned once more, the grimace of the hauntingly familiar face in the battered pickup remains in focus in her head and at the top of the pull's bellowing tongue. She envisions the rest of the truck smashing in around him: the bed, the grill, the fenders, and the hood crushing themselves around his face in the window, entombing him. The mess of metal and man crunches further and further inward, metal screeching, glass shattering, until it looks as though it has wrapped him in a metallic coffin. She can't figure out what he has to do with the pull, but the persistent image of him reeks of coming trouble. And, both she and the pull know it.

These thoughts have spun her brain around in her skull for the past few hours. Now the sun barely touches the sky under the curtain of evening. Even as she scales the gate and drops herself into the church alley, it still consumes her attention. She lets her shoulders and head lean against the brick as her body slides downward until she sits on the ground. There is a slight relief as her shoulders remain pinned to the bricks. Her weighted-down mind is less heavy. There is a tiny beam of light creeping into the alley from a crack between the ajar door and its frame. She sees it in her periphery, but she has no desire to investigate; nor does she have faith that anything beyond it could comfort her now. The light crease grows wider despite her lack of concern.

She sees a man with a tightly-fitting collar stepping through the church's illumination into her darkened alley. It is the man she saw yesterday morning; the one who brought her a sandwich and some water—her ears remember the crinkling of the cellophane. No doubt, he is also the one who left the door open with instructions on small notes. Her fatigued mind recognizes a smile, but she can't bring herself to move as he approaches. She wants to scream for him to leave her "loneliness unbroken." But, she remembers not from which poem the words came, nor does she realize how similar she feels to their narrator. Besides, there is a portion of her, somewhere beneath the sorrow, the anger, and the rage, that wants to find out what part he will perform in this tragedy.

His mouth moves its third line to her, "Welcome back. I've been waiting for you." He waits for a response. She consumes the words, but has nothing to say about their taste. He continues, "How can I help you?"

To her astonishment, she speaks, "I don't think anyone can help me."

"What if I tell you I've heard that before?"

"No, padre. You've never seen anything like me."

Nodding his head affirmingly, "Mmm-hmm. What if I told you that that is the devil's greatest trick?"

Laura's eyebrows curl asymmetrically.

The man continues undaunted, "You feel like you're different."

She wants to scream a thousand things to defend why she feels that she is different and is justified in doing so. She could leap off the building and show him. She could grab him and inflict any number of horrible things upon him, but she holds her mouth still.

"You feel like your thoughts and temptations are worse than everybody else's. That they are unique. You feel that you're dangerous. That there's something inside of you that is so foul, so evil, that you are beyond help."

Her face is surprised, although she tries to hide it as he proceeds.

"I know because I hear it everyday. From teenagers to little old ladies to hard working family men to college girls to homeless addicts; I hear it from all of them. It's the devil's most devious trick. To make each of us feel alone and monstrously different, to keep us from talking to each other about it—to make us think that even telling someone else about our wicked thoughts would ruin them too. If we'd all just talk about our darkest fears, we'd realize we're all the same and gain hope and strength for ourselves in knowing that we are not alone, that we are not damaged goods, not monsters, not an emotional mutant. But instead, we don't talk about it, and it keeps us from getting help, makes us give up on trying and give up on hope."

Laura's alert, absorbing pupils shrink, and her head drops to her chest at the mention of hope.

"And even worse, it is an insult. It's a disgrace to the One, who created all, for us to believe that we could possibly do anything so terrible that He couldn't fix it. That somehow we've grown larger than Him—that somehow we could create something bigger than God, whether it is good or bad. It's blasphemy. It's a perverse vanity. And it keeps us lost."

She stares at her boots, soaking, absorbing, not entirely agreeing, but feeling a warmth of truth in the words.

He continues, "If you feel like this, I can't help you. No person on earth can help you. But, I certainly can bring you to the only One who can."

Slowly, she looks up from her boots to his face, verifying his sincerity, "Padre, I don't call anyone father. I never have."

"I wouldn't ask you to."

"'Rene, I just don't know what else to do with this one. Today was just horrible," he says as he sinks into her couch with thousands of book titles calling out to him, asking him to solve the mystery of each, when he has just about given up on the one before him.

"Yeah," concedes Irene in a whisper.

Andarus continues to think aloud, "But, we've got to do something. Or quit. One or the other. I think we've run out of stall tactics with the chief."

Irene tosses her head side to side quickly, snapping herself to action and says, "Well, let's review what we know about her already."

Andarus nods his head tiredly.

Irene explains, "We know she hasn't accessed her credit cards or bank account since all of this started. Her out-of-town business has been abandoned and closed since she left. Her local stores have been open yet have not been able to contact her. She is not registered at any hotel or motel in town. So, the question is still 'Where is she?'"

Andarus's face slides into his hands, and he rubs his eyes roughly. Irene's index finger and thumb squeeze her bottom lip in the center as she thinks.

"Hey, Andarus."

He looks up at her, dropping his hands to his lap.

She continues, "How much money could she have on her?"

His eyebrows change position, and he sits more upright in the sofa.

He says, "I dunno. She didn't have much in her personal account before all of this, and it hasn't been accessed. So, I'd say not much. Not much at all."

"Yeah, me too. But, it's been eleven days. Even if she's been homeless, wandering this whole time or has found some other place to stay, what is she eating, Paul? How is she living?"

She looks at him hoping for a solution, not knowing he will end it with four of the creepiest words that she has ever heard him utter.

"Maybe, she is stealing food from here or there. But, we haven't had any reports of petty crime that have matched her description, and we've got every officer in town keeping an eye out for her. Twelve days is a long time to forage for yourself through questionable means without being noticed, especially given the way she has been behaving. Eating, sleeping, living—maybe she simply isn't."

Chapter XXXI

No one expected to see her back here, especially not exuding energy and acting as her old self. For a while, it seemed that she could not think or feel anything else except the hum of terror buzzing between her ears. It is an eerie miracle as Debbie once again sits behind her desk.

"Great to have you back, Deb," says Andarus with Irene standing to his right, "Maybe now we can get this place back in order."

"W-e-l-l," says Deb in a suspense building manner, "It won't be for long; I just put in my two weeks notice."

His jaw slacking open, "What?"

Her face loses its sheen for a moment as she elaborates, "Well, Paulie," she is the only person besides his third grade teacher to call him "Paulie." And, the second grade teacher was called "an old bag" for her efforts, but he has tolerated Debbie's calling him that pseudonym since his first day on the job. "When I was unconscious, all that I could dream about was painting; so many pictures in my head over the years that I've got to put onto canvas. So many ideas that I've got to try to bring to life. It's time for me to retire, Paulie; don't need the money anymore, just need to work on some dreams for once…I came back 'cause I wanted to help, to put things right before I go, to rejoin the team. Plus, I needed to prove to myself that I could go back to normal if I wanted to, that I'm not running away from anything." And, looking at Paul and Irene closely, she adds, "And to kick a couple of dummies who don't see something good right in front of their faces."

Warm awkwardness. Toes wiggle in shoes. Smiles crack broadly.

Andarus starts, "Well, I'd be lying if I said I wouldn't miss you, Deb; it won't ever be the same around here without you. But, I'm happy for you; I really am. I've always said you were too good for this place."

Looking deeply into Andarus, Deb says, "The most important jobs that are underappreciated by society are usually picked up by people who are too good for them."

Andarus blushes.

She certainly never expected to see herself inside a church again. Before the incident she prayed every night. Ever since meeting Gabe years ago, she had found the strength to deal with issues of faith. But, she has not had it since the physical numbness and emotional overload of her recent loss.

"Mrs?" asks the priest, who has introduced himself as Virgil.

Quickly, she stabs, "Call me Laura."

"Laura, I have no interest in trying to get you to join our church, neither am I interested in trying to force our beliefs on you. Nor do I want your money, either now or later. A church is supposed to be a refuge. You showed up on my doorstep—well, in our alley, and I want to help you."

Her face is still devoid of belief, but it holds steadily, not hatefully.

"I know you have problems—we've already touched upon that last night. The only thing I can do to help you is to give you the truth. I'll give it to you as neutrally and plainly as I can, but sometimes the truth is going to coincide with dogma. I could care less about formality and institution, but I am not automatically against them when they happen to be correct."

"And, what if you don't know?"

The priest's lips wriggle at the question, but he responds, "Then, I'll have to tell you that I don't know, but I'll try my hardest to find out for you."

Discussing theology in a church is a long way from where she would have envisioned herself heading recent days ago while in a motel room or a supposedly unoccupied house. In her rambling teenage years, she willfully ran from it, not even thinking it fair for her to have to deal with the weight of eternity and the one grand question that has piqued mankind since the first pair of human eyes opened to strain at the brightness of day. Survival was heavier on her mind then, and her flight from Riverview was of primary importance. But, when she met Gabe, he truly felt like a gift, one that she couldn't ignore, and she wanted to know from where he came to her. Through all of the years that followed, her faith had been strong. Only in the last two estranged years, in a tiresome dance with a fledgling business, had her focus drifted slightly away from the eternal question and the answer that had found her. Her prayer had continued, but her attention to it in her life had dwindled.

She is aware that these recollections would not be allowed to come so freely if the pull were swarming her. In fact, the pull is silenced; its presence is off her. As she stares at Virgil, she vows to pay attention to the consistency of the pull's absence while she is in the church. Although she is savoring its lapse in attendance, she knows it is brooding somewhere, creating a plan to torture her for entering where it cannot follow.

"Padre, what if you don't believe my story? I'm certain it's not like one you've heard before."

As Laura's lips moved, he noticed her eyes have none of the trepidation in talking about her misdeeds that others always have during these talks. Her pallid face is like an ice-covered landscape with two rogue eyes of defiance blooming out of season, somehow more beautiful in their obscure, frosty vista.

"Laura, something unusual has certainly happened to you, and I believe that. If not, I don't think we would have met in this way. But, if you tell me something that I don't believe is true—something that has happened to you, I'll have to try my hardest to believe you anyway because it is real to you right now. If I don't think your experience matches up with reality, I'll have to tell you that it is unlikely. If I'm not honest, what good can I do for you at all? But, know that I care that it is real to you. More importantly, I believe that I am supposed to help you. So, know that I am present, I am listening, and I want to help you."

Laura's pupils turn with a slow current as words flow from her, "My family was murdered, and my daughters were raped; so I prayed for vengeance…"

A pale, skinny man of nineteen years old with dusty-looking blonde hair and thin-framed glasses sits across the desk from the two detectives.

"Thanks for coming in, Jeff."

"It's okay," starts Jeff, "I'm glad that you guys are done with my car already."

"Well, we've gathered about all that we can from it, so it's yours again. We just wanted to ask you a few questions."

"Yeah, sure."

"Why were you at Daisy Slykovsky's funeral? How do you know her?"

"I don't know her very well. I would see her around at concerts—we must've listened to the same exact bands—she was always at the same ones as me," hesitating before continuing, "I drove her home once. Her boyfriend and her got into an argument at a show; he pushed her to the ground in front of the stage. A lot of people saw it. She was pretty embarrassed. Her boyfriend left with another guy; I think he was scared of getting arrested or security guards or something. So, Myles and I helped her up and gave her a ride home. We didn't talk much, just told her that if she ever needed a ride to a show to let us know, which really was kind of stupid since she doesn't have either of our numbers or know where we live. But, we felt sorry for her. I remembered thinking that I wouldn't treat her that way if she was my girlfriend. But, I didn't have any girlfriends at all, so what would I know…"

"But, Jeff," starts Irene, and his face brightens at hearing a female voice say his name, "You came here with a girl today—she's waiting in the lobby for you now—isn't she the girl that was with you at Daisy's funeral?"

"Yes, she is my girlfriend," says Jeff beaming. "It's really been weird. I never had the courage to ask a girl out, and it always bothered me. I knew I wasn't Don Juan, that I'm kind of a dork, but what irritated me was that I never even tried. And, like with Daisy, why would she be with someone like that jerk? She could've been with me—I wouldn't treat anyone that way, but it was never even a choice because I never opened my mouth. That's what bothered me." Jeff pauses and looks at his hands which are clasped together on his lap, "Something happened with this whole carjacking thing. When she touched me…I don't know how to explain it, but…it woke me up. I thought I was going to die, and I wasn't really scared, not about dying. I had this horrible feeling that I had wasted my life, that I had failed myself by not doing any of the things that I wanted to do, by being a coward. So, I started asking out girls in my classes at Riverview U. The first time I was still nervous and got shot down. The second time the girl agreed to a date—it was pretty weird and awkward, nothing happened. But, when I asked out Tonie, I was more comfortable, and she didn't care that I wasn't smooth and sure of myself. We've been together every day since then."

"Good for you, Jeff," offers Irene.

"Yeah, it's bizarre how such a terrible thing can change your life for the better, made me realize what I needed to do to be happy. It's weird."

Andarus adds, "Yeah, Jeff, it is. But, why did you feel the need to go to Daisy's funeral if you didn't know her that well? How did you know about it for that matter?"

"I saw her obituary in the paper—I was flipping through the Living section to get to the comics, and I saw her picture. I wanted to go because I felt sorry for her. She seemed so sad and miserable every time that I would see her. She kind of reminded me of me, but I got a second chance to change mine—she didn't get one."

"Not many of us do," offers Andarus with more feeling coming out his vocal chords than he knows, "Well, it sounds like things are going great for you now, Jeff. You are very lucky to be uninjured and with a positive attitude. It takes courage to change your life."

"Thanks," says Jeff starting to blush.

Irene explains, "See Debbie at the desk; she'll make a phone call and tell you where you need to go to pick up your car."

He nods and rises from his chair, silently shaking both detectives' hands and turning to the door.

"Hey, Jeff," sings Irene brightly, "you take care of that girl."

"I will. I promise," says Jeff smiling.

Something about Jeff's change warms Irene's insides, and the strength of his response makes her believe that he will.

"That's a heck of a story, Laura," says Virgil as he strokes his fingers over his chin, "A lot to believe. A lot that's hard to believe. And some things…"

"That you don't want to believe," offers Laura.

"No, no. Just a little scary to believe, honestly."

His response calms the storm that was brewing inside of her as she was awaiting a different answer. He sat in front of her listening to her tale, trying very hard to withhold any reaction. At moments, his face looked bewildered, but he quickly returned his façade to neutral as best as he could manage. She did not spare any details that were important, nor did she censor any of its ugliness. It was a story that was not easy to experience without expressing some emotion, but Virgil gave it a strong effort. She stopped her tale at the killing of Daisy, so he knows nothing about her attempts to kill herself. Despite herself, she is anxious to hear his complete response. She is uncomfortable with the anxiety, as it is one more emotion that she does not wish to feel, but she holds onto it because maybe it could lead to a path to her family.

Finally, his voice appears, subtly reverberated by the high ceiling of the empty church, "Laura, I believe what happened to your family is true, and I am deeply sorry for it. I read about it in the paper; I remember. I also remember reading about the deaths of the two teens, followed by the death of the girl. It seems hard to believe with you sitting before me telling me that somehow this was a divine wish granted to you, and that now you are dealing with its aftermath. Forgive me, I am trying, but this is a lot."

Dozens of charged remarks find their way into her head, but she responds only with, "I know."

"I'm supposed to report murders to the police, Laura. Confidentiality does not protect a murder confession."

"I know," repeats Laura.

"Yet, you don't seem at all afraid."

"There's nothing they can do to hurt me now…if they could harm me at all, I would welcome them with both arms, so I could get to my children."

Completely puzzled, he asks, "What do you mean 'if they could do you harm, you would welcome them'?"

"I've tried many ways to get out to my family and nothing works."

"You've tried to kill yourself?"

"Yeah, padre, several different ways."

"Laura, many people have trouble actually committing suicide; it's nothing to be ashamed of—it's a good thing."

She leans forward placing her face close to his, her hair dangling before her, shielding most of her eyes from him, leaving them but a tiger's heartbeat beneath its stripes, "Have you seen your sidewalk, padre?" she asks as she points to the tall ceiling above them.

Realization sparks across his face, "You didn't?"

She lifts her hand upward and makes a falling noise as she brings it crashing down upon her leg.

"How? How can you..?"

"Yeah, that's one I'd like to know, padre. Do you think you could ask for me?" she poses, suddenly doubting any ability that he may have to help her.

Much faster than she thought he could move, he thrusts his opened hand at the top of her chest. Sliding it quickly to her left side, he holds it there tightly. The stinging cold that others have felt when coming in contact with her is there on his hand, but his tolerance for it is much higher. His eyes grow wild as what his hand reports seems to defy logic.

"My God. Laura, you're not breathing! Your heart's not beating. You're not!"

"I haven't eaten or drunk anything since my family died either. Explain that one too."

Slowly, he pulls his hand from her chest.

"I…I believe you."

"What?" asks Laura having trouble believing his response.

"I believe everything that you've said. How could I not?"

"Sometimes it's easier to pretend it's not there than to deal with it. If you don't want to believe, I'll go away; it won't be your problem anymore."

"No, I believe, and I can't deny it. God have mercy on me if I do…If you're not alive, then this isn't a matter for the police anymore. My dear Lord, this isn't even a matter for me; this is between you and God."

Her face contorts at his response. She feels that now it is coming out, that he can't help her and doesn't even want to try.

"But, I'm in this. I'm here to do God's will, and He has brought you here. So, I am in this. I pray for His strength to help both of us…and I thought you just didn't like tuna fish and water."

Prayer has not appeared to be a consolation to her since her transformation; it has not even felt like an option. But, as a result of his earnestness, she is willing to listen, even if it turns out to be nothing more than the breeze whistling through a graveyard.

Chapter XXXII

"So, what else of importance do I still not know about you?" asks Virgil.

"Well, my real name's not Laura, it's Jennifer. I started going by Laura just before I left home when I was a kid. And, my maiden name is Oren—I've always hated that name; it belongs to my dad, not me."

"So, technically your name is Jennifer Oren Bonney?"

She nods. His face becomes busy.

"Laura, do you realize your initials spell Job?"

She sits without reaction. Then a realization comes, "So you think God knew this would happen to me when I was born, and the name is no coincidence?"

"Just because we have free will doesn't mean that God is not aware of what choice we will make before we make it. But, in order to have free will, we still have to be provided with the opportunity to make our own choices. So, possibly, but, I don't put too much faith in details that may or may not be coincidence. If you're looking for proof of a grand design by God, there are many things that are too obvious to ignore—things that are much more undeniable than one's initials."

"Yeah, like what? Impending death, crime, abuse, hatred?"

"No. But, there are other things. The fact that nature itself is in balance until man screws it up; it is quite interesting that we are the only creatures in it with a soul, yet we're the only ones capable of disturbing or destroying its balance. That implies that we are by design the masters of our surroundings, and consequently, we are responsible for it."

"Fascinating, padre. Simply fascinating."

"Well, what about thunder? Any man who claims the thunder has never scared him has lived a spoiled and sheltered life away and hiding from the storm, or he is a liar. For, thunder can creep unannounced upon anyone and crash with such force as to rattle one's bones from within. That type of jarring frightens all in the moment that it strikes. The insane, who cannot comprehend, still feel it; those who hear other voices, are momentarily deafened; those who think they're already dead because they have nothing to live for, instantly find themselves clinging to this gossamer that we call life.

In one fleeting instant of the phenomenal sound like mountains being thrown, all of our science, all of our reasoning, all of our laws, every piece of arrogant invention that has ever been made by the hands of man cannot comfort that innate inner acknowledgement and fear that there is an almighty being beyond our understanding—and how many of us are ready for His reckoning?"

A brief silence settles so thick that it seems to make the room spin slowly, and he resumes, "We can deny it all that we like and claim it is only unrefined ignorance and antiquated superstition. But, eventually, we each will be all alone and the godsmack of thunder will shake the scales of our lies from our misguided, self-righteous and sophisticated eyes—and there will be no denying."

"The things I've seen lately have been much scarier than thunder."

"Well then, what about all of these things that you have been through? How do you explain the power that you were granted without there being a higher power to give it to you? How many people do you know who have been shot in the head without the bullet doing any damage to them? How many have jumped off buildings and mangled the sidewalk but not themselves? What rationale do you have to explain all of this?"

"I don't know…maybe love conquers time and space."

"If that were true, Laura, then you'd be able to bring your family back now or to have saved them before anything bad happened to them at all. No child would ever be harmed as long as a parent loved them, and that simply isn't so."

"Alright, maybe I'm just tainted—hopelessly stained from all of this. Maybe I have seen all that I need to believe, but I'm not capable of it. Maybe I can't forgive enough to be able to see it."

"Well, believe and love are two different things. Every demon in hell is painfully aware of God and believes that He is real, but there is no love for Him. But, for us, there is the example of the Israelites coming out of Egypt. They saw miracles and plagues. They saw the Red Sea part before them and manna appearing from nowhere to sustain them in the desert. They witnessed the angel of death kill every first-born son except for those of the faithful who followed God's directions. But, when they were tired and impatient with the journey, they grumbled at Moses who led them out, and they quickly tossed aside all of the unexplainable things that were done for them. Only Moses held fast to loving and obeying God, only he remembered the significance of what he saw. Despite all that they had witnessed, they convinced themselves it was not true. So, no matter what we see, we can rationalize and discredit even what we once believed to be true—what we saw right in front of our eyes. Nothing that can happen to us in life can force us to believe; the interpretation lies in our own hands. That's all part of our free will."

"Well, it's part of me right now. So, where does that get me?"

"The Bible is written in the same way. It can confuse the intellectual but be perfectly clear to the simple. It is strength and freedom to the believer and repression to the cynic. But, what most people miss is that if it were any other way, it could not possibly be true."

"What?"

"Well, if in reading the Bible we were given information in a way that we were forced to accept it, it would remove our free will. We would have no choice; we would be being programmed like robots. It is presented in a way that it can be accepted by the believer wholeheartedly and rejected by the skeptic. A person of great intelligence has no advantage over one with limited mental ability. Anyone anywhere in the world can accept or deny it as easily as anyone else. All are equal; all have free will, and all are equally equipped to make the decision for themselves."

Laura huffs.

"Now, believing in the Bible, at the moment, is irrelevant. I'm not trying to convert you. The immediate point is simply that, no matter what you have seen, you can deny God's existence altogether. How we interpret or rationalize the unnatural or unexplainable grants us acceptance or denial of a higher power. Or, if you do not deny that God exists, which is no different than the demons in hell, you can still deny Him your choice. Your choice to follow, your choice to love, your choice to honor cannot be taken from you no matter what you have seen or been through. That is the true power of free will. Think about all of the things that the Israelites saw before entering the desert: a river turning to blood, plagues, the death of every noncompliant parent's first born, yet, not long after being out of Egypt, nearly all of them turned away and were trying to concoct their own god out of gold. The point of the story is that we don't believe when we see miracles; we only choose to recognize miracles around us after we believe."

Disgruntled and curious, "How is anyone supposed to believe in something that they can't see until they believe in it?"

"There are things that we can see that spark the belief."

"Like what, padre, priests and pretty churches?"

"Well, the fact that we have the ability to be sarcastic is a good example too, Laura. Or, the fact that we have a sense of humor—it is not practical or productive, but it is so essential to being human. But, what about the immune system? It is an amazingly complicated system. One could easily make the argument that it is too complex and too essential to have developed that way by chance or that no creature could have survived to have the opportunity to evolve without it being intact in the first place. This would indicate a grand design by a creator from the first creation of physical life."

"So, you don't believe in evolution? Really?"

"No, I didn't say that at all. I deem it to be irrelevant. What I said is that the necessity of an immune system for a creature to have the ability to be around long enough to evolve is evidence that there is a creator. Whether the creator decided to spring forth life through evolution or a traditional creation story is completely not important to me at all. I've never really understood why people get so upset about this subject."

"You can't be serious."

"Yes, I am. If evolution is proven beyond a shadow of a doubt, it is still only a theory of development; it does not explain where the initial creatures came from. It does not explain where the earth came from, or any physical matter at all. If everything evolved from a tiny, microscopic particle and it exploded through a big bang and life sprung forth from there, it still would change nothing for me. That infinitesimal particle still had to come from somewhere, and then something had to push it to move. Something non-physical definitely created something physical. Physical matter could not have always just existed; it had to come from somewhere. There had to be an unmoved mover."

"Not convinced…"

"About what part? Or all of it?"

"Not convinced about the part where any of this proves that the creator, or unmoved mover, is benevolent at all. Where does it prove that He cares? Or even that He is a He? How does any of this affect my situation? Why should I care about someone who has left me in such a position?"

"This is what all of this has to do with you: many people have come to me over the years pleading for God to grant their wish, to save them from some trouble. They always say, 'If God saves me from this, I'll do whatever He wants for the rest of my life.' Sometimes the trouble comes, but sometimes they do get their wish and are spared what they were trying to avoid. Either way, most go back to their old lives and ways, soon forgetting their promises. The existence of God is something that we all seem to know somewhere deep down, but we have the ability to ignore it if we choose to. Some of us come up with complicated, intelligent, and creative ideas to avoid it—theories that would make great movies or books, but are nevertheless still not true. Take an atheist for example. A man who has made a conscious effort to exclude any mention of God from his life, not even saying 'God bless you' when others sneeze. Acknowledging God has been removed entirely from his culture. But, throw him into an immediately life-threatening situation, and he will instinctively call out to God. If he dodges the impending crisis, he usually returns to his regular life, never minding that he called out to a being of whom he says does not exist. Rationalizing it as panic, as some socially programmed response, as a nothing, calls for no effort, no change, no responsibility, no subjecting oneself to a higher power. It's a blind elevation of the self over what one knows to be true. This person is as self-driven and blind as some early Christians who opposed the earth rotating around the sun. To see something is true and to deny it for political, social, or selfish reasons is vain, lazy, and irresponsible…"

"Padre, I believe God exists, although I am pretty angry with Him about my current situation. The problem is He seems to have stranded me here. I'm stuck. I don't care about other people's religious issues right now. What does this have to do with me being stuck here away from my family?"

"It's not an issue of religious theories or doctrine; it's an issue of spirituality. And, we're all a part of this; none of us are excluded."

"How?"

"Every time I feel agitated or annoyed I have a choice; the same choice as everyone else. I can act how I want to, do what I feel, say what I want to say, and it sounds like I have the right to do so. But, that self-righteous thought process has hurt people since time began. We'll all agree that none of us are perfect and that people should not make important decisions while feeling emotional, yet we think it's perfectly okay for us to put someone in their place when we are emotionally upset. Isn't hurting someone's feelings, possibly for life, an important decision? Aren't we incapable of making that decision responsibly at that frustrating moment? Yet, we feel we are entitled to it."

Grinding her jaw, she warns slowly, "If you're trying to tell me that I had no right to hunt down my family's murderers because I was emotional, then this is going to get ugly."

Her words project a heaviness on Virgil, but he continues, "No, Laura, that's not where I'm going with this one. Hang in there with me; it's coming to a point. I promise."

She folds her arms across her chest, but her attention is open and waiting.

"When I am irritated and upset, I have a choice. I can rationalize it to myself that I am justified, have done no wrong, and have the right to let off some steam on the person responsible for my discomfort. To vent. Or, I can look to my God and ask what does He want me to do. His command is for me to treat others in the same way that I want to be treated. So, my other choice is to stop thinking of how I've been offended and to think about how I would feel to be the other person. What would I do if I were them? Are they having a bad day? Does no one love them at home? Has anyone ever loved them? Sometimes simply asking 'Why are you being so rude to me?' will cause the person to open up. It usually makes them feel better just that you asked, and often it points out their unkind behavior in a way that makes them want to change it. Most people would agree that making sound decisions results from having inner peace, but how many of us truly have it? More importantly, how many of us actually have the real thing where it stays with us even when the world is being its most difficult? That is why it is so important to be aware of the choice to resist one's emotions and urges to submit to a higher power—an inner peace, to maintain self-control over one's environment. We are not our own little gods, and, when we act that way, we make a horrible mess of the world around us. My concern with the atheist is not about his religion—frankly, that's none of my business; that's between him and God, or him and the universe—however you want to look at it. My worry is how is this person going to act when he or she does not feel like doing the right thing? Or, how is this person going to act when he or she honestly believes they are right, but are terribly wrong? All humans are fallible and subject to passion. Without bowing down to something bigger than oneself, one will become an unchecked tyrant in an extreme situation. The choice is to act as a little god and obey one's own desires or to surrender to a higher power and act beyond human nature and impulse. I'm a priest, and I face this every day. When I am frustrated, I have the same choice. And, to be completely honest with you, I know some priests who do an absolutely lousy job at it. But, it is a challenge every day to every person. When I fall down, I apologize to the other one involved, pray for more strength, and get back up and try again."

"My challenges should be over."

"If you're still here, Laura, whether you're breathing or not, there is still a challenge before you."

"Like what, padre? What else do I have to go through?" It's another moment when she would be crying if her body would melt enough to permit it.

"I agree you've been through your share of peril. Horrible things that I can only imagine. But, you've worn yourself out doing your own things and obeying that 'pull' that you described to me. You've been a slave to your desires and an inner emotion pushing you."

"My only desire is to be with my dead family."

"But, how have you tried to get there? Have you asked God what He wants you to do? His way is the only way out of this, and, just like all of our daily struggles, it is not easy. But, it is never more than what we are capable of doing. When we're on our own, we're flailing in the dark because we are merely human and are blinded by our own driving emotions. We're either debating incessantly like Hamlet or vaulting into evil deeds through rationalization like Macbeth. When we seek God, we are on the path to do what needs to be done; doing the right thing becomes more important than oneself. Some truly amazing things grow out of acknowledging that there are things bigger than oneself. Without it, we are all little dictators, emperors spinning around slamming into each other, damaging all around us trying to force our vision upon everyone else. With it, one would die to protect one's family; one would die to protect one's neighbor; and one would die to protect freedom."

"But, I would die for my family. I would have died for my family; I'm dying to die so I can be with them now."

"Yes, Laura, but that is what you want—your desire. And, I'm not saying you don't deserve it, but you're not going to get there through your own actions; no one ever does."

"Well, what am I supposed to do?"

"That's one that I don't think I can answer for you, but I will pray about it. I think you need to ask God on your own."

"I don't know if I can."

True hopelessness has a smell. It's something like sweat, hunger, and adrenaline, and it hovers around her.

"Well, what about your children?" asks Virgil as the smell drifts to his nostrils.

"Watch it, padre."

"No, no. Stay with me. A few moments ago, you asked how does any of this prove that God is benevolent. But, were your children not perfect gifts? Can you honestly say that they, the wonderful little miracles that they are, are only the sum of a work that you and Gabe did on your own? Did you not produce something greater than a part of both of you? Could you and Gabe create anything else that you would consider to be perfect?"

He pauses as she shakes her head in a negative agreement, and then continues, "If you could, you'd be the first people ever to make anything that is completely perfect besides a child. Can you say that there was nothing divine or sacred in your children?"

"Okay, so children are sacred. Not many would argue with that. But, what does that have to do with the fact that life is random, and God is not answering my question? I'm stuck here, padre. I'm trapped. I'm not alive, yet I can't die. I'm forever exhausted, but I can't sleep—at least not any restful sleep. Only torture waits for me behind my eyes. My brain aches with puzzles and riddles and horrible images constantly, but I never solve this problem. It's like I'm forgotten."

"Limbo is not a forgotten place, Laura. I admit I've never heard or seen anything like what has happened to you. And, honestly, who knows if it has ever happened before? But, anytime a person is trapped between one stage of their life and the next, they feel tremendous stress. People caught between jobs, graduating college but not knowing what to do, people dealing with the loss of their families, people not knowing what they think about God; all of these people are in a limbo of sorts, and they all feel miserable. But, it passes for them. Eventually, those, who look for it, find their way, or, if you think like me, they are shown their way. You're not forgotten, Laura. We just have to find your way. I don't believe that you are banished. There has to be something left for you to do."

"Damn you, padre. Can't you ever let me have my moment?"

"No. If you mean can I let you soak in a pool of hatred, no, I can't let you. Not unless I sell my compassion right along with you."

"If there's something for me to do, why am I suffering so much now when I don't even know what it is that is left for me? Why would God put me through this when all that I want to do is be with my family? Have I not been through enough? Why not tell me specifically, so I could get it over with? Why all this cruel withholding?"

"Laura, you asked for an amazing thing. A supernatural thing. When you asked for it, you were not concerned with the consequences. You prayed for blood, Laura. It was blood that you deserved, blood that you, if anyone, had a right to receive. But, you were granted it. I can't tell you why God answered you in a specific way then. But, I can tell you why He's not answering right now; you prayed for blood—now you have to pay for it."

"Yeah, how am I supposed to do that? I've tried to kill myself. Several times," she says thinking of the ruptured sidewalk as she unintentionally nods her head at the front of the church.

"Smashing all that is around you in an attempt to enact your own desires."

"Wasn't what I was trying to do," she says, pausing before continuing, "I was trying to wipe my shadow off the face of the earth."

"Laura, that is not the first time that you've referred to yourself as a shadow. If you are indeed a shadow of yourself, then it is no wonder you are trapped and cannot find a way out. Shadows cannot move on their own. To move a shadow, the original object must move—the real object. We need to move you, the real you—the you before all of this, to move what's left of you now."

"She's dead, padre."

"I know."

Chapter XXXIII

"So, padre, I always wanted to know: is hell burning hot or a cold burn like a frostbite?"

"Why do you ask?"

"Curiosity. I mean, it's different for each person, like a customized torture to one's fears, right?"

Virgil watches her mouth as she speaks. She is not smiling, but she is also not frowning; she holds her lips perfectly level. There is some excitement in her eyes.

"You're fantasizing about what you put them through, about how they're suffering right now, aren't you?"

The corners of her lips turn the slightest bit upward, and she asks, "Do you blame me?"

Shaking his head, "I have to tell you that the hate, the vengeance, the enjoyment of it are all eating you alive, rotting you out; can't you feel that?...but, no, Laura, I can't say I blame you for anything. I am not your judge, but I can tell you that you're destroying yourself."

"There are worse things, padre, and I hope you'll never know."

"Laura, I can't pretend to know. But, I do know that losing your eternity for anything is not worth it. And, what if you have, Laura, what if you have?"

"Well, if that's so, what do we even have to talk about?"

"I didn't say it was too late. I just meant that you're in danger, and we don't know how much time you have to change it. No one ever knows that."

"And what hope do I have of that—of changing?"

"We always have hope, Laura. That's faith."

"How can I have hope? Part of the beauty of being human is being able to write our own stories. Our choices of what we do every moment between life and death. I'm stuck here and all of my efforts to get to the one place where I can find solace only serve to mock me. My story is in red ink on blood-soaked paper, a ghost's voice in the wind."

Hesitantly and with the shimmer of compassion in his eyes, he leans forward, lightly touches her forearm, and says, "Laura, how can you expect to hold the pen to finish your story with so much blood on your hands?"

For the first time since she stepped into the church, there is a flash of bright color in her eyes. Brown-green flakey flashes of pain. Rage and anguish. Truth and comprehension. She realizes that he has touched her twice now, and nothing bad has happened to him.

An hour later…

Laura says, "I was only there trying to make a better life for Gabe and the kids."

Father Virgil reaches out and grabs at her wrist, "But, it's not the natural order of things…"

She interrupts irritatedly, but feeling the sincerity in his hand at her wrist she keeps the volume of her voice to a speaking level, but the tone reveals her emotion, "Natural order? How could we care for those kids—send them to college, on Gabe's teacher's salary?" pauses briefly, "Gabe loved his job, and his students loved him—they were all better off from him being there. He could've done lots of other things to earn more money, but he would've always regretted it. I couldn't do that to him: I just couldn't…"

Virgil interjects, "I'm not questioning your intentions, Laura. I'm just trying to explain why it hurts. Some of the most terrible things the world has ever been subjected to were done under the blindfold of good intentions."

Gritting her teeth, she grumbles, "Go on, *padre*."

With a sigh he begins, "It's not your fault that they were killed. There was nothing that you could have done. Even if you were at home with them when it happened, there would not have been anything that you could have done to stop it. You would have died right alongside them. You can't blame yourself for that."

Laura shakes her head and thinks about the lost possibility of dying with her family and being with them now in the afterlife, instead of being locked in her current state of suspended reality in between what she was and where she longs to be. She imagines their three faces, free of the hell that they endured immediately before they left the world to which she remains chained. She can see them reaching for her and smiling. Longing. The whole world is her holding cell, and she feels more worn out with each passing moment. Inner strength fading, misery constant. But, she does not speak it as she braces herself for what Virgil has to say next.

"What you did have control of was what you did with the time that you had before they died."

At this, Laura's eyes course with energy while they focus on his face. They absorb every motion of his mouth and every emotion in his eyes as he speaks. He does not flinch or react but continues with his words.

"Running a business out of town when you had young children at home was not a necessity. And, it certainly was not for Gabe, or the kids: it was for you."

"You bastard," whispers out of her mouth like the last word of the dead or winter's subtle breeze exhaling through a wooded path as it surrenders its final dried leaf to the cold ground.

Speaking softly now, "That may be, Laura, but the point is true. You can't tell me that moving hundreds of miles away from your children was the best thing for them—or for your husband for that matter. You're far too smart to believe that yourself."

"I know…it wasn't supposed to take that long. It was a setup in a new city; I was only supposed to be there for three months and turn it over to Judy to manage it. But, she moved to California with her husband who got a better job, and no one else knew how to run things. I couldn't quit that fight. That debt would've caused all three locations to go bankrupt. It was my fight, and no one else could help," says Laura speaking faster than he has ever heard her speak before.

"Yes, Laura, but why did you get into that fight? Were two successful gyms and a teacher's salary not enough to support a family of four? Even if you lost all three gyms, were there no other jobs? Would the girls have starved or been out in the rain if you just came home?"

"I wanted them to have things that I never had. I ran away from home to get away from a bad situation when I was fifteen. I never wanted any of that for them."

"Yes, I know. But, the truth is that since you were not there by your own choice, they often felt starved for a mother, who was too busy to be with them, and unprotected from the innumerable things that only a mother can tend. They needed you, not the gym. The gym was for you. Your pride. Your benefit. No matter what your intentions were when you started it; this is where you ended up."

Sounding wounded, "But lots of mothers work. Some get divorced. Some die. What about them? Are they all terrible mothers? Are all of their children hopeless? Are they all doomed?"

"Laura, I don't think for one second that you were ever a terrible mother. And, no, a child without a mother around is not hopeless and destined to be miserable. But, a child, whose mother is not around by her own volition, will absolutely be burdened with a lot of pain and issues: feelings of being unloved, inadequate, and unimportant—at least that they are not as important as the new life or the work that the mother chooses to give her time instead of them. Think about it: if Gabe could've worked at a school a hundred miles away from you and the kids and made fifty percent more money, do you think that would've been good for your children? How hurt would they have been to see him that much less?"

Laura's head drops slightly from her primal stare at his face.

He continues, "They knew that you loved them, Laura. You were there with them during every moment for the first few years of their lives. And, I am sure that you were amazingly kind to Daniella and Susanna. *They knew you loved them, Laura.* You're hurting because you know that they missed you terribly and that you missed out on most of the last few years of their lives. And, it was all your choice; it was all within your power. The last two years were not the fault of the murderers. You have got to accept that; then you can let it go. It's the only way. You can't keep this hatred twisted up inside you; it'll slowly rot yourself away."

Her eyes are pools of disturbed water, constantly stirring. Waves of pain crash with currents of rage, each struggling for dominance. To Virgil, it looks like blocks of ice crashing into each other, gliding over the oceans of her pupils. And, he wonders what unseen horrors swim below the thin surface that he can see. The thought of the finned fears and razor-toothed vengeful impulses that lurk behind her eyes causes him to squirm in his pew with a quiver up his spine as he struggles to maintain his emotionless, neutral countenance that he has cultivated through years of hearing the worst sins of mankind confessed. As tiny as the movement is, she sees it.

She leans closer, stares firmly in his eyes, and, with the rasp and tone of someone who has been in the desert for weeks, says, "You expect me to not blame the unholy creatures who did this to my family?" now screaming, "To my *babies*? To my *Gabriel*? Is that right, padre?"

As her voice bounces around in the high ceiling and off the wooden pews and stained glass windows, he responds calmly, "No, Laura. They are to blame for what they did; they are responsible to God for it. But, they are not responsible for the time that you wasted before they did it. No one is promised tomorrow. Ever. It is our burden to live each day as our last. Part of your hatred for them is rooted in blaming them for your own wasted time. They ended your story before you had a chance to make things the way that you wanted them. But, you had every day for the two years before that to say the things that you wanted to say, to do the things that you wanted to do. Hating them is going to destroy you. It is a cancer; you can't contain it—it will consume you," Virgil pauses and a level of compassion overpowers his voice, "Laura, I can't begin to understand what you are going through. I'm not even going to pretend to see everything that is at work inside you. But, I know this is true; you have to forgive them or you'll never get out of the quicksand that you're in," pausing again, "You're not going to thaw out of this frozen state with more coldness."

Her fist squeezes itself, and it shakes. She stares at it and back to Virgil. She feels the rage pulsing inside of her, and she closes her eyes, drifting and dreaming as its angry current pulls her along a twisted landscape. Flashes of her recent bloody aggressions bounce in and out of her mind. Giving into it for just a moment feels like some form of a release. Allowing the current to toss her downstream is much easier than standing and fighting it as she has been, which has constantly and unmercifully been draining her every second since completing her task. Flashes of violent possibilities for the immediate future tantalize and taunt her fatigued consciousness. She tries to stop her downward flow in this bloody fantasy, but she cannot gain a foothold. Not being able to halt or even hinder the fast drifting and flowing gives her a feeling of vertigo. Images of her fists flying in anger bombard her. They are all she can see. She tries to let them go, but her fingers remain clenched in a tight fist. She tries to stop the flashing images of blood and release, but they come faster. She knows she has to open her eyes, or they will completely pull her under, drowning her in the rage until it becomes her. But, she is afraid that she has let it go too far to safely open them. She fears what little control she has left.

Eyes open. Swirling. Disheveled. Tornadoes of sight. Whirlpools of perception. Only faint glimpses of what she used to be remain. She stares at him. Virgil pulls his head back slightly. She thinks she will lunge. The mental floods demand that she focus on his head and to silence the words that penetrate and lacerate her. It screams to rip out the tongue. Blood. It wants to crack open the rivers of blood. She forces her head to look at the floor by his feet. She stands.

"Virgil, you are right about one thing; you have no idea what I've been through."

And she walks directly to the doors, both fists clenched.

"This scares me, and I don't know how to say it," says his eyes that are as faded blue as a painting, which has been placed in direct sunlight for a forgotten number of years, of a tiny ship surrounded by the gargantuan ocean. His mouth moves not.

Surrounding the blue circles is a yellowish discoloration of the white. It is a subtle hue, much like the teeniest ring-shaped overspill of coffee soaked into a thick, blanche napkin. Andarus has often wondered if it is a remnant of a past illness. But, how does one ask the person closest to oneself, "Did your father have jaundice?"

This visit has been one of the better ones in recent memory for Irene. Her father has been relatively subdued. While he still certainly has contributed more than his portion of the conversation, he has been content to allow others to lead the discourse for awhile. Irene has not deluded herself into thinking this behavior means he has changed or suddenly become more interested in what she has to say, but she has used the opportunity to talk about what is going on in her life. It wasn't until he just nervously asked them about work and his silent, uneasy response to Andarus's pat answer that she realized his unusually considerate demeanor is a result of his fear over the graphic newspaper account of the murders at the Bonney house, the No-Tell Motel, and the vacant home on Sanctuary. His reason doesn't bother her, but his not being able to vocalize it does make her tender.

Andarus has been the conductor, keeping the conversation moving. Whether it is innate or a result of his years of questioning witnesses and suspects, fueling an exchange of words is easy for him. Whether pleasant conversation in trying situations like this one or getting a rise out of someone who has irritated him, he has been able to do both easily whenever he has desired. Talking about what is going on inside of him has always been another story.

"So, Martin, you went to high school in the northern part of the state, didn't you?"

"Yeah, I did. Went to Teddy Roosevelt High School. We always had us a rivalry with the school across town—there was only two of us back then. In fact, mah senior year, one day this fella named Timmy Bradfield said he was gonna win the state cross country meet. Boy had never trained a day in his life. School across town had this slickster city boy who'd won the race three years in a row. Our boy Bradfield had never been on a track; he went home to work on the farm with his pop everyday right after school, but he knew. He got it in his mind he was gonna whup that slick showboat from across town…"

Irene reaches over, grabs Andarus's hand, and squeezes it tightly. It is a story they've both heard on nearly every visit to see her father together. Andarus wonders if he honestly doesn't remember telling the story before or if he doesn't care if it's being retold, simply enjoying performing it again. Irene is positive that he knows he's told it before and will gladly subject anyone to it who will listen until one would grow deaf. The hand squeezing helps keep her from screaming her frustration at the top of her lungs in the nursing home. Although, even if she did, she is quite sure he'd start in on the same story the next time Andarus and she walked through the door.

"…and that boy Bradfield came through that finish line, barefoot, without anyone near him for a hundred yards. Ole slicker boy didn't even finish. He knew he was beat, and couldn't face the crowd. He musta been hiding up in the trees somewhere along the course, waiting for the rest of us to head outta there, which was a good idea 'cause we'd a let him had it that he'd been beat by a farm boy with no fancy training. Just guts. Bradfield won on guts."

The story always ended the same way. The only plus to the familiarity is they both knew exactly how much longer they had left of the story. The familiar words were like landmarks on a trip, counting down the remaining distance. Although it was never planned out, visits to Irene's father typically lasted one hour, almost to the minute. If he was in a particularly cantankerous mood, the visit only would last about twenty to thirty minutes, but these moods rarely surfaced when Andarus was there with her.

Ending the visit is typical—have to get home to get some sleep for work the next morning. There are no secrets whispered to Andarus this time, just a troubled look on Martin's face and lips that start to move several times, but his mind shuts them down. Irene notices the premature death of sentiment as it is sacrificed on her father's lips. Her face is sad and overloaded as they walk down the hallway. It does not lift from her until Andarus slides his hand over the center of her upper back, gently caressing the area between her shoulder blades. It lifts, and she smiles.

She wishes the wind blowing under her outstretched arms would take her away or blow her into pieces. Oblivion. Her soul's grown too heavy for the air. And, she has no doubt the ground will crack and split before her fall if she tries to fly again from off the rooftop on which she stands. The retreating rays of the setting sun only count off seconds in her infinite sentence. Fatigue grows like an unchecked creeper vine. Its unwanted roots absorb all energy that was left for her resolve. Despair is her hope as all that she loathes is trapped inside her eyes. She strains to remember the outline of what she desires, the little of it that remains: three faces far away. Shadows blend into shadows, and, for the first in a long time, the pull's cackle does not clash; it reverberates like an organ in an asylum, insane fingers seducing reality down a secluded path; heavy frown becomes pointed grin, an evil tenor now has a soprano accompaniment, light chorus turns to lamentful dirge, discord becomes harmony, a negative harvest, dark sunshine, black daisy, poisoned soil. Light touches not what grows inside her.

His head wonders why he is still there so late. Both of their eyes know why they are there, and he sits on a couch pretending to watch a mediocre movie with her closer to him than what has become protocol. Her right shoulder lightly touches his left, and both tingle in the dimly lit room that is bathed in the electronic glow of the flickering screen. He looks to the hundreds of stories that are contained in bound pages around the room, and he wishes just one of them could give him some lines to say, or that some wise character would give him some sage-like advice and the reassurance to enact it. What are worse than his chronic loneliness in the dark hours are moments like this where he is reminded that it does not have to be that way; there could be a different existence for him. But, to bring it to life, he would have to do things of which he does not feel confident. If he is hopelessly doomed to be alone, then maybe there is some valiance in accepting it with stoicism. But, this is an undeniable reminder that it simply is not so; he could act now. He could purposely touch her, kiss her, and tell her thoughts that he has never allowed to breathe the outside air. He could act now, and possibly fail, but at least he would have tried—that would be easier to live with. But, he keeps himself chained to something that he can no longer see and can barely even remember. He drags around the empty case of a past promise that has long disappeared, refusing to free himself. Despite his repressive resolve, the tingling becomes more than excitement. It is a pulse, a register of his happiness, and, at the moment, it is but one more reminder that he does not live the life that he wants to, nor one that he would wish upon anyone else.

Equally delicate, but unique in her own way, Irene sits, as classically beautiful as a maiden in a fairy tale. She is surrounded by a thousand journeys that she has taken in her mind, recorded on the pages of her eclectic library that surrounds the two of them like a forest around a campsite. In nearly every tale, the characters that should be together find a way to make it so. Yet, here she sits on a sofa feeling much like a wallflower in her own living room, yearning to no longer be unnoticed, or at least unpursued. She also has little interest in the movie on the modest screen, yet she wishes it would not be so close to ending.

On the street again, her eyes burn with intensity. They take in the dank, unnatural lights of the drag and swirl them into a kaleidoscope of raw emotion. Before she started walking, while she dwelled in the church alley, even the torturous, unrestful sleep of the pull's torment would not come to her. Instead, she remained awake, eyes dryly open as they were raked over with images of the sloppy and haggard-looking driver of the pickup truck from three days before. Now, her soul feels like it is in as much disrepair as the driver's face; battered, bloody, bandaged, swollen, unshaven, and wrenched in its own agitation. Virgil's message is still not sitting well in her mind, and the pull's ferocity is unusually strong as the priest's words hang around in her head.

The dingy bars are identical to her last jaunt down Cellar Street. It looks like the same cars line the curb in a slightly different order, and, as she walks past the all-ages music venue, it seems to be the same kids loitering in the fenced-in, outside area of its courtyard just beyond the sidewalk on which she travels. Inside of it near the fence, one of the teens is particularly nervous, his mouth slightly unhinged and still, with the eyes of a child who has seen a parent become enraged for the first time. A young hand shakes in a jeans pocket. It calms itself still as she walks on without looking in his direction.

Despite the similar surroundings, it all looks different to Laura. Darker. The sound of her shoes smacking the sidewalk, the intrusive brightness of the streetlights, and the smell of the garbage cans and random litter are all harsher on her senses than on the previous trip. From out of the urban mire, a car grabs her attention. Its deep rumbling engine tingles her ears before she can see any of it. It is a bright red sports car, a Camaro. It is the type of car she used to love to race in the years before she met Gabe, wandering around in her rusty GSX, trying to drive into a place that might accept her, one that might understand her. The Camaro is an 80s model, an IROC, and definitely not stock. The windows are down, allowing the unseasonably cool weather to breeze over its passengers. As the car approaches, its stereo can be heard. She knows the song but cannot place its name. As the car nears, she can see it has four passengers. The driver is the guitar player from the band at the bar the other night. Sitting next to him is a brunette who must be his girlfriend. Her blue eyes shine in the streetlight. In the backseat is the bass player, and next to him sits Demure with her fiery red hair. The car comes to a stop in front of Laura as they wait for the light to turn green. Laura looks through the window into the back seat and sees Demure lean over and kiss the bass player on his cheek. Red drops to green, and the sixteen-inch wheels chirp very subtly as the car pulls away. The song's energy strikes a memory in her brain; it is the charging opening song that the local band played at the bar. It's the one that was playing when Meelynn fled to a bathroom and a monster followed a young girl into a refuge. Her attention shifts. The pull screams for Chris. She resumes her course to the bar, knowing that this is no random excursion.

As she approaches the familiar haunt of her youth, the alley contains people in a circle. Elbows move and heads face downward, but it is nothing out of the ordinary for this place. There is a light fixture above the circular group extending from the brick wall of the alley, but it has never worked since before Laura started going there. The only light to hit that darkness at night has been a quick flicker of a match or a lighter. 'Meaty' Gino is not at the door, unless he has shrunken four inches and has learned how to relax. The new keeper of the gate is smiling as he nods patrons inside without checking their IDs. Laura wonders how long this will go on before he has dealt with enough alcohol-induced incidents to turn into a smaller imitation of Gino. The line is shorter, but the crowd flows in slowly enough for there to still be a few people waiting to be nodded inside. Perhaps their trepidation in coming inside quickly has to do with past treatment that they received from Gino, which still leaves them weary of darting past the doorman without individual approval.

Laura is about to test out the new gatekeeper's resolve when something grizzly comes her way through the opened doorway. It has its arm around the waist of a girl slightly older than the one from the other night. It is the driver of the truck, and, although he has removed some of his bandages, he matches the face in her head. The new girl has long black hair and a look in her brown eyes that exudes a lot more confidence and comfort in her situation. The pull coils inside of Laura as grizzly and brown eyes step past her and make a hard left, walking down the sidewalk in the opposite direction from which Laura has come. Her eyes watch them as their walk has a sway to it.

His right hand is now placed at the small of her back, and her left arm is flung upwards around his shoulders. Chris's hand lifts off her back, and he looks as if he will pull it to his side. Her body drifts slightly from him in their sloshy, sidewalk stumble. Her wispy stare is looking at the approaching squares of the sidewalk just ahead of their moving feet, which remind her of silly puppet feet flinging forward ahead of their bodies, but his head is staring at her. His face is crinkled up around his nose and eyes. Her body strays a little farther from him, and he quickly places his hand back on her.

Without a thought, Laura follows, staying a half block behind them. The pull pushes her onward, singing a song that is as creepy as it is happy.

The hatred builds in her as she remembers the disheveled girl with smeared tears in the grimy stall. The happiness of the pull's ditty scrapes at her with the sentiment of "I told you so." Irritation in not finishing the job slides over her. She has the weight on her chest of needing to cough, but her body is far too numb to allow it. The pull dwells in the weight that is upon her, as do the words of the priest, and she is unsure of which she wants to listen to in her miserable situation. But, right now, she'd much rather hear neither of them inside her.

Chris is the perfect target for her frustration, for her desire to unleash what is inside her upon whoever is responsible for her torment. While she can't see how he could be the one who caused her misery, he deserves the attack more than most and as much as any other ill-willed miscreant fishing for some depravity in the dark waters of the night. She looks upon him walking unsteadily as a hunter waiting for its prey to wander into range. His hand lifts and returns to the small of the girl's back twice more. Then, suddenly, he stops, and leans his back against the glass window of an overpriced antique store, the type of high-dollar boutique that inhabits Cellar Street besides its colorful drinking establishments. Laura stops and conceals herself in the recessed doorway of a dress shop two stores down, close enough to hear them, and she watches with her dynamic eyes peering over the edge of the building.

Brown eyes smiles at him, reaches a hand up to his receding hairline, and says, "Come on, lover, let's get to your place."

She belches quietly between dark red lips underneath her hand, which covers her mouth from being seen by his trepid eyes.

He smiles but cannot hold its shape for long, "No, I don't think we should."

Not smiling with her inviting mouth anymore, but trying to force her lips to maintain a grin, she says, "No, really, I'm fine with it. We should go. Besides, you said the stuff was at your place; let's go party."

"I just don't feel like it anymore. Think I want to be alone."

"Excuse me? *You* wanna be alone?" she shrieks.

"No offense, Joanna, but I wanna be alone."

Her face tenses, and she bellows, "You conceited old fart. The only reason I was going anywherez wit you was you had some stuff for a party. I got me a boyfriend, and he's a lot hotter than you. Helluva lot hotter. But, he's a broke ass. Try to take some pity on an old geezer, and this is what you get. *You*—you're turning me down?"

A car whizzes past, interfering with Laura's ability to hear the conversation, which continues, "…ck you. You were lucky. Stupid, old ass."

Joanna waits for a response from him. Seeming somewhat disappointed, she mutters something that Laura can't hear, and she starts to walk away. She stops three feet from Chris, whose head has dropped to his chest, turns, and walks back to him. He still looks at his feet, pondering over where they will take him, until she again stands in front of him.

"Look at me, …" she says, the last word being inaudible to Laura.

He lifts his head to look in her face. Before they quite reach her eyes, her thin, bony hand smacks across his cheek, the sound moving across the uppity storefronts just as its upscale shoppers do during the day. Immediately the nail marks on his cheek become fiery. He says nothing. She flails her hand twice more, but misses him. Taking another shot, she connects with a sting, this time striking blood from the wound on his battered face. He still says nothing.

"What kinda man are you anyway? Can't keep it up, pops, is that it? Afraid you can't handle a young girl anymore? Just as well—I mean, just look at you….pfffh. You—*you*—saying you don't want me to come home with you? Pfffh. To hell with your dumb ass. Pathetic, nasty, old man."

Joanna turns back toward the bar and keeps walking this time. Stomping fast with anger and without the support of Chris's shoulder, she stumbles much more than she did earlier. She catches a blurred vision of a woman standing by the entrance of a closed store. She slows her pace to get a better look. Joanna sees two eyes that move in a most unsettling way in the shadows of a locked entrance. All of the adrenaline and gusto have left Joanna, who is wishing anyone were with her now, including the one she just slapped, to step between her and what she sees. The eyes swirl at her, and she feels the hot, fluid of fear running down her legs. Embarrassment is a feeling that she has no time for, and she runs toward the bar down the street, not looking behind her to see if the woman in the darkness is following.

Stepping out of the recessed, shadowy entrance, Laura glances down the sidewalk. Chris now steps in the direction in which he was originally walking with brown eyes. His chin still remains pressed against his chest. He approaches an intersection without looking upward. Laura follows.

Unsteady feet step off the curb onto the street. Headlights wash over them, and the blare of a horn shakes his eardrums. He stops moving forward and retreats toward the curb. The hulk of rolling metal passes him, and obscenities flood out of a window that is sliding down into its door cavity. His hand raises up in the vehicle's direction with all of his fingers extended, not being able to pull some down to leave one, lone and raised. His chin remains unmoved on his chest. He steps back into the street, again not looking for a safe path first, but this time he reaches the other side without conflict.

His walk is much different than when he stormed the girls' bathroom the other night. His shoulders are hunched; his head is down. His daring, glaring expression does not look for trouble as it has so often in the past following a round of drinks. His head points just before his feet, but his mind is somewhere else, somewhere inside, which drenches him in discomfort.

Her mind has two fronts. She struggles to think of her family, but her memories are suddenly hard to reach. When she does manage to grab onto a tiny recollection of her three precious ones, the pull twists it into a piece of nightmare, yanking her away from them and returning her attention to the drunkard walking a half block ahead of her. It flings memories of the other night at the bar into her head, and even imaginings of girls whom he has attacked before. No matter how much she fights the calls for violence, the hatred simmers, and its steam fills her lungs.

The buildings become familiar. Laura knows she has seen them before. The neighborhood is uninviting, and graffiti spawns across the sides of buildings like a vine. A rusty rail that is not fastened tightly to the steps sways as he climbs. Chris makes his way up them. She watches from a distance in the parking lot. The door. She remembers seeing it. The apartment letter H. It was a recent destination. She remembers the window.

Chris opens the door with a shove. He steps inside and clumsily tugs the key out of the handle. As he begins to close the entry, an uncanny feeling tingles at the back of his neck. Pulling the door open and sticking his head out into the balcony, he looks down the stairs and around the parking lot. He sees no one there and shuts the door. Click goes the deadbolt.

Laura perches herself on the thin lip of the window. The hole that she had left on her previous visit has been patched with cardboard and duct tape, looking more like a botched third grader's project than protection from the elements. It is made of two pieces of cardboard and unevenly torn strips of gray tape. One of the strands of tape, which is meant to connect the two pieces of cardboard in the center of the window, hangs limp inside the bedroom apartment, leaving an unblocked slit into the night. The streetlight in the distance flows through it in a rectangular beam as does Laura's gaze. The purple curtains lie on the coverless bed, devoid of their former beauty, never to be hung again.

She's been pulled here for the kill, but it doesn't feel right. The uncertainty leaves her restless. Things wrestle with her mind; tears in a stall—she remembers them vividly. But, there is something else that is moving inside her. It hasn't attached itself to a memory or even a reason. Something that whispers for her to hold off, passively pleading, nearly drowning beneath the pull's screams. Then, there it is.

Inside the room, a tiny book opens in his hands, and his lips move as he deciphers the words. Glossy eyes and a lack of illumination make his task challenging. His fingers reach backward, fumbling around underneath a lampshade. A faint click cracks the air in the room, and light enters the darkened chamber. As he pulls his hand back to him, it snags on the lampshade, pulling it off the nightstand. The lamp crashes to the floor, and its base shatters into jagged, little pieces and dust. The cable still runs from the bulb area to a tiny piece of its broken lamp base and then to the wall outlet; and it still burns. Shaking his head and muttering curses, he remembers when his ex-wife bought the lamp and brought it home. She was so excited that it matched the comforter in the baby's room so perfectly. He grumbled about the cost, as he did with most things related to his newborn daughter, and eventually his wife lost all of her excitement about the baby girl too, and soon for the girl's father as well.

The book's cover is a dark floral print; in the dim room with the only light coming from the feeble bulb on the floor and the lone blade coming from the shoddily patched window which lands near Chris's feet, it looks as if its petals are burning in the light's glow. On the opened pages close to his face, the words ignite. His face feels their burn, and he cries as he has only done alone in the bathroom and occasionally sprawled on the couch after a potent bender.

Laura's awareness is intensely heightened. The sound of the crashing lamp reminded her of when she broke through the window in the first place looking for Daisy. It took all of her strength not to lunge back into the room, smashing the feeble cardboard barricade covering her entrance. The urging has been going on for so long that it sounds natural to her now. It nudges her to leap into the room and upon the miserable creature inside and give him a taste of what he has forced others to swallow. There is little that she can think of to hold back the logic. The urging seems justified. Why should he not be made to face the same horror that he has brought upon so many: the lonely, the lost, the inebriated? Wouldn't justice leave the world a better place? How many girls would be spared his vile traps if she would end him now? Her resolve is running out of weapons to fight the pull. She saw the effects of his prowling in the bathroom; she cannot deny it, and she knows that the terror on the face of the girl was minimal compared to those who were not fortunate enough to have someone save them.

Sounds of whispering and weeping creep to the slit in the window. It is from within and without as Chris makes the noises on his knees in the room and the pull pleads inside her mind, whistling and swirling like the wind. The two noises coincide in a whirr as if they were a legion speaking to her in unison. It builds. Rises. And, its peak nearly shatters her eardrums.

Her feet hit the cardboard, sending it flying into the room at speed. Her body dives through the opening as smoothly as a paper plane, and haggard eyes stretch and pulse at the memory that has formed in front of him. He remembers the speed and the strength in her movements and his helplessness in resisting her attack in the bathroom. She looked tired and distracted then; now, she only looks angry.

She is anxious to pounce onto him, but he has remained kneeling, clutching onto the book. Chris resembles a penitent animal sitting on the floor, clinging to the text as if it were a bone, keeping its head down, refusing to look up at the angry master. While staring at him, that something, the thought that she cannot exactly assign to a memory or an idea, calls out to her to hold off, to wait, to feel out the situation before dismembering it. She couldn't be any less happy about trying to feel anything, but it is the only voice that she can hear above the pull. So, she stares at the man on his haunches, waiting to find out what he is doing, as torturous as it is for her to have to drudge through the experience.

He recalls quite well who she is and what she did to him the last time they met, yet his attention remains on the book, as if it is a portal in which he can escape from her if he needs. He has a total lack of attention for Laura standing before him with the night blowing subtly through the hole she has just made. The pull's fire is so hot that she feels like she is melting in the anticipation of the attack. But, the new voice inside her has gained strength in watching Chris's demeanor and his soft response to the hostile interloper standing before him. It whispers for her to wait and to listen. Its softness cuts through the roar of the pull, and for the moment she'll let it continue to speak.

"This was hers," he says, without taking his eyes off the pages suspended between his fingers. His sobbing surrounded by soundlessness is the chorus to his speech, and, when it has placed enough weight on the words he has just uttered, he continues, "Never knew it was so bad for her…never knew. Always seemed like a bad day—just a bad day; a bad day never killed anybody…was every day. Every damned day."

The sound of one breathing heavily and sobbing is all that can be heard in the room.

He starts again, "Do you know how it feels to read a story and hate the bad guy—you really want him to get his, and then you remember that it's you?"

His words stir something, and, although she has decided she would not speak, her tongue and lips do not obey, "Yeah, I think I know a little bit about that."

"Do you? Do you really know how sick it feels?"

His sobbing ceases as he waits for a response.

"Yeah, I know."

"Hmmph," he starts as the tone of her voice convinces him of her sentiment, "That's why I'm not afraid of you. I remember you; I know. But, I also know I deserve it. Reading these pages—I can't ignore it. Hell, I want it to happen to the bastard who treated my daughter this way. And, it's me. It's all me…"

His sobbing smothers his speech.

"You do deserve bad things. That's what drove me here."

His head nods, still staring at pages filled with journal entries documenting disappointment, sad little pictures that are aesthetically appealing but still ooze despair somewhere in the details. They mimic teenage female doodling except for the depressing air that surrounds them; a twist in a line, a harshness to the shading, an elongation of a facial feature, and cartoonish turns to deranged.

His voice makes the sound of a blade sliding on a sharpening stone, "Some of it I don't even remember…I dunno; it must be true; the other stuff's true. No one would make up things like that. No girl would think of her daddy acting like that—not even as part of some story or a game. No. No way; must be true."

The pull's volume becomes too much for her, and its will is her speech, "What is true? What did you do?"

"I knew sometimes when I'd been drinking that I'd hit her a few times. Hated myself for it, but I knew it happened. Never stopped it. More I did it, more I hated. More I hated, the more I did it. Everybody gets hit sometimes…never shoulda touched her though. No girl should have her daddy touching her. Ain't right. Never. Didn't remember."

The pull swarms as the words taint the air. Laura steps directly before him; the tips of her boots are close to touching him. Nausea builds inside her. The situation ignites a deep hatred; one that would be burning now even if the pull had never invaded her. Her nails push against her palms in tight fists. Her eyes spin with rage; memories fly about in their gust: unwanted pictures of her childhood, the lifeless bodies of the remains of her family, the girl in the stall whimpering and wounded, Daisy's nail marks on Gabe's arm, a chain between Chris, Daisy, and Gabe.

Her hand blurs forward and squeezes his gorge nearly shut, lifting him to his feet. His hands hold onto the book, which is now waist level between the two of them; his head struggles to keep an eye on the pages. As she tightens her grip, his breathing stops, his face reddens more than its natural rouge hue, but he does not look at her. His response antagonizes both her and the pull within.

She lets go of his throat. Gasp and wheeze get his breathing started. His vision stays on the dark, flowered book. Instinctively, she grabs it, yanking it away from his hands. The anger from the other night returns to his face, and he whines in something close to a howl.

"Give me the book!" he screams.

The pull is electric inside of her. The whisper is still there, but it is not audible anymore.

"Give me the damned book," he says, his alcohol-soaked breath pelting her face.

She stares at him, eyes swirling, and he howls again. He reaches for the book with both hands, but she stops his forward motion with a lightning kick to the chest. The breathing stalls again as the kick sends him crashing against the dresser, his feet crushing the bulb of the fallen lamp. Darkness grows. The only light sneaks in through the forced entrance in the window.

Her pointy smile reflects dimly from the outside light, "What if I rip it up?"

"God, don't. Please. Don't you dare."

"Oh, no. Don't you call out to the One whom you have had nothing to do with for so long."

Those words are heavy with truth, and his tongue can't lift them.

"Oh, yes, I think I should rip the pages to pieces and toss them into a fire. After all, she ripped my husband to pieces."

Her mind is wild as she stands before the man wrecked on a shoddy dresser. He breathes like a cornered pig who has surrendered to the realization that there is nowhere else to run. He had heard the other night watchman talking about the murders of a teacher and his family. The newspaper article was very graphic, and it had set people talking. When Daisy had been missing since then, he thought she might have known something about it. Maybe that boy or his friend that she had been trying to keep him from finding out about had done it. He saw the boys dropping her off in the parking lot a few times; he knew they looked like trouble, but they didn't look that much different than himself. And, that made him angry that he could not say anything. Besides, with his nightshifts, there were not a whole lot of rules that he could have enforced on her anyway. Commanded respect does not truly exist; it only appears to be useful when one is around to enforce it, causing the other person to pretend compliance. As soon as the commander is away, so are the charade and any semblance of admiration. Earned respect is the only kind that is real, and he knew he hadn't paid for it, leaving him with no power to govern her while he was gone. It also occurred to him that maybe she could have been the next victim in the murderer's rampage. He didn't really believe it to be true, but he knew it was a possibility. Yet, he did not call the police, not with his record and background. And, he didn't go looking for her either. Now that he looks for her in the words and sketches of a small book, he can see that she had trouble finding herself too.

The pull speeds up its attack; this time tossing images to her mind of Chris's sloppy walk with the brown eyes of Joanna. Laura's thin eyebrows raise the question, and her mouth follows.

"You're a phony, a total hypocrite. If you cared so much about this book and your lost daughter, why were you out getting drunk and trying to take home some young girl? Why were you drinking and trying to get laid instead of being here and reading this book? You're a pretender; nothing about you is real."

"Well, what about you? Did you follow me all the way from the bar?" A stare like a brick wall is her only answer, and he continues, "I just can't deal with all of this. Since her momma left, it's been a hard ride for me. Never knew what to say to a little girl—don't know what to talk about. I tried to bring her up hard just like I did so she'd know what was going on around her, what people were really up to. But, it kept her away from me ever since she was old enough to stay away. I can't deal with all this."

"What does that have to do with you getting drunk and chasing young girls?"

"Can't face this. I was sticking with what I know. I've always drank, and chasing girls has always come with it too. Was trying to get my mind off of what I read in this book when I came home from work. Today's shift, well I guess it's yesterday's shift by now, was from six to two a.m., and the other guy replaced me at two so I could come home. When I got back here, something pulled me in this room. I saw the book on her shelf, never noticed it before then, and I started reading it. The things in it twisted me all up inside. Wanted to stop reading but couldn't. I was stuck to it. The more twisted up it made me feel, the more I had to keep reading. When I got to the one where I crawled into her bed, I just about exploded. I put the book down on her bed and got myself a beer. Then another, and another. I drank seven of them and felt nothing. They didn't even taste right to me anymore. Tasted too much like water. So, I went to the bar and tried it there. I did shot after shot. There's a new girl behind the bar, and she let me run a tab—didn't know any better. I racked up one long bill; shots, beer, hard drinks. None of it did anything to me."

Laura's voice leaps ahead of her patience, "But, you were stumbling; I saw you. You were nearly hit by a car."

"Yeah, it's hard to pay attention where you're going when your head's someplace else."

Those words bring her mouth to a close.

He continues, "You stumble on the outside when you're stumbling on the inside, ya know? Sometimes it's alcohol; sometimes it's other stuff; and sometimes it's from the drinking you did to forget the other stuff. But, tonight, it wasn't alcohol; it was my head."

He lifts himself into a better position, propping his elbow on the top of the dresser and leaning his weight on it. His body hurts where it crashed into the furniture, but it is not much of a concern to him.

"What about the girl?" poses Laura.

"Same thing. Sticking to what I knew. Trying to do the same old thing to keep me from drowning in all this—get my mind off of it. But, she didn't feel right either. And, it wasn't her. Two weeks ago, shi—I'da been all over her. I was just doing it to do it. I wasn't excited—didn't really care. Was hoping it would help, that I could feel something besides what I read in the book. Nothing worked. It's still there—I still feel it. S'why I don't care what you do—I need that book. Gotta finish this thing. Right now nothing's right; it ain't no place to be."

"What if it'll always be that way, Chris?"

Hearing her say his name stuns his brain, causing a momentary hesitation, "I dunno; I think it just might end up always being this way. Don't think I can be like this. Don't think I wanna be at all if it's gonna be like this. But, I gotta know what happened to my girl, even if I'm the miserable s.o.b. that done it to her."

Laura continues, "Beer has no taste, alcohol has no effect, and your touch is numb to girls—that's why you don't wanna live anymore?"

"No," he says as he thinks about what that 'no' actually means to him. "I don't really care about all that right now. Gotta finish looking at what my girl was trying to tell me—to tell anyone. Something's wrong with her being gone and no one reading her story—especially me. Didn't pay it any mind while she was living it, least I can do now is to read it."

"And, what about when you're done?"

His face is pale and still, "Don't know that one. Maybe, I can't live without my old ways. What the hell could take away liking women and alcohol? How'd this happen to me? Maybe I'm being punished for what's in there," he says pointing at the pages bound in the dark floral cover, "Maybe there is nothing else for me after the book. Maybe my story ends when her diary book does…Got no family, don't do anybody any good. I dunno what good it'd be for me to be 'round anyway if I can't live my life the way I always have."

"It would've done Daisy some good a few years ago."

His head drops to his chest, his lips mouth the word "yeah", but no sound comes forth. Somewhere beneath the toxicity of his eyes, she sees a swirl of her own misery, like oil in mud.

Without thinking about what she is going to say, words slip past her lips, "I've got some things I wish I had done differently about two years ago. I think that's gonna eat at me until I'm not here anymore."

His head lifts half the distance to her face, stopping at the book that is now in her left hand, "You're not completely here anyway, are you?"

"No."

"Not like you," he says in a quiet gruff, "But I ain't all here either."

Words fall like water, when she would much rather be a dam, "You are a terrible person; I'm not going to lie to you. You've done a ton of harm to God knows how many people. But, you've lost the taste for the two things that have driven you to all of that trouble. Don't you see there's some design to what's happened to you?"

His body sinks from its elbow's perch on the dresser to plopping itself upon the floor with his back leaning against the bureau. The words stun herself as much as they have shocked the mess of a man on the floor. A grand design is something that she has revoked since the call came to her office in what seems to be an eon ago, another life, a green-tinted story from one's childhood.

To her amazement and his fearful captivation, more words flow, "But, all of this is within your control. If you are to continue being a monster, then it's no one's fault but your own. You have the power to behave in any way that you see fit. This book," she says, shaking it softly in her hands as his eyes follow it intently, "makes you sick. You know what is awful in it; no one needs to help you. You know what should not be; you just need to figure out what should be. The complete opposite might be a good place to start."

Her words blanket over him like snow, encompassing him, chilling him, and fitting him perfectly. He knows not what to say. His thoughts are digesting her words and considering what has been heretofore undreamed of for him: the possibility of living a different way, breaking the pattern that started in his family long before him. The only other emotion that is given air to breathe is the yearning to regain the book.

Her voice slices through his thoughts, "If you don't…the pull will bring me back again, and there won't be anything to talk about next time."

It screams within her head to strike. *He'll never be any different. You're allowing him to abuse other girls. He'll never make it sober. End it. End him. Now. Get rid of him. He's no good.* She fends off its forceful reasoning, and the pull becomes more enraged. Grabbing a fistful of heinous images, the pull tosses them in her eyes, each a tiny particle shining in its horrific graphicness. Phantasmagoria consumes her. Her commanding face is now only one of great pain. Her lip quivers, and her eyes are strange.

A flash of memory returns to Chris too. He remembers her spell in the bathroom in which he tried to attack her. His anger surfaces again on his face. She has the only thing of value to him now and possibly the one thing he'll value for the rest of his life. The opening for action, this small moment taunts him like a young, flirtatious girl who has just begun an experiment with drinking in an adult world. It is a familiar setup for him. His own inner voices urge him to lunge and to silence her. How dare she suggest that there is any other way to live? He's been this way his whole life, and so had his parents been during their lives. His hand trembles as his usual urges nudge him to move.

Laura stumbles at the barrage of nightmares that attack her consciousness. Her hatred rises as she knows this attack is upon her because of the piece of garbage on the floor before her. Had he not lived such a miserable and selfish existence, the pull would not have brought her to him in the middle of the night, demanding his life. Had he not been such a lousy father, maybe her children would still be alive. Maybe the other two deviants would not have held such a grudge against Gabe without Daisy's involvement in the tale. The pull's voice has overcome the calm whispering, and the drive rises to embrace violent means and rid herself of the horrors that block her vision. As her hatred surges, her eyes clear, her balance returns, and she sees the unlikely scene before her.

Chris's back still leans on the dresser. His hands are clasped between his knees like one in prayer, and his face shows pain but not wicked intentions. The pull screams for her to dive at him and rip him apart before she can absorb the meaning of what she sees. His window to attack her has closed, and he fought the urge to jump through it. The only movement that he has made has been within himself.

The pull has intensified its screaming to unbearable levels. She can feel that the whisper is still there, but she cannot hear it. She knows what she will be put through if she does not act. The book feels warm in her icy hands, and a vision comes to her of a chain between her, this world, and the corpses of three teenagers.

Chris has not looked back to her face since she began stumbling. Rusty, late October flowers drop through the air. The book lands against the pouch of his belly, and his hands clasp at it in reflex. He stares at it, lifting it to his eye level. It truly is the book that he needs and dreads. One that he wishes he could unwrite. He notices no one stands before him. He glances to the window and sees nothing but a jagged hole into the night.

Chapter XXXIV

An elevator dings, and doors open for her destination. This floor, full of familiar equipment, looks less like a dead end this morning than it has in the past. Something has happened, and this current existence seems optional instead of mandatory. She knows this new one is not the one for her, and she has always held out for the real thing. But, how long can one go without seeing a color before forgetting that it ever existed?

A short while later…

The color of his eyes is dense and electric in a way that she has not seen in a long while. They don't look faded and irritated; it's as if they were suddenly unveiled from behind the filmy, bloodshot curtain of life. Although they are alive, it is not with the same emotion that she has been scouting for.

Her voice has a timber of annoyance beneath it as she speaks, "It's just a movie, Andarus; it's not that big of a deal."

"If that's so, then why are you so irritated with me?" he asks.

"You honestly don't know why I'm aggravated?"

"No, not specifically."

Her eyes match his in a stare, "I'm aggravated because I told you about the stupid little date because I was trying to be courteous of your feelings, and you've been giving me attitude."

"Well, you don't see me dating anyone on the force, do you?"

"No, Paul, I don't see you dating anybody…and, I, I don't see myself dating anyone either. I don't know how you can live like this, Paul; it's killing me," she says as the last two words squeal in her throat. Her eyes well up, and it takes a great deal of strength for her to hold the burst inside.

Vexed he is, but much more so at himself than in anything she has done. Part of him feels affirmed that she felt the need to tell him that a rookie officer had asked her out in the elevator that morning. He knew something was up by her behavior; her responses were just slightly slow, and she kept repositioning her lips from one shape to another; sucked inward, tucked to a side, then tucked to the other side. Despite the repulsion he feels at the actual message, he feels special that she felt the necessity to relay it to him quickly. If she felt the need to tell it to him, then she thinks that her personal life is his business. He likes this almost as much as he hates the idea of her going out with some guy, especially one whom he may see daily.

She continues softly in volume but stern in tone, "I just told him 'maybe', Paul. Not that that's any of your business anyway."

He adjusts his tone to gentle and says, "It just doesn't seem appropriate, 'Rene, to be dating someone at work."

Her face fluctuates from enraged to hurt, all of her shaking subtly like a reflection on the top of the ocean. Many things come to her mind, all trying to escape through her lips that are currently sucked in at the right corner and sandwiched lightly between her teeth. Eventually one of the waves of emotion rushes over her levee and floods out of her.

"Paul, you know why I'm upset, and, damn it, I think I know why you're upset too. But, what's so lousy about all of this is that you won't say it…"

Her lip trembles jarringly and it looks as if she is trying to compose herself to speak further, but she does not. She rises out of the chair in Andarus's office, digs in her purse, and comes out with her keys and a crumpled receipt. She tosses the receipt in the small trash can in front of Andarus's desk, and she walks out of the room.

Left to his thoughts, Andarus is a mess. His emotions, too, resemble waves at sea. One crashing into another into a big, meandering, chaotic current.

Glancing at the trash can, he sees a crumpled receipt at the top of the tiny heap with half of a name and the end of a phone number written upon its visible flap.

"Aww, no! Damn it. 'Rene!" he cries out, but she is not there, leaving him feeling hollow.

The phone rings, jarring his heart and echoing through his emptiness. *Could it be Irene?* Could she have called from the parking lot to talk to him, feeling as miserable as he does? The ringing has stopped, but the red light remains lit indicating someone has picked up the line. The light then flashes as it is put on hold. Red is a tricky color. It can symbolize warmth, heart, and even love, or it can be scorching, a reflection of hell itself.

Jackson calls from the eating area, "Andarus, it's for you."

Excited at the prospect, he feels that his voice has abandoned him.

Jackson continues, "It's the chief."

The emptiness floods upon him again, but it brings his voice back with it, "Tell him I have an appointment with a bench."

"With what judge, Andarus?"

"Biggest one in town."

The night before had been a marathon, a venture into torment. It was what she knew it would be when she leapt out the window, except for the ending. The long, lightless hours with the pull were quite unkind, but slowly the whispering gained more strength, not through volume, but through its ability to maintain Laura's focus. The pull's screams became more frantic, but quieter. It has not lost its ability to make hell appear before her eyes, but its voice is not as powerful, at least not at the moment.

She sits. Her mind is as boggy as the path around the edge of the park. The rains stopped seven days ago, but the sunken path under the shelter of trees has barely dried up at all. The record rainfall drowned the earth, leaving deep, sloppy footprints filled with dirty water encircling the recreational area, foreboding most from crossing its stagnant moat-like outer circle and entering.

"Never know who's gonna be sitting next to you on a park bench."

She looks to her left to see the detective plopping down next to her. The humor doesn't quite touch her, and, as she looks over his countenance, neither does fear of being apprehended. She does wonder how he got so close without the pull or her senses giving a warning.

"Kill anybody today?" asks Andarus nervously.

"It's early yet," she says, with the corners of her lips staying straight and flat.

Feeling the silence start to paralyze in an emotional hypothermia, he forces his question out, "While we're talking about it, why didn't you kill me when you had the chance in the office?"

She glances back at his face, and he continues, "Or in the car that night?"

"Andarus," she says remembering his name like one does when involved in a crash with another, "I never wanted to kill anybody…just had to be."

"Yeah," gasps out of his mouth in an exhale, "that's what I thought…but, then why did you come back to the office the last time? There was no more information for you to receive. You had to be finished the…you had to be finished by then."

"Was trying something out."

Silence echoes one more round.

"Did it work?"

Laura's head holds perfectly still, "No, still here."

A large squirrel stands on its hind legs, watching them on the bench. It holds still until a small squirrel runs up behind it. The large squirrel turns and barks at the approaching youngster, and the youngster squeals and retreats.

"Shouldn't you be smoking?" asks her familiar yet unsettling voice.

"Excuse me?" responds Andarus.

"Every detective that I've ever seen in a movie or read about in a book has always smoked cigarettes."

"Well, life's not always like the movies, Mrs. Bonney."

"Yeah, sometimes it's much worse."

"Besides, I have enough vices," ignoring her comment.

"Like what?"

Looking into her face, "Like not being able to let a case go. Sticking my nose into something dangerously unreal," his voice dropping lower, "Focusing on everything except my life."

"Be careful where you stick your nose; trouble might find you. Besides, you never know who's sitting next to you on a park bench."

A half minute of stillness creeps on them following her throwing his line back at him.

"I…I understand why you did what you did, Laura. I can't say I would've been any different."

Looking to the sky, "Wish someone else thought that way too."

"You know if I don't bring you in—or someone else to blame for all of this, I'm gonna get fired—well, at least demoted."

"Good luck with that."

"Hey, I never said I was gonna try…well, actually I did tell someone that I would try to bring you in."

"Someone? You shouldn't lie to your partner, Andarus."

He stares down at his knees.

Laura continues, "Saw her at the funeral; I could tell…she's a good shot."

Sighing, he says, "It wasn't a lie; I meant it. I *was* going to try, but I didn't like it. I wanted to make this town feel safe again, to give people closure, justice. That's just it though—it's not justice; it's obeying the law, and I can't make them the same thing. This all has just been haunting me. Things going on with you are not rational or even explainable; I figure maybe you were given these abilities because you were right. Plus…I just don't feel right about trying to bring you in."

"Tell me what you knew about the kids that killed my husband."

"What difference would that make? They're all dead now."

Her eyes start to spin with emotion, "Trying to make sense of all this."

"I've been working on these cases for years; there's not much to make sense of."

She leans, moving her head closer to his with her eyes building with emotion and movement.

He starts, "They were angry with your husband about giving them their last detention that resulted in them being expelled."

"Knew that. What else?"

"They all come from lousy families."

"Knew that too."

Placing his hand to the edge of his chin, he says, "Hmmm...Daisy had some crush on your husband about a year ago. It had to be how they talked her into this. She's never been in any type of trouble—none at school, none outside of it."

"Found that out, too; it explained some things," she says as she remembers the chain that appeared to her while she was holding a sad book in the dark.

"Like what?"

"Just an image in a dream that came to me...while I was awake."

"Yeah...I haven't been one for sleeping either. Can't seem to find the energy to find the peace to sleep, and can't get the energy because I can't sleep."

"I know a little about that," she says with her mind going over the early events of the previous night. She shifts her weight on the bench as the old wooden boards begin to dig into her.

The smaller squirrel approaches the big one again; this time he moves slowly and quietly. The larger squirrel notices his movement, but he is satisfied with the young one's current, calmer approach.

Andarus looks to her with a face that shows the troubles of his heart.

Without a thought the words come to Laura, and she says, "Call her. At least one of us can be free."

The phone rests awkwardly angled downward in his hand like a sword in the palm of the inexperienced. He wants more to have it done than to be doing it. He holds it as uncertain as an eleven-year-old boy using it to attach himself to a girl for the first time, yet he calls for something else.

The number is familiar enough for his fingers to remember dialing it, but distant enough to feel that he is visiting a part of his life that has passed, like returning to a childhood home that is inhabited by new people. As the phone rings, reality seems to be dynamic and able to be manipulated. As his call awaits an answer, his life feels more like a game that is still being played than an unbreakable routine, to which he has been accustomed for quite some time.

The voice that comes through the receiver is a crisp audiograph to match a fuzzy memory in his head. Its familiarity tugs at his raised guard to lower its defense and open himself up to the person he has called. Memory reminds him to keep it where it is, and emotion pushes him to respond to the lone "Hello."

"Hi, Karen, it's Paul."

A soft gasp comes through the tiny holes pressed against his ear, and it is followed by, "W-e-ll, Paul, how have you been?"

"Same as always; busy with work, up at night. How've you been?"

Hesitation is followed by, "I-I've been really busy too. Very busy in fact. Paul, why are you calling?"

"I don't exactly know. I just wanted to say some things."

"Well, okay. That's fine…It's not that it's bad to hear from you; it's just so unexpected."

"I bet it is, Karen; it's been awhile. A long time."

"Yeah, about three years now."

"Yeah, I think that's right," he answers knowing exactly how long it has been.

"So," she says softly, "what is it that you want to say?"

Ideas and emotions fill his brain, although he can't match them with words to bring them out of his head and into the phone.

Finally he starts, "There were a lot of things that I was sorry about. Like the work invading into our private plans all the time and me being so worn out when I would be at home. Tickets to events that we never got to go see because a case came up. Lots of things. That wasn't fair to you, but that's my life; don't know if I can live it any other way."

Her voice answers, "As much as I hated the hours that your work took away from us, I never blamed you, Paul. All the good that you did, bringing justice to those poor lost families—no, I never blamed you. You wouldn't have been the same person if you didn't care so much about catching the bad guys and protecting the rest of us. I just knew that I couldn't live that life with you anymore. It did make me miserable, Paul…I'm sorry if this hurts to hear, but it's the truth."

"I don't like hearing it, but I've known it was true for a long time now."

Silence slides into the conversation.

"Well, what about you, Paul?"

"Huh?"

"What about you? I don't blame you for the work that made me unhappy. Do you blame me for your work making me unhappy?"

"No, never have. For a long time I blamed myself. Then I realized that that wasn't the biggest problem. The biggest problem was me not apologizing for things that I knew had to hurt you. For not being able to say things that were going on inside of me. For me not to tell you a thousand things that you needed to hear. I still blame myself for that."

"Paul, you need to forgive yourself. If you don't forgive yourself, you'll never get past all of this; you'll never be able to move on…Paul, are you seeing anyone?"

"No," he says as he thinks of someone for whom he does have feelings.

"My God, Paul, tell me you've dated someone—anyone since we split up."

"I don't really want to talk about this."

"Paul, you called for a reason: to say some things to me that you needed to get off your chest. This is important. Have you dated anyone since we separated?"

Words follow an exhale, one like a worker dropping a heavy load into its place, “No, Karen.”

“No?” she repeats, “Are you telling me the truth?”

“Have I ever been one to lie to you?”

“Oh, Paul, I just don’t want to believe it; it makes me feel guilty. I know that doesn’t make any sense, but it makes me feel bad about myself. It’s like you put your life on hold for me, and I’ve…”

“What does this have to do with you, Karen? We’ve been divorced; you have every right to do whatever you want. It’s not like I’ve been calling you every day trying to get you back.”

The words sting the air, and neither’s mouth ventures to send any more statements for a moment.

“Damn it, Karen, I’m sorry; that didn’t come out right. That’s not what I meant.”

“No, that’s not why I’m being quiet; Paul, I’m getting married next week. I wanted to call and tell you, but we haven’t talked in so long. I honestly didn’t know if you cared, or, even if you did, if it would be a good idea to call you out of the blue and tell you that I’m getting married again.”

“It’s…it’s okay. I’m really glad that you’ve been able to find happiness again. Really; I’m glad for you.”

“Paul, are you sure? It seems like this would be hard.”

“Well, the tiniest bit of me might be bitter-sweet about it, but I’m mostly happy. I don’t quite know how to explain it, except that it means I didn’t wreck your life.”

“Of course you didn’t wreck my life. We just didn’t work out.”

“Well, there’s only so much time in life, and you gave a few years to me. Time for careers. Time for spending time together. Time for children. A family. You lost time with me; I’m just glad that there was still enough left for you to be happy.”

“Paul, you know what? There’s time for you too. I’m okay; I’m going to be happy. There is nothing for you to feel guilty about. We weren’t good together; it didn’t work out. It wasn’t your fault, Paul. You owe it to yourself to be happy.”

“What if? What if I do the same thing to somebody else? What if I take years away from somebody else only for them to realize that my lifestyle is not going to make them happy too? What if they’re not as lucky as you? What if they end up miserable for the rest of their life? How can I put someone else through that? Nothing’s changed; I’m still me.”

“Paul, Paul, Paul. Slow down there. First of all, anyone, who knows you now, knows your lifestyle already. I met you before you were working so many hours. I watched you study ferociously in college, but I thought things would settle down once you graduated. But, they sure didn’t; that was only the beginning. But, someone who knows you now should know what she’s getting into. Secondly, you could just tell her this is how it’s going to be and make sure she can handle it. And, if she tries and can’t, that’s her decision; every person has a right to make their decisions in life. You can't worry about that—that would be the woman's choice to be with you. As long as she isn't being deceived, which I don't think anyone would be with you, it's her choice. And, you're wrong about something else, Paul."

"No surprise there. What is it?"

"You said nothing has changed."

Glancing around his gloomy living room, "What makes you think that's not true?"

"You called, Paul. You haven't done that since the divorce was final. You apologized; you've talked about how you feel. You're not the same anymore; you're something new."

Chapter XXXV

"No, I think you may be something new, but you're not completely gone."

Laura responds, "Everything that I've loved is gone; where else can I be but gone too?"

"Is everything that you've loved gone, Laura?" Virgil asks as he glances up to the sun setting in the horizon which casts an interesting glow into the church alley in which they stand.

She doesn't like the taste of the question, but it still makes her feel guilty for her previous comment. Yet, she makes no effort to take it back. Right or wrong she is feeling things out, and that feels better than lonely hours in an alley or long, dark, wandering nights, devoid of sleep or even the most simple dream. Nightmares cling to her; like scent on a prey, she cannot wash them off, and the source of her torment remains on her heels. A shot in the dark is the hope of the hopeless, but at least it is a shot. So, she waits to see what it will hit.

It is by no means uncomfortable weather as the sun sets on the fading late summer evening, but Virgil suggests coming inside, and she concedes with a silent nod.

Hours later inside the church, Virgil sits in the first pew, closest to the altar, and Laura sits in the second. After a long streak, there is a lull in the conversation. He waits for her to talk and watches her demeanor for the unspoken. She wraps her arms across her chest and begins to speak of the haunting mallogos with which the pull persistently attacks her. As she describes the sadistic images, her taut, thin biceps tremble slightly, and their movement interrupts the priest's thoughts. He stares, fixed upon her arms for a moment, and she is unsure as to why.

"Laura, are you nervous?"

She raises an eyebrow, and poses, "I've already crashed, padre. What is there to be nervous about? The terrible thing has already happened."

"Well, quite often the aftermath is worse than its original cause. But, I've never seen you act nervously before tonight. So, if you're not nervous, why are your arms shaking?"

"Oh," she says with a small laugh of which Virgil has not heard from her in their previous conversations, "this may be a church, Virgil, but you keep it cold as hell in here."

He does not laugh at the response, but continues to stare at her.

Laura offers, "Don't take so much offense. It's just a figure of speech."

"No, that's fine. It's just that you're cold. I mean, *Laura, you're cold*."

The words pierce her consciousness.

"Oh, God. I do feel cold. I feel it," she says, sliding her hands over her upper arms. Her fingertips sense the tenderness of her skin as they slide over, "Virgil, I can feel it. Maybe, I can…"

He interrupts her, "Laura, no, that's not the way."

"Maybe, I can get the hell out of here."

Softly, shaking his head, "Laura, no."

"This could be it! I can feel the cold; my fingertips are alive again—I can feel them. I can die now. I can get to my family!"

"Laura, that's not how it works. How do you know that you'll get to the same place as your family? They were murdered against their will; you're murdering yourself. What makes you think you'll end up in the same place when you're taking a different path to get there?"

"Got to get out of here. I'm not some depressed girl who's just been broken up with; it's my family, my children, my husband, my life that I'm trying to get to—I'm not running away from anything."

"Please, Laura, no. Don't do it this way. We don't know what's going on inside of you or why you were granted the powers that you had, or maybe even still have some of, so you can't just try to crash into heaven. That's not promised to us; we can't show up with a man-made deed and expect for the gates to fling open. Don't jump off this cliff; we don't know where you're going to land."

"Anything's better than this; can't sleep. Every break from consciousness is a nightmare like nothing I could've imagined before. No family, no desire for life. A dark voice threatens me with horrible visions if I don't do its will. There's nothing for me here; anything's better than this."

"Is it? Is it really? Have you thought this out? You just said you've had nightmares that you could not have imagined before; how do you know that there will not be more than you can imagine now when you cross over? Why are you assuming this? Maybe there is another life for you here; maybe you're not supposed to leave now."

Tears fill her eyes, pupils shining underneath their gloss. They are still uncommonly vibrant, and they swirl slowly and unnaturally. But, they are closer to how she appeared before any of this happened. She strains to hold the tears inside. Maybe, it is a result of her not having been able to cry since she got up from the floor in her office that she feels it inappropriate to let a tear slide out now. All of the hideous things that she has been through are a flood of tragedy to which she does not want to add the liquid of her tears. And, she fears letting them fall now, as if they will chain her to this world.

"All I've done since things were finished with Daisy is to ram myself against all that is around me, trying to break through this place to get to the next. I can't fit into this world again; it can't be meant for me. I've killed three people; my family has been murdered. What am I supposed to do? Go get a job? Go out for a drink? I don't want this! I've got a chance to check out; I'm taking it before something changes and this door closes."

"And, what if this door leads you to a place that is forever like what you've been going through? What if this door leads you to an eternity of horrible visions and images and being separated from your family? If you slam yourself against the world again and shatter yourself to another place, what makes you assume that it's going to be a better one?"

"The desperate urge for something better. Some peace. There has to be peace somewhere."

"Well, I don't think you're going to find it by tearing yourself to pieces."

"And I don't think I'm going to find it if I stop looking for it."

"That's actually exactly how it works a lot of the time."

"What?"

"That's how we live our lives a lot of the time; we work so hard to make things easier. Someone will work tremendously long hours to retire five years earlier, but in the process they make themselves miserable, they miss irreplaceable events with their loved ones, and they wrack their bodies out; they could easily end up taking five years off their life. The overwhelming effort to make things easier can steal all that is wonderful from us. Another one is a person, who blindly leaps from one relationship to the next, desperately searching for the perfect person—this one will never find what they're looking for. They are always in transit from one person to the next. They get into a relationship without putting any thought into who they are with. Often, it is with a person whom they are poorly matched, because the relationship started out of a need to cling to the next person he or she could find, often the first person he or she could find. So, they are in relationships with people who are not right for them, because they lunge into them blindly, never having the opportunity to find someone better suited for them. And, since they are compulsively always in a relationship, they are never single, which would give them the opportunity to find someone that could make them happy. And, they are never available for someone else, who could truly love them, to have the chance to ask them out. It is a downward spiral. This person can never find an appropriate partner because they are so blinded by the obsession to have a good relationship that they never have the chance for it to happen. If the person would remain single and hold out for the right thing, then the opportunity for an appropriate partner is there; they can find each other if they both hold out. The guy who wastes most of his life by overworking in the effort to make things easier has missed what he was working so hard for. The happy moments in life are all around us all of the time. We can't decide to miss them for years in the hope that we can enjoy all of them that we would ever want once our task is finished. If there is food on the table and a roof overhead, a person can stop working. Everything that we work for after that has to be scrutinized carefully. We work to provide the essentials for life, and, after that, we are assumedly working for things that will improve the quality of our lives. Well, if we're missing what makes us happy in life in an attempt to make our lives better, we've missed the point. In other words, we missed what we were trying to catch because we were so obsessed with looking for it," he breathes deeply and continues, "This is why I don't think you're going to find what you're looking for by smashing into things blindly. I think you'll end up somewhere; I don't think it'll be what you're looking for at all."

All of his words still fill the air around her. She stares at the floor below her and a small crack that runs through the stone where the pew was bolted to the ground.

Virgil starts again, "I'm sorry, Laura. I didn't mean to give a speech, just didn't know how else to explain it. I know it's not what you wanted to hear."

"I'm not. I'm not starting over. I'm done with all of this, Virgil; I swear it; I'm done."

"Well, let's try and figure this out; I'm not God. I don't know everything. Just because I could see that the path you were going to take is the wrong one, it doesn't mean that I can see the right one, or certainly that I can see all of them. Let's see what we can figure out; there has to be some sign, some guidance as to what you should do."

Laura's eyes hold firm to the crack by her feet, and her brow is full of more despair than hope. But, she listens.

"When did you start to feel things? I mean physically—when did the numbness fade away?"

"I remember feeling a chill at the park yesterday—well, it was two days ago by now. I didn't think about it until a minute ago, sitting here talking to you. I remember it was overcast and chilly sitting down on the bench, but I didn't realize it was anything special until now. Before all of this, I was always a bit cold; it wasn't anything unusual. That's why I had this jacket with me in August—always wanted something on my arms at night. But, I felt it in the park; I definitely felt something, even if I didn't know it at the time."

"Was there anything before that?"

"Yeah, when I left here two nights ago, I found Daisy's dad."

"Oh, my God, Laura, tell me you didn't."

"No, I did. Tracked him down to his apartment. But, relax, padre; I didn't kill anybody."

Relief rushes over his face, and, realizing that she must have seen his reaction, he says, “I’m sorry, Laura. Of course you didn’t. I shouldn’t have assumed.”

“Well, hold on there. The pull did lure me there. In fact, it wanted me to attack you before I left the church. It was angry with me for not attacking you after our conversation—the one about me letting go of the hatred and accepting responsibility for the last few years. It was so enraged with me that it tormented me for half the night until I followed its direction. Wandered the streets until I found him. He was coming out of a bar—one I went to when I was a kid. I followed him home. It was the second time that the pull had brought me there. It urged for me to kill him. It threw ugly images into my head; it reasoned with me that the world would be a better place without him in it. And, it was hard to argue against it; it was honestly hard to imagine that the world is a better place with a man like Daisy’s father in it. He drinks, he’s violent, and he takes advantage of every girl he can get his hands on. But, when I found him, he was reading his daughter’s diary and crying. He knew I was the one; he knew I could have killed him. But, he didn’t care. He didn’t care what I did to him; he just wanted to finish reading his daughter’s story. The pull screamed for me to kill him, but underneath the crazy screeching of the pull was another voice; it told me to listen and be still. Somehow I could reach past the pull to the quiet voice, and I didn’t harm him. I told him if he didn’t change his ways and the pull brought me back again that I’d kill him. And, that’s true, padre. That’s true.”

“Why didn’t you kill him?”

“His pain over Daisy was not entirely unlike mine. He regrets his life, pretty much his entire life. I regret being away from Gabe and the kids the last few years. You were right, padre. You were right…”

“I’d rather be wrong and have things be easier on you; I promise you,” he responds softly.

“The quiet voice made me believe that he’d change. And, maybe I’m an idiot, but I still believe it.”

“It’s not often that we change ourselves in such a big way; but we can. We certainly can, and that’s part of what’s wonderful about being human. You’ve changed, Laura. I can see it in your eyes. You can feel things again. You showed mercy to someone who probably had done nothing to earn it. You fought the pull when it pushed you to attack me. You’ve gained control over the hatred that transformed you into what you were. Now it’s time for you to return to what you were before all of this.”

“I don’t want it; I don’t want to be here without them. It seems so sick to imagine myself with other people, carrying on like my family could be replaced, or at least that I could be distracted enough to forget and be happy again.”

“Well, how do you want to be when you see them again?”

“What?”

"Do you want to see your family as you were when you killed their killers? Do you want your girls to see a murderer? Someone whose body is too numb to feel them? Or do you want them to see their mother that they remember? Do you want to embrace Gabe with hands that pulse with the pull's hatred, or do you want them to move with love?"

She still stares at the crack, which suddenly seems more like an opening, a winding path, than like a weakness or an imperfection.

Virgil continues, "You've already started peeling this off of you. You can't stop now; you need to shed the rest of it. It means you'll be vulnerable, it means you'll lose that barrier that has kept you from feeling nearly all that is around you, and it means that you'll be human. You'll hurt, you'll feel all of it, and you'll be alive in this world without them. But, there is no other way. There is no other way for you to be you when you return to them."

She responds softly, "I did what you asked, you know?"

"What is that, Laura?"

"I've let it go."

"Really?" he asks surprised.

"I still hate all of this; this terrible thing. But, when I saw some of me in Daisy's dad. When I saw where she came from—learned some of what has happened to her, it's hard to see her as only a villain. And, the other two. I went to their houses after I left Daisy's dad, watched their parents stumble home from a casino or shout at a television and each other. For two days, I watched their lives. It's not hard to see why the kids turned out twisted. They're still guilty; horribly guilty—there is no excuse. But, I don't hate the same way anymore. It took a long time for it all to sink in—went to the park every day to think in between watching them."

"Do you regret what you've done?"

"Not at all."

Virgil sits silently.

"If I hadn't done it, who knows who else they would've hurt? When they would've been stopped. It could've gone on for God knows how long. They deserved every bit of what they got from me. And, I'd do it again. I came out of a bad place, too, and I didn't do the things they've done. But, I did have Gabe…I did have Gabe…"

"And, they didn't have anything?" he asks.

"I sure as hell didn't have anything until I found Gabe, but I held on. I was waiting; I was fighting, and then he appeared. They didn't try; they embraced the sins of their parents and became even worse. I fought it when I was their age; I didn't go rape children and kill an innocent man. I fought all of that anger; I fought it alone until I met Gabe. It was a long time alone."

"Is this why you can feel things again? Is it because you've let go?"

"That's when it started, yeah."

Virgil's pupils hold still as his mind turns, "I guess you're on your way then. Don't know how much else I can help you."

Their thoughts give birth to a moment of silence.

"Virgil, why did you help me? I've done terrible things; things that you're supposed to tell people not to do. What made you want to help me?"

"Well, if I judged who I decided to help and who I didn't, I wouldn't be doing what I'm supposed to be doing. And, secondly, if I refused to help people because they had done the wrong thing, I'd never help anyone, including myself. That's part of being human; we make mistakes, sometimes terrible ones. But, we have the ability to change, to better ourselves as a result, and hopefully the world around us too. I admit, I've never helped anyone with something as morbid as this, but, if anyone ever had a reason to kill, as horrible and ugly as it is, it would be you."

"Is that the truth, padre?"

"I can't say it's right, Laura, but I've never been in your shoes. And, I certainly can't blame you," he pauses, absorbing his words and verifying how they make him feel, "Yes, Laura, it's true."

Laura smirks for a moment, letting his response settle inside her. The cold air gets to her, and she sneezes.

Virgil quickly offers, "God bless y-"

He catches himself quickly and looks her over intently.

"You're breathing," he says watching her chest rise and fall.

"Yes, I am."

"Then, you've unfrozen yourself," he says raising his hand to his chin, "You're almost you again."

"Yes, but I can't stay."

She is finally before him. It was a long night. He is surer than he ever has been, but he's never been such a mess around her. The self-defeating comfort of indecision, the "maybe I should or maybe I shouldn't" and the "it's not the right time", has left him. The clarity of knowing what he wants to do is married to the need to bring it into existence. All that remains is for him to do it, and that is what makes him a mess of choppy breaths, unsteady words, and clumsy movements. He knows she'll see it. What she'll think of it, he does not know.

Her face is painted in shadow; she is drenched in its sadness. It is six fifteen a.m., and she has no reason for being early except a need to be here. She does not have any specific remedy for their rift, but she wants to be there to see if one presents itself. She has resigned herself that if she is the one to bridge this gap, their relationship will never be real; it'll be something she constructed. Unnaturally forced. He has to reach for her this time, and she knows it. She is uncomfortable with leaving it all up to him, and, even though it's killing her to stand by and watch what happens, she doesn't want it to happen if it's not real.

It tears his heart to watch her face, so beautiful and sad. He can remember the first time her gentle presence lit a flame inside of him. It was not long after she came to work at the precinct. She seemed nice, almost too nice to believe for a girl who was so beautiful. Her intelligence was as sharp as anyone he had met, and she could be funny in her own observational way. All of these things left Andarus uneasy about his new partner. He had never known a person to be so attractive and possess those qualities, nor had he ever known anyone who knew such a person. He was waiting for the real her to surface; some snide, snobby comment, a frustrated moment, a sordid detail about her personal life, some conceited quip. So much did he feel this way that he was quite businesslike and curt with her, right up until he watched her walking back to the squad car. They were investigating a case, and Irene entertained a young boy outside while Andarus questioned his mother. It was hot, and it was summer; both Irene and the boy were sweaty. Upon leaving, the child threw his arms around her neck, kissed her cheek, and said, "You come see me again."

She said something softly to the child that Andarus did not pay attention to hear. But, as he opened his door to the car, he looked in her direction; she was still walking slowly, a good ten paces behind. He could see her lips moving with a child's smile that appeared so delicate upon her beaming face. It looked as if she was rehashing her discourse with the boy, going over her words and hoping that she said all the good she could say, and gleefully enjoying the interaction, savoring every high-pitched syllable. Suddenly, she wasn't the seemingly self-sure, gorgeous woman who was intelligent and overly kind, but she was also vulnerable and delicate. She was not domineering, condescending, or calculating, and he felt ridiculous for ever assuming so. All of this made her inwardly stunning, which outshined even her appearance. She was no longer too good to be real; she was real. And, where he expected her to be callous, she was soft. Realizing how rough and distrusting he had been with her, being one more filthy weight threatening to shatter her gentleness, he had never felt so terrible around Irene as at that moment, that is, until this past weekend.

"Irene, I'm so sorry."

"Save it, Andarus. I'm here to work; I'm okay."

"Well, I'm not okay; I feel terrible. I'm sorry for the things I said; they weren't what I meant to say."

"Seems like that's been a consistent problem with us."

"It's been my problem for pretty much my whole life. I'm sorry that I hurt you with it."

"Who said I'm hurt?"

"I did. I can see it. I've felt it since you left the office on Saturday."

"Oh, so, it's because I left. I get it; you missed your partner. Well, I'm back; I'm here to work, so don't worry about it."

"That's not it. The way I acted, the things I said; they would've hurt me too."

"What?"

"If you would've told me the same things I said to you, I would've been hurt."

"What did you say that was so terrible, Paul? We work together and that's it; I was silly to be upset at all. I should've known where our boundaries are."

"That's not right. There's more than that, and I've never said it."

Her eyes fill, and her hand moves to cover a tear crawling out of her left eye. She wipes it away and looks into him.

She asks, "Then, what more is there?"

"We…I…I have feelings for you. It's not that we work together or are friends; it's something else. I feel horrible for going so long without saying it; that must've been the worst thing for you—that's what was so bad about Saturday afternoon—I never said what I needed to say, that had to hurt you…"

Through a trembling smile, she says, "Say it, silly."

"I love you, Irene. I have for a long time now; I've been a complete wreck this whole weekend thinking I lost you," he looks toward his shoes and back to her face again, "I love you."

Smiling completely now, still with full eyes, she says, "Paul, I…"

Debbie blasts through the intercom, "Andarus, we've got a description that matches Mrs. Bonney as a jumper on top of a church on 40th Street. I don't think anyone else picked up on the description; they're treating it as a regular jumper. A car is already on its way out there; what do you want to do, Paulie?"

Andarus looks at Irene helplessly.

"I know, Paul. We've gotta go."

He nods his head, but he is slow to move.

She grabs his shoulder and nudges him toward the door, adding, "We better get down there fast." She notices the top of the file cabinet is completely cleared off, and she smiles as she follows behind him.

Pulling out of the police station less than two minutes later…

"I hope we get there in time to catch her," says Irene, thinking of the long jump to the sidewalk.

"'Rene," he says as he gently reaches across the console and touches her forearm, "I'm not sure what I want to do if we can catch her; I'm not sure that there's anything that we can do to her anyway."

"I know," she says uneasily, "I'm starting to feel that way too."

"Really?"

She nods.

With a surprised yet relieved countenance, he asks, "How did this change of mind come about?"

"It was a long couple of nights, Andarus. Long nights."

A short, speed-filled, noise-blurry drive places them at the curb of the church behind another police car. The car in front of them is empty. They step out of the vehicle and look directly up to the rooftop. Laura's body casts an angular shadow onto the street as the sun breaks strongly over the top of the church.

Irene says, "The other guys must be around back or inside trying to get up to the roof. Whoever called this in must be with them too—don't see anybody else."

Andarus and she keep their eyes on Laura as they step to the front of the edifice. His left foot stumbles on the broken sidewalk.

Glancing at the severe crack that has snagged his shoe and all of the tiny fault lines that surround it, he says, "Looks like she's tried this before."

Irene glimpses to the sidewalk and then back to the roof. She has no words, but she reaches out and grabs his hand.

As her feet leave the rooftop, the rain breaks in front of the rays of the sun, falling for the first time since she last left the zenith of the church. She falls through the air as displaced as a feather floating through the depths to the bottom of the ocean. A flash of light bounces off a peaceful smile that sees three faces beyond the concrete below. The light spreads like a fire over her body, a blaze of illumination, far more intense than the rising sun coming over the top of the church. The brightness makes her nearly unbearable to look upon, but the two on the sidewalk can't turn their squinting eyes away. The blinding radiance reaches its apex and then is snuffed out instantly. She vanishes with the light. A few stray particles sway toward the earth below, twinkling in the morning rays.

The sun beats, and the rain mists softly; her hand remains in his.

"My God, I don't believe it!" she exclaims.

Andarus responds, "It's hard to believe any of this…we've shot her in the head, watched her jump out of a third-floor window, and just witnessed this; all of this makes no sense, and, yet, it still is."

She nods, and her mouth remains open as she watches the few shimmering particles drift, slowly making their course through the air.

"Well, Irene, I can tell you this is true; you're going to be asked to accept a promotion sometime tomorrow."

"No, Paul," she starts, but knowing that it's the truth.

"I'm going to file a report trying to explain this. No games, no gang violence, no lies. I'll be gone by the end of the day."

"Me too, then."

"No, 'Rene, don't quit because of me."

"I'm quitting for me, Paul; I don't want to work there without you, but, even more than that, I don't want to be in your position in a few years. I don't want all of this trouble; I don't want that life."

He nods his head softly, "We'd make a heck of a pair of English teachers; high school, maybe even college professors."

"Yeah, you've always been a little too well-read for a detective," she says looking into his eyes, noticing the absence of the sunglasses.

"Well, I haven't tackled anywhere near as many pages as you, but I've read a little bit. You know, when you can't sleep at night…"

She turns and looks at him, tugging lightly on his hand, "Do you think you'll be able to sleep now? *Now*, that you know someone loves you too?"

He pauses for a moment, watching the last of the sparkling bits of dust land on the sidewalk.

"It's a strange world, Irene. There's lots of terrible things in it to keep most of us living like we're dead, keeping us distracted, focusing on things that don't matter, but I'm willing to give it one more try. How about you?"

As her fingers slide tightly between his, she says, "You'll have to shoot me to keep me off this one, Paul. You'll have to shoot me."

Join us Online to Discover
even more about

by

Lewis Aleman

Target us at

www.LewisAleman.com

for more author info, details on the upcoming prequel, free downloads, & a lot more Cold Streak goodness.

I Would Like To Thank...

Miss Antonia Tunis for her constant love and encouragement. My immediate family: Ron and Flo Aleman, Ronnie, Tommy, Austin, Alexis, Ronnie Jr., and Tony Aleman.. All of my former students and fellow teachers for their encouragement and support. To those who have taught me for creating a spark and a love of writing, specifically Mrs. Verdigets, Mrs. Shaeffer, Mrs. Adams, Mike Boudreaux, Mr. Musselwhite, Mr. Guiterrez, Mrs. Barton, Patty Richard, Mrs. Robarts, Tom Lapre, Dickey Dufor, Lynn Sylbernagel, and Sue Owen. And to all of my friends whom I am very fortunate to have and are far too numerous to list without unintentionally leaving out someone very dear. But, here's my best shot at it: Steve, Amy, Kurt, Wendy, Bert, Stacy; Craig, Kelly, Brian, Jack, & Suzanne Lebaron, Curtis, Nikki, Kari, Jason, Presley, Meghan, Big D, Donovan, and the rest of the crew, Rashad, John Q John, Jonathan, Mark, Brandy, Joy, Amanda, Johan, Stefanie and the Bowers family, Mr. A.J. & Mrs. Billy, Mike & Lori Rodrigue, Tony Gusler, Lennie Dufrene; Fran, Dave, Melvin & Loretta Lagasse, the entire Catalanotto and Aleman family including many aunts, uncles, and cousins, patrons of the former Lewzworld Comix, Brett & Erica Badinger, the Credo family, Johnny & Marsha Maestri; Keith (who always pushed me to work harder by being better than me at nearly everything), Mary, & Ronnie Hicks; Brian Bernos, Wayne & Audrey Ovella, Sarah & Mindy, friends from LSU, the entire Prather family, my old friend Laura W., Dave Dauterive; Nicole & Lori; Swensen's people, Jason Hardy and the CC Team, Bill, Mary, & the Martin family; all fans of Quiver music and the other bands with whom I've played, everyone who has read the preview online, The Legacy @ LSU for publishing my short stories, Todd's Music Express, Bill & Colette of the former Hammerhead's, the defunct 106.7 The End for playing my music, and Anthony G. for always trying to help out a former teacher. To my wonderful students in The Writer's Club; you guys always motivated me even though I was supposed to be the mentor.

To God for blessing me with all of the above people, giving me the strength to finish this book, always guiding and protecting me, and for the person reading this now.

For those that I have inevitably left out, I'll keep a running list on my website, and I'll catch you in the next book.

And, most importantly, thank you, the reader, for reading my book; I am forever in your debt. Send a message to me at www.LewisAleman.com, and I'll be happy to personally tell you so.

LEWIS ALEMAN was born in and still resides just outside of New Orleans. He graduated from Louisiana State University with a BA in English which encompassed a specialization in Creative Writing. While attending LSU, he published several short stories and poems in various magazines and anthologies. At 19, he was offered a publishing contract for his first novel, *Alone*. After college, he taught high school English for five years. Then, he decided that he needed to finish this book. Currently, he is fast at work on the prequel to COLD STREAK, entitled RAGE.

All upcoming works, events, and news are updated on the website listed below. Also on the site are excerpts from other works, press/reviews, free stuff (screen saver, desktop, avatars, etc.), and a frequently updated blog.

He can be contacted through his website

WWW.LEWISALEMAN.COM.

Printed in the United States
117373LV00001BA/95/A

9 780980 060508